'Okay, here we go again,' Grundy said in Serbo-Croat. 'Your name, please?'

The sniper did not answer.

Grundy repeated the question in English and German.

Then he touched the sniper's torn face and stepped back. The man's head bent lower and the chair he sat in started to shake. Grundy signalled to Horst and Yves to steady the chair. The sniper cried out when Yves touched his wounded leg. Then Grundy caught him with a fist across the side of the face and the sniper's face opened again and he cried out and fell towards Horst. Horst steadied him.

'I said, your name, please?'

The left side of the sniper's face was streaming blood and the sweat beads on that side had spread out in lines and mixed with the blood. There was a deep cut to the right of his eye on that side, too, where Grundy's nail had caught him, and the punches had opened it.

'Anythin' to say?' Grundy said.

It was the twenty-second time Grundy had asked him a question. Again, the sniper did not answer, but this time his lips opened and closed two or three times as if he was talking to himself and on that Grundy made a decision.

'Okay,' Grundy said to Yves very slowly in Serbo-Croat, 'okay, he's not gonna say anythin', this is a waste of time and effort, just cut his fuckin' balls off.'

*Books by Conor Cregan
and available from Coronet paperback*

With Extreme Prejudice

About the Author

A former journalist, Conor Cregan has written three previous novels. He has travelled widely in Bosnia and lives in Dublin.

House of Fire

Conor Cregan

CORONET BOOKS
Hodder and Stoughton

British Library Cataloguing in Publication Data

Cregan, Conor
House of Fire
I. Title
823.914 [F]

ISBN 0 340 62306 3

Typeset by Palimpsest Book Production Limited,
Polmont, Stirlingshire
Printed and bound in Great Britain by
Cox & Wyman Ltd, Reading, Berkshire

Hodder and Stoughton
A division of Hodder Headline PLC
338 Euston Road
London NW1 3BH

This one's for Ivana, Marija, Vanja, Yves,
Mirsat, William, Mak and Natasa

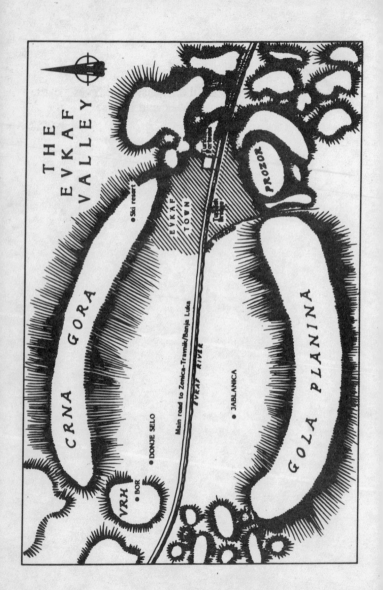

The unbelievers take their fill of pleasure and eat as cattle eat: but the fire shall be their home

The Koran

Bosnia-Hercegovina: 1993

The house was still on fire.

Frejzo Ceric looked up through the smouldering floors to the charred roof beams and the small orange flames that licked the black wood. A single ember fell three floors and settled beside him. He watched it until it went out, then turned his eyes to the window frame and no-man's-land and the dawn mist. Then he checked his equipment.

When he had checked his equipment for the third time, Ceric huddled closer to the pocked wall, rested his shaven head against the broken plaster and looked at each of the other Bosnian soldiers in turn.

Then he forced a smile at the old man beside him.

Mirsat Pasic was bald and fat with a long, dry face pocked with holes and scarred with lines like the building and the ground around him; one of his ears had no lobe. His clothing was a mixture of military and civilian: combat jacket, jeans, wellington boots, sheepskin overvest – he had been a shepherd before the war and his webbing was old Yugoslav People's Army leather.

He had an AK47 in his lap and carried his spare magazines right around his body in canvas pouches and wore a long steel hunting knife strapped to his leg.

One of the old man's hands touched a cheap walkie-talkie on his front shoulder strap, the other pulled a pack of Turkish cigarettes from his pocket. He took out one of the cigarettes, looked at the Irishman beside him and offered him one.

The Irishman shook his head.

'No,' he whispered to the old man. 'No smokin'. *Rauchen Verboten. Chetniks sehen.* Remember what happened to Saki.'

Mirsat Pasic did not understand the final sentence so he smiled and looked at Frejzo Ceric to see if it was a joke about the Japanese drink, then watched Luke Ryan give a lecture with handsignals.

Ryan's weatherbeaten skin, hidden behind a black growth somewhere close to a beard, seemed impenetrable, Ceric thought, and the bones under it stuck out as if they were a warning of something more dangerous. His eyes sat still and slightly sunken in their sockets and his hair was dark, dirty and shoulder-length and tied with a black bandana. His combat uniform was maybe a size too big for him and his webbing was German army surplus. Everyone called him the poet because he carried a poetry book some girl had once given him. But he never read from it.

Ryan winked at Mirsat Pasic, then looked at Frejzo Ceric.

'Tell him Saki was the pen name of an English writer called Hector Munro,' Ryan whispered to Ceric. 'He wrote humour with a bit of whip in it.' Ryan made a gesture with his hand. 'He was in World War One and there was this fellow smokin' and Saki – the name comes from the Rubaiyat of Omar Khayyam – Saki shouted at him to put the cigarette out or a sniper'd get him.' Ryan smiled. 'A sniper shot Saki. I have a feelin' he'd have got the joke.'

Ryan looked at Mirsat Pasic's eyes while Ceric whispered an explanation of the Saki story into Pasic's ear. Pasic grinned.

'What is the time, Luke?' Frejzo Ceric mouthed over Pasic's shoulder. He was not asking the time; he just needed to speak to Ryan.

Ryan raised the fingers of one hand.

Ceric nodded and untied the bandana he wore, unfolded it and then refolded it and tied it back around his shaven head. Then he checked his rifle and ammunition and took in deep breaths through his nose. It was his first attack and he was very frightened.

He watched Ryan and wondered if the Irishman was frightened, too, but Ryan's eyes had acquired a quality that did not give feelings away easily and anyway the foreigners were never frightened, everyone knew that: they had come to fight and they liked to fight. Ceric was a conscript.

Frejzo Ceric concentrated on his own fear.

Mirsat Pasic tapped Ryan on the hand.

'Womans, Deutschmarks?' he whispered.

It was a private ritual between them whenever they had time to kill, and Ceric, who was new to the whole thing, was envious of it. He watched Ryan again because Ryan had taught him about war and trained him to be a soldier, and that meant something there.

Ryan shook his head at the old shepherd.

'No Deutschmarks, Mirsat,' he whispered, 'and no woman. No woman, no cry.'

Mirsat Pasic tapped his chest.

'Many women,' he said. '*Vielen.*'

They both smiled. Frejzo Ceric smiled, too, but he could not hold it for long enough, so he dipped his head and said a prayer and thought for a brief moment about a girl he had loved from a distance when he was younger. And he said a prayer for her, too.

Then the very squat officer at the other end of the room nodded to Ryan and Ryan nodded to another foreigner who nodded to the men around him. The squat officer raised his hand and the thirty men in the room slowly lifted themselves off the broken floor and prepared to leave.

They moved from the house into the access trench in the village and crawled along the red mud to their front line twenty metres ahead. Then, one by one, they climbed out of their forward trench and ran through the mist and the cover of a small oak wood and from the cover of the oak wood into the open ground between the lines.

Their boots were covered in wet oak leaves, and their breath mixed with the early morning mist.

The Serb line was at the base of a mountain called Vrh. Vrh commanded the western end of the valley the Bosnians were trying to hold, and the valley controlled the main road from Banja Luka to Zenica. The Serbs were all around the valley and they wanted the road.

The Serbs had captured Vrh at the end of the summer. They had captured it in the spring, too, but the Bosnians had taken it back then.

The Bosnians moved in single file at ten-metre intervals towards a cemetery. Most of the headstones were smashed and many of the dead had been disinterred by the impact of mortar and artillery shells. The decomposing bodies of two soldiers lay across each other against half a headstone.

One hundred metres out, Frejzo Ceric could see the barest outline of two ruined houses through the mist. The Serb forward trenches at the base of Vrh ran between the remains of these houses and an orchard of shattered plum trees and then twisted back into a pine forest which ran up the mountain behind.

Ceric could hear his heart beating in his mouth.

There were fragments of vegetables in the open ground between the lines and the remains of wooden huts, with chicken wire and digging tools lying in the mud among the shell holes. The shell holes were full of autumn rain, and Ceric skipped to avoid them and slipped in the wet mud as he advanced.

He glanced left and right to Mirsat Pasic and Luke Ryan and then focused his eyes to the point in the mist where he knew the Serb forward trench was.

Behind him, the sun was trying to smile through the mist across the shoulder of the mountains at the other end of the valley. There was a town called Evkaf at that end of the valley, and the valley and the river running through it were called after the town. Evkaf is a Turkish word meaning pious foundations, or land given over to finance religious institutions and good works.

One hundred and fifty metres.

Frejzo Ceric moved faster, and the men around him disappeared and reappeared in the mist, their boots beating a desperate rhythm in the mud.

Two hundred metres. They were at the cemetery. Pasic had dropped behind Frejzo Ceric; Luke Ryan was ahead of him. The excitement almost lifted Frejzo Ceric off the ground.

Two hundred and fifty metres.

Frejzo Ceric was shaking. He could see the razor wire and the top of the Serb trench.

They had them.

Then '*Pazi*!' a voice yelled.

Shit!

A square hat with an eagle motif and a red, blue and white Serb badge came up over the top of the lookout's parapet.

The Serb fired nine rounds and Mirsat Pasic sank to his knees in the mud in a single movement.

He tried to get up but part of his thigh bone had been smashed; he tried to raise his AK47 but the feeling was gone from his hands and he could not control himself any more; he let the rifle slip into a small shell hole, sank forward into the mud and started to urinate. Blood ran from an exit wound in his lower back over his leather belt and down his kneeling legs and he tipped over into a shallow shell hole.

Frejzo Ceric dived.

Three Serb heavy machine-guns opened up and rounds hit a tall man on Ceric's left and two cousins just in front of him and a butcher behind them.

Small trench mortars from the Serb lines joined the machine-guns and rifles, and more Bosnian soldiers fell dead around Frejzo Ceric. The Bosnian attack stopped as if it had slammed into a wall.

Frejzo Ceric fired a burst from his rifle but he had pushed the fire selector to full automatic and most of the magazine emptied itself in three seconds. The AK47 almost fell out of his hands and all his rounds went over the heads of the Serbs he was firing at. He scrambled into a shell crater.

The Serb trench mortars gave way to heavy mortars and then mountain guns from the back slopes of Vrh and from another long mountain to Ceric's right called Crna Gora. Shells hit the ground every few seconds and the shouting and screaming echoed the firing and it felt to Frejzo Ceric as though the whole world was tearing apart.

Then the Bosnians began to retreat.

Soldiers picked themselves up and ran, crawled back on their bellies, on their backs, some wounded, some dragging wounded, firing short bursts, throwing grenades into the mist and smoke. Some of them shot their own men or were shot by their own men, and the mist and the smoke of battle and the noise held Frejzo Ceric frozen on the knife edge between terror and elation.

And he was scared in a way you can only be scared when you are running.

When you are attacking you are the hunter and you have all the arrogance and assurance of the hunter. You get high on your hunting skills and it is all a great adventure. And if you are afraid your arrogance can cover your fear. But when you are running all there is is running and getting away and you are so scared they will catch you that you do not want to stop for anything, no matter what.

Men around him were scrambling from hole to hole on their stomachs. Frejzo Ceric threw himself out of his hole and rolled and dropped his rifle and crawled back for it, then scrambled into another hole.

He heard a cry for help.

'*U pomoc!*'

He ignored it. The terror inside him was absolute. He threw himself out of his hole.

He saw a hand grab a man's boot but the man kicked the hand away, and the hand caught a second man by the belt and the second man fell dead. Then the hand caught Frejzo Ceric.

'*U pomoc!*' the voice shouted again.

And Frejzo Ceric was looking at Luke Ryan.

'Help me!' Ryan roared.

Frejzo Ceric could feel the Irishman's breath on his face and through it he could see Mirsat Pasic lying in the shell hole beside him.

Pasic was on his back in red muddy water up to the sides of his mouth, eyes open wide. And Frejzo Ceric wanted Mirsat Pasic to be dead.

'No, no, he is dead, he is dead!' Ceric said.

He tried to kick at Pasic as if to prove his point. Three Serb rifle rounds hit the ground beside them. Ceric kicked at Ryan then.

'Let me go, let me go, he's dead, do you not see that?' he yelled at Ryan.

But Ryan would not let him go.

He watched Frejzo Ceric's face lose its colour and thought the small spots on the young Bosnian's chin were going to pop like rivets and the face would just come apart.

'Help me!' Ryan shouted again.

'Jesus fucking Christ, Luke, Jesus fucking Christ,' Ceric said.

Ryan pulled him into the shell hole.

Ceric listened to Pasic's chest and then cursed Ryan and Mirsat Pasic silently. He put his hand near Pasic's gut and Pasic's skin collapsed like ripe fruit or wet papier-mâché.

Then Pasic began to scream.

At first it was a low scream, like air escaping from a tyre, but as the firing broke it got louder.

'Ah, fuck, shit, fuck, fuck . . .'

'Cover me!' Ryan shouted at Ceric.

Ceric thought for a few seconds and Ryan noticed the sweat on his face. Then the young Bosnian nodded.

Ryan took Mirsat Pasic by the collar and Frejzo Ceric reloaded his rifle. He checked the fire selector this time, fired a burst and rolled into a hole to the right. He then fired three covering bursts and threw three grenades.

And Luke Ryan began to inch along in the mud on his back, pulling Mirsat Pasic and firing his rifle with one hand.

The firing was fractured now, like the angry roaring of wild animals.

Ryan shouted for a medic.

Frejzo Ceric fired another burst from his rifle, crawled out of the shell hole he was in and and threw a grenade.

Then he shouted for a medic.

Ceric fired more bursts and Ryan dragged the old shepherd for fifty metres, then rolled into a hole and called for support from the Bosnian lines. He could not see Frejzo Ceric any more because of the mist.

'*U pomoc!*' he roared.

From the mist ahead of him, Frejzo Ceric yelled something in Serbo-Croat that Ryan could not understand.

It took Ryan twenty minutes to reach the oak wood and the Bosnians there threw out a rope and helped pull Mirsat Pasic the final few metres to the forward trench.

There were wounded and dead everywhere in the oak wood; the wounded in the forward trench lay on the remains of picnic benches from the oak wood, the dead in the long grass between the trees. Three of the dead had been killed by the same mortar shell. Their skin was pale and cold and you could feel it beginning to harden. Two of them had their eyes open and were staring at each other as if they knew something no one else did.

And Frejzo Ceric was still in no-man's-land.

The mist was lifting slowly all the way to the Serb line but the Bosnians still could not see Frejzo Ceric.

Ryan yelled for Ceric. He fired covering bursts over head height and went to go back out into no-man's-land. A Bosnian sergeant pulled him back just before eight Serb rounds hit the ground in front of him.

Five minutes passed and the fractured firing continued and Ryan kept yelling for Ceric.

Then Frejzo Ceric shouted back for cover fire.

Ryan picked himself up, fired a magazine, reloaded and fired another, and yelled at Ceric to move. Ceric came out of the hole he was in and rolled into another.

Five more Bosnians fired cover shots and yelled at Frejzo Ceric to move again and Ceric came out of the second hole and rolled into a third.

'Come on! Come on!' Ryan shouted.

He was desperately reloading again.

More Bosnians joined the cover fire.

Frejzo Ceric pulled himself out of the third hole and fired a burst and rolled again into a fourth hole and fired again. But he was out of ammunition now.

'More cover!' Ryan yelled at the soldiers around him.

And more Bosnians fired more covering bursts and Frejzo Ceric came out of the fourth hole and rolled to his left towards the remains of a headstone beside the cemetery.

He picked himself up and Ryan thought he saw a word on the young Bosnian's lips but he was still too far away to be sure.

Then a round went through Frejzo Ceric's leg and he went down.

And all the firing stopped.

Ryan moved out of the cover of the oak wood but the Serbs opened up on him again and he had to dive back into the trees.

Heavy firing started again.

Frejzo Ceric picked himself up and started to crawl and lift himself on to his good leg. But another shot hit him in the arm and he spun, another shot hit him in the other leg and another shot hit him in the shoulder.

'Luke!' he screamed and the scream fractured on the firing and the cold of the morning.

Ryan crawled out into no-man's-land again but the Serb fire sent him diving for cover behind a grass embankment, cursing.

Two other Bosnian soldiers tried to move out into no-man's-land and they were killed.

And Frejzo Ceric moaned and shouted for Luke Ryan.

He tried to crawl in the mud. The Bosnians shouted at him to keep moving. They fired more covering volleys.

When Ceric had made five metres the Serbs shot him again in the leg and then in the lower back, at the spine. He screamed in agony, cursed and shouted and the Serbs shot him again.

Then he was just crying.

For two days they tried to get to Frejzo Ceric, but the Serbs drove them back each time. And on the third day Luke Ryan shot Frejzo Ceric dead.

The attack had been the fifth failed Bosnian attempt to retake Vrh that autumn and they had lost forty-five men.

1

The map of the Evkaf valley on the wall shook under the shelling, and one of the small flagged pins marking the Bosnian front line at the village of Donje Selo below Vrh fell to the ground.

The flag was followed by fine dust from the ceiling and small drops of water from a burst pipe. The water ran from a very fine crack in the flaking ceiling, down a twisted covered flex and over a dull light bulb before dripping on to the concrete floor.

A very fat man with pale skin and a white beard, dressed in full combats, wearing a German Luger sidearm, lit a cigarette, bent down and picked up the flagged pin and stuck it back into the wall map.

The Bosnian army colonel beside him shook his head.

'Please, Grundy,' the colonel said.

Then Jusef Husic stood up from his desk and replaced the flag a couple of millimetres forward of the position the fat mercenary had picked. And for a moment the Serb encroachments into the valley made the Bosnian positions there look like a deflating balloon.

'I need all the ground I can get, Grundy,' the colonel said.

The valley was about five kilometres long and because it shrank from three kilometres wide to under one where the town wedged itself into the eastern end, it looked like a tear drop. Grundy was considering this.

Husic reached into Grundy's cigarette packet, pulled one out and held it for Grundy to light.

'A habit of field command,' Husic said then. 'I did not smoke when I was a lawyer. I wonder how many a general smokes.'

He went back to his desk and sifted through some papers. They were damp and stained and were held in place by a small Bosnian fleur-de-lis flag on a heavy metal stand.

'It doesn't much matter where you put your flags, Jusef,' Grundy said. 'Without Vrh, we just won't be able to hold Donje Selo if they keep pushin' into us on Crna Gora.'

Grundy ran his finger along the long mountain that provided a wall for the north side of the valley.

'Eventually we'll have to shorten the line here and if we do that then Donje Selo's theirs for the takin'. Only a matter of time. Not terrific prospects, are they, Jusef?'

Husic stood up again and walked over to the leather armchair across the room to the left of the blast door. The door led to a concrete corridor leading to scores of other rooms, workshops, administration offices, store rooms, cells. The complex lay under an old Turkish fortress at the east end of Evkaf and ran deep and wide like the roots of a great tree. Some of the tunnels had not even been opened yet. Husic said they would open the deeper tunnels when the Serbs were in Evkaf so that they could perhaps link into the sewerage system and fight from the drains.

He sat down in the leather armchair by the blast door, finished smoking a second cigarette and threw it on to the concrete floor. Grundy watched him.

Husic had that stain of melancholy in his olive skin that some Balkan people seemed to carry like a birthmark, Grundy thought. The colonel was very thin and his body was something like bent wire. His hair came down over his forehead and covered the tops of his ears. His lips were grey and dry and he always held a spare cigarette, which he never smoked, behind his right ear, under a few strands of hair.

Husic slapped his hands together.

'I will not shorten the line,' he said. 'I cannot. You do understand that, Grundy? *Rascistiti teren.* How do you say that word in English – ethnic . . . ?'

'Cleansing,' the third man in the room said.

Husic turned to the very sallow young man standing at the wall beside the leather armchair.

Hasim Kusturica stooped slightly to one side from a bullet

wound to the lower back. He wore camouflaged combat trousers and a black combat jacket with a green t-shirt underneath it. A folding butt G3 rifle slung around his shoulder rested on spare magazine pouches at his waist and four grenades hung from the front shoulder straps of his webbing, while two were loose on the waist belt at the back. He had a walkie-talkie and sunglasses hanging across his chest and wore a $250 pair of running shoes.

Kusturica had been born in Evkaf but had run away to Sarajevo as a teenager and become a gangster. He earned his stripes in Sarajevo as a low-grade enforcer and debt-collector, acquiring, in the usual manner, a black German car, a black German dog and a taste for black designer clothes.

When the war came he was still in Sarajevo and he fought in Dobrijna and around the Hotel Bristol, making some money on the side supplying black market equipment and food around town. At this stage of his career he was fighting alongside Juka, who was achieving legendary status around Sarajevo as a kind of Robin Hood figure cum resistance fighter. Unfortunately for Hasim Kusturica, Juka had an even bigger appetite for contraband than he did and there had been a falling out one night in the Holiday Inn when Juka shot Kusturica. Juka had been on crutches at the time and weighed down with metal pins from battle injuries. Otherwise he probably would have killed Kusturica.

Kusturica left Sarajevo, along one of the overland goat-track trails the Bosnian army had set up to link its Sarajevo command with the rest of its territory, and went home. He arrived in Evkaf with someone else's black German car, a new black German dog, three loyal followers from his Sarajevo days, a bootful of Heckler and Koch weapons and ammunition, a dramatic reconversion to Islam and new name to go with it, Muhammed – Muha for short.

Once in Evkaf, he formed a small private Muslim para-military force, the Black Berets, and, in the early fighting around Evkaf, spent more time leaning on people for money and dealing in the black market than fighting the advancing Serbs.

There was one attempt to disarm the Black Berets, but Muha

had about a hundred men around him then and they were just too well equipped to disarm.

Then the Serbs pushed deep into the valley south of the river as far as a tributary called the Thread, and began making ground on Crna Gora.

Muha's Black Berets moved into position around an old ski hotel on Crna Gora and led the defence of the mountain from five Serb assaults. Muha was wounded three times and more of the young men in the valley joined the Black Berets.

'Yes, Muha,' Husic said, 'ethnic cleansing, Grundy. I will not permit it. Anyway, where do we fall back to? There are thirty thousand people in this pocket, Grundy. We are surrounded, cut off. If we withdraw, our people will be at the mercy of the Chetniks. We must hold the line on Crna Gora and we must hold Donje Selo. And, yes, we must retake Vrh. There is no choice there. But it is a matter of priorities now.'

'So let me do what I want,' Grundy said.

'I am considering it. But it is a luxury I can ill afford at this time, Grundy. Anyway, we must prepare for their next move. Where will they attack next?'

'Flankin' along Crna Gora. Has to be. Then when they secure enough of it, down on Donje Selo. There's no mystery here, Jusef. It's straightforward. We're goin' nowhere, and they're cuttin' into us piece by piece.'

'Like a chocolate cake,' Husic said. 'It has been a long time since I have had a piece of chocolate cake.' He smiled but the smile could not compete with what was on his mind. He pulled himself out of the armchair and walked over to the wall map.

'You will leave soon, Grundy?' he said.

He touched the map.

'No, I will not, Colonel.'

Husic looked at the mercenary for a while. The moonlight silhouettes, he thought. It was the same with all of them – the foreign volunteers, international fighters, mercenaries, whatever they called themselves. Grundy had arrived on a bus from Zenica before the Serbs cut Evkaf off. He spoke fluent Serbo-Croat, with an accent somewhere between New Jersey and Vienna, and had definitely fought in Angola and probably in Nicaragua. Most of the rest of his men were even vaguer. And they never told you why they were there.

It definitely wasn't for the money: they got a hundred marks a month when Husic could afford to pay them. And much of the time he could not afford even that. So he paid them what he could when he could and they scraped whatever they could from the black market and other sources.

That made them even more unreal.

They all had a ghostly quality, as if they had appeared from a time-warp and would disappear back into it when their business was done. Husic could not understand why he placed so much faith in men about whom he knew so little.

'You do not long for chocolate cake then?' Husic said to Grundy.

A heavy shell landed above them. The room shook again.

'How many has that been today?' Grundy said.

'Three hundred and twenty-five,' Muha said. 'We must attack on Crna Gora, Jusef. Before the Chetniks do. Let me do it. Push them off Crna Gora and my men can then take Vrh.'

'And who will push them off Crna Gora, Muha? That's where they're concentrated. Look at our perimeter. I don't have enough men to hold all of it. We have attacked and attacked – everywhere. They're still coming.'

'There are enough men in this town,' Muha said.

'And what do we equip them with? This fighting in the Lasva, with the Croats, it has taken all eyes off us. Travnik, Vitez, Gornji Vakuf, that's all the international press want to know about. Why are we fighting the Croats when we should be fighting the Chetniks together? I heard one of our units got help from the Chetniks to shell the Croats. Can you believe that? We have become animals fighting over fragments of broken bone. Anyway, Muha, there are only boys and old men left here. Anyone fit is with us or has run away. Can you get me more weapons, Muha? A few heavy guns, maybe. Corps have nothing for us. So we are a brigade in name only. Fuck Corps. And fuck the United Nations – why won't they let us buy weapons?'

'Like I said,' Grundy said, 'if we control Vrh, then we can hit 'em on Crna Gora from two sides, Jusef. Five failures against

Vrh – hell, the last time Muha's and my boys didn't even get out of the trenches – the Chetniks're not gonna expect another move there. And not from behind.'

'I was willing to go the last time,' Muha said.

'Yeah, you were,' Grundy said, shaking his head. 'Look, we have to turn 'em, that's basic strategy, and the only way to really turn 'em is to come in behind 'em, here, Jusef, on Vrh. Another frontal attack anywhere would be damn near futile.'

'And marching how many kilometres through these mountains is a great idea?' Muha said.

He pointed at the mountains south of the valley. Then he stared at the colonel.

'Give me more men and we can push the Chetniks off Crna Gora, Jusef. My men are motivated.'

'And the Chetniks aren't?' Grundy said. 'You think they relish the thought of wakin' up with you standin' over 'em with all that mujahideen shit? If they weren't motivated before they sure as hell are now, Muha. Karadzic must love you. Hey, maybe you're workin' for him. So you go right ahead, Muha. Attack. It'd solve one of our problems, Jusef.'

'Hey, why don't you piss off, Grundy, why don't you?' Muha said. 'We don't need you. Any of you. You fucking Christians, you want to see us all dead, you want to kill all of us. You are shit. Mercenary shit.'

'Yeah, I'm a Chetnik spy, too, Muha, sent to undermine you. It's a double bluff, we're playin'. I get a million Deutschmarks when I bring your head in on a plate. Cuts their costs in half.'

'Stop!' Husic said.

He slammed his hand down on the table.

'We are fighting the Chetniks, gentlemen, please remember that. And, Muha, my wife is a Christian. You want her to go? My son? Milan is a Serb name. My daughters? That is what the Chetniks want. Are you a Chetnik? Maybe there are countries who want us all dead, maybe . . . I hope you are wrong, Muha, I hope that. But Grundy is here . . . he is here and his men are here. I thank them for that.'

'And, for the record, Muha, I'm a Jew,' Grundy said. 'A wanderin' Jew. The accent's the result of one too many years stateside and far too many years everywhere else, but don't make a decision on it.'

Muha's eyes opened and he stepped back and closed his mouth. Then he looked at Husic who brushed his hair back from his forehead.

'You are a Jew?' Husic said.

Grundy scratched his hair. It was whiter than his beard and it highlighted a kind of ironic squint he had in one eye.

'I am, Jusef,' he said. 'Solomon Grundy. There's a rhyme about me but I don't have it with me. Born on a Monday ... somethin' like that. You look surprised.'

'You are joking?'

Grundy looked at his feet.

'I don't see any cloven hooves and I don't have any horns. Here's my membership number.'

Grundy pulled his sleeve up. There was a number tattooed on his left forearm, just below the elbow. It was distorted.

'There's a black and white movie of me after my initiation somewhere. I haven't seen it in a while.' He pulled his sleeve back down.

Husic looked embarrassed. He frowned at Muha. Muha slumped into the armchair and slipped his rifle into his lap.

'I would like to take Vrh,' Husic said when he had regained himself. 'I would like to push them off Crna Gora, I would like to throw them out of this valley and I would love it if we were relieved from Zenica. But right now, for today, I just want to hold what I have. Anyway, can we afford the losses of another attack anywhere, without more certainty? Some of our men here have pistols, Muha, pistols. We must think about holding them first. We must. Maybe we can hold them for the winter. A few weeks and we will have winter snow. Why do the UN not make us a safe zone, Grundy? Why not? I have begged the UN to make us a safe zone.'

'I don't know, Jusef, I don't know. I'm not the fuckin' UN,' Grundy said.

Then he shrugged.

'One day at a time, sweet ...' he said then, in English.

Husic asked him what he meant.

'It's a song about a man askin' help from a Jew who thought

he wouldn't die,' Grundy said. 'Let me do what I wanna do, Jusef. Let me hit Vrh from behind.'

'This Jew, Grundy, what became of him?' Husic said.

'He died, Jusef, he died.'

Husic looked at Muha and shook his head.

'You are the commander of special forces, Muha, what do you think of this idea of Grundy's – is it feasible?' he said.

'Like I said, it's an idea for desperate men.'

'And we are not desperate?'

'Not when we can still attack from here,' Muha said. 'Perhaps we could use the river for a diversion. Make them think we are going for Vrh and strike at Crna Gora.'

'And the Serb boom across the river?' Grundy said. 'It's rigged to blow. Any diversion on the river wouldn't last long enough. The Chetniks'd cut it to pieces before you could take advantage of it on Crna Gora. Vrh is the key, Jusef. And I'm talkin' about comin' in back here, behind it, where they don't have mines on the banks, where they're not expectin' anythin'. Fifty well-armed men oughta do it. Get fifty men in there, around the Bor mosque—'

He pointed to the village at the top of Vrh. '—and the Chetniks would have a hell of a job gettin' 'em out. Then your frontal picks a spot in their line and you pour everythin' you have through it to link up with the men on top of Vrh. Look, we go behind their lines here, to the southeast, and come this way around the valley to here. What's that mountain called?'

'Sljiva.'

'Yeah, the plum,' Grundy said, in English. Then he switched languages again. 'Appropriate. And then we attack Vrh from there and you hit 'em from the front. It'd be just enough to turn the line – spook 'em – scare 'em – and – then maybe we get 'em.'

'But this is a thirty or forty kilometre march, through high mountains, perhaps through deep snow,' Husic said.

'Thirty-five, at the least. Ten out this way, fifteen down this way, ten back this way. But I'd say more.'

'Maybe you will just walk away,' Muha said.

'Yeah, sure, Muha.'

'Fifty good men?' Husic said. 'That is difficult.'

'We'd need 'em to secure the bridgehead. Block Chetnik reinforcements gettin' to the line. And you'd have to throw everythin' into it, Jusef. Stakes are high here.'

'And risk losing the valley.'

'We'll lose it anyway.'

'The international community?'

'You wanna live on a reservation? If we can get into that mosque and hold Bor and turn the line on Vrh, then maybe we have a chance. That's assumin' we make it through Chetnik lines and up their asses. Muha's right, it's the wildest plan I've ever come up with but there's a small advantage there and it's worth explorin'. We gotta have an advantage, Jusef, we gotta do somethin' they don't expect, you see? You ever heard of Otto Skorzeny?'

'The fascist?'

Grundy went over to Muha and stood beside him. Muha fingered the fire selector on his rifle. Grundy looked into his eyes, then smiled and held the smile and then frowned. Muha put the fire selector into place. Grundy squatted.

'I don't want you to take this personally,' he said.

Muha tensed and began to move his rifle towards Grundy's chest. 'And you must not take this personally.'

Grundy smiled. Muha looked up and down his body. Grundy then raised his hands.

'*Odjebi*, Grundy,' Muha said.

Grundy leaned in. He ignored the expletives.

'*Odjebi*, Grundy,' Muha said again.

Grundy smiled. He lowered his hands. Muha's eyes were moving fast now over Grundy's body. He followed the hands down to Grundy's waist.

Then Grundy leaned into his face and kissed him on the lips.

Muha pulled back and cursed again, and Grundy snapped his rifle from him and turned it on Muha.

'Bang, you're dead, Muha,' he said.

He put the safety catch back on the rifle and handed it to Husic.

'It's a tad blunt but you see what I mean, Jusef?' he said.

Husic placed the rifle on the table and Muha jumped out of

the armchair, wiping his lips and cursing Grundy. He grabbed a Skorpion machine pistol and threatened to shoot Grundy, but Grundy had his back turned.

'I just taught you a combat lesson there, son,' Grundy said. 'Do unto others as they would not do unto you. Do somethin' unexpected and there's an openin'. It's always there – it's short and sweet but it's always there. That's what Skorzeny said. And he knew what he was talkin' about. Tito'd tell you that. Skorzeny almost got him once.'

'Put it away, Muha,' Husic said.

'We're fightin' in mountains, Jusef,' Grundy said, 'we oughta adopt a more mobile strategy, like Tito did.'

'Tito did not have to defend thirty thousand people.'

'No. But you know what Frederick the Great said: he who defends everythin', defends nothin'. Look at these mountains outside the valley. You could run a division through some of the mountains here and no one would notice. Chetnik lines are thin on this side, smugglers get through all the time. Right, Muha? How do the smugglers get through the Chetnik lines, Muha?'

'You are a smart man, Grundy, you work it out. I shoot smugglers and black marketeers when I find them.'

'These mountains are very hard for men, Grundy,' Husic said. 'Men can lose themselves and die in these mountains. Especially when the snow comes. All the way to Jajce it is like this. Many have died. And there's so much we don't know about the Chetnik lines.'

'That can be remedied.'

'The attack would have to be so well co-ordinated . . .'

Grundy sensed he had a little more of Husic on his side now and he started pointing at the maps.

'Of course,' he said in English, 'and we'd have to find some people who know those mountains like their old woman's box.'

Grundy saw the colonel did not understand. He went back to Serbo-Croat again.

'It doesn't matter, Jusef, it doesn't matter. What I'm tryin' to say is it's about as long a shot as you can try – but it's so long it just might work. Any Serbs you can get would help. In case of unforeseen trouble.'

'No Chetniks,' Muha said.

'They're not Chetniks, they're Bosnians who are Serbs,' Grundy said.

'No Chetniks.'

Muha stared hard at Husic. Husic dipped his eyes.

'How much you chargin' to leave Serbs in this town alone?' Grundy said.

'*Odjebi*, Grundy,' Muha said. 'And fuck your mother.'

'If I told you about my mother you wouldn't say that.'

Muha was about to reply when there was a dull knock on the door. A young man with short light hair came into the room, carrying papers. He wore battle combats, double-strapped boots and a combat overvest, and he had a small automatic pistol strapped to his waist. He was Milan, the colonel's son and his aide-de-camp.

'Milan,' Husic said. 'I must talk with Milan, gentlemen. I will give your proposal very serious consideration, Grundy. And yours, Muha. And yours.'

When Grundy was at the door, Husic called him back. 'So which camp were you in, Grundy?'

'Mauthausen,' Grundy said.

'So you do know how we feel?'

'All my life, Jusef, all my life.'

Outside, in the darkness, a shell landed behind the fortress and a pillar of smoke rose over the north wall and then arched and split and fell to earth against the silver moonlight. Muha bowed his head and grimaced while the noise of the impact toured his ear canals.

'Sandjak,' he said to Grundy.

A thin cloud of dust was falling on the fortress. Grundy picked himself up from where he had been crouching and moved towards two makeshift armoured cars which sat against one of the fortress walls beneath the remains of one of the square towers.

The two men stood against the wall.

'Husic,' Muha said to Grundy. 'He is from Sandjak.'

Sandjak was a Muslim area in Serbia.

'He lives here,' Grundy said.

'Sandjak is Chetnik,' Muha said. 'Sarajevo is full of Sandjak people. They smell, you know. Peasants. Like many people here. We could have broken out of Sarajevo but they didn't want us to. The Ustasha were on Igman.'

Ustasha is a term of abuse used by Muslims and Serbs to describe Croats, much like Chetnik is used for Serbs and mujahideen for Muslims. The Ustasha were fascists allied to Germany, who ruled much of Croatia and Bosnia during World War Two. The Chetniks were a Serb nationalist organisation who fought the Ustashas and the Communists, often at the same time, during World War Two. All the hatred from that war and some more carried over to the 1990s.

Muha shook his head, pulled out a packet of cigarettes, lit one and offered the packet to Grundy.

'Your plan,' Muha said, 'you think it will work?'

'Jesus, Muha, what is it with you? You want this valley to fall?'

'Jusef is considering it. He says he will just let them in and see what the international community will do. What do you think they would do?'

'It depends on the time of year. Who's tryin' to get elected. What's on television. What's your fuckin' game, Muha?'

Another three Serb shells impacted near the fortress and they crouched down again.

'Who are you to ask me? You are a motherfucker, Grundy.'

'Yeah, it takes one to know one, Muha. Maybe that's why you hate me.'

Muha drew on his cigarette and a large calibre artillery shell flew over and hit a shop in the market place, the *carsija*. Glass showered the streets and small splinters landed around Muha and Grundy. Grundy watched small pinpoint cuts appear on the back of his hand and tiny bubbles of blood emerge around the slivers of glass in the skin.

'No,' Muha said, 'I hate you because you can go, Grundy. Because you can just go. Because you are outside – even here, even now – you are outside: you, UNPROFOR, NATO, the Europeans, the Americans, the UNHCR, the Red Cross, all of you, you are outside, looking in, telling us how it will be, what our futures are. And you would deal with the Devil. And I am inside and I will not.'

'And everyone who isn't with you is a Chetnik or an Ustasha? Many Muslims supported the Ustashas during the revolution – the Second World War. There was a Muslim division in the SS. And the Ustashas killed maybe two hundred and fifty thousand Serbs.'

'Not enough,' Muha said.

'You want an Islamic state? You?'

'*Allah u akbar*. Zionist.'

'Jesus, Muha, I think you must have been nicer when you were just a two-bit debt-collector beatin' up on old women. Now, you make me feel sorry for the Chetniks. That's a hell of a thing.'

They sat down by the wall in the shelter of one of the improvised armoured cars and smoked. They did not talk again and when the shelling was over Muha spoke into his walkie-talkie. He went out through a small entrance in the fortress walls that might have been an old gate position or just a hole blown in the wall by a Serb shell.

'Your operation is still on tonight?' Muha said to Grundy.

'You know everythin', don't you?' Grundy said.

'That is my job. Good luck.'

Muha got into a small black BMW and drove through the market place, the *carsija*, in the Turkish end of town towards the Habsburg centre.

Grundy looked up at the fleur-de-lis and white-stripe-on-blue Bosnian flag flying from the fortress.

2

And the yellow flames from a black wood stove seemed to
jaundice everything that night.

The cellar walls were dripping water and there was a damp
odour under the acrid smell of the charred wood and the
lingering smell of battle from the village of Donje Selo above
ground.

A pipe ran from the wood stove in the corner of the cellar
up through the house to where moonlight licked at the black
ribs stretched across the remains of the roof. The men in the
cellar had drilled holes in the pipe to disperse the smoke from
their stove so it would not give away their position.

Luke Ryan finished taping a spare magazine to the one he
was about to push into his Heckler and Koch submachine-gun.
The spare magazine was upside-down to the insert magazine
so that the feed end of each overlapped the closed end of the
other by a few centimetres.

A dark-skinned young man with Indus features finished
making camouflage patterns around his beard and then
stepped towards Ryan, holding a small tin filled with mud,
soot and cooking oil. He spat into it and mixed it with his
fingers again.

Then he reached out with his thumb and started streaking
camouflage on Ryan's face. Ryan watched the young face and
saw how the muscles in the cheeks tensed and the brown eyes
dipped below the level of Ryan's eyes and the small beads of
sweat at the top of the trimmed beard grew bigger and rolled
down between the hairs of the beard. He could have been
something from a Kipling story, Ryan thought, but he was
from Newcastle and even though he claimed to have fought

in Afghanistan everyone knew he had never been anywhere near the place.

When Tahir Khan got to Ryan's forehead, he smiled.

'Remember man that thou art dust and unto dust thou shalt return,' he said.

'You remember it, too,' Ryan said.

He stepped back and snapped his magazine into place, cocked the MP5D submachine-gun and put it on safety. The MP5D is the silenced version of the MP5. The silencer is an integral part of the weapon and helps with the balance when firing. They had loaded their weapons with hollow point ammunition because anyone they had to kill that night had to be killed quickly: when a hollow point round goes into the target it fragments and tears the vital organs to pieces like an explosion.

'And your webbin' pouches are too far forward,' Ryan said then. 'Stay still for a bit. Side and rear, side and rear, Tahir, keep it all there. You can't crawl with a heap of gear hangin' from your chest and your gut. Do it up again. I don't want this to be your first and last trip over there.'

Ryan shook his head and sighed. He had seen four like Tahir in as many months. The others were all dead. And he could not remember all their names.

Tahir Khan looked at the other men in the cellar, undid his webbing and moved his ammunition and equipment pouches into place. Then he pulled his black boiler suit in close to his body, tightened his webbing straps and checked the two grenades he carried and the small knife in the inverted sheath at his shoulder.

'You can use that?' Ryan said.

He touched the knife at Tahir's shoulder.

'I know what to do.'

'That wasn't what I asked.'

Ryan went across the room and looked through a heap of magazines and cassette tapes and pulled out an old shoe box. He opened it and pulled out a leather holster and an automatic pistol.

'It's a Tokarev,' he said. 'It's pretty old and the round is 7.62 by 25 mil. I could only get you a couple of clips but then again you'll only need one round. I use the same weapon.'

Tahir looked at the gun.

'Here, take it,' Ryan said, 'you need a personal weapon – and for Christ's sake, if you do have to use the damn thing, put it in your fuckin' mouth, you hear?'

Tahir smiled.

'Sure I'm dead already, Luke. Went to me own funeral, I did. Mujahideen, that's me. Look . . .'

He opened the top of his boiler suit. There was a large tattoo covering his chest. It was a sword with flames around it and the legend: '*Allah U Akbar*' across it.

'Yeah, terrific. But you're no fuckin' good to us dead. There's too many fuckers wanna die here and not enough wanna win. And I'm fuckin' serious about the personal weapon, I'm damn fuckin' serious. I've seen what happens when you don't have one. Yves, tell him about your mate, go on.'

A short, heavy-shouldered man turned from checking his weapon, shook his head and stubbed the cigarette he was smoking into the ground. He had a boyish face, if you discounted the scars and his expression of melancholy, and his lips were pure Gaulois. Except he wasn't French.

Yves was probably Belgian, though Grundy said he might have been Algerian Pied Noir. He had feminine eyes that lit up when he was happy and shrunk to almost nothing when he was not. He had been in the French Foreign Legion and he still wore the green beret and the winged hand and dagger beret badge of the 2nd Regiment Etranger de Parachutistes. In his belt he carried a Siberian Kandra, which is like a butcher's knife, but sharpened on both sides, and he said he could take a man's head off with one swipe.

'He was a Frenchman,' Yves said to Tahir Khan, 'a para like me, you know? And the Chetniks, they took him near Zadar in Croatia maybe two years ago. He was a good soldier, good drinker, you know? They are fucking *barbares*, the fucking Chetniks. So they take him and they peels him – yes? – they peel his skin like a potato – all of it. Yes! And then – then they let him go. He lives for maybe a few hours. They are fucking animals. It is best to kill yourself.'

*   *   *

They went into the water with a rubber raft, well upstream, behind a small pine wood which had been hit by mortars that day and torn up.

The night was cold and the wind was picking up in the valley and they could just smell the broken-tree sap and the resin from the pine wood before the wind carried it down river.

The Evkaf river had burst its banks and because the embankment on the south side was lower than on the north side, there was an area of about three hundred metres to the south that became a small flood plain. And the flood waters were an oily sheen on the valley floor.

Ryan lay in the raft. Low crescent-moonlight sank into the darkness to his left and spread out on the oily sheen of the flood waters and Ryan felt the cold of the water bleed into his skin and then into his bones and his marrow and he had a headache that was like burning and the water was pulling him away from the bank. He pointed his weapon forward.

The river was high and fast and dirty and it carried the raft several hundred metres downstream. Yves and the fourth man in the team, a very tall blond who said he was German and called himself Horst, steered the raft to the south bank of the river while Ryan and Tahir Khan covered the front.

Horst's real name was Willy and he was Czech. He said he had been a Foreign Legionnaire but he did not know the words to '*Le Boudin*', the Legion's song. Yves said he was a deserter from the Czech army but that was only a wild guess. Anyway, it did not really matter who or what Horst really was, what mattered was that he was there and could use a rifle and a fibreglass longbow, because he had been some kind of archery champion, and he wasn't a bad soldier. He liked to keep himself to himself when he wasn't working, as if he had even more to hide than the others.

The flood waters carried them over the south bank of the river and the first Serb minefield, which was supposed to be half a metre under water now. Just the way Grundy had said, Ryan thought. And he felt his body tense in expectation.

More and more now it was just the way Grundy had said,

as if Grundy commanded the war somehow. Ryan was finding it more and more difficult to distinguish the war from Grundy and Grundy from the war and his reasons for being there seemed to gravitate to Grundy and vanish into the fat, bearded man. And Ryan did not want that.

When they were coming to the edge of the flooding, Ryan slid out of the raft on the right side and steered it to where the land rose again.

The rise was covered in limestone rocks deposited by the flooding river, and Ryan anchored himself and the raft there with his knife.

He lay in the shallow water and covered the rest of them out of the raft.

Tahir went ahead of Ryan, to his left, and took up position in the wet grass. Ryan watched him and made a judgement.

He waited for Horst and Yves to slide in before he moved ahead of Tahir.

The land on the south side of the valley was mostly farmland and there were crops still rotting in the fields, fruit orchards covered in decayed fruit and lines of poplars on the small roads between the villages.

The four men went along the new river bank for a hundred and fifty metres, past a small field of rotting potatoes, river flood water lapping at the edge, depositing rocks and silt in a small bank. And none of them was quite sure if they had fully cleared the first minefield.

They lay flat for a while and listened and then moved over ploughed ground in single file and through a grass field.

The Serb village they were after was called Jablanica. It was about a kilometre from the river and shaded by poplars and beech trees. It got its name from the poplars.

Jablanica was a target for two reasons: it had an electricity substation which fed the Serbs in the villages on the south side of the river and a new ammunition dump right beside the substation. Blow the ammunition dump and the whole village – electricity sub-station included – would go with it.

For a brief moment, the image of Frejzo Ceric entered Luke Ryan's head and he stopped everything. It was the first time he had killed one of his own. He had joined the war to fight the Serbs, not even to kill them so much as to fight them for what they were doing, for their superiority, for their brutality, for the inequality of the struggle, and because no one outside really seemed to give a shit beyond proffering handouts; and he had ended up killing his own. And that had broken something inside him.

He thought about it some more and then found he had to rest on Grundy for support again. He cursed himself.

The ammunition dump was in and beneath a stone barn at one end of the village. The barn was protected from assault by a huge earth embankment running right around both it and the electricity substation. The substation was in a small concrete-block house. The stone barn belonged to a house which had been owned by the only Muslim family in the village. The family were gone and the house had a circled M on it.

An earlier Bosnian frontal assault across the river, which had ended with ten dead to the mines and fifteen more to triangular mortar and machine-gun fire from the mountains, had opened a small path into the second Serb minefield on that side of the river, which the Serbs had not repaired.

And Grundy had figured the Serbs would never expect a night raid there now, not with the autumn flooding and after all those losses.

Ryan was on his stomach, hoping Grundy was right and knowing he would be.

He slid down into a gully and the light of the low quarter moon slid along his back in a line and touched Yves's face. Yves rolled to Ryan's right and Horst went to his left and Tahir covered the back door.

It took three hours for Ryan and Yves to pick a path through the rest of the second minefield.

Three Serb patrols passed close to the minefield and one of them stopped for a smoke and a drink and a piss. Yves rolled into a hole in the minefield where three Bosnians had died during the failed infantry assault and felt some Serb piss splash on his face. The dead Bosnians' personal effects were scattered around the hole and Yves picked up a pair of worry beads and a wallet and stuffed them in his pockets.

When Ryan had cleared a path through the mines with his knife, he moved from the minefield through a series of smashed sheds and barns, over a stone wall, past an old pig pen and across three small gardens littered with shell fragments, vine branches and rotten vegetables.

He stopped at the earth embankment in front of the stone barn and fell on his stomach.

There were two sentries, one at either end of the stone barn. Ryan signalled to Yves. Technically Ryan was the leader of the raiding party but there was a certain democracy among the foreigners and no one obeyed an order in the field if they thought it was wrong. Except an order from Grundy. They all obeyed Grundy, no matter what.

Yves moved.

He was moving through a garden when he heard a door open in the stone barn. Yves went down on his belly.

There was a cough and the sound of boots on large stones from behind the stone barn, and then some talk and the sound of boots scuffing. The sound died in an exchange of gunfire down the valley and then there was silence again.

Ryan looked back at Yves and pointed in the direction of the Serb who had left the stone barn.

Yves drew his hand across his neck.

Ryan nodded and signalled to Yves to take the two sentries at the barn with Horst. Yves signalled to Horst to follow him.

Horst moved.

Then Ryan signalled Tahir and told him to flank left of the Serb who had come out from the stone barn. He hoped the Geordie had a tenth of the skill he boasted.

Tahir nodded and moved. Ryan rolled over and flanked to the right of the stone barn.

There were two sentries, one at either end of the stone barn.

Yves rolled over the embankment and crawled to the barn. Horst went up to the crest of the embankment and at a count of three stood up and shot the nearest sentry. The man fell back against the stone wall of the barn at the same time as Yves killed the second sentry.

The Serb who had left the barn was young and he had his hands in his pockets and was walking along a gravel path when Tahir and Ryan caught up to him.

Ryan was further away but he could see Tahir's silhouette against the trees and it got so all he had to do was look at a certain place and he knew Tahir would be there.

Then the Serb stopped.

Ryan fell to the ground. He could feel his insides trying to get out, and he buried his mouth in the hard ground to stop the sound of his heart jumping out. The Serb looked round. Then he turned into a plantation of tall trees to his left.

Tahir had dropped to the ground and Ryan could see his outline against one of the smaller trees. The trees were moving in the breeze and there was the sound of gunfire from across the valley. And then more footsteps.

Another Serb came from the village, very quickly.

Ryan crawled a few metres on his elbows and then rolled in beside two rocks and looked over for Tahir.

And they watched the two Serbs.

It was quick and except for the rhythm of the sounds Ryan was not sure what had happened. He looked over at Tahir and pointed to his knife and drew his finger across his neck. Tahir nodded. Ryan pulled his knife out and started to crawl towards Tahir.

Then, suddenly, Tahir stood up and fired his sub-machine gun.

Six silenced nine-millimetre rounds entered the darkness and there was the noise of splintering wood and something like tearing leather and a low thud and a wheeze and then the two outlines collapsed against a tree.

Ryan cursed to himself. He signalled to Tahir to go and check the two Serbs.

Tahir moved forward with his weapon extended and Ryan rolled over and flanked right of him and came into the trees from the stone path. He crunched gravel on the path and nearly slipped trying to get off it.

Tahir stood still and listened, then moved again.

Ryan stood away from him and then lay down and covered the Serb village ahead. He could see a caravan on the main street, next to a house with three huge holes in its wall.

And Ryan wanted to get up and run then, and the feeling was so strong that he nearly let go of his bowels trying to fight it. Come on, Tahir, come on, he kept thinking.

The young Serb they had followed from the stone barn was lying beside a tree with his combat trousers down to his knees and his jacket down over his shoulders. Three rounds had hit him in the chest and the white t-shirt he wore under his jacket was deep red in the silver moonlight. One of his fingers was twitching and Tahir, who had never killed anyone so close before this, watched it twitch for a few seconds and then put a round into the young man's head. Luke Ryan could smell the gases from Tahir's weapon.

Tahir was turning to the other Serb who lay face down in the grass beside his lover when the boot caught him in the shin. A second kick came in behind his left knee when he turned, and his knee folded and two rounds left his MP5D and hit dead leaves and branches on the trees overhead. Tahir moaned and hit his head on the trunk of the tree, as the Serb pulled himself up and tried to yell.

But one of Tahir's rounds had caught him below the neck and part of the fragmentation had torn his larynx, and another round had punctured his lungs so that he could not get anything out but a breathless wheeze; and when he tried, blood blocked his throat and choked the wheeze down to something the sound of the wind could cover.

And the wind was stronger now and there were small drops of rain on the wind and they were cold when they touched Luke Ryan's face.

Ryan rolled and aimed and fired at the Serb staggering towards the village.

He fired three single rounds and the third round caught the Serb in the right shoulder and spun him against the high stone wall of the house with the holes at the end of the village. The Serb fell backwards and cracked his head off the wall and tried to pick himself up and yell again.

The pale blue of pre-dawn was spilling over the mountains at Evkaf and the sharp cold of that time of day had come with it and he could feel his body chilling and wanted to scream louder than he had ever screamed in his life.

Ryan picked himself up and went after the Serb.

The main street of the village had a small *kavana* and about six habitable houses. The rest were holes held together by masonry and the street was strewn with rubble and glass and the glass cracked under the Serb's feet when he ran. There were two burnt-out cars in the middle of the street with their bonnet hoods up and their wheels burned off. Some of the rubber from one of the cars had liquefied and then resolidified in a kind of long lump further down the street.

The Serb fell, half picked himself up and staggered up the street, touching the ground with his hands. And Luke Ryan stopped and watched and fired again and missed.

Then another Serb appeared out of the house with the huge holes to Ryan's right, with his rifle levelled. Ryan swung. Five rounds killed this Serb and he fell back in the street where he had stood. The Serb who came after him was still loading his rifle when Ryan shot him through the head. He smashed into a wall and fell through a hole in the house.

Ryan caught the wounded Serb at the door of a brown two-storey house with a huge red, blue and white Serb flag draped from the first-floor balcony. The flag had a cross and four mirror-image Cyrillic Cs on it. The Cs stand for *Samo Sloga Srbina Spasava*: Only Unity Can Save the Serb.

There were shutters on the windows of the brown house and sandbags, three deep, out in front, but Ryan could see light through the gaps in the sandbags and shutters, pinpricks of light, and they touched the face of the Serb he was chasing when the man reached the front door.

The Serb banged once on the door and Ryan shot him across the back and then the chest. The Serb was twenty-two and from Belgrade and had come to fight for the Bosnian Serbs because he thought it would be a great adventure. He had taken part in a massacre of Muslim and Croat civilians near Zvornik early in the war and when he was sliding down the sandbags with sand pouring over his bloodied face he tried to think of these things but his mind could not do it.

Ryan followed the Serb down to the ground and watched him die.

Then the door opened and another Serb in olive green combats, carrying a folding-butt AKMS and eating a plum came out. He was in his thirties, his hair was dark and oily, his face long and his eyes green. He had a few days of stubble and he carried a side arm in a small leather holster. He had no boots on and there was a beer bottle on the floor behind him.

He got the first syllable of a warning to the edge of his lips when the first round hit him in the mouth; the second round caught him in the right side of the chest and the third hit him dead centre in the spine. He tumbled in the doorway, fell over his beer bottle and dropped his rifle and Horst stepped on him, running into the house.

There were three Serbs at a table, drinking beer, playing cards and listening to the BBC World Service on the radio. The reporter was describing a Serb advance in southeastern Bosnia and a night's shelling in Sarajevo.

Horst shot the man nearest him in the head. One of his friends reached down for his rifle but the safety catch was on and it was lying on the floor and Horst had put two hollow point rounds into him before he could get to the weapon. The third Serb did manage to get his pistol out and was aiming it at Horst. Luke Ryan shot him from the doorway, and the man flipped back in his chair and sprawled across the tiled floor and his blood ran along the grooves of the tiles and gathered around a waste basket.

'What the fuck has happened?' Horst said.

Ryan shook his head and stared at Tahir Khan standing in the doorway, gasping for breath, holding his hands high in apology.

'Shut the fuckin' door,' Ryan said.

Tahir shut the door and Ryan moved to the stairs, covered by Horst. The smell of spent ammunition was everywhere and it mixed with the sweat Ryan could smell from his own body and the sweat of the dead Serbs and the dry heat of a storage heater.

'Cover me, Horst,' Ryan said.

Horst nodded and covered Ryan up the stairs. Then Tahir covered Horst around the downstairs rooms.

Upstairs, Ryan turned the door-handle of the first room and slowly shoved the door open with his foot while he held his MP5D extended with one hand. The light from the landing entered the room ahead of him. It was a small room and the far wall had a hole in it where a piece of metal had come through.

Ryan saw more holes and a bed turned over and pushed up against a window and smelled the musty smell of the room. There were three mattresses on the floor showing signs of use. He checked the wardrobe, then left the room and closed the door.

Downstairs, Horst came out of the cellar, sweating. He began to drink the remains of a bottle of wine and eat some some dry beef and told Tahir to cover the front door. Tahir began to apologise, but Horst put his finger to his lips. Then he went looking for more food and equipment.

Above him, Ryan moved slowly along the wall to the next room. He was about to put his hand on the door-handle when the toilet flushed to his right.

He swung round and threw himself against the covering wall as the door opened. The Serb collapsed back on to the toilet bowl behind him when Ryan fired.

Horst heard this and moved over to the bottom of the stairs and took position.

Ryan just kicked open the next three bedroom doors and sprayed the rooms. The bullets tore velvet furniture, sandbags, mattresses and kitbags. There were ten automatic rifles standing against one of the walls.

'Luke!' Horst whispered.

Ryan came to the top of the stairs and mouthed a curse.

Horst made a sign that told him to hurry up.

Ryan gave him a finger and moved round a corner to the last bedroom door. He turned the handle.

Then he thought he heard breathing.

He held himself and pushed the door. To his left there were six boxes of books, stacked on top of each other and a pile of old 78 records.

There was breathing.

The room was darker than the others because the window was completely sealed with mattresses and none of the landing light had made it round the corner into the room.

Ryan reached into his pocket, pulled out a small rubber torch and clipped it on to his weapon. He directed the beam into the room and moved along the far wall. Then he stopped.

The breathing again.

He waited.

It was still there.

He pushed his weapon in and fired.

The bullets hit sandbags and mattresses and furniture and pieces of equipment.

Then Ryan crouched and moved low along a wall with his MP5D extended.

The torch beam touched a bed and a heap of clothes and then moved across a couple of chairs. And then Ryan heard the breathing again.

He rolled across the floor and swung the MP5D to where he thought the breathing was coming from.

He just held his fire.

The girl was huddled in a corner between two chairs.

Ryan cursed quietly to himself.

There were clothes shredded in front of her and she was wearing a blanket. Her face was bruised, but it was a beautiful face, even with the bruising, and she had deep brown hair with Pre-Raphaelite curls that touched her shoulders. Her skin was brown and her body was beautiful enough to make Ryan keep looking at it, even under the blanket. And her eyes looked like something very precious.

Ryan swung round the room again and then back to the girl.

'Jesus,' he said. 'How are you?' he added in Serbo-Croat instead of 'Who are you?'

She did not reply.

'Do you speak English?' Ryan said then. '*Govorite li engleski?*'

The girl nodded, very slowly, as if she was not sure what her answer would result in.

..yan could not take his eyes off her and felt that if anything had happened then he would still not have been able to take his eyes off her.

'*Da . . . da . . .*' she said. She nodded harder as if to emphasise what she was saying. 'Yes. *Molim, u pomoc*. Please, help me. Muslim, I am Muslim. You are English? *Armija BiH?*'

'Yeah, yeah, *Armija*,' Ryan said.

She smiled. Then she directed her eyes to the door.

Ryan swung round and fired but nothing happened. The magazine was empty.

Horst pulled himself up from where he had crouched. He whispered a curse and rubbed his mouth.

'Jesus Christ,' he said. 'Come on, we must get out, Luke. Kill her.'

'No, no, please, do not,' the girl said. 'Please, do not kill me, please. I am Muslim. I am Muslim.'

'Luke, kill her for God's sake!' Horst said.

He raised his weapon. The girl crouched.

'Please, no,' she said again. 'I am Muslim.'

And for an instant Ryan saw Frejzo Ceric again and he told himself what he had told himself for weeks.

'No, Horst,' Ryan said. 'No.'

He stood in Horst's way. Horst thought for a few seconds and then lowered his weapon.

'Fuck, shit,' he said. 'Okay, it's your head, Ryan. But tie her fucking tight. And come on.'

He turned and left the room.

Ryan thought for a few seconds, switched magazines, snapped the cocking lever back and set the MP5D for single shots.

'I'm sorry,' he said to the girl.

He pulled some cord from his thigh pocket and moved towards her.

'Stop, you fucking pigshit bastard,' she said.

The girl had a knife pointed at him.

'You help me, you fucking pigshit mercenary bastard. You think I will stay here with these? Help me, you shit. Fuck you, you bastard.'

Ryan just looked at the knife shaking in her hand.

'Okay, okay, keep your damn voice down – shut up,' he said. 'Are you gonna kill me?'

She held the knife up for a moment and then shook her head.

'Help me, please. Help me. Please.'

He lowered his weapon and reached out and the girl lowered the knife and Ryan took her hand in his.

'Okay, okay,' he said.

Tahir was covering the front door and Horst was collecting food and weapons when Ryan brought the girl down. He had dressed her in combat trousers and a torn shirt.

'Jesus Christ, Ryan, you get a fucking blow?' Horst said.

'Shut up, Horst,' Ryan said. 'She's a fuckin' Muslim.'

'Oh, sure, and you know this?' Horst said.

The girl looked at the three dead men in the room.

'They keep me here,' she said to Horst. 'I am Muslim and they keep me here. Please!'

Horst kept shaking his head.

'Do you know what this is?' he said to Ryan. 'Chetnik brothel. She is a whore. Yeah?'

The girl dipped her eyes.

'Please,' she said again, 'I am Muslim, please. Yes, they keep me here. Use me.'

She pointed to the cellar door.

'You are a fucking asshole, Ryan,' Horst said, 'a damn fucking asshole. Fuck her and kill her.'

'No,' Tahir said.

'Who the fuck asked you?' Ryan said.

Tahir looked at the girl.

'Men have authority over women because . . .' he said.

'. . . because He has made the one superior to the other,' she said, 'and because they spend their wealth to maintain them. Good women are obedient.'

She bowed her head.

'That's from the Koran,' Tahir said. 'The Sura on women. She's probably tellin' the truth.'

'You will take me, please?' she said to Ryan.

Ryan nodded and a relaxed pleasure took over his face. Horst kept shaking his head.

When they had collected all the food, arms and ammunition they could carry, Tahir opened the door and moved into a cover position on the street. Horst followed and moved out of the village.

Ryan looked at the girl and her precious eyes and her Pre-Raphaelite curls and smiled. She did not smile back.

'Sorry,' he said. 'I have to do this.'

Then he pulled two gags from the thigh pocket of his combat trousers, stuffed one in her mouth and tied the other round her head.

He booby-trapped the house and when they reached the stone barn Yves was sitting on the floor, setting explosive charges.

There were three dead Serbs beside him. One was decapitated.

Yves looked at the girl and smiled at Ryan.

Ryan shrugged.

'We found her. She's Muslim. She wants to come.'

'Funny war for funny life, yes, Luke?' Yves said.

Horst stuffed his pockets with the vegetables and beer that lay around. Then he found a knapsack beside a small cot and bottles of plum brandy in a cupboard and some cream cheese and bread wrapped in newspaper. The bread was stale but he took it anyway.

Ryan looked at the girl again and touched her hand and asked her if she was all right. Her head made no reply.

'Okay, let's move,' he said.

Yves took some grenades and some thin wire from a pouch in his webbing and laid booby traps around the stone barn and the substation, and when they were all out, he put a wire across each of the doors and a second hidden to the right of them that would go off if you disarmed the first.

Then they moved off towards the river.

Horst led off with Tahir behind him, then Ryan and the girl. Yves covered them from the earth embankment while they made their way back through the minefield across the markers Ryan had left.

It was very quiet and Luke Ryan expected something to explode or someone to shout and then start firing but nothing happened. Somewhere in the foothills of a long, bare mountain to their right, called Gola Planina, they could hear singing and there were a few shots from the mountains on the other side of the river but nothing happened.

They made the girl lie face down on the raft and Ryan got in with her and the captured rifles, ammunition and food. He lay beside her and she loosened her grip on the knife and rested her head on his arm. The other three stayed in the water. They paddled east up the flooded area for almost a kilometre before moving into the river proper. The river took them downstream again, very fast, and they only made the north bank at Donje Selo.

The sun had not risen over the mountains yet and the light was soft and the cold was hard. Ryan gave the girl his jacket and she leaned her head on his shoulder for a few seconds. Then the stone barn at Jablanica exploded.

3

The Evkaf hospital was a grey Titoist building wedged in between two Habsburg blocks at the end of a winding street where a bus used to run from the main square, the Bratstva i Jedinstva Trg. The two Habsburg blocks were destroyed and the flagstones on the winding street were pocked with shallow mortar holes and a bus stood burnt out where it had been hit by a machine-gun burst on the first day of the war.

Luke Ryan kept close to the walls of the buildings. He could hear the odd sniper bullet whistle overhead and a mortar round impacted to his right, but the worst of the morning's shelling was over and people were re-emerging on to the streets.

He passed a *'Pazi Snajper'* sign at a junction and sheltered behind a wall of wrecked cars and cargo containers before following a line of shell holes across the face of one of the Habsburg blocks beside the hospital. The brown face of the building was gouged out and behind the brown there was a yellowish stone and then a powdery white, and the powdery white spilled on to the street in small trickles.

One of the Habsburg blocks had been an apartment building and the whole front of two of the higher apartments was gone. Ryan could see a bed and a picture and a Playboy magazine centrefold stuck to one of the walls. Someone's calendar had fallen into the street and it lay sodden in the gutter. It was a Croat calendar with a picture of some Wagnerian types on horses standing at the Dalmatian coast, looking out to sea. The caption said: The Arrival of the Croats. He picked it up.

The hospital had red crosses all over it. It was built in concrete and, unlike the Habsburg blocks around it, was meant for war. There were impact holes from every type of weapon in its front but the concrete was very thick and well angled against attack. Only the few rounds that went directly through windows had done damage inside the hospital. The window spaces were all metal plate and board and sheet plastic now and some of the contents of the rooms had spilled into the hospital forecourt.

Inside, the smell was a heavy rotten smell partially masked by disinfectant and cleaning fluid and anything else they could get to cover it up.

There was fast talking and a scream and low moaning Ryan could not identify and then he was looking into a room at an amputation. Then a nurse shut the door and there were only the voices again.

And that was the way it was now for Ryan, the war, like hearing voices behind a door.

And you think you know what is going on behind the door from the voices, he thought, but when you open the door and enter the room you find out you are not so sure any more.

Ryan put it down to fatigue – he had been fighting for nearly a year now without a break – but it was more than that, something more basic. He went through it all now: his first action, the first time he saw someone killed, the first time he had killed, all that kind of thing, as if it would reinforce whatever was failing in him.

Doctor Mihalj Dutina was sitting on the floor in a corridor on the second floor of the hospital. He wore a white coat covered in bloodstains and had a stethoscope around his neck and a white face mask hanging free. His head rested against his knees and it was only when Ryan bent down to him that he realised the doctor was asleep.

Dutina was rare in two ways: he was a Serb who had stayed loyal to the Bosnian government and he was a qualified surgeon in Evkaf. He had worked in Germany and France for twenty years, mainly as a psychiatrist, and had come back to Bosnia to wind down. He was in his sixties and balding and his chest became irritated in very cold air. But the thing that got to him most was that he was broke and alone.

He had brought home nearly a million Deutschmarks, a wife and two sons. He put the money in a bank and sent his sons to university in Sarajevo. And the day before war broke out his wife went to visit relatives in Banja Luka. Both of his sons were in the Serb army now, his money was in a Serb bank which had closed and he had not heard from his wife since the outbreak of the war. His wife was a Muslim.

When Ryan shook him, Dutina opened one eye. It was bloodshot. He looked around and rubbed the eye.

'You are early,' he said to Ryan. 'What is your blood type?'

Two orderlies rushed a stretcher past them. A child's scream rang through the corridor. Formaldehyde hitched a lift on the cleaning fluid and open flesh.

'I don't know,' Ryan said. 'I came to see someone.'

'You do not come for give blood?'

Ryan shrugged and looked up and down the corridor, hoping he would see the girl he had brought over from the Serb lines walking towards him.

'I'm lookin for a girl,' he said. 'Administration don't know her. No one here does.'

'What girl? What is her name?'

'I don't know.'

'Look, I am need you *fur blut*,' Dutina said. '*Bitte. Fur blut.*'

He pointed down the corridor and then stood up, rubbed his eyes again and massaged his face. He put his hand on Ryan's back and said please in English and German.

'Yeah, sure, okay,' Ryan said.

He was still exhausted from the night before and he had not slept because he could not get the girl with the pre-Raphaelite curls and the green eyes out of his head.

He followed Dutina down the corridor to a staircase and down the stairs to a basement. They walked along a stone corridor with two small wall-lamps, covered in wire, at either end. Ryan could see the bricks in the walls seeping water.

Then Dutina pulled out a key and unlocked a thick metal blast door and they entered a dark room.

The doctor lit a candle. There were three couches and a sink and a small beer cooler in the room and there were no

windows. The room was cold and it did not have the smell
of the rest of the hospital.

'You have good *blut*?' the doctor asked.

'Yeah, you know, red.'

'I mean, no hepatitis, HIV, etcetera, etcetera?'

'Not that I know.'

The doctor pointed to a couch, took a squash ball from his
pocket and gave it to Ryan. Ryan hesitated.

'Please – to lie down,' the doctor said.

Ryan's combat fatigues were stained with mud and oil and
he looked at Dutina and then at his uniform and at the couch.
Dutina walked over to a cupboard on the wall, took some
newspapers out and spread them on the couch.

'Now, to lie down, *bitte*.'

'I don't know my blood type,' Ryan said.

'*Es macht nichts*. I have no *blut* – blood. *Verstanden*? I have
asked for blood. I need blood. All blood. All hospital has blood
geben. *Bitte*, my English . . . I am very tired . . .'

Dutina shook his head, took a bottle from the beer cooler
and put it on a bench beside the sink, then took out a clear
tube and a needle.

'It's clean?' Ryan said.

'Boiled,' he said. 'It is okay. I need blood.'

The doctor was arranging his equipment. He hung the bottle
out of a metal stand and connected up the tube.

'Squeeze, please,' he said.

Ryan started to squeeze the squash ball and Dutina took out
a dirty handkerchief and tied it round Ryan's arm above the
elbow, then found a vein and put the needle in and connected
the needle up to the tube.

'*Herr Doktor*,' Ryan said, 'the girl I want, she came here
this morning, she had bruises, cuts, maybe other things. The
police brought her here, I was told.'

'Which girl? What wound?'

'Muslim girl. Very beautiful. Green eyes, brown hair, curls.
The most beautiful girl I've ever seen.'

'Yes, yes . . .'

'Yeah . . . ? Where is she?'

'I do not know. I do not remember her, perhaps another

doctor ... Do you know how many people have green eyes in Bosna?'

He tapped his head.

'She was maybe raped, I think,' Ryan said. 'She was very beautiful.'

'More womans raped than have green eyes,' Dutina said. 'Very bad. They are not Serbs who do this; Serbs are not like this. I am Serb. I am not rape women. It is terrible. I am shame. I am shame.'

'You're not a Chetnik.'

'My sons are with Chetniks.'

'They are not you.'

'They are my sons.'

When he had taken Ryan's blood, Dutina took a bottle of iodine from the beer cooler and put some on a piece of tissue paper he had in his pocket and wiped the needle mark on Ryan's arm. Then he replaced the squash ball, the dirty handkerchief and the piece of tissue paper in his pocket.

He told Ryan to lie still and placed the bottle filled with Ryan's blood in the beer cooler, then took the needle and the tube and put them in the sink.

'I have no tea, no *kuchen*,' he said. 'I have *rakija*. You came for to see this girl?'

'No. Mirsat Pasic, from Donje Selo. He is wounded in the leg and stomach.'

Ryan pointed to the positions of the wounds.

'Muha man?'

'No. *Armija*.'

'I am sorry. I am afraid,' Dutina said. 'Muha mens come this morning. I am afraid. I hide.'

He wiped his brow.

'Mujahideen,' Dutina said. 'They want to kill me. I hear them. They call me Chetnik. They want to kill me. But I am necessary. Doctor.'

'Mirsat is not mujahideen. He's not much of anything right now. He was with Mustafa Spahic's company in Donje Selo and Spahic is a raja, like you.'

Raja is a name rural Bosnians give urban Bosnians, and it means they are soft.

'All *Muslimani* are *raja*. You see ... ?'

The doctor pointed towards the carsija end of town.

'When the Turkish here, they – *muslimani* – were – *ubermensch*. *Verstanden?*'

'I know. But that was then. Mirsat's a shepherd. He's dying, I think. The girl?'

Dutina wasn't listening.

'Chetniks afraid,' he said. 'It is fear. Of Ustasha. Of mujahideen. They are afraid of everything. Always armageddon. My sons Chetniks. You kill many Chetniks, Ryan?'

'Where's that *rakija* you promised?'

The doctor went over and searched in the cupboard. The bottle of *Sljivovica* was half full and he wiped the top before handing it to Ryan. *Sljivovica* is a plum brandy, often home-made, usually potent and always available.

'If Muha's men give you trouble, you come to us, okay? Have you told the police?' Ryan asked.

Dutina threw his eyes up in the air and sighed.

'Muha is *policija*. *Ja?*'

'Yeah,' Ryan said. 'I forgot. Jesus, my head's a bit light. How much blood did you take?'

The doctor smiled.

'Drink,' he said.

Mirsat Pasic was lying on a stretcher in a top corridor of the hospital. The rooms on the side of the corridor facing Crna Gora were empty and their doors shut and reinforced with pieces of steel. Some of the doors and some of the steel patches had holes in them. Some of the steel patches had other sheets of steel fixed across them. Once or twice a piece of shrapnel or an armour-piercing round had gone through everything, even the far wall. You could trace the path of a projectile through the hospital, and if you looked into the rooms that were closed off, their windows were gone and they were wrecked.

Mirsat had no left leg and his right foot smelled faintly of gangrene. He smiled and lifted his hand. Ryan took his hand and shook it.

'Womans, Deutschmarks?' Mirsat said.

Ryan shook his head. His felt slightly dizzy and out of breath and he could not figure out what he was doing there because Mirsat Pasic was dying and it was better to leave the dying to die and not let any of their misfortune rub off on you. That was one theory anyway. There was another that said you were reinforcing your own good fortune by being with a dying man because he was dying and you were not and that said something about what would happen to you. It was all bullshit but it kept men going and some carried charms and went through routines before going into battle to add to the effect.

'*Rakija*,' Ryan said to Mirsat.

He had brought along Dutina's *Sljivovica* bottle. He took it out of his pocket and looked round to see if anyone was watching. The corridor was lined with men on stretchers and beds and in between them were piles of grey blankets. They had a musty smell which, added to the rotting from the gangrenous limbs and the disinfectant, made the choking atmosphere sharp.

'*Musliman*,' Mirsat said.

Then he smiled and the black hairs on his face stood up.

Luke Ryan put the bottle to Mirsat's lips – they were grey and dry and wrinkled. Mirsat held the brandy in his mouth, wiped his lips and handed the bottle back.

'*Allah u akbar*,' Ryan said.

There was a well of tear water in one of Mirsat's eyes and he winked to stop himself crying and part of the liquid dribbled out the side of his eye and back into his hair. His hair had lice. You could see them. One of them hopped on to Mirsat's face and then disappeared in a smile and a movement of the stubble on his face.

Mirsat swallowed the *rakija*.

'*Kaputt*,' he said.

Then he coughed and winced and Ryan knew he should not have given him the alcohol to drink. He thought maybe he wanted to do more than just be with him when he was dying. Suddenly, a woman slapped him on the shoulder.

'Christ, what are you doing? That man has severe abdominal wounds and internal and external haemorrhaging. He has no bloody stomach.'

Ryan turned fast on his heels. The woman shoved past him and bent over Mirsat.

She spoke without looking at Ryan.

'You stupid bastard, who the fuck said you could give him that? Jesus, you bloody people . . .'

She was about ten years older and two inches shorter than Ryan and her hair was blonde and tied at the back. She wore a white coat and had a stethoscope around her neck and her eyes were misty. She grabbed Mirsat's arms and pinned them down and he started to convulse.

'Come on,' she said, 'get him, quickly, get hold of him.'

She pointed at Mirsat's leg.

Ryan put his hands on Mirsat's leg and Mirsat kicked out. Ryan could see the black colour of the skin at his foot.

'I said hold him – both hands, stupid. Push. His fucking wounds will bleed now. Oh, shit!'

Blood seeped through the sheet over him, first as a dot, then a spot, then it spread and you could see it move across the individual threads of the sheet. Ryan shoved down on Mirsat with both hands and the old man tightened and screamed and the woman reached out and grabbed a handful of sheet and shoved it in his mouth.

'You stupid bastard,' she said to Luke Ryan again. 'No alcohol. This man has no insides left.'

She touched her stomach.

'No *rakija*. No fucking *rakija*. Jesus Christ . . .'

Ryan's head was lighter now and he watched her mouth without hearing all the words. She had a beautiful mouth and he did not take his eyes from it.

He pulled his Tokarev automatic from its holster, removed the safety, cocked it and pointed it at her.

'Fuck – off,' he said. 'Fuck off nice and slowly.'

She stepped back.

'Oh . . .' she said.

She had a sallow, angular Balkan face and it reddened.

'You had a bad night, Luke?' she said. 'You look awful.'

'I'm lookin' for someone.'

'And you're annoyed.'

Now Ryan blushed and the lightness in his head made his

hand shake. He lowered the gun and replaced it in the holster. Natasa Ruzic slammed her hand against his chest.

'Well, you could have killed this man,' she said, 'you stupid bastard, Luke. And you ever pull a gun on me again and I'll make you sorry. You think you scare me?'

'Let him have a fuckin' drink, Natasa,' Ryan said. 'He's dyin'.'

'Tell me something I don't know. Here, give that to me, give it to me.'

She took the *Sljivovica* bottle from Ryan's pocket and drank from it.

'You fucking soldiers, you fucking bastards. See what you cause?'

'Shut up, will you? I'm not feelin' so good. Dutina took all my blood, I think.'

Mirsat convulsed again and cried out through the sheet, then bit his lips and passed out.

'Come on,' Natasa said. 'Help me get him down to theatre.'

'He's dyin'.'

'You want to put a bullet in him? I'll walk to the end of the corridor. If you do, say so. If you don't, then help me get him to theatre.'

She stared at Ryan's sidearm.

He shook his head.

'I'm lookin' for a girl, Natasa,' he said. 'She has green eyes.'

'Don't tell me that, Luke,' Natasa said. 'I don't want to hear.'

Ryan sat outside the operating theatre two floors down. There were some minutes when he must have passed out because he felt that time was jumping in his brain. When they had patched up Mirsat Pasic again, two orderlies moved him back up to the top-floor corridor. They asked Ryan if he wanted to go with the old man. Ryan said, no. He was feeling very thirsty now.

Natasa Ruzic came out of the theatre, rubbed her eyes and sat down beside Ryan.

'Don't they teach you about gut wounds? Alcohol – it's the

worst, you know. Makes the heart beat. Causes bleeding. Good for passion, bad for wounds.'

'Yeah, I'm sorry,' Ryan said. 'You're lookin' pretty.'

She sighed.

'I have a sty – or hadn't you noticed?'

She pointed to her eye and it was purple at the lid. Her eyelashes were big, and even with the sty they made her eyes beautiful. Ryan didn't care. He just wanted a woman then. And the girl they had found in the Serb village? Well, that could wait.

'He's your friend?' Natasa said. 'The old man?'

'No,' Ryan said. 'I don't know him.'

'It's good he's asleep. I hope he dies asleep. I have no morphine to give him. So what's been happening to you, soldier?'

'I've been thinkin' of you.'

'You need to wash, Luke, you need to wash and maybe put on some weight and you'll look even nicer.'

'You're lovely.'

'You're just saying that to get into me.'

'Yeah.'

'Who's the girl?'

'I don't know. She had green eyes.'

Natasa looked away as if she was not interested in hearing more.

'How's Grundy?' she said then.

Ryan shrugged.

'You look a bit lost, Luke Ryan, you look like someone on a roundabout who can't figure out which exit to take.'

'I think I'm in the wrong war,' Ryan said.

'They're all the same. Only the individual reasons change.'

'I came here to forget,' he said.

'What?'

'I forget.'

He smiled.

'You're not a professional soldier, Luke?' she said.

He shook his head and laughed.

'I was – am – a religion teacher. To twelve-year-olds. Yeah! But I always wanted to be a journalist. So I came here to make

my name. Yeah! Then I saw the Chetniks shoot some people
... I'm on sabbatical from my school. Kind of extended leave.
You can do that.'

'I bet you write well,' she said. 'You must.'

'And you smell beautiful, Natasa,' Ryan said.

She kissed him.

'That's on account,' she said.

Ryan kissed her back and this time they held the kiss
for longer.

'You are a man of very strong emotions, Luke Ryan,' she
said. 'But your lips are dry. Here ...'

She licked her finger and then wet his lips with it. They
kissed again.

'Which room can we use?' Ryan said.

'Oh, you pick one – and make it sound nice.'

'I'm serious.'

'Yes, you look like a man who's serious, Luke. But you're too
tired. You wouldn't know it was me. So on second thoughts, I
won't sleep with you now. I don't want you to feel cheap. I'd
be using you and I don't want to use you. What day is it?'

Ryan shrugged. Then he blew air from his lips and closed
his eyes.

'Hey, Luke, you're not being very mannerly,' Natasa said.
'A gentleman does not fall asleep in front of a lady. It's bad
enough when they do it afterwards, it's damned unforgivable
if they do it before. Hey!'

'I'm sorry. I gave blood to Dutina.'

'Mihalj always takes too much. Drink lots of water.'

'UN get anythin' in?' he said.

'Some food. I was thinking about hopping on one of the
trucks going out. Why do we do it? I don't know. Well, I do
but I like to pretend I don't. Very English and very Balkan.
My problem.'

'You still want me to shoot him? Mirsat Pasic? The
old man?'

'Too late,' she said. 'I have to go. We'll see each other again,
Luke. You will want me. I'm jealous of that girl.'

'She's gone.'

'Good. I ...'

Natasa saw the two figures out of the corner of her eye before she heard the words shouted up the corridor.

'How's the best piece of ass in BiH?'

Natasa swung round. Grundy was coming along the corridor with Mihalj Dutina. Dutina was stooped and rubbing his eyes. Grundy had a pronounced limp in his left leg and his head seemed to move independently of his body.

He took Natasa in his arms, swung her round and kissed her.

'Bet you can't live without me?' he said.

'I've been seducing your friend,' she said.

'He's not my friend,' Grundy said.

'We're going to have an affair, aren't we, Luke?' Natasa said.

'Yeah, sure, why not?' Grundy said. 'Jesus, you look like shit, Luke, Mihalj steal your blood?'

'It is gone,' Dutina said. 'You are AB positive. Here, write it on your jacket.'

He handed Ryan a felt pen and Ryan tried to write his blood type on his uniform. But he could not manage it, his hands were still shaking.

'I took a litre,' Dutina said. 'I am sorry. Drink water, Ryan. You will be okay.'

'Here, let me,' Natasa said.

She took the felt pen and wrote the blood type above Ryan's chest pocket and below his left shoulder and kissed him gently on the lips.

'You had a bust up with Muha last night, darlin',' Grundy said to Natasa. 'Unwise.'

'His heavies were pinching UN supplies again,' she said.

'Well, watch it.'

'Muha doesn't scare me.'

'He should.'

'He frightens me,' Dutina said.

'I have to work, Grundy,' Natasa said. 'Anyway, I have a feeling you're going to start all that tough stuff and I really couldn't stand that now. I'll see you. And I'll definitely see you, Luke. We're this close to our affair. That gun thing did it for me. Turns me on.'

'Stethoscope turns me on,' Ryan said.

Natasa walked away and the three men followed her until she had disappeared around a corridor.

'You get any pay for last night, Grundy?' Ryan said then. 'I need some cash.'

'You goin' anywhere?'

'Some time. Any luck with Husic?'

Grundy shrugged.

'Maybe, maybe not.'

'What the hell does the fucker want?' Ryan said. 'I mean, last night's little pop isn't gonna do more than stop the Chetniks readin' at night. His people were all handshakes and stuff like that this mornin'. I couldn't take it. Jesus, would you get me some water, Mihalj? I'll give you a pack of cigarettes.'

Dutina nodded and went into the operating theatre. Two patients were wheeled in soon after him and five nurses had an argument with a doctor in the corridor. Ryan and Grundy moved into a small annexe corridor and sat down.

'He's comin' our way,' Grundy said. 'Jusef. He needs coaxin'. He's a cautious man. Still holdin' out for the world to come and help. But the world just wants a deal. Muha isn't helpin' things. Who was the whore you brought in?'

'She wasn't a whore.'

'Yeah, well, you shoulda fuckin' killed her, you know.'

'My call. She's one of ours.'

'So who is she?'

'That's just it, I can't find her. Intelligence said the police had her, the police said she came here and here hasn't heard of her.'

'Shit. You shoulda called me.'

'I was tryin' to sleep. I thought she'd be around.'

'Always the way with women. And, Luke – Natasa, she can't help it, you know. She can't help it. You should remember that.'

Dutina came into the annexe with a plastic can of water. He gave it to Ryan. Then he sat down and pulled out a cigarette. Ryan drank and Dutina smoked.

'Muha men,' he said. 'They kill me?'

Grundy shook his head.

'You're too important, Mihalj. Even Muha knows that.'

'Karadzic, Muha, they are the same people. All this is because of them. Yes?'

Grundy shook his head and took one of Dutina's cigarettes.

'All this is because of Diocletian,' he said. 'The Roman emperor.'

'Yes,' Dutina said.

He nodded.

'What do you mean?' Ryan asked.

'Simple. Diocletian divided his empire and the rest is this,' Grundy said. 'Oh, I know Antony and Octavian did it before him and Constantine moved the focus east after him, but Diocletian was the man. You heard of Diocletian's Tears, Mihalj?'

'Sure. That is for children and foolish men.'

'Let's drink to children.'

'What're you bullshittin' about now, Grundy?' Ryan said.

'Diocletian had to marry his only daughter, Valeria, to this underboss guy he'd taken on to help him with the Roman empire, a fella called Galerius. Now this Galerius was a vicious bastard, real animal, maybe a Chetnik, and Diocletian wasn't all too pleased at givin' the guy his only daughter to poke. But the empire was the empire so he sent her off to her new husband on the Danube and about a month or two later he sent her a kind of sweetener, under the watch of a unit of the Praetorian Guard.'

Ryan was drinking from the plastic can again. He stopped and some of the water ran down his front. He looked directly at Grundy.

'That's it,' Grundy said, 'that's Diocletian's Tears. Whatever it was – most people say it was silver – there's silver mines round here – it never got there. It never got to Valeria. It vanished.'

'Here,' Dutina said. 'In Bosna.'

'Right near here, near Evkaf,' Grundy said. 'An old Roman road from Diocletian's palace in Split to the Danube runs right through this valley, right across Evkaf. There's a museum with a piece of it down town.'

Grundy smiled.

'Sure, that's why I'm here,' he said. 'Didn't you guess? You don't think I'm here to fight for truth, justice and the American way? That right, Mihalj?'

'The tears are for children and fools,' Dutina said.

'It's a story, Luke,' Grundy said, 'it's a story. Jesus, don't look so serious, man. It's just a story.'

'So there's no treasure, no tears?' Ryan said.

'There's always tears,' Grundy said.

Grundy and Dutina started to laugh. And Luke Ryan felt foolish and held back his laughter until he could not resist the laughter infection any more and when he did give in he felt better.

'So what's next?' he said to Grundy as if he did not mean it.

'We keep up the pressure – on Jusef anyway,' Grundy said.

There was a rumble of artillery and the siren went and Ryan heard shells hitting the tower blocks at the west end of the town.

4

Later that day, the Muslim girl Ryan had brought over from the Serb lines sat on a bed in an apartment in the centre of Evkaf, watched by her brother.

She crossed her legs, pulled her hair back and double wrapped an elastic band on her fingers, then slipped her hair into the elastic band and combed her loose curls behind her ears.

She walked over to a table and picked up a roll of Deutschmarks, counted them and pushed them into the small pocket in the front of her jeans.

Her ponytail fell forward over her shoulder and the Pre-Raphaelite curls she had pressed back behind her ears slipped out and touched the tops of her ears, caught her earlobes for a moment, then fell forward with her ponytail.

There were two china cups with floral decorations on the table. They were sitting in deep china saucers with gold rims which sat on a red table rug with animal motifs sewn into the edges. The rug hung down low over the table and covered it, except for the mahogany feet which spread out on a varnished floor and left small indentations in the varnished wood and tiny scratch marks where it had been moved during a heavy Serb bombardment one Saturday.

Across the floor, where the sun's rays touched a cracked mirror and threw twisted shadows on faded wallpaper, a small fire of pine cones was burning in a high metal fireplace. The girl knelt down and watched the flame lick up at the black metal wall behind it and then spit and shrink back to the pine cone. There was no warmth.

The girl shook her head and cursed the fire and felt the

sharp end of a whistling wind on the back of her neck. She went over to the window and checked the barricade and found a hole between two chair seats and a pillow. The pillow had become dislodged and she pressed it back in place, reached over to an old armchair and, taking a cushion, rammed it in to secure the pillow. The barricade ran up to just over head height so the sun could come in when it was available. The sun was disappearing into the mountains to the west – giving the Serbs more warmth, people said. Even the sun is against us, they said.

The girl sat back on the bed. It was pushed in next to a veneer wardrobe. The metal frame had been scratched with initials and graffiti and was slightly buckled by a shell impact in a room below which had turned it over. All the occupants in the room below had been killed and no one went into that room any more.

The girl checked her small rucksack. There wasn't much in it: a plastic comb, some low-grade soap, a lipstick, two spare pairs of panties, a bra with a tear in it, one Tampax, a bar of chocolate, some single cigarettes, a plastic lighter and two books. One of the books was *Bosnian Story*, by Ivo Andric, though she had it under its original title, *A Travnik Chronicle*. It was dog-eared and damp and three of its pages had gone on a fire the day before. Most of the bookshelves in the room had been denuded to the needs of various fires. The family who owned the apartment had started with potboilers first and worked their way up to Nobel laureates, classics and religious texts. An open Koran lay beside the fire with five of its pages torn out.

'You do understand why I can't let you go?' the girl's brother said.

She did not look at him across the room. He picked a pine cone from the wicker basket beside him and threw it on to the fire. Then he stood up and went to the table and picking up one of the china cups, swirled the *turska kava* grit around in the bottom and replaced the cup in the saucer.

'And you'll stop me?' she said.

She reached into the bottom of her rucksack and pulled out

a knife. The knife was clean except for what looked like rust on the very tip.

'Yes, of course,' her brother said. 'Or will you use that on me, *draga*?'

'I don't think I could,' she said. 'I was going to – over there, but I didn't have to. I was lucky. You must be lucky in life. Take your chances, no matter what. I believe that.'

'You must stay, Emira. You must,' her brother said.

'Must I?' she said. 'You know I am so used to people telling me what to do I'm almost glad to hear that. But I don't really care any more ... Fatima's dead, Fatima Mulic, did I tell you that? I saw them kill her. You and her were sweet on each other, weren't you?'

Her brother's face showed no emotion. His pupils expanded, minutely.

'That's not the issue,' he said. 'Please, *draga*, even if you did go there is a good chance the Chetniks would catch you again. And if they catch you now, you will wish they did kill you, *draga*.'

'Please don't call me *draga*. You keep calling me that. I'll get through. Maybe you could ask Allah to protect me. You're in good favour there, I'm told, Hasim.'

'You will call me Muhammed, please. Muha, if you like. Most people do. It is more affectionate. But my name is Muhammed now.'

'Of course. Very appropriate,' Emira Kusturica said. 'The Chetniks say they will kill you slowly, Hasim. Do you want that? Maybe you should come with me.'

'Very touching, *draga*,' Muha said. 'I might be tempted, but more pressing business here keeps me from accepting your offer.'

'I didn't really mean it, Hasim.'

His pupils narrowed.

'They killed our father, they raped our mother, they killed her, they raped you, they raped Amela, Amela is gone, and you want to know why I stay. I stay for them.'

'Bullshit, Hasim. You were never there for them. Where were you when Daddy was telling us to be brave, Hasim would come? Where were you when I had to stand and watch Amela and Mama being raped? Six of them, Hasim, six of them raped Mama, and she cried and begged me not to look when they were doing it, begged me not to witness her shame. Her shame! And then they laughed and shot her like a dog while they were talking among themselves, one of them just drew out his pistol and turned around and shot her. You weren't there, Hasim, I was. And I'm going, I mean it. Away from all this shit.'

'It's against the law. We're not allowing people to leave. That's what they want. The Chetniks. We'd be helping them. And how would it look for me? Muha's sister leaves in the middle of the night when the Chetniks are at the gates. I will not permit it. I have a position here now, *draga*. I have a reputation. I am an important man.'

'So stay here and be important. I choose to leave.'

'I can have the police arrest you. I have that power. It is not personal, *draga*, it is policy.'

'I think I heard that in a movie, Hasim.'

His left cheek reddened very slightly.

'We are letting no one leave, *draga*,' Muha said. 'You think if we told people they could all leave, they would stay? And then the Chetniks would have our town. Our town.'

'It's not my town. I hated living here. I preferred Banja Luka. Think about it: I preferred Banja Luka to this place and you know what Banja Luka's like? But then again, what would you know of that, you never came there, Hasim.'

'I was busy, making a living. They offered to sell you.'

He made what passed for a smile. It was a very laconic gesture. Emira did not respond.

'The Chetniks,' Muha said.

'How much?'

'Ten thousand. Almost three times the usual price. I said I'd give fifteen if they could find Amela. But they couldn't find her. Then they said twenty for you alone and I knew they would never sell you. I've known you were over there all summer. I say this only so you will be aware that I knew, that I had it in my mind, that I was thinking about you all the time, knowing they had you, wondering if they would . . .'

'If they would what, Hasim? Didn't you know? I was having

a wild time over there. Oh, yes, I was having a party with the Chetniks, Hasim. They throw the best parties. I wondered why they brought me here. All summer, Hasim? My God, you must have some kind of small imagination if you knew I was there all summer and you did nothing. You can use your imagination, Hasim, or does Islam expect you to give it up? Well, let me brief you on what was happening over there. We were their entertainment in the evening – there were ten of us – the good-looking ones, they said – and we were the officer's fun and games. Some bastard got drunk in August and shot three of the girls. Just shot them. It's just about time for the night shift to have their recreation now. I know the day by the customers. At least the food was good.'

She laughed.

'You don't mind that I was their whore, Hasim?'

'You were not their whore.'

'You know this? They moved us around in our own armoured car. Yes, we had that, we became celebrities. Two of the girls killed themselves, cut their wrists with broken glass. I told your intelligence man all this, it makes good reading. I don't want to talk about it any more and I don't want it in the press, Hasim, it cheapens it all.'

'We would handle it delicately. People should know.'

'You think they don't? You know, one of the girls who killed herself, she was so scared when she was doing it, she asked me to help her, to hold her wrist, so I did, and I ate bread and drank from the bottle she took her piece of glass from. And she took a long time to die and she talked all the time. The other girl cut her neck and she died very quickly. I'm sorry, Hasim, I'm sorry, but I think if I don't get away from this fucking war and this fucking mess I will gladly do that to myself. You look thin, you should eat more, Hasim. Perhaps you should have told them to kill me.'

'I'm angry, Emira,' he said, 'You think I'm not angry. I'm very angry. But I'm angry for all of our people, for all of our women who have been raped, for all of our people who have been murdered. I must be angry for everyone, Emira, I cannot be angry just for you. You must understand. You must be strong. You are strong, Emira.'

'Am I? I don't think so. I don't want to be strong, Hasim, I want to be out of here and living in a nice apartment in a nice city where no one shoots at me when I come out to buy bread in the morning. I want to be in a place where I have hope. I have no hope now, Hasim, I have nothing, I am in neutral.'

'It would be good, though, if you would talk to our press. Let the people know how Muha's family has suffered. Maybe we could get you on the international airwaves, you know, the BBC, Sky, CNN, that kind of thing. When you are ready.'

'You're not listening to me, Hasim, you're not listening to me. I hate this place, I hate it all, I want to go away.'

'There's nowhere to go from here, *draga*, nowhere. The Lasva fighting with the Croats has closed off the coast to us. We're surrounded. You want to go to Travnik or Zenica? Sarajevo?'

'Yeah, sure, Sarajevo. Maybe I can get a job with the United Nations. I speak very good English, I could be a translator. Or with the international press. Then I can get out with the United Nations. I will get out, Hasim, I will get out.'

'You're tired, Emira. I'll send a doctor. And you won't get very far with a hundred and fifty Deutschmarks, *draga*, things cost a little more round here. Stay, eat, rest, build your strength, try and find old friends, maybe find something you can do for the army. There's always work to do.'

'You want me to be a fucking soldier?'

'Please, please, you must not use that tone or those words to me. I'm offended. I think you should consider it – the army. We don't take women in the Black Berets, for delicacy's sake, but the army has room for women, jobs they can do. There are some who fight. We don't make them. We're not Chetniks.'

'That's what they say, the Chetniks: "We are not mujahideen".'

She placed all her things in her small bag, looking at each item before she packed it.

'You should look up your old friends,' Muha said. 'There are a few around, I think. Uncle Alija is around but we don't talk much. I don't think he likes me.'

'Hasim, I'm tired. I want to think, you know, I want to think and to wake up without being afraid. I think I need a shrink. You know a good shrink?'

'Karadzic.'

'That's not funny. One of the doctors at the hospital, he was a shrink, I heard. Maybe I should talk to him.'

'No, not that one, he's a Chetnik. His sons are in the Chetnik army. Maybe you met them.'

'I wouldn't know. I have changed, Hasim. Maybe more than I know.'

'Haven't we all? You're my sister, Emira, all I have left. I have no family except you. I feel this. Please, try and look at me as something more than a teenage delinquent.'

'I think you like all this, Hasim, I think you have found your world and you do not want to give it up. You are very thin. I thought you'd be fatter. The Chetniks said Muha was a gangster, so I thought you would be fatter – oh! Speaking of fat men, Crni Bokan raped me. He was with other men and he pretended he didn't know me. Maybe he was scared, maybe he was something else. He didn't hurt me. I was grateful.'

A single tear came from her left eye and she dug the knife into the rugs on the bed.

Muha moved beside her and put his arm over her shoulder.

'Hey, hey, *draga*, you think I don't know what those bastards did to you? You think I don't want to go out there and kill every one of those motherfuckers? If they keep winning, we'll be in a reservation, one big refugee camp, for a hundred years. We'll be like rare zoo creatures. People will come from around the world to throw food at us. Sure, I used to think Islam was some stupid thing left over by the Turks, like the architecture, just there, with no real meaning except for a few old men and their women. Then they tried to kill me for it, for being Muslim, and I said to myself, what is this thing that someone would try and kill me for it, it must be something damn special. So I read and I listened. Do you understand me? Hasim is dead. Hasim was a foolish boy. Muha is here now. And if we do not stop them here, they will drive us all out of Bosna or kill us. They hate us. It's better to die for something you believe than to be killed for something you know nothing about. That is logic.'

'And I must wear *chadur*?'

'You may wear what you like, within reason, but you must stay here now. I must insist. We are a family. We are all

that is left, you and I. You should see a doctor again,
I think.'

'I will see the United Nations woman tomorrow.'

He pulled back just when she was leaning into his shoulder.

'You should always see one of our own doctors.'

'Whatever.'

'You are okay, Emira?' Muha said then. 'Grundy's men
treated you well? With respect?'

'Sure. At first, I thought they would kill me. They didn't
come for a whore. It was difficult.'

'You're not a whore. They're mercenaries and you know
what mercenaries are like.'

'So why do you use them?'

'It's Husic's decision. He's a weak man. They're good
soldiers. But you must always remember they're not us.'

'They were gentlemen.'

'I think not. Your sense of humour was always more secret
than mine. You must believe Allah will be with us, Emira,
in this fight, and if we must die, then we will die here.
But we will not move. I will not be cleansed like some
sewer rat.'

'And I don't want to die. I would rather live somewhere
else.'

'As a piece of refuse?'

'I don't give a shit. How many times did I fight with Mama
when we were kids? How many times? You must come to
the mosque, Emira – I will not go to the mosque, Mama, I
am a Communist like Daddy. Well, I am not a Communist
any more. It's always the way. How old am I, Hasim? See,
you don't even know that. You know, when I first heard
them talking about Muha over there I knew it was you.
They didn't even have to tell me about you. I knew. I
thought they didn't know who I was. It is so easy to be
very wrong.'

'I can have a guard placed here. I will do it if you go to
leave. Do you want that?'

'And what must I do not to have a guard?'

'You must promise me you will not try to leave. This is a
difficult time for us, *draga*. Maybe this whole battle will be

decided in the next weeks. One way or another. If we do not hold them, then you are free because I'll be dead. But I must ask you to stay. Please, *draga*.'

He touched her hand and she slipped hers from under his and laid it on top of his hand and he did the same, and she repeated it and they did that until you could not tell which hand was under which.

'I hate Uncle Alija, too,' she said, smiling. 'He's a mean old bastard. Does he still fart a lot?'

'All the time. He drinks too much. I tried to get him to stop but . . .'

'So you're not all powerful?'

'Not yet.'

'So who else is dead?' she asked.

'Safet, Safet Pasalic . . . Fisdret Azdic . . . and Arif – Arif Raskalji. They were all killed last year. Safet died running at a machine-gun nest. He was yelling a football song. He liked you, didn't he?'

'I don't remember him much, Hasim.'

Muha looked uncomfortable. He stood up and walked across the room, holding his back. There was a combat jacket rolled up on the floor against the wall.

'What's this?' he said.

Emira shook her head. 'It must belong to one of the *stranci* – the mercenaries. He gave it to me. I'd forgotten. I forget a lot of things. It's easier.'

'I'll take it. I'll get you better clothes.'

'He was good-looking. I liked his hair.'

'Don't say that. Please.'

'I'm trying to tease you, Hasim. The way you used to tease me when we were kids.'

'I'll be a general soon, *draga*,' he said. 'And when we've driven them back from here we'll march to Sarajevo. You'll be with me then, *draga*. When I enter Sarajevo. I can see it now: the Sarajevans will cheer me and throw flowers in my path like a Roman emperor.'

'And will a servant ride with you and whisper in your ear that you are only a man?'

She promised him she would not leave, but she did not

mean her promise when she made it. He kissed her and gave her food and said he would call again. There was a man standing in a doorway across the street when Muha left and Muha nodded to him.

5

Luke Ryan watched Jusef Husic's mouth move and struggled with a rough translation of the colonel's rejection of Grundy's plan.

Grundy showed no emotion.

Ryan stirred his *turska kava* and lifted the cup to his lips, and it was a bitter taste. Then he thought of the girl they had brought in from the Serb lines again and the bitterness left his mouth for a while until the vibration of the next Serb shell. The girl came back easily, though, and his thoughts rested on wanting her, and the want built in him like a surge of excitement he did not want to control. He sipped his coffee again.

The small *kavana* off the main street in Evkaf, the Ulica Marsala Tita, was boarded up and the owner, who was swarthy and square-faced, was polishing one of the metal tables with a rag and rubbing the lower part of his back at the same time. The light in the *kavana* came from four candles and the thin shafts of daylight that made it through the boarding at the windows. And the shafts of daylight showed the smallest particles of dust around the *kavana* owner.

Jusef Husic drank from a small glass of *Sljivovica* and, cutting a small piece from a sugar-coated cake, lifted it to his mouth.

Another shell landed in the Bratstva i Jedinstva Trg, two streets away. The ground shook again.

'One would think they knew when I took my breakfast,' Husic said.

Then he smiled.

'They probably do,' Grundy said.

Husic nodded.

'They are perhaps a little crazy because you – the other – night, Ryan,' he said in English.

'Or happy because of you,' Ryan muttered.

Husic was not listening hard enough to understand. He looked at Muha and switched back to Serbo-Croat.

'I think you would agree, Muha, it was a text-book special forces operation. And now they know what it feels like to have no electricity, no damn hot water in the morning.'

Husic laughed then.

Muha dug a ballpoint pen into the metal table and turned up the corners of his notepad.

'If there is nothing else, I have business to see to, Colonel,' he said.

Husic looked around at the other men at the table. All the faces showed the boredom of the daily routine of Husic's breakfast briefing. Mustafa Spahic, the major commanding Donje Selo, drank two extra glasses of plum brandy and an officer from a loyal Croat unit, the Kralj Turtko Kompanie in the southern suburbs of Evkaf tore up small strips of paper and laid them out in a line on the table. A Serb officer with the mountain soldiers picked bread and dry beef from a plate and dipped them in cream cheese.

'Of course,' Husic said, 'I am too fond of my breakfast, I think. You understand why I have to turn your suggestion down for now, Grundy? For now.'

Grundy picked up his glass of *Sljivovica* and downed it all in one.

'That is your privilege, Jusef. It is not for me to question.'

'I think you were a politician before you were a soldier, Grundy,' Husic said.

'No, Jusef, always a soldier.'

'Well, I have to be a politician, too. That right, Muha?'

Muha nodded.

'Muha's right, Grundy,' Husic said then. 'Crna Gora, that's our immediate problem. They are making their move there. You said so yourself. If we can fight a competent holding action there, till the snow comes, then we can deal with new possibilities in the new year. But Crna Gora is where the threat is now and I must deal with that. That is the smart move, as you Americans say.'

'If I am American.'

'Of course. The shadowy life of the international mercenary. Very melodramatic.'

'You're makin' a mistake, Jusef,' Grundy said.

Husic turned to Ryan again. Ryan was trying to remove the grit of the coffee from his teeth.

'You think we make mistake, too, Ryan?' Husic said in English.

The girl left Ryan's thoughts and the bitter taste returned to his mouth.

He took a drink from a glass of water, looked at each of the officers around the table and then at Husic.

'Yeah, Colonel, you're makin' a mistake. But you've made a million mistakes, so what's another? Sure declarin' independence and goin' to war without an army beats everythin'.'

'We were attacked,' Muha said.

'And now we're down to a finger and a few freckles like this valley,' Ryan said. 'Maybe we've lost and we just don't know it. Or I don't and you do Colonel. Because sometimes I get the feelin' you're scared to even look like you might win. All this victim shit is gettin' to you. Is that it? There's no angle here, Colonel, there's no fuckin' way out, it's very pure, win or lose, that's it. Tell me somethin', Colonel, which is better for you – to hold the valley or to bring the UN or NATO in on our side – 'cos that's it, isn't it? You're pissin' hard against the wind there, Colonel. Pissin' hard.'

Husic did not reply. He leaned towards his son, who sat quietly behind him, for a better translation of what Ryan had said and to give himself some time to calm the situation. But Muha would not let that happen, even though he agreed with much of what Ryan had said.

'And you are a strategist?' Muha said to Ryan. 'Which army do you come from?'

'Same one you do, Muha.'

There was a silence while Husic talked to his son again.

'So, Ryan, you will appreciate we are at something of a disadvantage due to the international arms embargo and the

fact that the Chetniks have all the heavy guns and tanks?'
Husic said in Serbo-Croat then.

Ryan asked Grundy for a translation. Grundy translated
and told Ryan to shut his mouth. But Ryan did not.

'So let's stop sittin' on our arses, waitin' to be put down,
colonel,' Ryan said, 'because that's the way we're goin' here.'

Husic did not ask for a translation this time. He just looked
at Grundy.

'You are loyal, Ryan,' he said in English. 'I like. But not all
good is. Yes?'

Ryan drank some more water and looked at the faces again.
One of the officers who understood English was explaining the
conversation to another who did not. Ryan stared at Grundy.
Grundy's head was shaking slightly. Ryan steadied himself
and turned back to Muha.

'You got that girl we found the night before last, Muha?'
Ryan said then.

Muha dug his ballpoint pen into the table again. Grundy
touched the table with his thumb, as if he was trying to make
a bigger hole than Muha.

'Military police say they gave her to the civilian police,'
Grundy said, 'the civilian police say they took her to the hospital, the hospital didn't know anythin' about her yesterday, and
now this mornin' the hospital people say, yeah, your men took
her, Muha. And nobody has a name for her. What is this?'

Muha stared at his featureless reflection in the metal
table.

'I don't know this, Grundy,' Muha said. 'If the police took
her then she is a police matter. It's not my place to interfere.
Correct, Colonel?'

As well as being the commander of Bosnian special forces,
such as they were in the valley, Muha was also in charge of
internal security in Evkaf which, in effect, gave him command
of all policing. This and Muha's membership of the Bosnian
Government party, the SDA, gave him a degree of power that
made even Husic nervous.

Four heavy shells landed in quick succession nearby and
broke concentration.

'This is true, Grundy,' Husic said then. 'Milan?'

He turned to his son and whispered into his ear. Milan whispered back and then shrugged.

'She was cleared by intelligence, they gave her to the military police and the military police gave her to the civilian police, I expect,' Husic said. 'All very normal. If the police let her go then that's it. I believe she was a victim of rape and other crimes. I am right about that at least, Ryan?'

Ryan looked to Grundy who translated. Ryan nodded.

'And her name?' Grundy said. 'Who is she?'

'Ask intelligence or the police,' Husic said. 'I don't know it.'

'They don't either,' Grundy said. 'Yeah, they take a three-page statement and forget to ask her name.'

Husic shrugged the way Balkan people often do when they don't want to talk about something.

'Maybe they lost it,' Husic said then, 'we have thousands of refugees in this town. Thousands. The system is stretched to breaking point. Muha?'

'Very possible. We do not give our own people what you call the third degree, Grundy,' Muha said.

Grundy looked around the table.

'Yeah, sure,' he said then, 'I hear she was a whore. Definitely your type, you have to admit, Muha.'

The social temperature in the *kavana* dropped through the floor.

'Is she all right?' Ryan said then.

Muha shrugged the way Husic had.

'Well, I wanna question her, Muha,' Grundy said. 'I wanna know who and what she is and what she knows about over there. Hey, how about we sell her to you? How about that? How much?'

Muha lengthened his jaw and his eyes looked as if they would swallow light. He looked at Husic.

'You should not make jokes about Muslim girls the Chetniks use for their pleasure, Grundy,' Husic said. 'The girl has been questioned by our intelligence, now she is a free civilian. That's normal. We get many people from the Chetnik lines. The ethnic cleansing. We treat them all the same way. I will make inquiries and when I have information you will be informed. For now, you may have her statements to our intelligence, okay? But you do not need to question her as if she is a criminal, I think.'

He looked at Ryan.

'She was bad hurt, Ryan. Yes?' he said in English. 'Girl.'

Ryan nodded.

Grundy scowled at Ryan.

'It is not a crime to be raped by the Chetniks,' Muha said

'What is a crime these days, Muha?' Grundy said.

'Betrayal, Grundy. Only betrayal.'

'Well, I wanna question her, Muha,' Grundy said.

'Do you think she is a Chetnik spy or something like that?' Husic asked. 'Obviously, they do not treat their spies very well.'

Husic smiled at Muha.

'We don't make our women suffer any more than they have to,' Muha said.

'I realise you are disappointed, Grundy,' Husic said, 'but there are more important matters than the fate of one abused girl, don't you think? I would prefer if you would concentrate your energies on helping me fight this war. This source we talked about, you have made progress?'

'It's comin',' Grundy said. 'You'll be the first to know.'

'And I, Grundy,' Muha said.

He grinned.

'If you need my help . . .'

'No! I wanna see the girl, Muha,' Grundy said.

'Well, then I suggest you go and find her. There are only thirty thousand people in this town to choose from. It should not take too long.'

Grundy and Ryan walked back to an apartment in the centre of town during a lull in the shelling when the small arms came into use. They spoke between the rifle fire.

'You were a great fuckin' help,' Grundy said. 'What the fuck did I say about Jusef? I mean what the fuck were you about?'

'I don't know why the hell you bring me to those things when I speak about fifteen words of Serbo-Croat and all of them involve sexual positions or drinks,' Ryan said.

'Well you've put a fuckin' spanner in my moves, I'll tell you. Just keep your damn mouth shut if you've nothin' constructive to offer. You fuckin' shut up when I was havin' a go at Muha about the girl. You started the fuckin' thing and that was when you shoulda come in.'

'You didn't have to call her a whore, Grundy.'

'Yes, I did. I want you to go try and find her.'

'Yeah? You're jokin'? Just like that? And what about this job?'

'Ask around about the girl, Luke. Do as you're told. See what you can come up with.'

'You know I haven't a hope without Muha's help. You tryin' to shove me, Grundy?'

There was a certain hidden desperation in Ryan's voice that surprised even him.

'Look, it's just all this shit Husic's peddlin', like he's anglin' for a deal or somethin' – and Frejzo – Frejzo Ceric, the guy I had to shoot. I can't find anyone who knew him at all, know that? No one. What the fuck is it here?'

'Look, there's two halves to the people in this world, Luke, those who believe Kennedy was shot by a conspiracy and those who believe he was killed by a lone nut. One of them has a shelf life; the other goes on for ever. Get me? All bets are off here, Luke. This is the twilight zone, you know that? You gotta put aside what brought you here and concentrate on what keeps you here.'

'And then you turn around one day and that's all there is, Grundy.'

'Your problem, Luke. Now do you do what I tell you or bug out? Your choice. Always. Know what I mean?'

'Yeah, don't I just.'

'He'll come good. Husic, he'll come good. Meanwhile we keep workin'.'

'What the fuck is it with you, Grundy, what the fuck is it?' Ryan said.

'Just it, I suppose.'

The apartment was a couple of rooms in the attic of a turn of the century Turkish building built in a pseudo Moroccan style. Most of the ornamentation had been blown off the building and there was furniture piled up at the apartment windows and pieces of kit scattered about on the floors with weapons and ammunition around them.

The beds were positioned in the shape of a cross and Grundy's had three grenades with the detonators taken out and a heap of back issues of *Soldier of Fortune* and *Penthouse* and some videos on top of a Bergen lying on it.

Grundy cleared the bed with one sweep of his arm and lay on it and, picking up a bottle of beer from the floor, drank it and threw the bottle at the wall.

'He said no?' Yves said.

Yves was stripping two AK rifles, oiling the parts and then placing them on a towel beside his Bergen.

'I was thinkin',' Ryan said, 'maybe they wanna lose. Maybe it's more than just the lack of weapons and stuff. Maybe they're guilty about what they did when the Turks were here. I mean they're like soupers in Ireland – people who changed their religion to stay alive, get ahead or keep land.'

He was unzipping his combat overvest. The zip had caught.

'Maybe everythin' the Chetniks say, about the Muslims and the Turks and the Croats tryin' to wipe them out, all that paranoia shit, maybe that's the way it is or was – it's all the same here, isn't it?' he said then, 'and we've just been suckered by a well-played con pulled off by people who know their time's up and want the world to come and say it's okay. Maybe that. You know? I mean these Muslims here, they're nothin' but the leftovers of the bastards who collaborated with the Turks. Aren't they?

'And then when the Croats were doin' the Serbs in the Second World War, who the fuck did the Muslims support? The fuckin' Ustashas. I mean they were fuckin' SS. Ah, fuck it, Grundy, fuck it.'

Grundy sat up and threw another beer bottle at the wall.

'Whatever happened to the defenceless Bosnians against the Serb aggressors?' he said.

'I wanna win, Grundy. I wanna win.'

'There's all kinds of winnin',' Grundy said. 'You ever really think what we'd have to do here? To win? I told you, Luke, remember what I said about Kennedy. That's the problem with people like you, Luke, you like it laid out simple and rational. And when it isn't you start losin' the faith.'

'I haven't lost anythin', Grundy,' Ryan said. 'I'm where I am – I'm here because I wanna be.'

'Sure you are. My plan'll work,' Grundy said.

'If they wanna help the Chetniks cut their throats,' Ryan said then, 'then fuckin' let 'em. It's not in my contract that I have to follow them to hell.'

'I think you'll find it is, mate.'

Luke Ryan turned to the skinhead Englishman in his late thirties lying under a combat jacket on the next bed. He was deathly pale and his eyes were a very cold stratospheric blue. He pulled a bottle of *Sljivovica* from under the combat jacket and drank from it, then passed it to Ryan.

'Very philosophical, Spit,' Yves said. 'Very *intellectuelle à gauche*. I think you are perhaps an idealist. Or a psychopath.'

Spit smiled as if he had been complimented. He had been a Royal Marine some time in his life and had killed a man in London – he couldn't go back to England because of it. Earlier in the war he had fought with the Bosnian Croat militia, the HVO, in Mostar until a knife fight with a relative of a local warlord had forced him to leave. He still wore the Croat chequered crest, the *sahovnica*, on his t-shirt.

'Too fuckin' right,' Spit said, 'that's me. What's a fuckin' *gauche*, Froggy?'

'It's a direction, Spit,' Grundy said.

Spit pulled off the wooden Rosary beads he had round his neck and swung them in the air.

'Do to them what they've done to us – that's right?' he said. 'Eye for eye, tooth for tooth, life for life.'

'And what have they done to you, Spit?' Yves said. 'The Chetniks?'

'Well, they scared the shit outta me down Mostar way. But these people . . . well, we're evenin' things up 'cos the rest of the world won't, right, Grundy, man?'

'That's right, Spit.'

'But we're gettin worse than nowhere,' Ryan said. 'Fuckin' goin' back.'

'You say that like we're supposed to win,' Grundy said.

Ryan shook his head.

'So what's the point?'

'We're soldiers,' Spit said.

'That is right,' Yves said. 'Very simple. We are soldiers, we fight war. If we take a moral perspective, then we are destined to fail, you know, Luke. We always do in a war like this. If we lose, then we fail because we have lost for our side, and if we win our side will do to the Chetniks what they have done, *peut-être*. So we fail also.'

'That's bullshit!' Ryan said. 'So why aren't any of you over with the Chetniks then?'

'You think they're Martians out there, Luke?' Grundy said. 'The Chetniks? Ask around this town. The people here know who they are. They're friends, neighbours, workmates, lovers, husbands, brothers, sons-in-law. They're the same. That's why they do what they do and why our side'll do the same if we get on top. The Chetniks know that. That's the way war is here. We do it to them in one generation and they do it to us the next. And so on. The closer you are to somethin' you hate, the more you have to destroy it.'

'So what the fuck are we doin' here, Grundy?'

'That's your problem, Luke. And Natasa's mine, by the way. You hear me?'

'She didn't say it to me,' Ryan said. 'I'd say she prefers me to some half-crippled geriatric walrus, wouldn't you, Grundy?'

Grundy threw another bottle at the wall.

'Skilful,' Spit said. 'Pistols at dawn. My money's on Grundy.'

'You don't have any money,' Yves said.

'Well, next Chetnik we take apart, you can have my share.'

Spit rolled off the bed, grabbed a beer and sat on the floor.

He had full combats on and wore two Brownings and had a Beretta stuffed into the front of his combat trousers. He wore a shoulder holster with another pistol in it and a knife in a sheath in his webbing at the collarbone and another knife in a sheath strapped to his leg and two grenades on the front of his webbing. And he wore running shoes and white socks.

'When are we gonna go out and get that scalp, Grundy?' he said.

'Well when we do I hope to fuck I'm not standin' beside you, Spit. How many times I told you not to wear grenades like that? You fuckin' tryin' to get us all blown to hell? Jesus, man, I oughta fuckin' cream you you know, save the fuckin' Chetniks the effort.'

'What would I do without you, Grundy,' Spit said. 'Cheers, mate.'

He took the grenades off.

'So we're goin' after that scalp, then?' he said.

'Soon as we get the word from Horst. One step back, two steps forward. You know you should take care about who you pick arguments with, Luke.'

Ryan was lying on his back now.

'Look who's talkin',' he said. 'And you can have her, Natasa. I don't care.'

'Wouldn't mind dippin' myself in there, if you don't mind, Grundy?' Spit said. 'Wouldn't mind her at all, that Natasa. Nice bit o' skirt.'

'Which would you prefer, a fuck or a kill?' Grundy said.

Spit thought about it.

'Well, you know, a fuck's good, good tight fuck, but you can't beat a fuckin' kill, you just can't. This fuckin' thing on automatic, man – '

He picked up his AK.

' – there's nothing like it, nah! That's what I think. You gonna kill him, Grundy? This Paddy bastard?'

He looked at Luke Ryan.

'I'm thinkin' about it.'

'So whada you do, Grundy?' Ryan said. 'You just press on regardless? I mean they don't give a fuck about us, why the fuck should we do any better?'

'You know you're beginnin' to piss me, Luke,' Grundy said. 'I mean I'm a generous son of a bitch, but you're soundin' like you're out to rub me in the dirt. If you wanna go, then go.'

'I was thinkin' this mornin', tryin' to listen to what was bein' said, lookin' at all the faces . . .' Ryan said.

'You're not real, Luke,' Grundy said. 'Maybe you should go.'

'No, no – that's not it, Grundy, that's not it. I didn't understand most of what was bein' said and I didn't much care. I don't think I want it to end,' Ryan said.

'Wow!' Spit said. 'Fuckin' spiritual.'

'Any food, Spit?' Yves said.

Spit looked into a knapsack he had beside him.

The early morning sunlight came through the gaps in the sandbag defences in the apartment and it was a weak light and it touched everything at a thin angle, so thin you thought the light was going to disappear; in the afternoon, as the sun started to drop into the mountains, the thin light would get thinner and then there would only be the remains of the light until the light would not be there any more.

Spit pulled out a piece of dried beef, a bottle of Croatian wine and a loaf of bread and half a cheese burek.

'I took this from a bloke was killed in town yesterday. 'E musta been doin' black market. The burek's shit. I hate that shit, all fuckin' oil, man.'

'You're a ghoul, Spit,' Grundy said. 'I hope the fuckin' crows eat you when the Chetniks are finished.'

'Too thick skinned, Grundy, man. I'm a British bulldog, I am, you wanna see me bite? I'll eat the next fuckin' Chetnik we see, you see if I don't.'

'Yeah. You think I should kill this Mick motherfucker who wants to take my woman, Spit? You think I should rip his fuckin' head off and feed it to the dogs?'

'Yeah, Grundy, you kill the Mick and we'll eat him. Christ, I'm famished.'

Spit picked up a PK machine gun and started to strip it while Grundy broke the stale bread into big pieces and cut up the meat with his knife. Grundy carved the beef into fine slices and laid them out on a steel plate. Spit removed the PK barrel.

Then Grundy laid out the bread and the beef on the plate as if he was preparing it for a party, and went around picking up tin cups and glasses.

Spit removed the rest of the PK parts.

He started cleaning the machine gun parts while Grundy handed round the bread and wine.

'You think we'll hold 'em, Grundy, man?' Spit said after a few minutes.

'No, I don't think so, Spit,' Grundy said.

'Jesus Christ!' Ryan said.

He pulled himself off his bed and put a combat jacket on.

'Make a bit of 'avoc,' Spit said. 'Make a bit of 'avoc.'

'That's about it,' Grundy said. 'You comin' apart, Luke? Some boys aren't meant for this game. Damn exclusive club, you know.'

'No, Grundy, I'm not comin' apart,' Ryan said.

He did not know if he was telling the truth. It did not matter.

Spit had reassembled the PK and was fixing an ammunition belt into the weapon and chewing on some stale bread and dry beef.

'I reckon he's got that whore he brought in on the brain. Right, Luke?'

'She's not a whore,' Ryan said.

'Yeah, she's an angel,' Grundy said.

Grundy passed Ryan the bottle of wine and Ryan drank some wine and watched the darkness take the outline of Grundy's frame.

'*Stranci* – foreigners – aren't worth shit round here, Luke,' Grundy said. 'I think maybe Muha'll kill us before the Chetniks do. Maybe we oughta go over there and offer our services. Whada you think?'

'Dutina says you're a priest, Grundy,' Ryan said.

'Dutina's lookin' for a priest. He's been lookin' for a priest since this war broke out. You think I'm a priest?'

'I'll see you around then,' Ryan said.

He walked over to the door.

'You will or you won't, Luke,' Grundy said. 'It's up to you.'

'Don't patronise me, Grundy. I'll take so much . . .'

He was gone before Grundy could come up with an answer.

Fifteen minutes later Horst came in. His eyes were wide and he was sweating. He picked up some bread and meat and drank some wine.

'It is him,' he said.

Grundy smiled and rubbed his mouth.

6

In a middle-floor apartment in a tower block above the river at the very western edge of Evkaf, facing the Serb lines on the south side of the valley, Spit strapped on a kevlar vest, pulled another from the floor and fitted it over the first, then took a third and stretched it over the other two. When the vests were comfortable, he pulled a white t-shirt with a black-and-white print of Radovan Karadzic having oral sex with Adolf Hitler over them.

Then he took a helmet from the chair beside him, turned it back to front to cover his forehead completely and put a second, bigger helmet over it. He turned to the others and smiled as if looking for approval.

'Now let's see,' he said.

He picked up a British L96A1 Accuracy sniper rifle, checked the four .338 Lapua Magnum rounds in the magazine, snapped the magazine back in, pulled the bolt back and pushed a round into the breech. Then he went to the window.

The window area was sandbagged on the inside and then barricaded with metal at what was left of the frame and sandbagged on the outside.

Spit took away some of the sandbags on the inside, pulled out one of the car roofs wedged in the window as part of the metal barricade and then kicked out the next layer of sandbags.

The wind pushed into the apartment disturbing the damp, musty staleness and bringing with it a smell of burning.

Spit leaned over and passed the sandbags he had kicked out to Grundy who stacked them against a wall.

There was a long rainbow stretching from behind the mountains on the south side of the valley and single drops of icy rain flew with the burning smell on the mountain wind, touching Spit's face and legs when he stepped out on to the balcony.

The valley was green and grey but the green was a dead green and when the dead green turned brown higher up it looked as if it had never lived. In one field were lines of white stones and then thin trees which had lost most of their leaves and beyond them the remains of a village which was no-man's-land now.

Spit stood at the metal railings and faced a line of wrecked whitewashed houses in the village in no-man's-land on the south side of the river. The line of houses climbed towards the slopes and then there was a forest and that was where the Serb front line lay.

Serb snipers worked from the line of wrecked houses; the distance was about a kilometre, their maximum effective range with souped-up Russian Dragunovs.

'Say somethin' dirty, Grundy man,' Spit said. 'I wanna be horny for the bastard.'

'*Cinq minutes*, Spit,' Yves said. 'Begins now, okay.'

'Put on my Clash tape, Froggy,' Spit said.

Yves slipped a cassette into Spit's ghetto blaster and handed it out to him. The Clash broke the silence in the valley and Spit started to strut to the music. Then he took aim at the line of wrecked houses and fired a round. The houses were at the limits of the effective range of the Accuracy too, even with its .338 Lapua Magnum rounds, but the shot was never meant to strike a target. Just provoke a reaction.

'Come on, you bastard, put one in Spit!' he roared.

He strutted some more and shouted across the valley and beat his chest and put two fingers up.

'Fuck you!'

A few seconds of wind and silence passed.

Then a round whistled to the left of him followed by a crack on the valley floor from the line of wrecked houses.

'Skilful!' he roared. 'Where from, Grundy?'

From a small gap in the sandbags on the right side of the

room, Grundy watched the line of houses a thousand metres away with binoculars.

'Don't know yet,' he said, 'better keep movin', Spit. Go left. You seen which one yet, Horst?'

Horst was in a house in the southern suburbs of Evkaf, on the south side of the river, about three hundred metres from the line of wrecked houses the snipers used and five hundred metres from the Serb lines on the valley floor.

'Not yet,' Horst said on the walkie-talkie.

Spit leaned down and pushed up the volume of the music.

Another round came across the valley and hit the wall beside Spit's head and a piece of masonry fell out. The round ricocheted into an earthenware pot at the other end of the concrete balcony. The pot cracked and clay spilled out. Spit cursed, dived and rolled.

'Come on, Grundy, man!' he shouted.

He stood up, rammed another round into the Accuracy and took aim. Another shot hit a sandbag to the left of his head. Spit dived for cover again, without firing.

'Okay,' Grundy said, 'he's in the second house from the right, Spit. I can see his head. You got him, Horst?'

Horst's voice crackled through Grundy's walkie-talkie.

'Shit, he's gone,' Grundy said then. 'You got him, Horst? – wait, keep movin', Spit – yeah, he's back. Move over right, Spit, move over right. Yves, what's the time?'

'One minute fifty seconds.'

Spit was lying on his back. He checked his weapon.

'Hold it, Spit,' Grundy said.

'How much longer?' Spit yelled.

'Okay, over right again, Spit,' Grundy shouted, 'he's gone, he's movin' position! Is it him, Horst? Can you see?'

There was a crackle on the walkie-talkie.

'Affirmative.'

'Okay, hang on, Spit!' Grundy shouted. 'There he is again, third down. Go!'

Spit rolled over, aimed and fired.

'Shit, he's moved again, Spit, he's goin' left.'

'He's taking a new position,' Horst said over the walkie-talkie.

'Go left, Spit!' Grundy shouted.

Spit rolled left, stood up and fired a third round. Two incoming rounds hit the wall to his right. One passed through the gap in the window where he had climbed out to the balcony. It went over Yves's head, hit a cup on a shelf and embedded itself in the wall.

'Jesus Christ, they were close, Spit,' Grundy said. 'I don't think you're gonna make it, man. I want your boots.'

'*Trois minutes*, Spit,' Yves shouted. 'I hope he takes your fucking balls off, English.'

'I'll just keep playin' my music in the sun,' Spit said.

Spit started to simulate masturbation.

'Fuckin'—'

A round creased his helmet and knocked him to one side.

For a moment, all there was was the music and the wind.

Spit got up and laughed and looked back at Yves and shoved his last round into the breach of the Accuracy and fired without knowing where he was aiming.

'I make it third house down now, Spit. You got that, Horst? He's usin' the same pattern. Feelin' safe.'

'Let 'im fuckin' try and do old Spit,' Spit said.

'*Trois minutes* and a half, Spit,' Yves said.

Spit turned his head to the right to answer Yves. A round struck him in the chest and he staggered. Then another hit his chest and he spun and a third hit him in the back and he hit his head against the sandbags behind him.

'Spit!'

Yves grabbed the AK47 beside him and threw himself through the hole in the window defences and fired three single rounds and then two more and then switched the fire selector and let go with the whole magazine.

It takes about three seconds to empty an AK on full automatic and you have to hold on tight because she tends to kick up.

Yves's rounds went up and he cursed. They were always going to be off target because of the distance but he did not want them to be up.

He roared for cover and tried to load the second magazine which was taped to the first.

Grundy was already through to the balcony. He had a Heckler and Koch G3 and he fired covering bursts past Yves. Yves got hold of one of Spit's kevlar vests and dragged him through the gap in the sandbags. It was a narrow gap and one of the sandbags had been hit and was spilling sand and clay on to Spit.

Four small-calibre mortars burst to the right of the block, and they were followed by heavy machine-gun fire from a mountain position. Then Bosnian mortars and machine-guns returned fire and tracer skipped back and forth across the valley. The exchange went on for about six minutes.

'Oh, Jesus, Jesus,' Spit kept saying.

Yves tore the Velcro straps on his vests and Grundy undid his helmets.

'Oh, God, fuck, I'm dyin', I'm dyin'.'

Grundy poured some *Sljivovica* on to his face.

'Shut up, Spit, you're not dead,' he said. 'What was his time, Yves?'

Yves picked up his stopwatch. He showed it to Grundy. He had taken Spit's second vest off. Spit's body was bruised purple where the bullets had impacted and he said he thought some of his ribs were broken. He grabbed the rest of the *Sljivovica* bottle from Grundy. Grundy went back to watching the Serb sniper.

'Four minutes,' Yves said to Grundy. 'And forty seconds. Then you are inside, Spit. You owe us a bottle and a carton of cigarettes each. I will have mine now.'

'Champion,' Spit said. 'Cheers, mate.'

He raised his fingers but had to lower his arm.

'Let's see your booze and cigarettes, Spit,' Grundy said.

Yves lifted Spit from the floor and looked him over. Spit looked at his bruising.

'See that! See that!' he said. 'Fuckin' ace. Nuthin' fuckin' like it. Goes right through ye. Tell me a tart can do that. Bet that fuckin' Natasa gives good 'ead, Grundy. Bet there's nuthin like her 'ead. Yeah, Grundy?'

'Sure, Spit,' Grundy said.

'Christ, me fuckin' chest, me fuckin' head.'

Yves shook his head and smiled.

Spit smiled.

'Fightin' war, givin' grief, gettin' 'ole and 'ead. That's life, innit?'

'Okay, the sniper has moved again,' Horst said over the walkie-talkie.

'Right, let's go,' Grundy said. 'Spit, we're the bait, Yves, you and Horst, you're the hooks.'

'Ah fuck, Grundy, man,' Spit said. 'No rest, no rest . . .'

'They'll never kill you, Spit, you're a fuckin' monster.'

'Have to drive a stake through my sacred heart.'

They moved to the southern suburbs of Evkaf and took up position in a house beside the tributary called the Thread. The flood waters on the other side and along the river had started to subside and the tributary and the river had dropped slightly below the level of their banks.

They watched the sniper for another five hours. He fired at six targets in the town, killing a woman in an apartment and hitting a man near the river. The man was wounded in the lower back and crippled.

When the dusk came and the temperature fell, Grundy and Spit moved across the Thread into no-man's-land, towards a field of rotting wheat to the left of the flooded area. And they moved like dancers.

They moved from the shelter of a row of poplars along a broken road at the edge of the field into a dip in the field and crawled towards the wheat.

Spit was ten metres to Grundy's right. They kept that distance in case of mines or booby traps. If one of them tripped a mine or a booby trap, the other would escape, the theory said. Often the reality did not obey the theory.

Spit reached into his pocket and pulled out a second magazine for his AKM, checked it and taped it to the magazine in the rifle. The AKM is about two-thirds the weight of the AK47 and easier to handle on the move.

Grundy had an AK74. The AK74 fires a smaller 5.45mm round than the AKM's 7.62mm bullet, but it has a higher muzzle velocity, a higher rate of fire and tighter rifling which gives increased stability in flight; but once the round enters its target it tumbles. And the AK74 round has mercury in the tip.

The wheat field ran towards a line of beech trees and then green fields with long grass and a wall.

Grundy lay at the edge of the wheat, broke a stem of wet wheat and sucked on it. Spit moved for the beech trees.

The sniper hadn't seen them yet.

They crept forward.

The sniper was in the third house in the row which backed up towards a gradual hill with the remains of gardens and trees and machinery, and then there was a forest. The trees were tall pines with no growth for three or four metres on the lower part of their trunks, and you could see reflections in the raindrops on the needles. The ground was hard mud now because the temperature had dropped. The valley was disappearing in the dusk. The hard ground was cold and the cold took the heat from Grundy's body as much as the wind in the valley.

The sniper was two hundred metres away.

Spit stood up and fired on full automatic at the sniper and Grundy moved under the cover of Spit's rounds. Then Spit called for cover and Grundy stood up and fired three rounds at the hole in the wall from where the sniper was firing. Two of his rounds knocked pieces of masonry from the house. He called for cover and Spit stood up and fired again. Grundy ran forward and fell on his stomach.

Then there was movement along the Serb line in front of them and individual weapons loosed off rounds in their direction. A heavy machine-gun opened up on the Serbs from the Bosnian line and the Serbs replied in kind.

Grundy fired on automatic again and Spit ran forward.

A bullet went by his head and hit a tree, tearing the bark. Another passed close to his arm and he had to throw himself to the ground. He hit the hard muddy ground and tore his face and rolled towards a stone wall from where Grundy was firing. All around them the ground was punctured with limestone flints and pieces of shrapnel. Spit tucked himself into the wall and waited.

Grundy reloaded and stood up and fired, then dived for cover. A shot came at him and hit the ground five metres behind him. It threw up some flint. Grundy smiled at Spit and showed his fingers, one, two, three. Then they both stood up and fired at the sniper on full automatic.

When they got to the line of whitewashed houses, the sniper was already out and running towards his own lines. Grundy thought that maybe the sniper believed he was away because he ran as if he was expecting to make it to his lines. He was a small man but his legs were strong and he wore running shoes and had a green boiler suit that was the same colour as the grass around them.

Spit and Grundy moved left and right around the houses and took up firing positions and fired short bursts at the sniper.

The sniper stopped, dived, rolled, picked himself up and ran on.

Grundy could see his rounds impacting on the hillside around the sniper.

Then three or four Serbs opened up on Spit and Grundy from the trees above the houses. They shouted to their comrade and he shouted back for more cover and another Serb machine-gun fired. Its rounds went high.

Grundy ran for a shallow lie. Spit thought for a moment that Grundy was going to fall over on his bad leg. He went to shout something but Grundy signalled to him to stay put and cover the back. Grundy fell flat.

The sniper slowed down when he reached the first trees. He slung his rifle over his back and began climbing on all fours because the ground was steeper there.

The Serbs above him kept up their fire and two small-calibre mortar rounds landed behind Grundy and Spit. They watched different soils rise into the air when the mortar rounds hit and they could tell where they had come from. A piece of something hit Grundy and he looked down at the blood on his wrist.

The sniper staggered, cried out and fell back.

Yves and Horst had been waiting for him in the trees. Horst shot him in the lower leg from ten metres with two tungsten-tipped arrows from a fibreglass longbow. The two arrows went in almost touching. The sniper pulled himself up and tried to get his rifle levelled but Yves rammed the butt of his rifle into the sniper's face and broke the man's nose. The sniper staggered some more and then fell down on to his knees, spun round and fell back down the hill.

The Serbs above him called to him and stopped firing and called to him again and fired another volley. Then there was silence for a while except for some distant firing on the other side of the valley, and the sound of the wind. And the smell was of gun oil and cordite.

Then the Serbs started firing again, and Horst and Yves had to dive for cover with the sniper.

Eight Serbs were in the forest above them and they made an attempt to outflank them. Grundy fired at the Serbs and hit one but the distance was too great to see the result and the Serb just vanished in the shadow of the trees. The other two Serbs came under fire from Spit and ran off.

Grundy yelled at Horst and Yves to get the sniper down and then he was up and running and roaring at the top of his voice. He stood in front of the Serb lines, shouting, firing, covering Horst and Yves while they dragged the sniper to the cover of the line of whitewashed houses.

When Horst and Yves had made it back to cover with their prisoner, they shouted at Grundy to come back, but Grundy was caught, and when you are firing on full automatic and caught it is a hard spell to break.

Grundy wasted two magazines and then fell down to his knees to get another from the thigh pocket of his combat trousers and while he was doing that a Serb grenade rolled down the slope and exploded beside a tree. The blast went away from Grundy, but it broke the spell and Grundy pulled himself up, turned his rifle and, calling for cover, fired on full automatic and started to run for the line of houses.

The other three covered him from a whitewashed house. It was pocked with shell impacts and black where the impacts were, the roof was gone in strips and many of the roof slates were in pieces in the grass and mud around the house. There were red slates piled in neat rows in the garden, all of them broken.

A Serb fifty-calibre machine-gun hit the house and the rounds went through the walls. One burst took an angle off the top of the house and the bricks landed near Grundy, but the Serbs were firing too high and that was the only thing they damaged.

The Bosnian lines replied in kind and the Serbs stopped firing and dropped some mortar rounds near the line of houses, but they were long and short and they stopped after five minutes.

The mercenaries fell back through the broken wheat field, in the dusk, under Bosnian cover fire towards a Croat machine-gun position in the southern suburbs of Evkaf, dragging the sniper by his arms.

Grundy gave a Croat officer from the Kralj Turtko Kompanie a small bottle of *Sljivovica* and thanked him for his support fire. The Croat gave Grundy a salute and told him to invite him along if he had anything else in mind. Two of the Croats wanted to kill the sniper and another wanted to interrogate him. They argued with their officer and kicked the sniper when he was being dragged past their post to a Toyota four-wheel drive down the road. But the Croat officer stuck to his word.

The mercenaries drove over the only bridge left standing in Evkaf. It was an old Turkish bridge, called the Bridge of the Revolution, and it had been standing for four hundred years now. The sniper was bound and gagged and covered by a blanket on the floor. Horst kept his boot on the man's spine and told him not to move or he would damage the arrows in his leg.

Rows of whitewashed, red-roofed houses stretched to the tree-line on the mountain to their right, and then the trees took over and there were small streaks in the gaps in the trees which were the Bosnian approach trenches on that side. The Bosnian forward trenches were over the top of the mountain, where there were no trees. And the first snows had already fallen there. The mountain was called Prozor and it was the highest on the south side of the river. The Serbs held a piece of a smaller mountain beside it and their snipers operated from there, too.

A sniper fired. The round went wide and hit a house gutter.

7

Another sniper round came from the direction of Prozor across the river at about the same time the following evening and the dusk seemed to hang on to the edges of daylight until the very last moment. And as it got darker the shots came with the stars.

Luke Ryan stood at the door of a small white mosque and looked down at his open boots. A couple hurried along the footpath in front of him and two men stood in the shelter of a cargo container. Ryan bent down and tied up his boots and pulled up the collar of his combat jacket. The firing was punctuated by praying from inside the mosque and an old woman went down on her knees beside a fresh grave to his right.

He had been back to the hospital but Natasa was not there and he blamed her for not being there. And Ryan saw it all for something else: the voices in the rooms again. He had come to Bosnia knowing what he was there for and now he was trying to remember what it was he had come for. Someone had changed the problem while he was still trying for a solution. Maybe Grundy was right, maybe the job was all there was. Except the job took from the cause and soon the cause would be the job and Ryan did not know if he could take that. He was still outside them, Grundy and the rest, and they were slowly sucking him in, but he was not sure he wanted to go. And Grundy knew it, the way Grundy knew everything.

Ryan was very tired now and when he walked with his hands in his pockets and listened to the firing he let his shoulders fold and he felt his body shake and wondered if he could take any of it much longer. And he thought of himself in another place, at another time, where the worst that happened was nothing at all, and he could barely recognise himself or the place any more.

Then he thought of Frejzo Ceric, and he did not know why he could not lose that thought, and the Muslim girl he had found in the Serb house and her green eyes and her Pre-Raphaelite hair and her face and the way she moved and how she smelled. And somehow there was something between all these things. So he stopped thinking and stopped searching for her.

And then she was there, right in front of him.

Emira Kusturica was walking into a small side street off the Ulica Marsala Tita when Ryan saw her again.

And in the dusk it was the movements of her body that told him it was she.

The street was straight and dark and only the stars and the moon provided any light.

There were three burnt-out cars at one end and a rubbish heap which gripped your stomach in the middle. Most of the buildings were Habsburg vintage and most of them had no windows. Some had UNHCR plastic sheeting covering them and some had wood wedged in them, and most had masking tape holding in what was left of the window frames. There was a burst drain beside the rubbish heap and the dirty water was taking away small plastic bags and running around an empty tin of American cooking oil which had been brought in by the United Nations.

A tall woman in a black coat was picking at the rubbish heap and throwing things through an open door at the far end of the street.

'*Hej*!' Luke Ryan yelled. '*Gospodo!*'

Emira Kusturica stopped beyond the rubbish heap and stood with her back to him. Luke Ryan slowed when he approached her and put his hands back in his pockets. He shook more now because he was not absolutely sure it was her until she turned.

And Emira turned very slowly.

Ryan felt as if someone had injected him with adrenalin.

'Hi!' he said. '*Kako ste?*'

He smiled. She did not. She looked him up and down as

if she either could not quite remember him or there was too little light to recognise him.

'*Hvala, dobro,*' she said then. '*A Vi?*'

'Oh, I'm well. I thought it was you.'

'Yes, it is me – I. And I am not old enough to be addressed as madam.'

'Sorry, my Serbo-Croat isn't great.'

'No. So, what do you want?'

That caught Ryan like a punch. He just stared at her. She was clean now and her bruising had faded, but that could have been the darkness, and her hair was combed back and tied. Her eyes had a shade that looked romantic in the late dusk.

'Oh . . . just – just to see if you're all right,' he said.

'Yes, thank you, I am all right. I am sore but I am alive. Please, do not look at me like that. I know this look. I saw it – is that right? – I saw it every day. You are shaking. You are nervous?'

'First date.'

She didn't get the joke.

'I was lookin' for you before,' he said. 'I went to the hospital. You were gone. The hospital said Muha's men had you, Muha's men said the police had you and then the police said they'd let you go and didn't know where you were.'

'The police perhaps have more important things to do. Is there anything else?'

'No – I mean, yes, I mean, would you like a coffee?'

'It is dark. I have things to do. Do you have Deutschmarks?'

'Some.'

'I have not much money. You are always with the *Armija?*'

'Yeah, there's a few of us, foreign volunteers, international fighters.'

'Mercenaries.'

'Volunteers.'

'There is a difference?'

'It's a pay grade.'

Again, she did not laugh.

'You will give me your Deutschmarks, soldier? Give me your Deutschmarks and we will have our coffee some time ahead. I need Deutschmarks. I can leave coffee. You will give me Deutschmarks? Or do you want something from me?'

'Your English is very good.'

'I am a good student. I am a – and now I forget the word – I am out of practice. You look tired. You have been fighting today?'

'In a way. So where have you been? What have you been doin'? I can't believe I found you.'

'You ask a lot of questions. There is a bad smell here. It is not good to be out on the street now. In the dark. I do not like the dark. So, I must go. You will give me Deutschmarks ... ?'

Ryan kind of laughed out of surprise at her directness and a certain good feeling that she was talking to him. And for the first time everything Grundy had said went out the window.

'Yeah, sure,' he said.

He smiled and, reaching into his pocket, pulled out a ten-mark note and unfolded it.

'All I have now. I'm waitin' to be paid. There isn't always money here.'

'Oh, there is money here. It is hard to get, but it is here.'

He smiled. She did not. She looked right through him.

'I'm Luke – Luke Ryan, by the way,' he said. 'I'm from Ireland.'

He put his hand out.

'Where?' she said.

'Irska.'

'Ah – Bobby Sands, Jackie Charlton, Bono, U2. You see, I know Irska. IRA. Are you IRA?'

'No.'

'Why not?'

Luke Ryan could not think of an answer.

'Who are you?' he asked. 'I feel I should know. I'm sorry, but I've been thinkin' about you.'

'You have a right? You find me and you have a right to me? How do you say that? Finders keepers. I am the spoils of war, is that it? How medieval. You are medieval, Ryan? You are a knight?'

'I don't mean it like that. I just like you.'

'You do not even know me.'

'But I like you.'

'Oh, you want to sleep with me!'

'What are you so aggressive for? I'm not a Chetnik.'

'If you say.'

Ryan stepped back and raised his hands.

'Okay, okay, listen, I don't need this, I don't need this shit. I was just tryin' to be nice, you know, man to woman, that kind of thing. I don't need to feel like I'm a fuckin' wolf and you're little Red fuckin' Ridin' Hood. I don't need that. What is it with you people?'

She forced a smile.

'I know this story,' she said. 'It is a good story. Be honest with me, Ryan, be honest with me.'

He grinned.

'Coffee?' he said.

He moved his head.

She shook hers.

'Too expensive,' she said. 'A waste of money. So, thank you for what you did for me and thank you for your Deutschmarks . . . goodbye.'

'Look, what's your name? At least tell me that.'

'*Zovem se* . . . you undertsand this?'

He nodded.

'*Zovem se* Emira – my name is Emira – I will not tell you my other name.'

'Jesus Christ, what is this? Look, you're beautiful, I think you're bloody fuckin' beautiful. This whole fuckin' place stinks like a clap house and you're beautiful. You're beautiful.'

'Thank you. That is nice to hear. You are nice, too.'

'So what are you doin'? Who are you with? Do you have family here?'

'I am alone. Are you alone?'

'Yes. Where are you stayin'?'

'Why do you ask that? I do not ask you where you are going. I am going to an apartment in the next street. It is small. One room. An old couple gave it to me. Do you want to know their names, too? You are not with Muha Kusturica's men?'

'No. Are they doin' anythin' to you?'

'Of course not. But it is always good to know things. You

do not understand us very well, do you? Look at you. You
are a mercenary in a war that cannot pay you. A foreigner
in a family fight. You cannot even understand our language
properly and you are here fighting our war. This is crazy. I
want to leave. I want to leave and go far away and live, and
you are here, fighting this war.'

'I'm committin' suicide.'

She indicated that she didn't understand.

'It's a joke,' he said.

Do you want to die?'

'I came here to help. When the world wouldn't. Kinda noble,
don't you think?'

'I do not know what is noble. You have no more Deutschmarks? Dollars, maybe?'

'Who needs money?' he said.

'Okay, okay, thank you for helping me, Mr – say your name
once more.'

'Luke Ryan.'

'Mr Ryan. Thank you. I must go now. The dark.'

She backed off from him and faked a smile.

'Jesus, I thought I might see you,' he said. 'I thought I might
get a cup of coffee, for fuck's sake.'

Her face frowned and she ran a hand through her curls
and pushed her hair back, and Luke Ryan thought then
that she was very beautiful and he did not want to let her
go.

'You want to fuck me?'

'Don't say that.'

'Do not look at me the way you do, do not do that.'

'Just a coffee.'

'I am going away.'

'Where?'

'Anywhere. Away from here. The Chetniks will come, they
will come and they will kill you and they will kill everyone. I
have seen them, I have seen them kill people. They will kill
everyone. They rape and they kill, I have seen it. And they
will kill you, Luke Ryan.'

'If you're tryin' to scare me you're succeedin',' he said. 'They
have patrols and snipers all the way to Travnik. And it's a

hard journey in the mountains. People who try it die. You are beautiful.'

She dipped her head. Then she moved the Deutschmark note he had given her in her fingers and brought her eyes up to his.

'I was at university,' she said, 'I am clever, too. When I was fourteen, my father gave me a test and I am a genius – is that the right word? – I am a genius. And I go to the university and I study for the law – to be a lawyer because I am a genius. And I am home then. Banja Luka. Banja Luka is not a nice town. There is a nice Orthodox cathedral but it is provincial, like here. We lived in Jajce once. Jajce is very beautiful. There is a waterfall. Anyway – hey, my English is getting better – I am home and we are – were – eating dinner and the Chetniks come – came. First, they ask my father for money and they say we may go if we give them money. So my father, who was a good man – a gentle man and a good man . . .'

She dipped her head again and began to finger the money faster.

'So he shows them where some money is. My father was a Communist, you know, and we have – had – many pictures of Tito in our apartment. My father – he was a good man – a kind man. They killed him.'

She drew her hand across her throat.

'They made my sister and me and my mother look when they killed him. He did not die quickly.'

She dipped her head again and began to fold the money.

'He was begging them not to kill us and they were kicking him and my mother was screaming and two Chetniks had my mother on her knees. I remember all this, I remember it. I can see their faces, the Chetniks, they were Beograd Chetniks. Arkanovci, perhaps, I do not know. You have heard of Arkan? One of them had a – how do you say this?'

She touched her face. 'A mark. Brown.'

'A mole. You don't have to tell me this.'

'Shut up, please. Yes, he had a mole, yes, and when he was raping me . . . I remember the mole . . . I wanted to touch it. Then another Chetnik raped me and another and another and then . . .'

She started to open the note and iron it out in her hand. Her hand was slender and the fingers were dirty and some of the dirt from her fingers was left on the note.

'Look, I'm sorry,' Ryan said. 'Your mother?'

'Oh, they killed my mother – my sister is alive, somewhere, I think. I hope. I do not allow myself hope except for that. But I do not know where she is.'

'I'm sorry.'

'Shut up. You keep saying you are sorry. Why are you sorry? You did not do it. I know who did it, I saw them. Why are you sorry for something you did not do? You be sorry for what you have done. Have you done this?'

'No.'

'Then you do not need to be sorry. I do not need you to be sorry. I need money. Can you get me more money?'

'I don't know.'

'I have seen their guns, they have many more guns than you. You will be killed. I told the *Armija* intelligence man this. He was a nice man. I think he taught me at school many years ago. He did not recognise me and I did not know his name. I lived here for many years. This is my town. I hate it. Which town are you from?'

'Dublin.'

'I do not know it. Is it nice?'

'It's wet.'

'But no one is bombing it?'

'No, not at the moment.'

'Then it is nice. You think I could go there?'

'I suppose. We took some wounded, I heard. From Sarajevo. Not many. We aren't great at taking people. We like to go to other people's countries but we don't like them to come to ours for too long. We're poor.'

'This is poor, Ryan. This is poor.'

She sighed.

'We're fightin' well,' Ryan said even though he didn't believe it. 'The *Armija* have a good heart. Maybe we can hold this valley. We have a few tricks.'

'I do not really give a shit. Anyway, you say that to impress me. Maybe you think I will sleep with you if you impress me. Soldiers always want to sleep with girls when they are fighting. They are so frightened. I have seen this. Are you so frightened?'

'Listen, I just wanted to talk to you, I don't need the third degree. Jesus Christ, I'm sorry I asked.'

'What? What did you ask?'

'Coffee.'

'But you have no more money.'

'Yeah. So you won't have a coffee with me?'

'No. Who would pay? You are a lonely man, Ryan. You have a lonely man's face. It is dirty and you are tired and you are afraid – yes?'

'I'm constipated.'

Ryan made a gesture with his thumb and forefinger and smiled. She shook her head.

'But you would like to be with someone?'

He moved his right shoulder.

She stepped towards him and touched his face with her hand and then pulled her hand away and fingered the money again.

'I'd like to see you,' he said.

'Not possible – believe me.'

'Just to talk.'

'I will write you a letter from wherever I go. I will marry a rich man and drive a big car and someone will rub my feet every night – a different person. I think that is what I want most in the world. Over there, when I was with them, I used to dream about it – about other things, too, when I let myself, but always about having my feet rubbed. And sometimes I could feel it, and I could lie down and believe my feet were being rubbed and it made me feel like I was floating in the clouds.'

'My back,' Ryan said.

'What is wrong with your back?'

'I have the same dream about my back. I have a lousy back, I've always had a lousy back and all this lyin' around in holes and trenches screws it up and sometimes I want a few hours of someone rubbin' it. I miss that.'

'You had someone?' she said.

'Yeah. Up the side of the spine, between the shoulder blades and the spine, then around the neck and under the skull and over the head. It's nice.'

He stepped towards her and put his fingers to her head and rubbed her. She moved her head back and then dipped her head and he moved his fingers around her skull and under the back of her skull and down beside her ears and then down her neck.

'I like that,' she said. 'It is not as good as the feet but I like it. You are a gentle man, Ryan, you have very gentle hands. I have not felt hands like that for ... it doesn't matter. You must be very lonely to be in a place like this, Luke Ryan. I cannot imagine how lonely you must be.'

'Or crazy,' he said.

'They are the same thing.'

He took his hands away and she backed off.

'Thank you for helping me,' she said. 'Goodbye now.'

He touched her face again.

'You're very beautiful,' he said.

She pulled away from his hand and then went back to it and he rubbed her head again.

'Are you always a soldier?' she said.

'No, sometimes I'm worse,' he said.

'What do you mean?'

'I mean I have to do things I hate. I'm supposed to find out about you. Who you are. What you're doin'. Where you're goin'. I'm supposed to. I didn't think I stood a chance of findin' you.'

'You found me once, perhaps you are destined to find me always. You work for Grundy?'

'With. Who are you?' Ryan said.

She put her arms around him and rubbed his back.

'You will make me tell you?'

'No. I won't do that.'

She looked around her.

'Come — come with me,' she said.

She backed away from Ryan and reached out and took his hand.

The street was very dark now and the figures at either end were barely pencil marks.

She led him into a side street and then up a small alley and into a bombed-out apartment block. They stood under the stairs.

'You will please hold me now,' she said. 'Just hold me, okay?'

He nodded. Then he put his arms around her and she held him at the waist. She closed her eyes and dipped her head into his chest.

'Rub,' she said.

He moved his fingers under her skull and she touched his back.

'Your clothes are big,' he said. 'It is difficult.'

She undid his webbing and left it hanging loose from his shoulders and, unzipping his combat jacket, slipped her hands under his woollen pullover and put her hands to his skin. Ryan sighed and pulled her closer. Then she began rubbing his back.

'I like to do things properly,' she said. 'You are tight there. The muscles are bad. Keep doing that. It is very nice. I think my head is going to float. You smell of river water and fruit juice, I think.'

'You smell so beautiful.'

'You like me?'

'Yes.'

'Lean back, please ... Yes, that is right. And rub my shoulders, please. Maybe I will let you rub my feet some time.'

'I want to. Is that good?'

She did not answer. She dipped her head more so that he could push his hand inside her coat and rub her shoulders and she moved her hands up his back to his neck.

'God, I love you,' he said.

He moved in closer to her again and she pulled him to her.

'And you will always love me?' she said.

'Always.'

'And you would do anything for me?'

'Yes.'

He tried to kiss her and she pulled her head away.

'You are hard,' she said then.

'I want you.'

She pulled back from him.

'Okay, that is enough,' she said.

She shoved him away and stepped into the broken hallway of the bombed-out apartment block. Ryan felt exposed in the darkness and he tripped on something trying to do himself up again.

On the street, she shook his hand and backed off.

'Please, go now,' she said. 'It was nice.'

'But I wanna see you,' he said. 'I mean just you and me. I'll tell Grundy I couldn't find you.'

'And he would believe you?'

'Yeah. He would. I wanna see you, please.'

'Believe me, Luke Ryan, you do not. Goodbye.'

He made a move towards her.

'Please, please, go away,' she said. 'Please, I am asking you, please.'

'What is it?' he said then. 'You agreed to do the same for Muha you were doin' for the Chetniks?'

She looked at him for a few moments and then pulled the knife she had had in the Serb house out of her jacket pocket and pointed it at Ryan. He raised his hands.

'I'm sorry,' Ryan said. 'I'm sorry. I didn't mean it. I just wanna see you.'

He came forward. She lowered the knife and replaced it in her pocket. He touched her face.

'You're beautiful,' he said.

'Thank you for what you did,' she said. 'But my brother, Hasim, does not approve of you. You understand?'

Ryan's head moved as if he was trying to see the subtext.

'Hasim is Muha,' she said. 'Muha Kusturica.'

Then she backed off again and began to disappear into the darkness.

When she had gone, Luke Ryan stood in the street and listened to a gun battle develop down the valley. The single shots became short bursts and the short bursts became automatic fire and the calibres increased and there were rockets and grenades and then low calibre mortars and medium calibre mortars and then heavy calibre mortars and artillery.

'Away the lad!' the silhouette on the footpath said. 'You could get run over walkin' in the middle of the street like that, mate.'

'Where the fuck'd you come from, Tahir?' Ryan said.

'I'm everywhere, I am, don't you know that?'

'Grundy taken you on?'

'I don't think he likes me, Grundy.'

'Get rid of the tattoo. Want a drink?'

'I don't drink, do I?'

'Have I got pox?'

'You could buy me a coffee.'

'I've no money left.'

'I'll buy you one. I owe you it, I suppose.'

'You'll learn.'

'You look like shit, you know.'

A salvo of shells hit the *carsija* end of town and the ground shook under their feet.

'I feel worse,' Ryan said.

And he turned and walked away from it.

8

The room was an apartment block cellar. There were four chairs as well as the one the sniper was in, a wooden table and some water and clear alcohol in bottles against one wall. The room was dry and very cold and they had left the sniper in it for twenty-four hours, stripped naked on the floor, with a very white light, fired by a portable generator, and a ringing noise coming through a speaker system they had rigged in the ventilation.

Grundy leaned close into the sniper's ear and watched the sniper's temple pulsate and smelled the sniper's body odour and saw the small sweat beads cling to the stubble on the sniper's face. He had a square face and a high crown and his hair spread out in long curved lines and came back around and behind his ears. His ears were small and they had large lobes and he was cut behind one ear and the blood ran in a thin line down to his shoulder. The blood had coagulated and some of it had flaked off and fallen on to the collar of his olive green combat suit to mix with his dandruff.

'Okay, here we go again,' Grundy said in Serbo-Croat. 'Your name, please?'

The sniper did not answer.

Grundy repeated the question in English and German.

Then he touched the sniper's torn face and stepped back. The man's head bent lower and the chair he sat in started to shake. Grundy signalled to Horst and Yves to steady the chair. The sniper cried out when Yves touched his wounded leg. Then Grundy caught him with a fist across the side of the face and the sniper's face opened again and he cried out and fell towards Horst. Horst steadied him.

'I said, your name, please?'

The left side of the sniper's face was streaming blood and the sweat beads on that side had spread out in lines and mixed with the blood. There was a deep cut to the right of his eye on that side, too, where Grundy's nail had caught him, and the punches had opened it.

'Anythin' to say?' Grundy said.

It was the twenty-second time Grundy had asked him a question. Again, the sniper did not answer, but this time his lips opened and closed two or three times as if he was talking to himself and on that Grundy made a decision.

'Okay,' Grundy said to Yves very slowly in Serbo-Croat, 'okay, he's not gonna say anythin', this is a waste of time and effort, just cut his fuckin' balls off.'

Yves stood up, walked over to a canvas roll, unrolled it, pulled the Siberian Kandra from its sheath, ran his finger along the blade and then turned and very slowly walked towards the sniper.

The sniper's lips began to move again and his eyes twisted in their swollen sockets and his good foot moved and he searched for Grundy behind him. There was a minute when all you could hear was the breathing.

'Okay, okay,' the sniper said in Serbo-Croat. 'You win, you win.'

Grundy nodded. He signalled to Yves. Yves stopped. He did not put the knife away.

'Right, good,' Grundy said, 'that's better. I was beginnin' to think you were mute. Now, your name, please?'

The sniper was shaking and his leg wound was very swollen and discoloured.

Grundy's tone moved from threatening to irritated. The centre of gravity of the interrogation had changed.

'I said, your name, please,' Grundy said again. 'Look, I'm tired already and I'm not gonna ask any of these questions twice any more. You've decided to co-operate, so co-operate. Otherwise – you see this man here? – well, he will take you apart with that knife. You do recognise that knife? You should. You can take a man's head off with one cut. The other night – and you must know this, your people were screamin' about us on the radio – the other night he took one of your comrade's heads off with it. Now you want me to leave him here with you alone? You want that?'

'No, no.'

'Okay, so don't presume on my patience and don't insult my intelligence. I know what you are and what you do. You are a Russian, you are a mercenary, now what I want is your name.'

The sniper looked at Grundy and then at the others and thought and sniffled. There was blood trickling from his nose.

'Andre, my name is Andre.'

'What?'

Grundy touched the sniper's leg with his boot. The sniper winced and Grundy pushed his boot in harder and the sniper cried out and pulled back.

Grundy leaned in to his ear again.

'We will break you, no matter how long it takes, now matter what we have to do to you. You do believe that?'

The sniper nodded.

'Koniev. My name is Koniev,' he said. Then he nodded as if confirming it. 'Kill me, please, kill me,' he added.

'No way, son. You're worth money to us.'

'Look – maybe we can do a deal. I tell you what you want, you get me out of here. Soldier to soldier. You fix my leg, maybe I get you more money.'

'Middle name.'

'Fuck you.'

Grundy punched him on the left side of the face again and Koniev fell over and rolled in the chair and his wounded leg cracked off the concrete floor. The Russian screamed and tried to move, but his hands were bound behind his back and around the chair. Horst and Yves sat him up again. Spit sat at the door, smoking and drinking from a small bottle of *Sljivovica*.

'Now, just so we really understand each other, Andre – middle name?' Grundy said.

'Nikolaievich. Andre Nikolaievich Koniev.'

'Okay, okay, now just so we understand each other, Andre Nikolaievich, here you're a fuckin' Chetnik murderer. I put you outside on the street and they'll fuckin' rip you apart. There's no one here hasn't lost someone or doesn't know someone lost to Chetnik snipers. What I'm gettin' at here, Andre Nikolaievich, is you don't have too many friends right now, so you better start makin' some. You with me?'

'Okay, okay, what are my options?'

'Not great, Andre Nikolaievich. You slipped up. Very careless, son. Workin' a pattern like that. Got too cosy. You should never have been caught. We been watchin' you for days. That was an asshole screw-up for a guy like you.'

'You think I don't know. I was expecting maybe to be shot – not caught. That was clever.'

'You know what they call you here, Andre? Ivan the terrible. Everybody knows you. Well, they know your handiwork. You could say you're kind of a celebrity. But I wouldn't expect roses though.'

Grundy pulled the table in close to Koniev and took a map from under his webbing belt and laid the map out on the table.

'Now, Andre Nikolaievich, this is how it is, very simple, I wanna know what kind of strength you've got in each of the areas I point out. We'll do it systematically, so you don't get confused, and each time I think you're lyin' or holdin' back I'll hurt you. Deal?'

Koniev nodded and coughed.

'We'll start here: to the east, between this valley and the Travnik–Zepce line – your current dispositions there, please.'

'You going to break out that way?' Koniev said.

'You answer my questions. You give me what I wanna know and I'll see about gettin' that leg seen to before it gets black. You mess with me and I'll see the other one gets black first.'

'Like I fucking care,' Koniev said.

'Here,' Grundy said.

He pointed out the area of beech covered mountains to the east and south-east of the Evkaf valley, stretching towards Travnik and the battle lines in front of Zenica.

Koniev looked at the map.

'Fuck you. Go ahead, kill me,' he said.

Grundy leaned into him.

'Now you listen and you listen good, Andre – Spetznatz?'

The Spetznatz are Russian commandos, like the SAS.

Koniev nodded.

'Well, then, you know what'll happen,' Grundy said. 'I can make your life – or what's left of it – the most hellish thing you ever imagined. I can make it worse than you could possibly endure. You know that, don't you?'

'You're a bastard, Grundy. You're a bastard.'

'And you know my name. Good. Well, you know that I will carry out everythin' I say – to the letter. You wanna answer my questions?'

'Give me half an hour, Grundy,' Yves said in Serbo-Croat. 'I'll cut his balls into pieces. Feed him his own balls. Hey, Ruski, you should have had a personal weapon.'

'Jesus, I don't know anything,' Koniev said. 'I don't. I'm a fucking sniper. That's all.'

'Unimaginative,' Grundy said. 'You think I went to the trouble of gettin' you just for a few Deutschmarks and a bottle of *rakija* reward? Or maybe you just can't imagine how bad things can be for you, Andre Nikolaievich.'

Grundy brought his boot heel down on the Russian's leg wound and the bone cracked. Koniev screamed and the scream echoed around the cold room and Grundy caught his nose with a punch and his nose cracked. Grundy swung his left boot around and kicked the man under his right knee and the Russian toppled over in his chair again and screamed for five minutes, twisting in his chair on the cold stone floor.

Grundy picked up a plastic bottle of water and took a drink and poured some of the water over his right fist. One of the knuckles had split. He rubbed his knuckle with the water and the cut stung and the blood came out over the end of the cut and ran down his hand.

When he was ready, Horst and Yves pulled Koniev up again.

'You thinkin', Andre Nikolaievich?' Grundy said.

Yves poured some alcohol over Koniev. The alcohol cooled his skin and the pain was the first thing that told the Russian he was not dead.

'Now, Andre,' Grundy said, 'I'll make you a deal. You give

us what we want and I'll maybe even keep you alive. I can manage that. I have that power. Otherwise, I get pissed and just fuck you out on the street bound and gagged with a placard over you.'

'Go fuck yourself, Grundy,' Koniev shouted.

Grundy kicked the wound area again and punched the Russian twice in the face. Koniev passed out this time.

'Fuck, you're a tough shit, you know that?' Grundy said when Koniev was conscious and seated again. 'What the fuck are they payin' you over there?'

'One – two – three hundred Deutschmarks a month. Whatever. Maybe more when they have it. You?'

'I haven't been paid since July. There's the bounty on you we can collect. It's only cigarette and booze money really.'

'It's a lot in Russia . . . fuck you, Grundy. Jesus, why don't you just shoot me? Go on, shoot me.'

'Sure, I get paid either way. But who needs ammunition when you have an angry citizenry. I saw one Chetnik strung up a few months back. Kickin' and screamin'. Now you tell me what I wanna hear and I'll put one nicely in your head, clean, like. Otherwise, I really will fuck you out on the street and they'll rip you apart out there. The women are the worst. You want that?'

'No, no, please, please, no – look, kill me, okay, just kill me.'

'You say that like you know somethin'. And I'd say you do. You and I know guys like you don't just do sniper work. So answer my questions. You want some weed? I got a little. Everyone around here's on somethin'. I mean they have to move mountains to get flour in here but they got a heap o' dope, all kinds of it. Damn stuff is cheaper than beans. Now answer the questions or I'm gonna keep causin' you pain till you break.'

Koniev looked round him.

'Go get Muha, Spit,' Grundy said in English.

Spit stood up from his chair. He turned the doorhandle. The name, Muha, was enough to make the Russian go paler than before.

'Okay, okay,' Koniev said, 'okay, please – please. I don't

know much about it here –' he pointed at the map to the east of the valley – 'it's just mountains. Very hard land. We have the road as far as the front line – you know that – and that's all really. But we can't even use the fucking thing because of you, here. The rest is the mountains. We use tracks for resupply and there are positions on top of some of the peaks, and controls. To stop you. But it's not good to be between two lines. You know what I mean?'

Grundy sensed the Russian was probing. He slapped his face.

'So mark your positions,' Grundy said.

He undid the Russian's straps and gave him a pencil.

'With details,' Grundy said.

'You got kids?' the Russian said.

'Sure, somewhere.'

Grundy lit a reefer for the Russian.

'You wanna see mine?' Koniev said.

'No.'

'They're good kids. Why are you fighting for the mujahideen? Jesus, they're animals. I saw them, I saw what they did in Afghanistan. They fucking get a man and they fucking open him, you know? Fucking open him so all his insides fall out but he doesn't die. I've seen that, Grundy, in Afghanistan. And you, French? You were with the Serbs always. You were with Russia. Now you fight for Islam. You guys are fucked up. Wow, this is good. Shit, just kill me this way, please.'

'Okay, now down here, to Jajce,' Grundy said when the Russian had finished describing the Serb positions between the valley and the main lines between Travnik and Zepce.

'Jesus, it's the fucking same,' Koniev said. 'All the way to Jajce. The roads, the roads.'

'Write it in. Everythin'.'

'Villages, controls, patrols. That's it. You think we keep men sitting there? Bandits and smugglers are a problem. But we don't have enough men for all here. Just the roads. And no one goes up here –' he touched an area between the Evkaf valley and Jajce – 'except some old villagers, a few lumber workers and the bandits and smugglers. There are guards with the villages. Local boys. Jesus, the Germans and the Ustasha didn't have enough men for all here – ' the Russian swung his hand around the map – 'during the Patriotic War.'

Grundy switched to the north of the valley and had Koniev fill in information about Serb positions Grundy had no real interest in. Then Grundy went back to the east again.

The Russian argued and then tapped his head and looked at the remains of the reefer he was smoking.

'I think my head is going to come off,' he said.

'The questions,' Grundy said.

Grundy pointed to the map again. Then he kicked the Russian's leg again. The Russian let out a delayed action scream and then held his pain for a moment and then screamed again.

'Fuck you, Grundy,' he said. 'Fuck all of you, bastards.'

'This area – and these mountains. Here!'

Grundy pointed to the northwest of the valley.

'You'll let me go?' Koniev said.

'The questions . . .'

'You will kill me . . . ?'

'If you want.'

'Shit, this is good stuff. What are you going to do? Break out? Attack us? We'll make shit of you,' Koniev said. 'Jesus, give me more of the dope, hey!'

Grundy lit another reefer and gave it to the Russian. Koniev smoked it for a few minutes and studied the map and talked about areas where there had been fighting. And with each sentence the next one became easier.

'Look, if you won't let me go, you must kill me,' he said then. 'You must promise me this. Your word, Grundy?'

'Trade me some more and I'll think about it. How about around here, eh, this mountain back here, Sljiva, what kind of strength you got back there?' Grundy said.

'Jesus, how many men do you think we have? There's nothing there. We have nothing that far back. We have that territory. It is Serb land. Cleansed. All the positions are forward now. We haven't enough men for everywhere. The valley, the valley, that's what we're after. Everything is here. They're mujahideen, you know, the Muslims here. You listen, one day they'll come – mujahideen – they'll come to your country and yours and yours, Grundy. We are all infidels. I've seen what they do.'

The Russian smiled. Grundy made him go over old positions, slamming his hand each time he asked a question. Twice more he asked the Russian about Serb positions east of the valley. The Russian cursed.

'Now your positions south of the river here, just behind the boom,' Grundy said. 'All those little mountains.'

The Russian shrugged.

Grundy tipped the Russian's wound again and pointed to an area between Sljiva and Vrh.

'Jesus, you fuck, Grundy,' Koniev said, 'you better kill me, okay . . . okay . . . there is a camp here and in these villages here and here, in these valleys, there are some soldiers, yeah, around these mountains. We use these small valleys to rest up. There are camps. Men come and go to the line, you know the way. The artillery use this village, the military police, this one – there is a prison there. There are girls there, too, good girls. There are girls here, also. They move them around. The best go to the officers. I'll write it all in and you'll kill me?'

'Not for this shit,' Grundy said.

'Ah, fuck you, Grundy.'

'Fill it in. Fill it in and give me more. Your tanks, where are your tanks now?'

'We've got the tanks lined up back here, off the road behind Vrh, maybe ten or fifteen, I don't remember. We can't use them on Crna Gora or the front of Vrh and they don't want to come into the valley in force while you're on the north side of the river. They're too vulnerable. So they shell you in pairs. The tank commander's an asshole. Look, okay, there's a forward unit for a new brigade down here, near that mountain, Sljiva, but the troops haven't come, they're still around Sarajevo, I think. Like I said, we're stretched. The line is thin here because we're pushing at Crna Gora. Only the shit troops, old men and boys and queers, you know? You can move in the mountains. The roads are controlled, the mountains are free. Like in the Patriotic War. Like in Afghanistan. Now, you promise you'll kill me?'

Grundy nodded his head.

'Keep goin'.'

'This is maybe why the ethnic cleansing,' Koniev said. 'The mountains. You cannot leave the enemy in your rear. They must be cleared, all of them. What are you going to do, raid one of the villages? They're scared of you, the younger ones. The old men say you will come over at night and slit their throats. Many of them get drunk when they hear this. I was drunk last night. Hey, who was that fucker dancing on the balcony?'

'Rudolph fuckin' Nureyev,' Spit said.

He was leaning over the back of a chair, pointing a rifle at Koniev.

'I got stupid there. I didn't kill him, no?'

Grundy shook his head.

'Did I get anyone today?' Koniev said.

'A woman and a man,' Grundy said. 'He didn't die.'

'Shit,' Koniev said. 'Bad day at the office. Oh, fuck, this is wearing off. Give me another.'

Grundy lit him another two reefers and Koniev marked in troop dispositions and some details of the topography behind the Serb lines, and they drank from a bottle of *Sljivovica* and talked in generalities about the war.

'I'll miss my kids,' Koniev said then. 'You wanna see a picture of them? It's in the lining of my jacket. Fuck, I think I'm gonna pass out. Maybe you won't have to kill me.'

'I'm still waitin' for somethin' good, Andre,' Grundy said then.

'Oh, come on, please, you promised. I'm a fucking sniper. What the fuck do you want? Hey, you guys hit Jablanica the other night? That was good, that was really good. You stiffed a few military police. No one likes them, the bastards.'

'They were gettin' their balls off,' Grundy said.

'Yeah? Good. Now everyone'll be scared to get their balls off. Fuck, I think I caught something off one of the girls. What do you think? You can't be too careful, can you?'

'You're pissin' me about, Andre, you're pissin' me about,' Grundy said. He pointed east of the valley again, towards the Travnik–Zepce line, and did it three more times.

'Hey, man, I'm scared, I'm scared.' Koniev said, 'You'll fucking kill me?'

'Go on, get Muha, Yves.'

'Hey, Jesus Christ, I've written you a fucking novel. You want me to give you the soldiers' names? I don't know their fucking names. Most of them are from Prijedor and Banja Luka and Sanski Most. A lot of pricks from Bosanska Krajina. Farm boys and corner refuse. They've even got some jailbirds. Like the Ustashas down in Mostar. The Prisoners Brigade. Real shit.'

'Hey, that was one of my old units,' Spit said in English.

'What did he say?' Koniev asked Grundy.

Grundy shook his head.

'I could give you a spy. Hey, I give you a spy and maybe you let me go?'

'Maybe,' Grundy said.

He touched the wounded leg with his boot. The Russian cursed.

'Everyone throws out spies when they're cornered, Andre. And you're Spetznatz.'

'Hey, no, I mean it. I'm a businessman. New Russia. We can do a deal?'

'Shoot.'

'Very good, very funny,' Koniev said.

He looked around at the faces. They were impassive.

'You were talkin'?' Grundy said.

'I don't know the name. I was fucking this girl from intelligence. She told me. Nice girl. I think I gave her the clap I got from the brothel. There, that's it. That should do you. It's all I know. What's a fucking sniper going to know about spies?'

'Jesus,' Grundy said, 'Spetznatz, and you expect me to believe that? I didn't pick you for your good looks, Andre. I picked you because I knew you'd have somethin' to trade. Had my eye on you a long time. Throw him out on the street, Yves.'

Yves came round the back of Koniev and Horst stood the other side of him. Spit opened the door.

'Ah, Jesus, fuck you, Grundy, fuck you. Okay, okay, I was

supposed to cover someone a couple of nights ago. I do that kind of work when we send people in or take them out.'

'Who?' Grundy said.

'Hey, I don't know. I'm just support. You know, make sure there was no interference, shoot if anything went wrong. I don't know where and I don't know who. I just know that I was detailed for the job and then I was told I wasn't needed any more. So maybe and maybe not – eh? That's it, that's all I know. Now maybe we can deal.'

Grundy looked at Yves and there was silence. They hooded Koniev and retied his wrists behind the chair, then went over to a corner of the room and drank and talked for about half an hour. Koniev asked questions but no one answered him. Then Yves pulled out his automatic pistol and gave it to Grundy.

'I'm gettin' soft in my old age, Andre,' Grundy said, removing the prisoner's hood.

'Bastard.'

'You'd never make it with that leg the way it is. And you don't wanna get caught by the civilians here. You want a little time?'

Grundy went behind Koniev.

'Sure fucking do. I'm a Christian, amn't I? I believe in God. My old man, he's a fucking Communist. Old bastard. Don't screw up, Grundy.'

Grundy re-hooded Koniev and placed the automatic beneath the Russian's skull and told him to say when he was ready.

The Russian began to pray. They were slow prayers and his head moved when he prayed.

He had been praying for five minutes when the door crashed open and bounced off the wall.

Spit pulled his rifle into position.

The door rebounded and a boot kicked it back open.

'You would murder a prisoner, Grundy? That is against orders. What would the colonel say?'

Muha stood at the open door. Yves, Horst and Spit kept their seats at either side of the door. They had their rifles in their laps and their fingers on the triggers. Muha saw this. He called two military policemen in and two Black Berets followed them. Two more military police stood at the door behind him and more Black Berets stood outside them.

'You are a difficult man to find, Grundy,' Muha said. 'This is quite a set-up.'

'We have what we want,' Grundy said. 'So we're executin' him. He's a sniper. He's murdered women and children.'

'He is a prisoner, Grundy, you should have reported his capture to the military police. To intelligence. To me. You will please hand him over for further questioning.'

'I questioned him, I got what I wanted.'

'Prisoners are my responsibility, Grundy. Why was I not informed you had this man?'

'You're a hard man to find, too, Muha. I swear you just vanish sometimes. But then prisoners you get hold of do that, too, don't they?'

When Koniev heard Muha's name his hooded head moved left and right frantically.

'Grundy,' he said, 'please, please, shoot me, Jesus, please shoot me, Grundy, please . . .'

He tried to move but his wound and the bindings held him fast in the chair. Muha signalled to the two military policemen in the room to hold him.

'The prisoner, Grundy,' Muha said. 'You will hand him over to the proper authorities.'

He held out his hand.

'Grundy!' Koniev shouted.

One of the military policemen hit him.

'And what will you do with him, Muha?' Grundy said.

'That's not your concern. But I will leave with the prisoner. Alive!'

'For God's sake, Grundy, don't, please, I am begging you, please fucking kill me, please,' Koniev said.

'Shut up, you bastard,' Muha said. 'The question is, Grundy, do we all die here because of a Chetnik – well?'

Yves and Spit looked to Grundy for an order but Grundy did not give it. Horst moved his weapon. Grundy told him not to with a flick of his eyes.

'Where's Jusef?' Grundy said.

'I do not need the colonel's permission for this,' Muha said. 'I have the military police, they will take the prisoner. You want to fight them for him? For this piece of shit?'

'Fuck you, Grundy,' Koniev said, 'You gave me your word. Kill me!'

'Go get Husic, will you, Horst,' Grundy said.

Horst stood up and checked with Grundy again and Grundy nodded. Then Horst pushed his way out of the room.

'We seem to have a standoff, Muha,' Grundy said.

'I am tempted to kill you,' Muha said.

'You'd die first.'

'I can wait.'

'Grundy, you bastard,' Koniev said.

The military policemen hit him again. Then they waited.

Twenty minutes later there was talking in the corridor and the voices got louder and then Grundy could hear Husic's voice. Husic's son, Milan, pushed past two Black Berets at the door, followed by his father. Horst stood in the corridor. Jusef Husic looked at Muha, then at Grundy.

'What is this?' he said.

'The military police are collecting this prisoner, Jusef,' Muha said. 'He is a sniper, I believe. Grundy took him yesterday and did not inform anyone.'

'Well?' Husic said, looking at Grundy for a few seconds. 'So hand him over, Grundy.'

'I want him protected, Jusef. I still want information from this man.'

'You will hand him over to the military police, Grundy. Please.'

'You gave your fucking word, Grundy,' Koniev said.

'You know what'll happen, Jusef?' Grundy said.

'I will not argue with you, Grundy. This man is a sniper, he is a murderer, and you would defend him?'

'I'm not defendin' him. I gave my word.'

'Kill me . . . please!'

'It wasn't yours to give. You will deliver him to my authority. Milan, you will escort the prisoner. Does that satisfy you, Grundy?'

Grundy thought for a while and then put Yves's pistol in his belt.

When they were dragging the Serb out, he screamed and cursed at Grundy and begged to be shot.

Grundy was alone, drinking what was left of the *Sljivovica* and smoking his last reefer when Husic came back into the room.

'I am sorry about that, Grundy,' he said. 'But you must realise my position here. And with Muha. I cannot have you antagonising him for no reason. He is a powerful man here. And we need him. Maybe one day we will not need him but until then he must be handled with care. I know Muha is unbearable sometimes. I know all about him. But he is a good soldier. Perhaps he does things that in ordinary circumstances would not be tolerable – I am a lawyer, I know this – but we do not live in ordinary times.'

'We live in interesting times,' Grundy said.

'Very interesting.'

'We'll get paid for him?' Grundy said. 'The prisoner?'

'Of course,' Husic said. 'He's useful?'

'He's more than that, Jusef. If I'd had more time – Shit! I wasn't gonna kill him, Jusef, I wasn't gonna kill him. He's Spetznatz. You gotta play these boys like that. It's a game. And Muha'll fuck it up.'

'I'll get you more time with him. But now I want you and your men on Crna Gora – they are moving at us there.'

'And Vrh?' Grundy said.

'It is still in the deep freeze. In your strategy, the men who take the mosque and occupy Bor, Grundy, they would suffer heavy casualties?'

'Yeah.'

'And you would still do it? Why?'

Grundy smiled.

'On Crna Gora?' he said. 'As you order, Colonel. You want some?'

Grundy gave the end of his reefer to the colonel and as Husic smoked it the strain on his face began to loosen. Then he coughed.

'I wish to be friends, Grundy,' he said, 'but this thing with Muha, I cannot back you when you do this. You must realise that my first duty is to this valley and the people in it. I will do what is necesary to defend them. You cannot have a private war, Grundy. Not with the Chetniks and not with Muha. I will not tolerate it. That man will be treated like a prisoner, I will insist. But he is a murderer, he has killed women, children.'

'It's just a damn waste when Muha gets a prisoner, Jusef. He's not trained. Spetznatz'll fuck with Muha's people.'

'He will be well interrogated. Properly. I will insist.'

'You know what'll happen, Jusef?'

'What would happen to such a criminal in America?'

'He'd write his memoirs and have a movie of the week made about him.'

'Interesting times, Grundy,' Husic said.

'Pity the man who lives in interesting times,' Ryan said from the door.

He came into the room and stood leaning against the wall. Grundy passed him a bottle of *Sljivovica*. Ryan looked at the bloodstains on the concrete floor.

'I been tryin' to find you,' he said to Grundy. 'I shoulda been here.'

'Should you?' Grundy said. It wasn't a real question. 'Any luck?'

Ryan looked at the bloodstains on the concrete again.

'No,' he said. 'No luck. You?'

Grundy looked at Husic.

'We're movin' up to Crna Gora,' he said to Ryan.

9

The Serbs attacked along Crna Gora that night, and all the next day and into the night they shelled the mountain in the heavy rain. The shells tore holes in the forest lines and the red mountain clay and the limestone outcrops, and the rain-water poured into the shell holes and the shell holes swallowed the forest around them and the forest smelled of cordite and rain. The shelling and the rain kept the soldiers awake and they clawed into their trench walls for cover. Then the snow fell.

Before dawn there was a thin crust of snow on the ground which caught the moon in places and lit up the darkness of the forest, and the forest creaked in the wind, and when the snow stopped, the early morning sunlight crept in among the pines and spread out in long thin shafts through the woods. When the snow began to melt, the water from the melting snow snaked around the roots of the trees and into the ruts and through the pine needles.

The trench ran along a north to south line across the top of Crna Gora and then down where the mountain-top dipped and back up higher till it anchored on a limestone wall and the remains of a house, where the 50mm mortars were. Then it swung back at right angles above a deep hollow where they had dug mantraps and planted land mines.

There had been fire fights along the line all night and Serb patrols probed the line from early in the morning, supported by small-calibre trench mortars. When the snow came, the snowflakes got mixed in with the tracer rounds and the moonlight, flares and mortar impacts, and someone had died about fifteen metres down the trench from Luke Ryan. The Serb patrols had pulled back.

Ryan watched a stream of water eat the edges of a slab of hardened snow and then ducked his head, pulled his collar up and gripped his AK47 with his finger over the trigger guard. He leaned into the clay wall of the trench and, moving his feet in the muddy stream, felt the water enter his boots. Water drops tapped a slow beat on the forest floor from the pine needles on the trees and the virgin sunlight skipped along the branches on single drops of water.

There would be another barrage now.

Men had burrowed into the trench wall and the sticky red soil was sitting in uneven lumps behind the trench and in the water on the floor and over the logs of the parapet at the front. They could not see the Serbs yet but they knew they were coming: they knew how the Serbs were moving and how they would wait until the barrage had been laid down and how they would follow the barrage with grenade launchers and small trench mortars. How they would pick a spot they thought was vulnerable and concentrate their fire there to make a breach and how if that did not work they would try another spot and go on like that until they made a breach or were driven back.

Ryan watched the forest and let his eyes glance at the man beside him.

The man fingered worry beads and recited a Muslim prayer. He was a very ordinary man and wore a sleeveless combat overvest and three woollen pullovers and carried grenades and ammunition all over his body. Ryan had told him to move his equipment to his sides and back but the man either did not understand Ryan's pidgin Serbo-Croat or did not want to listen. Luke Ryan did not want to be beside him because of all the ammunition on the front of his body, but it did not really matter because all the local soldiers carried as much as they could in all the wrong places.

Fathers stood beside sons and cousins tapped uncles on the shoulder and asked them for a shot of plum brandy and brothers argued and exchanged family gossip and command structures withered among these family ties because they did not need commanders for what they were doing; and for some of them, the men coming to kill them were family, too. At this level it was a local war between people who knew each other and grand strategy did not mean as much as being surrounded and outgunned with nowhere to run. Ryan envied them this, and for all their amateurism he envied them their motive for fighting, their isolation, their sense of right, their common cause. It made order from the chaos.

The trench wall was buttressed for the last half metre by logs and there were small gaps in the logs along the line of the parapet to allow for crossfire. There was a dugout to Ryan's left and the dugout, too, was buttressed by logs and sandbagged with a half metre log-and-mud roof. Some of the sandbags were open and spilling their contents. And there was urine.

The urine was everywhere and it warmed the water at the base of the trench and stank out the dugout and made sitting in a dugout like choking.

No one sat in the dugout during heavy barrages, except perhaps to keep warm because the dugouts weren't much good against heavy calibre artillery and not great against heavy calibre mortars, so people preferred to dig alcoves into the trench walls and dig their heads into the clay and sit in the water and urine and say something like a prayer. No one wanted to be buried alive.

If you asked a man what his worst fears were, his first was always being captured – everyone was scared of that the most and everyone told you they would shoot themselves if they were captured. Sometimes when he should have been asleep Ryan lay awake, scared of what would happen if the Serbs caught him and he could not shoot himself. And this went hand in hand with his vision of what he had become.

Two shells impacted behind the trench and tore up some topsoil and dead needles and sprayed the trench with the topsoil and the needles and unmelted snow. Ryan swung round to see where they had landed. The other men near him tucked into the red clay wall. Two men, who had been civil servants before the war and who were white-scared, went to run and were grabbed by their captain, who said he would shoot them if they ran again. One fat man stood up on the parapet and began to fire his rifle. His section commander, who was his brother, pulled him down and slapped him across the face. There were two men scribbling notes at the far end of the trench and they handed their notes to one another. Above them, the blue Bosnian flag with the fleur-de-lis and the white stripe was hanging from a tree. Three more mortars impacted. Ryan tucked himself into a ball and went into his alcove.

Grundy was about four men up and he was on the firestep, at the parapet, watching the forest with field glasses. He had one rifle in his hand and a G3 slung over his shoulder. More men started to bury themselves into the wall of the trench.

If you asked a man what his second worst fear was it was being buried alive. And if you went into the dugouts in these trenches and a large calibre shell impacted on it or near it you stood a good chance of being buried alive. Another three mortar rounds came in ahead of the trench line and Ryan looked over at the dugout and wanted to go inside, but he was scared now and not able to make himself move.

The shells hit closer and showers of dirt and pieces of tree landed on the men in the trench. Someone further down screamed he had been hit and then a shell landed in the trench a hundred metres to the right of them and there was more screaming and some cursing and smoke and cordite hung over the trench line. Ryan dug his hand into the red clay and said a Muslim prayer he did not know the meaning of and asked Allah to keep him alive. He was afraid now and he did not care if people saw he was afraid because they were all afraid. One or two of them cried during the barrage when the shells switched from mortar to long range artillery and took away whole lines of trees. You could smell the sap and the pine resin on the cordite and the urine, and the men's tears spoke only between the shells and the cracking of the trees and the whistle of the splinters and shrapnel.

Ryan clawed at the wall of the trench alcove he had made for himself and he pushed himself into the clay so deeply he felt he would stick there and be buried anyway if a shell landed close by. And he was more scared of that than the shells because that could only happen to him but the shells had a couple of hundred other men to take and there were good odds if you were smart and lucky and he could stand those odds. But being buried only happened to you.

The mortar and heavy artillery shells came so fast you could not tell which was which and the whole mountain and forest seemed to be moving and there was so much muck and smoke and screaming that Ryan thought he was being buried alive and he said things he did not mean and pleaded and promised and prayed, and when the barrage had stopped and the smoke was clearing and he could hear the screams all along the line from the men who had been hit he looked around him to see if anyone had seen on his face what he had been thinking and if he could see it on the faces of other men.

A baker from a village in the next valley, where the Serbs had burned people in their homes, stood against the back wall of the trench with his rifle still in his hand and his head split open and streams of blood running in winding lines around his open eyes. His head shook and his left hand held his rifle which was dug into the floor of the trench. Down from him, a teenager had lost the right side of his body and Ryan could see the steam from his entrails rising from the water and urine of the trench. The line was not a line any more but a series of lines fractured by the barrage.

'*Pazi*, Chetnik!'

The Serbs attacked from the right, through the hollow, in an arrow formation, and ran into the minefield and the mantraps.

One of the mantraps was a pit of acid from a technical college in Evkaf, and a young Serb in olive green fell into it up to his knees. It was a deep pit and it was constructed so that the walls concaved and the Serb could not pull himself out. He screamed for someone called Todor. Four Serbs were blown up by the mines. They were heavy anti-tank mines and the Serbs made the mistake of bunching close together. And when other Serbs tried to go round the heavy mines they ran into anti-personnel mines and a crossfire from each side of the hollow.

Ryan leaned over the parapet.

A Serb came out of the smoke and killed the man next to Ryan. The bullet went through his head and he fell forward.

Ryan fired at the Serb and threw a grenade. The Serb staggered and fell and then fired at Ryan. His rounds missed and the blast of the grenade knocked the Serb forward into the Bosnian trench. Ryan watched the Serb try to pick himself up and reach around for his rifle. The Serb said something and spat mud and there was blood on his legs. Ryan lifted his rifle and shot him on the ground. The Serb jerked as if someone had bitten him and raised himself up on his knees and reached around for his back and cursed and fell forward into the water and mud.

Ryan fired over the trench wall again and emptied his magazine in two-shot bursts, shouting at the men around him to identify their targets. But the battle was breaking down and when he had reloaded Ryan fired the next magazine on full automatic. It emptied in three seconds and he pulled out another magazine and emptied that on full automatic, too, and four Serbs who were trying to outflank him around some trees ran right into the rounds.

One of the Serbs fell dead and another threw a grenade, but the grenade did not make it over the parapet and rolled back at him. A Bosnian soldier who had pulled himself up over the parapet beside Ryan caught the blast from the Serb grenade and their return fire. Ryan had ducked under the wall of the trench again.

He looked around him. Men were firing and ducking, roaring for support, running up and down the trench, screaming in pain and terror and excitement, and it was impossible to tell one from the other.

Grundy had his two rifles on full automatic and was firing short bursts from one, then ducking and throwing grenades and standing after the grenades went off and firing long bursts with the second rifle.

Tahir came running along the trench from the south end, crouched low, reloading a magazine.

'Fuckin' magic, man,' he said to Luke Ryan.

Ryan was down under the parapet, reloading. Breath steamed from his mouth and clouded his face and the sharp cold tore at his lungs. Mortars impacted ahead of them and dirt and rocks sprayed them.

'Where the fuck are you goin'?' Ryan said.

'*Allah u akbar*! *Allah u* fuckin' *akbar*, man.'

He sucked in the air around him in five deep breaths and whispered to himself.

Then he jumped up on the parapet and, throwing himself over the top of the trench, fell flat on his stomach and fired at three Serbs who had taken up positions in a hole about thirty metres ahead of him.

Ryan shouted curses at Tahir, then pulled himself to the top of the trench and threw his rifle over and sprayed the area in front of Tahir with one hand.

'Fuckin' magic!' Tahir screamed again.

'Get back in, you fucker,' Ryan roared at him.

He was pulling himself out of the trench to grab Tahir when he felt a hand grab his leg and pull him back. Ryan kicked out, but the hand was stronger and it dragged him down into the trench.

'Stay!' Grundy said.

Grundy clambered up to the edge of the trench parapet and opened fire and threw grenades in each direction, then reached out and tried to grab Tahir, but Tahir had rolled forward.

Ryan scrambled up after Grundy, fell against the parapet and fired to Grundy's right at two shapes trying to set up a machine-gun position between two trees.

The Serb mortars had stopped, the fighting was too close now and the Serbs could not risk hitting their own men. It was so close Ryan did not know what was happening beyond his vision which, in the smoke and the chaos, stopped at Tahir on one side and two of Muha's Black Berets on the other. One of the Black Berets was dead and had fallen over his comrade who was trying to get him off.

'They're cuttin' us to fuckin' bits, Grundy,' Ryan said, 'they're cuttin' us to fuckin' bits. You gotta make him do what you want, Grundy, you gotta make him go for Vrh.'

For a moment Ryan felt he was on the border of hysteria.

'Move down the line,' Grundy shouted at him. 'And gimme cover.'

Ryan stepped back.

'Tahir?' he said then.

'Fuck him. Move, Luke,' Grundy said.

Ryan was glad to obey the order.

He ducked and started moving to his left behind men who were up on the parapet firing in small groups. Some of the men were below the level of the parapet, just throwing their rifles over and pulling the triggers because of the intensity of the Serb fire. Ryan could hear rounds passing over his head and could see rays of sunlight in the trees over him and the blue sky unfolding from the morning clouds.

Then Grundy was behind him again, with Yves and two twins called Grebo, who'd had a rock band before the war and still wore their hair in plaits. Yves had a PK machine-gun with the ammunition belt over his shoulder and a grin like he knew something.

'Yves and I'll work into the trees this side,' Grundy said to Ryan, 'and you boys hit 'em from here. We'll get 'em in a crossfire when they work this way.'

Then he explained the plan to Fikret and Alija Grebo.

Alija Grebo said he wanted to go with Grundy but Grundy just shook his head and the bass guitarist nodded. The firing was almost solid now and Luke Ryan could not make out the individual weapons any more.

Grundy counted time on his fingers and then Yves and he threw themselves over the edge of the trench and Alija and Fikret Grebo followed them to the top and poured fire left and right of them in three-shot bursts. Then Luke Ryan came up and fired straight ahead at five to ten Serbs who were behind a dip in the forest and trying to crawl to the right of their position.

Ryan watched Grundy roll into a shallow mortar hole and then crawl his way slowly round the flank of the most forward Serb position. Yves followed, and they moved as if they were connected, and all the time the Grebo brothers and Ryan kept firing to cover them. Out of the corner of his eye Ryan saw that Tahir was gone from where he had been and there were two dead men lying beside each other in the trench at the door of a dugout. A grenade had killed them and it had gone off without Ryan even noticing it.

The dead men did not look disfigured and their rifles lay

side by side in the water and mud of the trench. The wall of the dugout had begun to collapse and two alcoves burrowed too close to each other and not butressed with wood had brought down some of the front wall of the trench and some of the parapet logs on to the bodies of the two dead men.

Ryan could see eight Serbs in the forward group on that side and they had their heads buried in the ground in front of them to avoid the Bosnian fire. One of them was shouting into a walkie-talkie.

Grundy was making his way wide of them and two of the Serbs saw this and each of them threw a grenade at him. The first overshot and landed in the Bosnian trench and blew away part of a parapet. The second landed and did not explode. Ryan had seen it land two metres in front of Grundy and seen the Serb come up from behind his cover and throw the grenade in Grundy's direction, but the grenade did not go off. Ryan fired at the Serb and missed.

The Grebos and Ryan were reloading when two of the Serbs stood up and fired from the hip with their rifles on full automatic and made a charge for the Bosnian trench. Fikret Grebo had a blockage problem and desperately tried to clear his weapon, and Alija was reloading when the Serbs charged. Ryan swung his rifle to bear on them but the remaining Serbs came out of their cover on a shout and all opened up on the Bosnian position at once. The rounds sent Ryan down into the trench and killed Fikret Grebo. He stood up when they hit and then fell back, and when he fell a Serb grenade caught his body and blew his right arm off. He fell back into the trench beside his brother.

The first Serb had made it to the trench when Ryan recovered himself. He pulled his rifle up and fired three rounds and missed him, and the second Serb threw himself into the trench and shot a Bosnian soldier Ryan did not know in the back. The Bosnian just fell forward in the mud and Ryan fired at the Serb in the trench. Two rounds hit the Serb and three more went wide and the Serb turned face on to Ryan and pointed his rifle. Alija Grebo shot him from where he was sitting at the bottom of the trench in the muddy water with his brother.

Ryan shouted for Grundy and more support and fired at the other Serb in the trench, but a third Serb shot him from behind and Ryan tumbled to the trench floor.

He fell into the water and went under and his head spun. For a while he let himself go and felt the peace of letting go and the warmth of letting go. Then the water became cold very quickly and he could see a boot beside him and hear firing, and he lifted his head out of the water and pulled himself up on to his knees.

The trench had been constructed in a zigzag fashion so as to trap attacking troops in a crossfire and prevent them from taking the whole trench if they managed to get into one part of it. Now that the trench system was broken by artillery and mortar fire this helped its defence.

Ryan saw a Serb moving in front of him round a corner. The man was carrying a rifle and holding a grenade and Ryan shot him in the back with his automatic pistol. He dug his fingers into the wall of the trench and moved towards the dead Serb.

When he came round the bend in the trench he ran into another Serb and shot him in the head. The man, who had a heavy Chetnik beard, fell dead almost on top of him. Ryan kept moving along the trench.

The Serbs were in the Bosnian trench right along the line and the battle had fractured even more now, into a score of mini-battles, and the noise from the firing and shouting had fractured, too, and Luke Ryan felt he could hear the different battles around him. But he was alone. His heart was near to exploding and his breath was sharp and raw and mixing with the cold air and the forest mist and the smoke of the battle.

He moved along one wall of the trench and found a rifle beside a dead Serb where the trench fell away down a hill and the trees were in close and you could see their roots coming through the wall of the trench. The Serb had fallen over the roots and his arms were out in front of his body, touching the furthest root of the trees. He was young and his hair was cropped and he had been wearing glasses. The glasses lay broken in the mud beneath him and his blood dripped into the glasses and the mud.

Ryan picked up the Serb's AK47, cleared the barrel and checked the magazine. Then he moved up to the parapet, pulled himself over, fell flat on his belly and aimed the rifle.

Rounds flew over his head from two firing positions in the forest and Luke Ryan fired off two rounds and heard a round go into the ground close to him. He saw the muzzle flash and fired at it.

Heavy firing came back at him and he was forced to roll over and fall back into the trench. His head was aching now and the ache felt as if it wanted to tear the top of his head off, and there was blood. He had not noticed it at first and then he thought it was someone else's, but when it kept coming he knew it was his own and he remembered he had been shot. And then he was looking into the eyes of another Serb on the parapet.

The Serb had him cold and Ryan could not even bring the rifle to bear on him. He was a middle-aged man with greying hair and a fat face with wide, excited eyes and brown skin. He wore a scarf at his neck and a long coat and the thin leather webbing of the old Yugoslav People's Army. But he died before he could shoot Ryan. He spun round first one way, then another, then in a frenzy. The rounds hit his neck and his head, broke two vertebrae in his spine and smashed his hip. He fell back in a cruciform position and his rifle dropped into the trench beside Luke Ryan. Horst stood over Luke.

'Shit,' he said.

He grabbed Ryan and pulled him down the trench to part of a collapsed dugout, slapped his face and splashed urinic water on him.

'Come on, man, come on, man,' he said. 'Pick your weapon up, man. Where's Grundy?'

'I think he's dead.'

'Shit. You cover me?'

Ryan took the rifle beside him and Horst made his way over the top of the trench parapet, fired a burst from his G3 and yelled for Spit.

There was a shout from the right, a burst of gunfire and then Ryan heard Grundy's voice.

At first, he thought he was imagining it but it grew louder

and then there was firing and Ryan was trying to keep conscious and finding his eyes closing. Then Grundy was in the trench beside him.

'You're alive,' Ryan said.

'I believe so,' Grundy said. 'You're hit.'

'I'm hit.'

They sat in the muddy water at the back of the trench. Grundy tied a rag he had torn from the uniform of a dead man around Ryan's head and the blood on Ryan's face dried and his hair clung to his head on the dried blood.

Yves came up the trench, climbed the parapet and fired his PK in a wide arc and screamed when he fired. The trench was refilling and men were sitting together in groups, exhausted, the dead still lying in the water and mud and the smoke and the smell of urine and tree sap and resin and cordite lifting to the roof of the forest.

'Oh, Jesus ...' Grundy said then, 'I'm gettin' too old for this.'

He pulled a packet of Marlboros from his pocket, flicked a cigarette up and handed it to Ryan. Ryan was going to give him the Saki story. But there didn't seem any point.

'We held them?' Ryan said.

'I'm too beat,' Grundy said.

Grundy took another cigarette out and then passed the packet to Horst who had fallen in beside Ryan.

Spit came crouching down the trench with his arm bandaged, muttering curses. He sat on a dead body.

Horst passed the cigarettes to Spit and Spit lit two and smoked them together. He sat on the legs of a dead Serb. The man's head had been shot away from behind and Luke Ryan thought he had perhaps killed him but he could not remember. He found he could not remember most of the battle and he tried desperately to recall something about it, but it came to him in disjointed flickers that made no sense. Then he thought of Tahir.

'Tahir,' he said, 'where's Tahir?'

Grundy shrugged. He was talking on a walkie-talkie to Husic at the other end of the line and Muha kept coming in. Grundy told Muha to butt out. Muha cursed him. Grundy switched off his walkie-talkie.

'Spit,' he said.

Spit was rifling the dead body he sat on, looking for anything valuable and passing the things he found to Horst.

'Grundy, man,' Spit said.

'Get me a body count along here and check out the sections that side of the line. I'll meet you back here in five minutes. Luke, get up there and keep watch. They'll be back. Yves – ' he looked up at Yves – 'Yves, down with me.'

'Anybody see what happened to Tahir?' Ryan said. 'Spit?'

'Fuckin' Paki, all fuckin' mouth. Maybe they have him. Bastard'll be wishin' they hadn't.'

Spit laughed.

'Well, they don't, man. 'Cos I'm 'ere. Champion, eh? Oh, fuck, I think me leg's hit, Luke.'

Tahir was walking along the trench with his head bent. His face was covered in mud and his bandana was hanging round his neck and his combat trousers were torn from the thigh down to the ankle. His boot on that side was gone. He sat against the back wall of the trench and slid down the mud.

Ryan moved towards him.

'Leave him, Luke,' Grundy said. 'Get on the wall. Spit, go check the line. Horst, see if you can do somethin' with this guy. Jesus, you dumb fuck, Tahir, you go chargin' off into 'em on your own, man, what kinda shit were you thinkin'? You gotta be the stupidest piece a' shit I ever met, you know that? You fuckin' do that again, man, and I'll put one into you.'

'Hey, fuck you, Grundy, I'm dead already, man, I'm dead.'

'Hey, go to fuckin' Muha if that's what you're into.'

Tahir gave Grundy two fingers. Grundy picked himself up and moved off down the trench. Ryan told him to back off.

Horst bent down and examined Tahir's leg, reached into a pouch in the front of his webbing and pulled out a pad of gauze and some antiseptic powder.

'It is a – what do you say there, Luke – in the meat?'

'Flesh wound.'

'Yes. Stitches. Higher and you would have no balls. You were lucky.'

'Allah's on my side, man. Hey, Luke, I've been shot, what do you think of that? Eh, man, I've been fuckin' shot.'

'Keep still,' Horst said.

Horst bangdaged the wound, then moved down the trench and disappeared around a bend.

'You been shot, too?' Tahir said to Ryan.

'Yeah, I think. I can't remember. My head's achin'.'

'I tell you, me stomach's beginnin' to feel bad.'

'That's shock. Puke.'

'He was mad at me, wasn't he? Grundy, I mean. I mean, I showed 'im I could fight, didn't I? I don't feel good, Luke. Where's Muha? I thought Muha'd be here. I feel dizzy, I do. Oh, Jesus, I'm gonna puke. I'm gonna fuckin' puke.'

When Grundy came back, Tahir had been sick twice and was shaking. Ryan had taken a long coat from one of the dead Serbs and wrapped it round Tahir to stop his shaking. The medics were moving him out of the trench on a makeshift stretcher.

'Okay,' Grundy said, 'we're down twenty-five. Fifteen dead. They've lost forty-five dead that we can count, and maybe there's more out there. How you feelin', Luke?'

'Like a sick bollocks, Grundy. I wanna puke, too.'

'Well then, fuckin' puke. Put your fuckin' hand down your fuckin' throat and puke. You can stay in the line is what I'm askin', Luke, you can stay in the line?'

'Always with you, Grundy, always with you.'

'Well, that's good. Okay, okay, here's how it is. They'll bombard us again, maybe all day and all night. If I was them, that's what I'd do. They tried a small move down at Donje Selo and they might try a bigger one tonight if they're feelin' up to it, but with us on their flank they'll always be lookin' over their shoulders, so here's where it's at for the moment. We're gonna shift a company down to Donje Selo anyway. That means we're even thinner here but that's how it is. Two-hour watches.'

'So what do we do?' Ryan asked.

'We sit tight. We sit tight and see what they do next. Everyone get some food and have a drink if you can. And get these fuckin' Chetnik stiffs outta here. Dump 'em behind us. Husic'll get a grave party to put somethin' over 'em before they start to stink up the place. Jesus, it's cold. You got any *rakija*, Spit?'

Spit handed him a silver flask and Grundy drank from it and passed it around. Ryan watched the drizzle dissolve the remaining hard snow and saw blood streaming into the snow and drizzle and run down the small hill below the trench. The twenty metres in front of the trench had five Serb bodies lying in it and Ryan wondered if they were dead. He shot two of them just in case.

Jusef Husic came along the trench with Muha, who had his chief Sarajevan sidekick behind him, a bald man called Celo.

Celo had a facial wound which had been patched up by a medic now, and he was chewing beech leaves, an old trick to keep off scurvy. The shortages of fresh fruit and vegetables in the valley made collecting beech leaves, even fallen ones, essential.

'They have attacked Donje Selo from the south side of the river,' Husic said. 'With two tanks. They shelled it from prepared positions in the fields and we could not do anything to stop them. I think they are trying to draw us off here.'

'RPGs?'

'Three fired, no hits. The front of the tanks are reinforced with tracks and tyres and they are protected by earth. The rockets just bounced off. Then, when they were finished, the tanks pulled back out of range. Donje Selo's on fire again. What do you think, Grundy?'

'I give 'em three hours to get organised again and an hour to figure out what they're gonna do now. Then we'll start gettin' it right in the mouth here again. Can you get us more men?'

Husic shook his head.

'I do not have more men, Grundy, I do not have weapons for more men. If I get more men I must take ammunition and weapons from you. Do you think we can hold here?'

'What about your men, Muha?'

'I need all I have to hold the right flank of this mountain. Look—'

He pulled out his map.

'That is where the forest is thickest, that is where they come at us next. And if we are weak . . .'

'Well, I'll tell you, Muha,' Grundy said, 'your time'll come, but this is the part of the line they think they can make a break in right now. They wanna cut down behind Donje Selo and this is the place to do it from. We're gettin awfully close to last orders, Jusef. So how about some men, Muha?'

'I cannot spare them for you.'

'Jesus. Look, Jusef,' Grundy said, 'soon the Chetnik tanks'll ride right into Evkaf along the scenic route. Sittin' here waitin' for it ain't gonna do anythin' for us except get more of us killed for lost ground. We're fightin' their battle for 'em, not ours. And for Christ's sake, start diggin' another line about two hundred metres back of here or this line's just gonna be one big grave.'

'But we can hold them now, Grundy?' Husic said.

He was crouched in the mud, running his finger around in the water. He pushed his hand through his hair and looked at Muha and Celo.

'I'm not a crystal ball, Jusef. I don't have any magic. But what you're doin' here, man, is whippin' yourself.'

'You may leave when you want, Grundy,' Muha said.

'So you keep tellin' me. You drink?'

Muha shook his head. Husic took some *rakija*.

'Like the guy said, they're murderin' us here, so we might as well go somewhere else and get murdered. It's as simple as that. Let me do what I wanna do, Jusef.'

'It is a wild idea, Grundy, you said it yourself,' Husic said.

'And what's this?'

'I need men and I need guns, heavy guns, Grundy,' Husic said. 'When will the international community allow us to buy guns, Grundy?'

'They'll have to be dragged screamin', Jusef.'

'I do not understand,' Husic said. 'Bosna is democratic, Bosna is western, Bosna is European, Bosna is in the United Nations.'

'And Bosna is Muslim,' Muha said.

'If they hit us a few more times like this one, Jusef,' Grundy said, 'we're gonna have to shorten the line here, and if we do that they're gonna be knockin' on the north flank of Donje Selo by the end of the week. For Christ's sake, lemme do what I said. Just gimme fifty men, that's all.'

He began sketching on the wall of the trench and making arrows.

'They wouldn't know what hit 'em. Think about it.'

Husic was looking at the sky.

'Are you sure they will come again today?' he asked.

'Sure I'm sure they'll come again.'

Ryan began to whistle 'Always Look On the Bright Side of Life'.

10

The third shell hit the hospital and Natasa Ruzic buried her head deeper into her knees and prayed. The cellar was cold and dry and had no windows. There was a small orange light on one wall and each time the building rocked the light flickered and Natasa closed her eyes until she was sure it was on again. The shelling had been constant all night, like the footsteps of some insomniac giant pacing up and down the town, and the shells had been landing every two minutes in a wide arc from the *carsija* to the tower blocks. And behind the noise of the shells was the rattle of gunfire from Crna Gora and Donje Selo.

There were fires down the valley at Donje Selo, people said, and those who had been mad enough to stand out on their balconies said the sky was red there. Three people standing on their balconies had been shot by snipers but the bodies had not been removed. Other bodies had come in all day, from the front at Crna Gora and from the town. And the wounded were everywhere, in the corridors, in the rest rooms, in the cellars, in the kitchens.

Another shell impacted outside to the right and Natasa felt it under her feet and the walls seemed to shake.

'One hundred and thirty millimetre,' Dutina said.

Natasa turned her head to him and tried to keep her eyes open. They were bloodshot and she was so tired now that she could not sleep even if she wanted to. And her clothes were still stained with the blood of the wounded and dying from the previous day. She could smell blood on everything together with a low-grade stench that made the cleaning fluid of the hospital stand back in disgust.

'That last shell was a one hundred and thirty millimetre shell. I can tell now. High explosive. Perhaps it will blow up an apartment or leave holes in a building.'

'You think I care, Mihalj? I'm afraid, Mihalj, very, very afraid. Do you know that?'

She looked around at the other staff members, huddled under blankets on the floor around the cellar, between the flickers of the yellow light, and she prayed the emergency generator would hold and the light would not go out. She found herself almost begging for the light not to go out.

Some of the people around her were sleeping. She watched them snoring and she was angry and wanted to kick them, only she did not have the energy.

There were bottles of water stacked in one corner and pieces of bread lying on sheets of paper beside each person. People picked up their bread and chewed it when they had nothing else to do. They did not eat the bread so much as suck on it, to make it last longer.

The smell of body odour cloaked everything. No one had washed and constipation was written on every face.

Another shell hit close to the hospital.

Dutina put his hand on Natasa's hand and squeezed it. She took his hand and gave it a squeeze back.

'I bet I'm more afraid than you are,' he said.

'How much?'

'I have no money.'

'Your next cigarettes. You think the UN will get a convoy through? What do you think?'

'You have asked me that before, I don't know. They won't come if the Karadzic men do this.'

'Yes, I'm sorry. I keep asking you, don't I? It's one of those things when you're afraid, you keep asking the same question. I'm terrified.'

'You're okay, you're with the United Nations. The Chetniks won't touch you.'

'It's not just that, Mihalj. Can I ask you something?'

'As long as it's not about women's problems. I get embarrassed.'

'No. I'm helping someone.'

'Commendable.'

'To get out of Evkaf.'

'Shut up, don't tell me any more. I don't want to know.'

'Okay, I'm sorry. I just need to talk, Mihalj, just that. It's someone who thinks they will be killed if they stay. I thought you'd understand.'

'Please, please, don't tell me anything that puts me at risk. I'm sorry, Natasa, I'm sorry. But a Serb here has to learn to stay alive. It's not the same for you.'

'And when the Chetniks come? I'm Croat, Mihalj. The Chetniks'll know that. They can tell what you are by looking at you. I heard there's a man with a dog, this Alsatian dog, and it can pick out Croats. I heard this from a woman yesterday, she said she saw it in her village in August. The Chetniks came and they lined them up and the dog picked out the ones they wanted. The United Nations and my English passport won't help me then. Jesus, I am afraid.'

'Don't say things like that, Natasa, please, don't.' He looked around him. 'They'll spread it and they'll say I was the one who told you and then Muha's men'll come and say I'm a Chetnik.'

'No. I won't let them. I didn't want to come this time, Mihalj, you know that? I had to get drunk to come down to the convoy from my hotel. I've been at it too long. All this. I remember being in such a hurry when it started. The excitement. I love excitement. I went to Ljubljana in '91 but their war was over when I arrived. They had a great war, the Slovenes, and the soldiers looked magnificent at the barricades. I had a handsome lover there – he was a deserter from the Yugoslav Army – and we made love under a tree in the Tivoli. People gave the soldiers drinks at the barricades. And girls stopped their cars and got out and kissed the soldiers. Ljubljana's a pretty town. With the castle. Like a small version of Prague. Do you know it?'

'Prague? Sure.'

'I meant Ljubljana. There's nothing I can do here any more, nothing. I know that now. And I cannot find the excitement any more. We just patch them up so someone else can kill them. If the United Nations get through again, well . . . do you think I should stay?'

'What's the time?' He showed he had no watch. 'I sold it to a Black Beret. He wanted it and he offered Deutschmarks. He would have killed me, I think.'

'It's ten past four. I'm cold. They won't kill you, Mihalj.'

'Your boyfriend will protect me?'

He laughed quietly.

'When the Karadzic men come, Muha's men will come here and say I'm a Chetnik spy and they will kill me. I know this. Your boyfriend, the Irac, he will not be able to protect me.'

'Ryan's not my boyfriend, Mihalj. I'm too old for those things. There are lines on my face, you know? There never used to be lines on my face. And my facial hair is increasing and getting darker. Soon I won't be able to deal with it.'

'You have very little facial hair. You're a good-looking woman. They will kill me, Muha's men. I know how they will do it. I should have stayed in Germany. Germany was a good country for me. I had a nice house and no one called me Chetnik and no one said they would kill me. I'll kill myself.'

'I'll kill you first.'

'Is that a promise?'

'No. He's probably dead now. Ryan. He's out there in that and he's probably dead with Grundy.'

'How do you know Grundy?'

'From Zadar. I was there and he was wounded. The Kolovare. Do you know the Kolovare Hotel in Zadar?'

'No. I hate mercenaries. They're just killers. I don't understand them. They are fuckers.'

'I knew one in Zagreb who wanted to die.'

'And did he?'

'No. He was wounded forty-three times, he lost a leg, two fingers and one eye, and he had a stand-up row with a Croatian captain who wouldn't let him back to the front. The captain kicked his false limb and Archie – that was his name, he was a Scot, there were a lot of Scots in Croatia – threw his crutches at the captain. They deported him, strapped to a stretcher. He runs a chip shop in Amsterdam now. He sends me postcards.'

Dutina leant his head back against the wall and pulled the grey blanket over his shoulders.

'My bowels have not moved in five days,' he said. 'I think maybe I have a problem.'

'Mine haven't shifted in three, Mihalj. I have laxatives I brought with me, you want me to give you some?'

'There's a man here – over there – he says he hasn't moved in nearly two weeks. I think maybe you should give the laxatives to him or we should try something else with him. Do you have lice?'

'No. Skin rashes?'

He nodded. Then he pointed between his legs.

'It won't go. My clothes, they haven't been washed. I'll have to wash them. Would you wash them? I can't wash clothes.'

'Jesus, Mihalj, you're a real new man, aren't you? He has a strong and beautiful face.'

'Him?'

He looked over at the man who hadn't had a bowel movement for two weeks.

'No, Ryan. I like his face. It's the face of someone I knew, I think. We're always looking for the faces of people we knew. Grundy was my lover in Zadar.'

'And now?'

'He's a good lover. He came to this war in a tuxedo, you know? Right from a wedding. With the French man. I think he's French, maybe he's Belgian, they're all the same to me. It's the thing with people, the more alike they are the more different they want to be . . .'

'. . . and the more different they are the more alike they want to be. In difference there is unity, in unity, difference . . . and so forth . . . can God build a wall he can't jump over . . . Are you in love with him?'

'With Grundy?'

'The Irac.'

'I've been married twice, do you know that? My first husband was a doctor until I learned not to marry doctors. They have no time for you. He had no time for me and I had no time for him, so we just forgot about each other. I can't even remember getting divorced but I must have because I got married again.'

'And the second?'

'Oh, that's Grundy. We're married, you see. It was a little crazy and I was drunk, I think. It was like this and the Chetniks were attacking and we were in bed with the window open and we could hear the shells landing down the coast and around the airport and suddenly the window blew in. I don't know where the shell landed and I don't know who died but I proposed to Grundy. We were married and then he went back to the front and that was that. I thought perhaps he was dead.'

'Didn't you care?'

'It wasn't that kind of marriage.'

'My wife is missing sixteen months now and I've heard nothing. I ask everyone who comes here, everyone. I asked a man yesterday just before he died but he didn't know anything. It's the not knowing, you know? You hear everything about what the Karadzic army are doing to Muslims, killing them, raping them, all that, and I don't know what's happening to my wife. And my kids are with the Chetniks. Muha, he knows this, he says it to me: Your kids are Chetniks, you are a Chetnik spy; but I say I'm not. I'm pretty scared, Natasa, I'm not a brave man now. I am too old.'

'I have a cold sore coming on.'

'I thought he was a priest.'

'Muha?'

'No, Grundy.'

'I suppose he is in a way, but not so you'd see if you didn't look at it from an angle. You have to look at everything about Grundy from an angle. That's where he's different from Ryan. Ryan is so straight you could move along him with your eyes closed. He's a man who's realised something. But I don't know if he knows what it is. Grundy realises that there is nothing to realise.'

'There hasn't been a shell in – shit, I wish I had a watch. But they have stopped, do you think?'

Natasa shrugged.

'I feel foolish wearing this.'

She undid the flak jacket she was wearing and let the front of it fall away.

'Thirty thousand people wandering around this town without one and little old me creeping in and out of the shadows with the very latest Kate Adie equipment.'

Dutina looked confused. He picked his nose without considering it and then, realising what he had done, looked embarrassed on top of his confusion.

'She's a BBC woman. It's something very English. My father used to say that when he started coming back here after Tito died: he could come back and meet people and they were just like he had left them, but he had this whole life they could not share. So if they kill me for being a Croat, I'll be really angry because I'm not even a real Croat any more. Just the name and the language and an accent that can cut stale cheese. Right?'

'Your father was Ustasha?'

'He never said. But I have a feeling he did things he would rather forget. We never went through Knin when we came to Split. We always came down the coast road. I remember my mother saying we should take the train and my father almost shouting at her. I didn't pay much attention then, I was going through a divorce. He would not come into Bosnia, my father – never. He died two years ago. I miss him. I'm not Ustasha. I didn't even know what Ustasha was until I came down here from London. Then I was in Split and I saw a young man walking with a girl and he was dressed in black and wearing a huge iron cross and I thought it was a joke. They were selling the iron crosses and other Nazi insignia at the market stalls around Diocletian's Palace – and pictures of Ante Pavelic. Grundy bought me a holster with the *sahovnica* on it and I used it to carry bandages and things. I didn't really understand what it all meant until I saw my first Serb necktie. But that was weeks later.'

'I was a partisan in the Revolution. The world war to you.'

She looked surprised.

'I am so old?' he said. 'I was young, fifteen. The Germans – the Ustasha – they came one day . . .'

He stopped and, taking up a lump of stale bread, picked

off small pieces from the crust and sucked on them. Then he offered it to Natasa. She refused.

'I have a medal, you know,' he said. 'Tito gave it to me. I liked Tito. He kept all this down. He was a strong man and he knew the people here and he knew how to keep them controlled. Because I have seen all this before. The Chetniks, the Ustasha, they were both with the Germans. Maybe it is some kind of shame that makes them fight like this now. They are trying to prove something. I am a psychiatrist – surgery, I left many years ago. Karadzic, he's a psychiatrist, too, at the university in Sarajevo. And with a football team, I think. Jesus Christ. And he's a poet. I don't like football and I'm not a poet. I don't like poets. And I hate poets who have power. Men who write should never be given power. They're dangerous. They have big dreams and they try to realise their dreams with power. I would kill Karadzic, I think. He's a bastard.'

He coughed.

'I'm not my father,' Natasa said.

'I know that. I worked in Germany. But I'm in the minority. I'm a Yugoslav. The sins of the fathers are paid back with interest in this land. I think I have athlete's foot. Do you think my sons have murdered?'

'No, Mihalj, not if they are like you. I would kiss you only it wouldn't be right here.'

'How long now without a shell?'

'Twenty minutes.'

Dutina looked around the room. A couple who had been holding one another when the worst of the shelling was coming in were under the same rug.

'So you don't love the Irac?' he said. 'I was hoping for a little romance. All the romance has gone from life.'

'I want him, how about that? I want him more than I could ever love him. Love complicates want. I'm romantic that way. We'll have a splendid affair, if he's alive. I do this a lot. I see a man, I want him, I get so I can't think about anything else. It's all very hot and steamy. More lust than romance. Anyway what's romance except lust with sugar in it. I prefer mine without sugar. Like me tea.

The couple who had been sleeping under the same rug

started to move and the girl, who was a nurse in the hospital, cried out and then they were moving together.

'It's all like that here,' Dutina said. 'Mere fornication. Fornication is so damned technical. When I was a partisan we loved. I can tell you that. We loved many times. It was a time of love. I didn't meet my wife until afterwards. She was a virgin. But when I was a partisan – well, we would have found a room on the top floor where the shells have come in from the Crna Gora side and we would have made love there.'

'I'll remember that. Love under shell fire.'

The couple on the other side of the room came noisily and quickly and a woman down from Dutina said they were like animals.

The shelling started up again for another hour and then stopped.

11

The walking wounded were sitting around on the grass outside the main door of the hospital. There were a score of soldiers and maybe thirty civilians, and nurses and orderlies were going around them with bread and water. Some of the soldiers had that stare Natasa had seen before and the stare looked past you or through you and it went on for ever.

One man would not look up from where he had his head rammed between his legs. He had been hit in the face and part of his right cheek had been blown away. They had saved the eye but there was a hole in his face and the morning cold burned at it. The men shook in the cold and the deadened wet grass made an attempt to stir in the morning breeze, but the wet was too heavy and the grass could not move.

The walking wounded were mixed in with armed soldiers who were not wounded but acted as if they were wounded or wanted to be wounded, and Natasa could not make out why they were there. She was going to say something about it, and a few of the nurses who had men at the front said she should, but when she looked closely at these men it struck her that many of them looked in worse shape than the wounded.

She watched a young boy who had been hit in the arm try to light a cigarette with what he had left and when the cigarette fell, a young girl with no right eye and a bandage around her foot, picked it up and gave it to him and he tried again. Then he dropped it again and she picked it up again and this went on for five more attempts. Then he cursed her and threw the packet of cigarettes at her and walked off.

Luke Ryan sat on a helmet that had been part of a monument which had been hit by the shelling. The helmet was filled with concrete and it had embedded itself in the grass. He had thrown up beside the helmet and one of his boots was still resting in his vomit. He did not see Natasa come over to him. She stood beside him for a few seconds until she realised he was not aware she was there.

'You're cold,' she said.

His head bandage had fallen down and the skull tear had peeled back flesh from his head and it was flapping in the breeze. There was vomit on his leg and he had his hand on his automatic pistol.

'I don't feel cold,' he said. 'They were shellin' us again. All last night. I almost got buried. You ever been buried? I think I screamed. Grundy pulled me out. Maybe I ran away. I don't know. You ever run away? I said I'd stay but I'm here now. You look tired. Am I cold?'

'I think perhaps you have little shock. Your head is open. You aren't bleeding. I'll get you a blanket.'

She went to get a blanket. She was picking her way through the people on the grass when she turned back to Ryan.

'Grundy is okay?' she said.

Ryan nodded.

'I am cold.'

She went on.

Inside the hospital, one of the stairwells and two of the lift shafts had been hit by rockets. The stairwell and some of the supporting wall had collapsed and the two lifts had fallen into the basement. Three of the hospital staff had been hiding at the bottom of one of the lift shafts when the rockets struck and now firemen were trying to get the bodies out. Natasa watched them for a while. Then she went upstairs for the blanket. The hospital had moved further into the centre of the building and down a couple of floors. And apart from the usual smells which she was used to now there was a smell of charred metal and a damp sharp tang on the air. Ryan was holding his head wound when she came back.

'I can't do you for a while,' she said. 'There are others who are more important. You shouldn't stay here, all of you, you should go somewhere safe. Who's in charge?'

Ryan shrugged.

'I'll get someone to move you into a basement. This isn't safe, they might start shelling again.'

'No,' Ryan said. 'No, no holes. I don't want holes. I want the air. I want to feel the air. I think we're really losin' this time.'

'Does it matter?'

'I have this.'

He touched his pistol.

'As long as I have this I'm fine. My mouth is full of muck. Got any more water? I need a bath. Got a bath? The muck's everywhere, it's in my fuckin' brain. Did I tell you they were firin' at us all night? Jesus, the trench collapsed down the line somewhere. I heard there's maybe a few lads they didn't get out, sleepin' in a shallow dugout. Fuck, I was just sittin' there in my hole and the whole world just swallowed me.'

'I have to go.'

'Tahir?' he said.

It took her a second or two to realise he was talking about someone.

'I don't know him.'

'He's from Newcastle. He was hit in the leg before. Maybe he came here. He's a mad bastard. Thinks they can't kill him, I reckon.'

'I'll find out if I can. You could move over there near the sandbags in front of the door. If they start firing here you'll all be killed. This is not right.'

'There's no room inside. Dutina threw us out. He's a mad bastard, too, Dutina. You think I could have *rakija* or is my wound too serious?'

'I think it's okay.'

'He died?' Ryan said then. 'Mirsat Pasic? The old man?'

'Yes.'

'You know where they buried him?'

She shrugged.

'One of the parks. Ask *Armija* headquarters or the town council. Whoever.'

'I'll do the parks. Christ, my head hurts. There's things I can't remember, small things, I know they're there and I just can't remember them and they're drivin' me mad. It's like I keep slippin' gears. You got time?'

'No.'

A shell impacted nearby.

'That was a big one. Where do you think that was? Across the river. Sounded like a tank round to me. Husic says they had tanks there, dug in. The Kralj Turtko Kompanie tried to get 'em out but they couldn't get near 'em with the RPGs. Maybe the Croats didn't try hard enough. Maybe they sold us out to the Chetniks. They're fightin' us in the Lasva, around Vitez. I saw it. You're Croat, aren't you? You sure you don't have time?'

'I have patients. I have wounded.'

A truck with two red crosses painted on the canvas cover pulled into the hospital forecourt and went to the right of the main building. Two soldiers jumped out and one of them shouted at three of the soldiers sitting with the wounded on the grass. There were two more shell impacts and everyone stopped what they were doing. Then, when there was no third, the soldiers started unloading the bodies.

The bodies were in a heap with their arms and legs entangled. Two of them had no heads and one had no legs; another had his stomach spilling out. The soldiers lifted them singly and brought them into a side entrance of the hospital to a makeshift morgue they had made in the cellars. Luke Ryan watched the soldiers unload the dead and saw their faces and watched them cover their mouths when they were lifting the bodies. And there was a high smell. Some of the bodies had been lying untouched since the week before, and the animals had eaten parts of them.

Another shell impacted. A doctor with a young face and old eyes and no hair on the top of his head came out and told everyone to move into the cellars. Then the siren started up. Some people shouted and screamed. Another shell impacted nearer the hospital and machine-gun fire opened up from the mountains and the valley floor. They could not tell if it was outgoing or incoming.

'Okay, come on,' Natasa said to Luke Ryan, 'I'll fix you now.'

They were moving patients down the corridors to the

stairwells to get them into the cellars. Natasa led Ryan up a staircase against the flow of people and hospital staff, talking and shouting over the sound of machine-gun fire and impacting artillery and mortar shells. The cracks were nearer and louder now and the small-arms fire was breaking glass somewhere nearby and the sound of it beat time with the footsteps of the frightened patients and hospital staff.

The room she took Ryan to was high up and back from the front of the hospital, but they could hear the shells landing in the town outside and feel the vibration of the impacts under their feet and smell the smell of the impacts.

She cleaned his head wound with a bottle of *rakija* and stitched it with animal gut and gave him two tablets and the small bottle of *rakija* she had used to clean his head wound.

'It was a crease wound,' she said. 'I don't think the bullet even hit you. It just passed close enough to tear your skin and give you a headache. They travel very fast, bullets, and the pressure and heat and sound can do this. It was very close. Perhaps it just touched the flesh, but no more. Any more and it would have taken the front of your head off. You were lucky. Normally, I would put you in a bed and keep you in for observation, but now I have nowhere to put you. The tablets are aspirin. The *rakija* will help. But you have a concussion, so don't drink too much in case there's a weakness.'

Then she took a bottle of water and wet a cloth which was hanging over a sink and started to wipe his face. It was scratched and she cleaned the small cuts and, using some of the *rakija* she had given him, rubbed it into the cloth and dabbed at his wounds. He winced each time she touched him.

'You didn't mind when I cleaned your bullet wound.'

'I can't feel things so good up there.'

'A Chetnik shot you?'

'He must have. Or Grundy did. But Grundy isn't sayin'. He's a mad bastard, too, Grundy. There's a lot of mad bastards around here. He's a fuckin' marvellous soldier, but, Jesus, there's a demon in there.'

'I know Grundy, Ryan.'

'I don't.'

'Have you ever been married?' she said then.

Ryan allowed a stream of memories to escape to his consciousness. They were random and the feeling was happy and sad at the same time.

'I lived with a girl,' he said.

'I've been married twice and I've lived with three men. I've had a daughter and three abortions. And I am forty and I have lines in my face and I have no womb. You want children?'

'I forget. I don't think about much except food and sleep. You have soft hands. You have a good smell. You have a good body. You're beautiful – I want you.'

'You are romantic, aren't you. You have a romantic face and you tell the truth, I think.'

But his truth went no further than wanting her. He examined her. She had a good body, he thought. Maybe her hair was dirty and maybe she had lines in her face and maybe the skin was looser than it should be but she was there and he wanted her.

Eight impacts hit the area around the hospital, so close together they sounded like they were from a machine gun.

'Mortars,' he said. 'They'll keep this up all day. Make us tired and hungry. They're softenin' us up for another hit, maybe. They can do that and watch the effect. We won't hold them. I was buried. I don't know if I ran. I wanted to run. Damn. I don't want to be buried again.'

'You should go back to being a journalist, Luke,' she said.

He shook his head and laughed.

'I never was one,' he said. 'The first paper I rang told me they had someone in Belgrade covering the story. In fuckin' Belgrade! I was ringin' from a battle on a public phone. The second paper told me they were monitorin' the situation from a wire service in Budapest. I was fuckin' unlucky tryin' to be a journalist. But I'm a good soldier. I'm a good soldier. Are you religious?'

'I love the excitement,' she said.

'The near death experience?'

'Yes. I think I enjoy the terror. It's hard to explain. But I feel whole in a place like this. I have never felt like that before. I can do things. There are no constraints. I can let go, live a year in a minute.'

'Yeah. There was a village ... the Chetniks came ... I was hidin'. I thought about comin' out, showin' my passport, takin' some photographs, you know the way they do it in the movies, make them think twice about what they were gonna do.

'They lined up the ones who didn't escape when they came, about forty of them, old and young mostly. Then a man in sunglasses came along and tapped people on the shoulder. "Ustasha," he said, or "Mujahideen". Maybe twelve were taken out this way. They were taken down to a river and told to strip. The Chetniks pushed them into the river and told them to swim. Then they shot them.

'They gang raped the women, I heard, but I didn't see that. Shot four of them. Necktied a couple. You ever seen a Serb necktie?'

She nodded. Ryan thought for a few seconds.

'I never came out and took photographs,' he said. 'You understand? I hid. And maybe I'm not up to it now. Not the way Grundy and the others are. I'm scared of that. I've failed at everythin' I've ever done, you know. Everythin'. I didn't even fuckin' believe the religion I taught. I'm damn good at this but I'm findin' it harder and harder to see the point. And I have to see the point. You think Grundy has to see the point? I don't.'

She touched him and nodded and then kissed his head.

'Did you ever find your girl?' she said.

'Nah. She's gone.'

'There's a bed,' Natasa said.

She pointed over to a hospital bed on the other side of the room. It had a mattress and no sheets and the mattress looked like someone had been on it for weeks.

'I want you,' he said.

'Dutina says we should,' she said.

'My head hurts. I want you ... damn ... what's your name again? I've forgotten your name. Damn! damn! damn!'

'Natasa, Luke Ryan, I'm Natasa. You have the softest eyes. Even if they are lost. Are you very frightened?'

He pointed at his automatic pistol and touched the holster.

'My guardian angel.'

'I'm cursed, you know,' she said. 'Do you believe in curses?

I believe in them. I believe in everything. I used to believe in nothing but now I believe in everything. If there's something new and I find out about it I believe in it. That's the war, I think. Can you tell me anything I should believe in? Maybe you know something.'

She kissed him and he kissed her neck and put his arms around her.

The shelling got heavier. There were three close impacts in front of the hospital and the metal sheet wedged in the window frame bent in with the third shell.

'It might not be good,' Natasa said to Ryan.

'We'll be good.'

'And then you'll go. And when you see me again you'll turn your eyes from me. I'm not as pretty as I once was. Oh, I know here and now in this war you think I'm pretty but I know I'm not that pretty any more. Have you been with many women, Luke Ryan?'

'Not so many.'

'Grundy wants us to be lovers.'

'You think so?'

'Of course. I know Grundy, remember. He said we'd sleep together. He said we'd be good. We could use the floor. My body is nice. But it was beautiful, I think.'

'I think it is now.'

'Don't let go of me,' she said.

'I won't.'

'Say you love me,' she said.

'I will. You too?'

'Yes. You like anything? I mean some men have things they like. I have things I like and I'll tell you when the time comes, I'll tell you and you must do what I like, will you?'

'I will. I'll do anythin'.'

'Don't say that. You may not be able to keep your word. Have you killed many Chetniks?'

'I don't know.'

'I think you know. I treated a prisoner, a Russian. He was beaten and his leg was broken. Muha's men had him and he was very frightened. They said he was a murderer. I could see they hated him, but I felt sorry for him. Is it good to kill?'

'I'm very dirty.'

'I'll wash you.'

She undressed and Ryan undressed and he thought her body was not very beautiful. She washed him with the cloth and then rubbed herself and put her hands between her legs before they held each other.

'You have a good body,' she said to him. 'I like your body. You must say you love me now, you don't have to mean it or believe it but you must say it and you must say it so that I believe it, can you do that? Can you say it so that I believe it. You have deep eyes. They're intelligent but you're a foolish man.'

'I don't think so.'

'I know you are.'

He lay inside her for ten minutes without moving, just feeling her skin against his and the touch of her hands on his back and the kiss of her lips. She began the moving when she could not hold herself any longer and when he had become excited enough and knew he would come if he did not take control of himself he pulled back from her and she came up to meet him and he thrust into her very hard and she said what she wanted and and he did it. She came first and Ryan thought he would not come on time to be with her and she was asking him to do things she wanted and he pushed harder to force himself to come and the excitement caught him suddenly and she came breathless and he came saying he loved her.

When they had finished, they lay together and then she made Ryan dress and told him to leave. She stayed naked on the floor and there were goosepimples on her skin and she was holding herself.

'Can I see you again?' he said.

'I'll tell you when. I think I'll stay here for a while and then I'll go down to my friends in the cellars and eat with them and get drunk and forget this place and this war. Tell Grundy where I am, will you. Tell him I'd like to see him. And tell him we made love.'

'I don't want to. I want this to be ours. It is ours and I don't want Grundy to know about it.'

'You must. Grundy has to know, so tell him. If you want

to see me again like this you tell Grundy. Your girl, Luke, you loved her?'

'I adored her.'

And he left her there.

12

The roof shook with the second impact and a stream of dried clay spilled from one of the pine logs to the mud floor and dissolved in the pool of water on the floor. Sawdust and wood-chippings floated down to the floor and floated in the water where the dry clay had dissolved. And the smell was of pine resin and *turska kava*. One of the men making the coffee took a billy-can filled with coffee and placed it on the upturned tea chest posing as a table. Muha poured the coffee into small enamel cups. Another mortar landed, and the dugout shook again and Emira Kusturica could taste the wood-chippings and the sawdust on the pine resin when she drank her coffee.

'I'm sorry I hit you, *draga*; you forgive me?' Muha said.

It didn't seem like a request. She touched her lips. The top one was swollen on the left side.

'It's only a small cut, Hasim. I forgive you.'

Celo smiled from where he sat on a plastic chair in the corner. A PK machine-gun opened fire to his right and there was shouting from the trench. Celo shouted to the men on the machine-gun to calm down and identify their target. He smoked a cigarette and dipped a sugared cake into his *turska kava*. His boots were undone and he had his head against the mud and log wall of the dugout. There was a three-centimetre cut across his cheek, held together with tape. The blood on the wound had coagulated and some of the scab had flaked away and fallen on to the white t-shirt he wore under his combat jacket.

'As you can see, we are very busy now, *draga*,' Muha said to his sister. 'I really do not have time to play the big brother role I perhaps should with you. I'm going to put you under guard – a guard I cannot afford, you know? But if you will insist on contradicting my orders and breaking your promises – I have no respect for people who break their word. People with no strength of belief break their word. I do not. This is a restricted area. You could have been shot by my men. You would definitely have been killed by the Chetniks, you know? They are down there, hundreds of them, down there, and behind them there are guns and mortars and more soldiers – what were you thinking?'

'I just want to get out of here, Hasim, I just want to get out.'

'And you think this will help you?'

He picked up a Croatian passport and threw it at her.

'It's the the the worst attempt at forgery I've ever seen. Where did you get it?'

'I bought it.'

'Then you were robbed.'

'I was desperate.'

'Who sold it to you?'

'I don't know. I put my own photograph in.'

'Yes, it figures. You could be shot here for having this.'

'It was for getting to the coast.'

'Well, I think you should apologise, to me and to Celo. I think you owe us that. We probably saved your life, you know.'

'It was nothing,' the bald Sarajevan said. 'She's a fine girl, Muha, your sister. Maybe she would make a man a good wife.'

'I take your point, Celo. Though I must insist on an apology, Emira. Apologise, please.'

His eyes narrowed and Emira tried to stare him off but found that she was growing more and more frightened of him with each second.

'I said, apologise.'

She held out for a few more seconds. Three heavy shells whistled over the position and struck rock several hundred metres behind them. Some of the rock fragments landed on the dugout roof. Dry clay and dust fell on Emira's head.

'Okay,' she said. 'I apologise.' Then she turned to Celo. 'I'm sorry, Celo – is that okay, Hasim?'

'And you will call me Muha, please. I don't know, Emira, I just don't know. I thought you'd be pleased to see your brother again. I don't understand you, *draga*. It must be fatigue, trauma. You've had a nightmare experience, *draga*, and I understand these things, I've read about them. You need a doctor. Tell me, please, where would you go? This is your home, *draga*, with me, with our people. You look terrible. Are you cold? Drink your coffee. Celo, see if you can find a uniform or something for her. Something clean, please. You see this hill here?'

He pointed to a small hand-drawn map he had in front of him. Emira leaned over the tea chest. She scratched mud from her face and held back a tear that was welling in her left eye. Then she sniffed, and her brother pulled out a handkerchief and gave it to her. She unfolded it and it was clean and white and had an M monogram in the corner.

'They have a position there, and it controls this gorge and this valley, here. You were going this way – yes? They'd have picked you off from here with a sniper. Already, ten, twenty people have died in this way. Just here. I've seen it. One time we watched five people try to run this way. Four of them were cut down by this sniper.'

Emira leaned back. The PK machine-gun opened up again and someone shouted that there was movement below them at the Serb line. Muha stood up and went to the door of the dugout. Celo had come back along the trench. He winked at Emira, and Muha dipped his head so Celo could whisper into it. The Black Beret making coffee asked Emira if she would like some more. She shook her head and he offered her the second half of a spinach and cheese *burek*. She took the *burek* and broke a piece off and dipped it in the remains of her coffee. Then she sucked on it.

'Okay,' Muha said to her. 'They're getting ready to attack again, *draga*, I would love to stay and chat but it's not possible. Perhaps later. I'll give you a man to guard you, *draga*, though I am stretched here now, but you are my sister and I owe you that. Please, do as he says, otherwise I'll be very angry. I love you, *draga*, you do realise that?'

'The fifth one, he got away?' she said.

'Sorry, *draga*, you've lost me again,' Muha said.

'The fifth one down there?'

She pointed at the hand-drawn map.

'Oh, no, *draga*, we shot him. It's against the law to leave without permission.'

Muha picked a walkie-talkie from the tea chest and a G3 rifle from a metal rack at one wall of the dugout. He checked the rifle and pulled a magazine from one of the pouches in his webbing and taped the magazine to the magazine in the rifle. Then he snapped the magazine back into the rifle and pulled his webbing from the wooden peg it hung on, tied the belt and tightened the shoulder straps. He pulled three grenades from a box beside the tea chest and hung them on his shoulder straps, then checked a Beretta automatic pistol in its canvas holster at his hip and replaced it.

'Okay,' he said, 'ready for work.'

He smiled at his sister. She grinned back. Celo came into the dugout with a combat jacket and a pair of black canvas trousers.

'All I could get,' he said. 'They're hitting us on the right, Muha. Two Bofors from hill seven for close support.'

Muha nodded.

'Put these on,' he said to his sister. 'We'll be outside. Oh, and one other thing, *draga*, you were seen talking to one of Grundy's men. What did you tell him?'

'We discussed many things.'

'I would rather you didn't do that. I have explained my reasons there.'

'He helped me.'

'So, you thank him and leave it at that.'

'I did.'

'Good. That's good. Now hurry up, *draga*, the war won't wait for fashion sense.'

He nodded to the Black Beret who had made the coffee and the man grabbed a rifle and left the dugout.

Muha was up on the fire step at the trench parapet looking through binoculars and talking into his walkie-talkie when Emira came out. The voice on the other end was excited and Muha kept telling him to calm down. Celo covered Muha with his rifle. Two heavy artillery shells landed in the trees ahead of them and a thin shower of dirt fell on the trench. Three Black Berets began firing to their right and a Bosnian mortar position fired five shells in quick succession. The shells landed down the mountain. The Serbs replied in kind. Emira stood close to the trench wall and watched men run up and down the trench, shouting, taking position, firing, giving directions. It looked a confused mess and she recognised some of the men around her but she could not put names to them.

A young Black Beret came running along the trench in a crouched position. He had a beard and his beret was low over his forehead and there was a green bandana tied beneath the beret. He had worry beads hanging from his epaulettes and a crescent moon badge on his breast pocket. Muha slid down from the parapet.

'Okay, *draga*, this is Murad, he's your escort from now on. I've told him what I expect. He won't interfere with your life, so long as you obey my wishes. I'll get down to you when I can. As you can see, it could be some time. Try and do something, *draga*, to help the war. There are plenty of things you can do. There's always work. You'll move back through our access trenches now. They're not as deep as this one, so keep your head down or some Chetnik shell will take it off. Murad knows what he's doing so follow what he tells you. And for heaven's sake don't stop moving until you have reached the hotel.'

He put his hand out and she took it and gripped it with both of hers. Then he took her hands and kissed them and then kissed her on both cheeks.

'You look after yourself, *draga*. I'll see you, okay?'

He nodded at Murad, and Murad tapped Emira on the arm and indicated she should follow.

They moved quickly along the trench for two hundred metres, passing small units of Black Berets on the parapet. Most of them were not firing, some of them were praying, others were shouting for information and directions, either into their walkie-talkies or just down the line. One young man snapped a magazine into a 7.92mm sniper rifle and, slipping over the top of the trench parapet, rolled to his right, covered by the fire of a PK machine gun. The Black Beret firing the PK stood high over the parapet and shouted when he pulled the trigger. A second man fed the ammunition belt to him, kneeling below the level of the parapet, leaning in close to the trench wall.

The access trench was less than head height and it meandered through dense undergrowth and concentrated deciduous forest. The trees were shedding their leaves and the leaves lined the access trench and piled up on either side of it. Sheets of plastic and old blankets were hanging at points along the access trench where the undergrowth and the trees were thin because of the autumn. Emira kept her head down and sometimes closed her eyes. The shells had begun to fall again. Every minute now.

They passed a Bosnian mortar pit, with soldiers getting ready to fire a 120mm mortar. They were dirty men and they held their ears, and one of them pulled on a cord and the mortar fired. Then they loaded another shell. Two Serb shells landed behind them, to the right of the access trench where it divided into three trenches and went off in different directions across the top of the mountain.

Three Serb shells landed behind them and then four in front, five to the right and Murad dived to the floor of the access trench and told Emira to get down, too. He did not have to. She was already down with her face in the muck. And the shells came in so quickly after each other that Emira could not tell the individual impacts any more. She heard a tree splinter and rocks shower the ground. A piece of thick reinforced plastic shredded and she could see smoke rising over the wall of the access trench and smell a half-eaten tin of fish and the remains of human faeces. She tasted the smoke of the battle at the tip of her tongue and felt the sting of battle in her eyes. And then it had passed them and moved to their right.

Emira pulled herself up to her knees and wiped the muck from her eyes. She brushed the leaves and pine needles and small stones out of her hair and spat out the taste of the shelling. Behind her, part of the trench had been obliterated by a shell impact. Smoke rose from the hole and there were milk cartons scattered around it. And a small tree had collapsed. Emira crawled forward to Murad. He was flat on his face. She touched his feet and he did not move and she touched his leg and felt it move, so she crawled further along his body and grabbed his shoulders.

He pushed her hands away.

'I'm okay, I'm okay,' he said.

His face was so white she could see the veins beneath his skin and she thought his beard would fall out. He rubbed the muck and stones from his face and pulled his beret back on. Then he crawled in close to the wall of the access trench and examined his body.

'Are you okay?' he asked.

Emira sat beside him. Six Bosnian soldiers came along the trench, going towards the front line. They did not speak, they did not even look at Emira and her escort. They were young men but they stooped like old men. Murad was taking deep breaths and looking at the sky. Clouds were coming in from the north.

'Maybe rain,' he said. 'Rain comes, battle stops. No one can see up here. That was close. You want a smoke?'

She shook her head. He pulled out a packet of Marlboro.

'United Nations,' he said.

'Let's go, please,' Emira said.

'Okay, okay. You got any *rakija*?'

'What would Allah say?'

'Allah will understand.'

'And Muha?'

'Muha's a little more difficult. But he isn't here, is he?'

'I don't have any. Come on.'

'Shit, you're just like him, aren't you?'

'You're not scared I'll tell him what you said?'

'Listen, I stand just as good a chance of Muha killing me for nothing as for something. I've seen it. He's a little crazy, your brother. Two months ago, he shot two guys for being late on duty. Just shot them. Their mothers went to Husic, Husic does this and that, gets the military police to look into it, the military police go and ask Muha if he shot these two guys, Muha says, sure, they were spies, they were dealing with the Chetniks, he has witnesses. And ten guys are brought forward who will swear that the two who were shot were trading with the Chetniks. The military police say fine and that's that. Except we deal with the Chetniks all the time. How the hell do you think we keep fighting them? It's a crazy war. And some of the guys with Muha, they're crazier than he is. Afghans, Iranians, Arabs.'

'So what are you doing still here?'

'Hey, you know it better than I do, you don't leave Muha. Anyway, where would I go? This is okay, though. I'll watch you. Gets me out of the fighting. I'm fine with that. We can have an arrangement. You sure you don't have any *rajika*? Dope?'

Another shell landed close by. There was a terrible tearing noise and the wind seemed to break the land in two and a cloud turned into a wave and engulfed them. Emira fell flat. Murad rolled over. He was covered in a thin layer of muck and it was still falling on him when he pulled himself up on his hands and knees. He was spitting out muck and trying to stand up. Emira watched him shaking the earth from his back and then the second shell hit.

Murad twisted in the blast and then somersaulted into the wall of the access trench and the trench collapsed on top of him. There was heat and cold in the same moment and the air left through a pin-hole. Emira dug her head into the ground and said what she thought was a prayer. It was a comic song she had learned as a child and she was still repeating it over and over again when she had recovered enough to pull Murad out of the muck by his feet.

He had been hit from his knee to his head on the right side of his body. There were seven entry wounds in his side and four exit wounds, two in his back and two at the other side of his body. The two in his back were the size of oranges and one of the side exits had torn away four ribs. They were sticking out of his skin. His right knee was almost gone and his neck had been lacerated on the right side. She could see the artery pulsating. It wasn't severed. His face was shredded on the right side and clean on the left.

'Fuck, I can't feel anything,' he said.

His eyes were moving around out of control.

'Am I badly wounded?'

Emira nodded.

'Get me to a medic.'

Emira called out for a medic.

'I'm going to lift you,' she said.

She tried to lift him and he screamed. She tried again and he cursed her.

'Get me a fucking medic. I can't feel anything in my leg now. Shit, that's bad.'

She called for a medic again. More artillery rounds landed to their right, then to their left. She pulled him along the trench, crawling herself. The shells landed either side of the access trench, throwing muck and bits of tree and rock across the trench. Murad moaned and cursed when she pulled him and all the time she screamed for a medic. None came.

They rounded a bend in the trench and it divided again, dipped down into a flat pine wood and snaked between the pines. There was no damage to this wood and the trees were tall and only the breeze moved them.

'How are you?' she asked him.

'I'm alive, I'm alive. I can't feel anything below my waist at all now. I'm not sure I can feel anything below my chest. Am I hit in the chest?'

'In the side. They're all in the side.'

'Maybe that's okay, maybe that's okay. If my chest is okay and my heart is okay and my head isn't in two then I stand a chance. I think maybe some of my organs have been damaged. I can lose a kidney and be all right, I can take damage to my liver, maybe. I was a medical student. Help me. I'm trying to figure out what's wrong. How are my legs?'

'Your left one is fine. Can you use it?'

'And my right?'

'Not great.'

'How not great? Shit, I'm feeling pain now, in my chest. I think maybe I have bleeding in my lungs.'

'I think so. Try and use your good leg to help me.'

'I can't. I can't breathe well, I can't breathe well. Hurry. Fuck, hurry. Shit, man, shit.'

'I'm trying. You weigh a lot.'

'Too many cakes. My damn mother.'

She shouted for a medic again. Murad shouted and cursed

and then slipped into unconsciousness. Emira pulled him for another five hundred metres. Blood trailed from his body along the access trench and she could hear his lungs fighting the blood beginning to fill them. Blood came out of his mouth in three coughs and he regained consciousness and coughed up more blood.

'Shit!' he said. 'I think my lungs are really fucked. I think my spine is fucked, too. I think I'm fucked. Shit, shit. I thought I'd get through, I mean, I thought I'd get through. Fuck. Fuck your fucking brother. I'm sorry for my language. You're a beautiful girl, Emira. How come a guy like Muha has a beautiful girl for a sister? I would have liked to have been your friend. I remember you when we were kids – you wouldn't remember me – right?'

'I'm sorry, Murad, I don't.'

'It doesn't matter. I don't feel so good. The pain is going but I don't feel so good. It's okay that you don't remember me; I wasn't very memorable. You'll remember me now, yes?'

'I will.'

'Just a prayer or two sometimes.'

'I'm not practising.'

'Hey, fake it, I don't care. I do it all the time. Listen, I have some stuff, things that are very valuable here, and a few hundred Deutschmarks in a box, stashed, if you want them. You take it all. Do what you want with it. I don't care now. There's a name with it. Just don't give it to Muha. I don't want that bastard making anything more out of me. Maybe it'll help you. Get you enough money, you know? The directions are in my pocket. I'll feel better if you have it. Clears my conscience. There's other stuff. But you look through it first, will you, make sure there's nothing embarrassing? I always think I'll die with something embarrassing on me I can't change. I don't wear underwear. I can't get any more breath. Oh, shit.'

'Keep still.'

'How about a kiss?'

She leaned over and kissed his lips.

'Hey, I scored,' he said. 'He hit you, the bastard.' He coughed more blood. 'Oh, fuck, I scored with Muha's sister. That's one for him . . .'

Two Bosnian mountain soldiers came up the access trench. Emira asked them for help. They didn't stop.

Murad was dead when the medics reached him.

Emira sat with him at the first-aid station, looking at him. She recognised the boots before she heard the voice and she did not look up when she heard it.

'He was always a bit of a weasel,' Celo said. 'Where are his personal effects?'

Emira nodded at the small imitation leather wallet lying on the grass and the set of worry beads. Celo knelt down and went through the wallet.

'You are lucky again,' he said. 'How about you give me some of that luck?'

'Fuck off.'

'I like that. Come on, I'd better get you out of here or Muha'll have my balls – and I'd rather it was you. Did he say anything?'

Celo gestured to Murad. Emira shook her head.

'Did Hasim not trust him?' she said.

'Fuck, no. No one did. But I'm here for more ammunition. Come on, I haven't got time. The Chetniks are hammering into us. I'll get you another escort. Leave him. And don't let it get to you.'

'It hasn't.'

Celo ordered two military policemen to escort Emira back to town. The order was copperfastened with a cigarette and a discussion about her features and character. And the mountain shook with the force of the Serb shells.

It started to snow and the snow came in large single flakes on the wind. The ground was hard and dry on that side of the mountain because of the wind, and the snow clung to the hard dry ground.

And Emira had to shield her face from the snow.

The walking wounded slipped on the new snow and the hard ground and the snow clung to their faces and then fell slowly to the ground. One man, on crutches, stood beside a tree and Emira watched the snow cover one side of him and he did not move. When Emira reached him, she saw his eyes were closed. One of his friends tried to get him to move but he would not, and when he had stood there for ten minutes he sat down and died. A group of reinforcements passed him with their heads down.

Horst left the men he was leading and watched Emira Kusturica talking to Celo. They did not see him.

In the distance, a house in Donje Selo was on fire.

13

The Serbs broke through at night, on the centre-right of the Bosnian line on Crna Gora, where the line dipped off the heights and wound down in a loop towards the next valley.

It was a steep face and there was a long stone wall and the remains of three houses. The Bosnians on that side were well dug in, but the Serbs brought all their artillery to bear in a single five-hour bombardment on that point and managed to get one of their mountain infantry companies up the steep slope and over the wall when the barrage was going down.

The barrage killed ten of their own men but they were willing to take the losses and when the Bosnians came out of their holes they found Serbs to their rear and the Bosnian line was turned.

A company of Bosnian mountain troops tried to circle round the Serb attackers, but the counterattack was a knee-jerk move and in the confusion the supporting Bosnian heavy mortars ended up firing on their own men. Then there was panic in the Bosnian line.

The panic led to more confusion and more panic and the line started to crumble in the forest on the north side of Crna Gora. Muha rushed men to plug the gaps and Grundy held tight to the left, but the breach in the line between them could not be repaired and the Serbs were pouring through.

Grundy said he was pulling back, to avoid being overrun; Muha ordered him to stay put; Grundy ignored Muha and began pulling his men back and there was a fifteen-minute shouting match over walkie-talkies in which Muha threatened to shoot Grundy if he fell back and Grundy said he would shoot Muha if he did not. Just before dawn, Jusef Husic

settled the argument and ordered the whole Bosnian line to
fall back.

The new Bosnian line was now back over half a kilometre
and the Serbs were in place to the north of Donje Selo now
and pushing into the Evkaf valley from that side, too.

When Grundy got to the ski resort on Crna Gora, there
were infantry and policemen digging fresh trenches and an
excavator pushing earth into a giant embankment in front of
the ski hotel. Men were filling sandbags and piling them one
on the other around three chalets which flanked the hotel. The
chalets were pocked with rifle and shell impacts and one side
of the hotel had collapsed.

The hotel was Muha's headquarters and it was sandbagged
up to the second floor and on the balconies of all the other
floors. It was a Socialist Realism building made out of
reinforced concrete and angled as if, when it was being
built, someone had had the idea that it might double up as
a headquarters or a barracks during a war.

The side of the hotel that had collapsed had been hit by
artillery and rocket fire for four days before it gave way, but
because the whole hotel was like a honeycomb inside only
that section gave way and all the other parts held fast. All
the windows in the hotel were blown out and replaced with
metal or wood or plastic sheeting.

On the side of the hotel that had collapsed, all that was left
were bare walls and the remains of rooms hanging on to pieces
of concrete floor. And the bare walls were pockmarked with
shell holes and rocket impacts and bullet holes, and the ground
below was a mix of masonry and pieces of bed and carpet and
furniture and light bulbs. There were maybe a hundred light
bulbs lying around.

A group of men on the right of the hotel were digging slit
trenches, but the ground was so hard you could not get the
shovels and picks into more than a couple of centimetres of
ground at a time. Some of the men had just given up and were
sitting on the ground as if waiting for a bus.

The demoralised men had left their rifles beside them
and the snow covered their rifles when it fell and the
men concentrated on small things like smoking if they had

cigarettes or tying a lace. Their eyes looked as if they were
so empty that the whole universe might fall into them and
disappear.

Three men held hands under a tree and two more just tapped
the ground with their spades while an officer tried to get them
to listen to his orders. Nearby was a car and a Toyota van and
they were full of men who just sat in them, waiting. Everyone
was waiting.

Jusef Husic was walking with a pronounced stoop now
which made him look shorter. His green eyes were small
and withdrawn and they were the colour of the green on the
mountains around the valley, a kind of dying winter green.
And he was chain-smoking.

Some of Muha's men stood around the foyer of the ski hotel
in small groups and when Husic passed one or two tried to
come to attention and one even attempted a salute. But he
couldn't remember the procedure from his conscription days
and it all looked stupid.

Husic's son, Milan, walked three steps behind his father,
wearing sunglasses, carrying an AK47 slung over his shoulder
and his father's briefcase in his left hand. Two military
policemen walked either side of Milan, carrrying their rifles
by the grips and smoking. Milan Husic had the same look as
his father only his eyes were brown and the look wasn't so
far gone.

The hotel foyer was a combination of marble and brown
carpet and the marble had a deader look than the brown
carpet. There was a taste of masonry in the air and a taste of
lime in the masonry. A huge chandelier hung from the ceiling
in stages, in great stalactite crystals looking as if they belonged
to a huge new-age temple.

Muha's men carried an assortment of weapons and wore
everything from combat fatigues to Manchester United track-
suits. They had white t-shirts underneath their clothes which
showed they were Muha's men and most of them had some
kind of black beret, but if you did not know they were Muha's
men you might think they were a bunch of gangsters getting
ready to go out on a hit.

The hotel dining-room had a large table stretching almost

its entire length. There were food trolleys lined up against one wall and chairs stacked against another and at the far end of the room was a small portrait of Alija Izetbegovic and a huge portrait of Ayatollah Khomeini. The tablecloth banner underneath them read: *Allah u akbar*.

Husic looked at the wall with the portraits and the slogan and tried to raise his eyes, but could not bring himself to do it.

Muha was bent over a map on the table and chewing gum. He had a Skorpion machine pistol lying beside him on the table and two G3 rifles slung over his shoulders. He had a shrapnel wound in the lower neck.

Muha looked up, acknowledged the colonel and his son, then turned to one of his own men and nodded at him. Then he went back to the map.

Yves and Spit sat in two of the chairs and smoked. Spit was examining Yves's knife and Yves took the ceramic plates from his kevlar vest and put them on the floor. The pocket that held one of the plates had torn and the plate was falling out of place. The vest was heavy and Yves only wore it when he was defending a fixed position or sniping. His boots were undone at the top and the laces were loose.

When Grundy came in, Muha's man pulled the doors shut from the foyer.

'How're you feelin', Muha?' Grundy said.

He slapped Muha on the shoulder without waiting for a reply.

'You never told me that Chetnik whore the boys brought in from Jablanica was your little sister, Muha,' he said. 'If I'd known that, I'd've definitely charged for the service.'

Muha looked at Grundy and then at each of the other faces in the room.

'It was not your business, Grundy,' he said when he had composed himself. 'And my sister is not a Chetnik whore. You wish to make an issue of it?'

'Hell, no. What do you think of that, Jusef? That little Chetnik whore turns out to be Muha's sister. Well, well, well . . .'

Husic said nothing.

'You're drunk, Grundy,' Muha said. 'I can smell it on your breath.'

'Just a tad tight, Muha, just a tad. And she don't wanna stay, little sister. Did you know that, Jusef? Yeah, I'll bet you did. She was tryin' to make it outta here when big brother caught her. What you do, slap her butt?'

He put his hand on Muha's shoulder again.

'Please take your hand off me, Grundy,' Muha said.

'Where is he?' Grundy said.

'Where is who?' Muha said.

'Grundy,' Husic said before Grundy could answer Muha, 'we don't consider everyone the Chetniks rape a whore. If we did, we would have a disproportionate number of such women in our society. I wish you would not talk like that. Muha's sister has been through what many of our women are suffering as we speak.'

'So you did know who she was, Jusef? Well, maybe you know where the damn Russian is, too, Jusef, because he's gone. Any ideas?'

'I do not know what you are talking about,' Husic said. 'What do you mean?'

'Yes you damn well do, Jusef. The military police don't have him any more. And guess what? They say the police took him away and the police say your men took him, Muha. Familiar ring to it, don't you think? So where the fuck is he, Muha? What have you fuckin' done with him?'

'I have done nothing with him,' Muha said. 'The Russian is in custody, undergoing interrogation. As far as I know there is a criminal file being prepared, too. All very legal. The last time I saw him he was lying in a hospital bed with a pin in his leg. A waste of time and effort and equipment in my opinion. What is between you and this fucking Chetnik murderer, Grundy? I have a war to fight, Jusef.'

'Well, find out what's happened there, Muha, will you?' Husic said. 'We've more important things to discuss now, Grundy, so drop it. But I don't want to find out there was any murder, Muha. I don't want that. Okay?'

'There was none, Jusef. He is being treated in accordance with the Geneva Convention. I swear it. My orders. We had more questions for him. But I will look into it. Perhaps there has been an administrative error. Something like that. These are difficult times.'

He turned on the walkie-talkie at his shoulder and called Celo. Celo came through and Muha told him to find out what had happened to Koniev.

'Celo will get to the bottom of this,' Muha said. 'I am not responsible for everything that goes on in this valley, Grundy, despite what you would like to think.'

'Maybe some honest citizens decided to deal with him,' Grundy said. 'The Russian.'

'That is always a possibility,' Muha said.

'Ah, shit,' Grundy said. 'I knew this'd happen. He was my fuckin' prisoner, Jusef. It's a fuckin' waste. Fuckin' myopic. Jesus, I bet you got your sister workin' for you down town now, Muha. Real money-spinner, that girl, I bet. Maybe you were gettin' a cut from the Chetniks. Hourly rate, of course.'

Muha turned to him, picked up his machine pistol and pointed it at Grundy's face.

'You will take that back, Grundy. Colonel, he will take that back.'

Yves had his weapon out and Spit was moving to a covering position at the other side of the room, towards the door. There was a silence. Grundy let Muha's barrel touch his face.

'Your men would not leave this hotel,' Muha said.

'Enough,' Husic said. 'I don't need this. Okay? Grundy, personally I don't give a shit what's happened to the fucking Russian right now and I don't know why you do, you've been paid for him. But it will be investigated. And Muha's sister is nothing to do with you.' He looked at Muha. 'And Muha, you control yourself, that's an order.'

Muha did not lower his weapon.

'I'm giving you a direct order, Muha.'

Muha looked at Husic.

'You're weak, Jusef. You let these bastards rule your mind. They're foreigners, Jusef, they have no concern here. They fight because they just want a war to fight. We're their toy and when they're tired of us they'll go and get another toy.'

He replaced his machine pistol on the table.

'So what did the United Nations say?' he said to Husic then.

'They won't come in until the fighting stops. I told them the fighting won't stop until they come in. He was British, the United Nations officer, they are hard to understand, the British, like the French.'

'Rule Britannia,' Spit said.

He raised a fist.

'They'll come in to count the bodies, Jusef,' Muha said. 'And maybe to preserve a few breeding pairs. You see, Grundy, you can make a joke. I do not have that privilege. They won't come until we throw down our weapons, Jusef. They're just doing the Chetnik job for them.'

'Can you do it, Grundy?' Husic said. 'Just tell me. This idea of yours?'

Grundy stepped back from where he was beside Muha and took his hand from the Luger pistol at his side and folded his arms. Yves lowered his weapon and Spit moved back from the door. Grundy looked at the map.

'Well, there's always a maybe involved, Jusef,' he said. 'But we're at the point that if we don't do it now, we can all pack up and head east. I'm not even sure it'll help any more, Jusef.'

He pointed at the map to the north of Donje Selo.

'They'll hit the village from all round and try and cut the link to town now. Just a matter of time. They moved those two tanks back into position across the river here this mornin'. Dug fresh pits for 'em. They might bring in some more. It's a shit of a position to be in, Jusef.'

'So we must attack before they can cut off Donje Selo,' Husic said. 'I don't want to, but we must. There it is.'

'That's about it. It's very simple now, Jusef.'

'Can you do it? Get in behind them?'

'Well that's it, isn't it? Will we still hold Donje Selo by the time we get into position? Can you attack in strength from the front if we do, Jusef? Can you throw everythin' into it? I don't want to be out there with nothin' but the wind for support. If you don't make a solid assault there, any move from behind'll be mopped up like spilled water. It's gotta be well timed, Jusef. And that's just one of the problems. We're really pickin' at straws now, Jusef.'

'Do you have any good news?' Husic said.

'Not really. I think I saw Elvis with the Chetniks this mornin'. Can't be sure, but it looked like him. If it works, then maybe we can push in behind 'em on Crna Gora and attack from here, too. Then we'd have 'em in a pincer. They'd have to fall back off the mountain. That and a good snowfall this year might secure the valley till the spring.'

'And then what?'

'We do it all again . . . maybe.'

Husic nodded and picked at his teeth with his fingers.

'Muha?'

'If the mountain companies had not run we would not be in this position. My men would fight to the death.'

'What do you want to do, Muha, line up everyone who ran and throw every tenth man off a cliff?' Husic said. 'Some of your men ran, too, Muha. And everyone else fell back on my orders. Anyone who didn't is lying on the grass out there. Concentrate on the issue here, Muha, the issue. We are responsible for thirty thousand people, Muha. We have decisions to make.'

Husic walked down the table and turned and came back.

'Okay, okay, we will do what you say, Grundy,' he said. 'We will throw everything at Vrh. I just hope to God we don't retake Vrh and lose Crna Gora in the effort. What do they say in English about the frying pan and the fire?'

Muha sat down on a chair, rubbed his eyes with his thumb and forefinger and looked at the map for a few seconds.

'If it is to go ahead, then I will lead it, Jusef,' he said.

'The fuck you will,' Grundy said.

'I am commander of special forces here, Grundy. And I will lead this.'

Grundy looked at Husic.

'No way, Jusef, no way.'

'Muha, I'll need your Black Berets for the frontal assault,' Husic said.

'And you will have them. Celo will lead the men from the front, they know what to do. But I go on this, Jusef, I insist. I will not allow fifty of our soldiers to follow these men across the lines on such a mission, I will not allow it. We do not know these people, Jusef. You want this whole valley in their hands? I go, Jusef.'

'Oh, for God's sake, Muha,' Husic said.

'It is for his sake, Jusef. Do you want to take it up with the party? With Sarajevo? I hold rank here, Jusef, in the *Armija*, these men are mercenaries, they fight for – I must confess I don't know what they fight for.'

'I'm an Arsenal supporter,' Spit said.

'I am an anti-Communist,' Yves said.

'And I'm a Communist,' Husic said.

'And I'm sick of this, Jusef,' Grundy said.

Milan Husic put his arm next to his father's and their hands touched.

'Okay,' Grundy said, 'okay, you go ahead and lead it, Muha, you do that. Best of luck. Come on, guys.'

Grundy started walking towards the door. Husic looked at Muha and turned on his heels.

'Stop, Grundy, stop, please,' he said. 'Muha, Grundy leads, that's my decision – that's my decision – but you will go, too, that's my decision also, Grundy. And Njofra. Njofra knows the mountains. He will pick the men.'

'You would see strangers make our decisions again, Jusef?' Muha said. 'The whole world makes our decisions for us.'

'Maybe, maybe, but Grundy commands this, Muha. He is experienced at this kind of thing, you are not. He will consult with you on all of his decisions; you are still the ranking officer. But we have no choices here, Muha. We have no choices any more. Grundy is here, he does not have to be here, none of them do. They are here and they are with us. Work with it, Muha.'

He pointed at the map. Muha went to turn away but he held his ground.

'Fifty men, Grundy?' Husic said. 'And the frontal assault.'

Grundy was going to try and argue Muha right out of the equation but he felt he had pushed his bluff as much as it would go with Husic. He wanted to do the job more than he wanted Muha humiliated.

'Five hundred,' Grundy said to Husic. 'More if possible. I don't care if they're armed with spears.'

Husic stuck his tongue out.

'I have less than two thousand men to hold this valley and maybe twenty per cent of them are walking wounded. If we take one in four men from other fronts and it doesn't work . . . ?'

'It won't matter then,' Grundy said.

He grinned.

'You ever seen the way the Germans operated in Belgium and France in 1940?'

He hit the map.

'It'll turn on a dime and if it doesn't work first time we all go down the shithole. But it's about all we have at the moment. When you're smaller than he is and he's holdin' a club and you're holdin' a twig – '

He smiled and spun round to Spit and Yves, then looked directly at Husic.

'– stick the fuckin' twig in his eye and kick his balls till they burst. The Germans found a spot where no one expected an attack, knocked a hole in it, poured into it and came in behind the allied flank. So they had to run or get caught. That's what the Chetniks just did to us here, Jusef. That's what we're gonna do back to them. It'll be tight. But for the hell of it, why not?'

'I have thirty thousand people who depend on me, Grundy,' Husic said. 'I cannot go for the hell of anything. This town has very little food and we are desperately short of weapons and ammunition. Hell is too close for me to joke about it.'

'Fifty men, thirty-five plus clicks through the mountains, hopin' the Chets don't pick us up and we don't all die of frostbite on the way. Then link up for a co-ordinated attack. Piece o' cake, I'd say,' Grundy said.

'Chocolate cake?' Husic said.

'Like the French marshal, Foch, once said, Jusef: "My centre is giving ground; my right retiring. Situation excellent. I am attacking".'

'Maybe you will just lead us into a trap,' Muha said. 'Maybe sell us out to the Chetniks. He makes such good friends with Russian murderers. He makes deals with them, Jusef.'

'And who do you make your deals with, Muha?' Grundy said.

'I am defending my home, my people. What I do, I do for them, Grundy. You cannot claim that.'

'You or any of your men fuck up, Muha, and I'll get mad,' Grundy said. 'Right now I'm damn tired and I can't think too straight when I'm tired, Jusef. And this doesn't go outside this room, Muha. Okay? So when you're doin' your deals across the lines, try not to mention it to the Chetniks.'

'You're a clever man, Grundy, but sometimes that's not enough,' Muha said. 'You choose to insult me here before your men, before the colonel, I will remember it. I will.'

'I hope you do. And make sure your men aren't high when they go in. I want fuckin' clear heads.'

'My men do not take drugs.'

'Your men take everythin', Muha. Includin' people's homes. You heard about that, Jusef? His boys threw three Serb families out of their apartments yesterday. What was the charge, Muha?'

Husic flicked his eyes over to Muha.

'Suspected Chetnik spies. The police have them. It's out of my hands, Jusef. Blame your Russian friend, Grundy. We are looking for his spy.'

'So your people do have him?'

'I was merely present when the military police and the intelligence officers questioned him.'

'Jesus, he was just tryin' to deal, Muha, just tryin' to deal . . .'

'You know this? There are many spies who come here as refugees.'

'You include your sister there?' Grundy said. 'Maybe she got cosy with 'em?'

'I will not be provoked,' Muha said. 'I have lost men today and I must see to their families. If the Serbs are innocent they will be returned to their homes. But don't think I don't remember these insults, Grundy. Don't ever think that.'

'I'm shittin' myself, Muha.'

Then Grundy slapped his hands together. He placed his finger on the map of the valley at Donje Selo and moved it into the positions occupied by the Serbs below Vrh. He moved his finger up Vrh to Bor on top and the mosque there, and kept tapping the map with his finger. Yves backed off to the door as if he was covering Grundy, and Spit was standing at the wall with his weapon cocked and his finger over the trigger guard.

'I want the Russian, Muha,' Grundy said.

Muha did not answer.

14

The dead were swollen and white.

They were laid out on stretchers and two of the stretchers were just combat jackets with tree branches inserted into the sleeves. And there was a smell. Some of the dead had been lying out for several days because the Bosnians could not get to them. That happened a lot and sometimes the bodies were left lying in the open for a couple of weeks and maybe there would be a spell of warm weather and the wind would carry the smell to the trench-lines and even down to the town.

The bodies were dirty and a couple were very bloody. The blood had dried into their skin and the mud had dried into the blood and any cuts and holes in the bodies were black and plugged with dried blood and mud.

Some of the bodies had plastic sheeting over their faces, others had blankets and combat jackets covering parts of them.

All of the dead were young.

One was a clerk from a meat store, another was a shop assistant and another was a photographer who wanted to be a journalist and was sending photos out to the news agencies with the UN when he could. His camera was still around his neck.

Another, a barman at a hotel in town, someone said, had the top of his head shot away and another had no arm. Two had their combat trousers torn at the groin and there was blood there.

And Natasa was standing in the rain beside the dead with a Bosnian captain.

She wore an anorak and boots and her scarf was loose and blowing in the wind.

Grundy stood for a while and watched her and felt something he did not want to feel. He glanced over at Spit and Yves sitting against a mud hill, stripping their weapons and checking their equipment – Spit was smoking – and Grundy envied them then.

The Bosnian captain went through the dead men's uniforms, looking for their identity cards and personal effects. He had a pad and pencil and he was taking down their details and pocketing their belongings.

'He has such beautiful eyes,' Natasa said, 'Luke. Did I tell you that, Grundy?'

'A hundred times,' Grundy said. 'I hadn't noticed. You're soundin' like a groupie, Natasa. Just get on with your work.'

'Hell hath no fury ... Grundy,' Natasa said. 'You need a little distance.'

'I always found that difficult.'

'They don't,' she said, pointing at the bodies.

'They are in gardens watered by running streams now.'

Muha walked slowly over to the line of bodies, holding an apple and touching the Beretta at his side. Celo and two bodyguards stood behind him. Celo wore sunglasses and cowboy boots and smoked a cheroot. He had two G3 rifles and two walkie-talkies and five grenades in his webbing, and the rain ran around his thick face through the pocks in the skin and down to his neck. There were water stains on his combat jacket at the shoulders and traces of bruising at one of the rims of the sunglasses.

'"He will admit them to Paradise", that is what the holy book says,' Muha said then.

He crouched down and looked at the dead.

Then he pulled a knife from his boot and cut a piece of apple and passed Celo the piece of apple.

'You want?' he said to Natasa.

'Whose is it?' she said.

'Mine, of course. You doubt this?'

'Oh, no, Muha,' Natasa said then. 'You're as honest as the polar day is long.'

He grinned.

'This is sarcasm, yes? Very effective. Most improper here among the dead. Their sense of humour is limited by circumstance. However, since you insist, you have not seen a spare Russian around the hospital, doctor? He does seem to be missing, Grundy, and so are the two men guarding him. Perhaps they have taken him elsewhere; there is some confusion in town at the moment. Down to you and your mistakes, Grundy, no doubt, and Jusef's rather middle-class character. However, we will trace the prisoner for you, no matter what. Celo will see to it.'

Muha looked at Celo who said nothing. The Sarajevan looked at Natasa.

'You look very pale, doctor,' Muha said then. 'Perhaps it is all getting too much for you. You should not keep Grundy's company so much. His sense of humour is tiresome.'

Natasa turned to Grundy.

'Your men had the Russian when I saw him last, Muha,' she said. 'He was in some distress. It wasn't funny.'

She flicked her head towards Celo.

'But if you want a joke I'll give you a fucking joke, Muha. Some bloody shit has stolen my new shipment of drugs and now I don't even have any aspirin. One fucking bag gets in for the first time in three months – the Chetniks took the last lot – and someone here fucking steals it. And now I have wounded lying on top of each other down there and some bastards have my drugs.'

She swung round to Muha again.

'What do you think of that, Muha?' she said.

'So report it to the police. I know nothing of this. You would be advised to hold your accusations around here, doctor. I see the traditional western intolerance for things Muslim is alive and well in the medical profession, too. We all operate under difficult conditions here. If you cannot cope with them, I suggest you ask for a transfer, doctor.'

'Don't try and frighten me, Muha. You may frighten the people here with your gorillas but not me. I do not work for you or the *Armija* or Sarajevo, I am with the United Nations.'

'Yes. And you come here and distribute your food and your medicines like we are farm animals. Maybe that is why people take your drugs.'

'They take my drugs to sell them on the black market. Oh, yeah, I know how it works. Someone'll turn up in a day or two and offer me my own drugs for a price. Sod all of you.'

'Perhaps they can buy weapons,' Muha said, 'perhaps a weapon and ammunition is more important to this valley than the sick and the wounded; perhaps there are people here who have to make such decisions.'

'Well you'd know, Muha, you'd know.'

'Ustasha.'

She swung round to Celo again.

'What did you say?'

'He said your family are Ustasha, doctor. You may deny this, of course, but we have the files. The Communists made many files, Communists like files. Franjo Ruzic, your father, was sentenced to death by Tito. Your mother was the mistress of a German officer after they had destroyed her village. Shall I go on?'

'Look, why don't you just fuckin' string her up, Muha?' Grundy said. 'Go on, fuckin' string her up.'

Muha looked at Grundy and Natasa and then turned to Celo.

'More sarcasm. Very popular with unbelievers,' he said. 'They were Chetniks, the other villagers, so I don't give a fuck. Maybe we should give your mother and father a medal. They were good soldiers. For Christians.'

'My father fought the Communists the way they fought him,' Natasa said. 'Grundy!'

'I won't defend the Ustashas, Natasa.' Grundy said.

'I hope you never come to me looking for a life-saving operation, Muha,' Natasa said then, 'you or your side-kick here, because my oath will be severely stretched that day.'

'Please, doctor, do not threaten me. You come here and make these accusations beside the bodies of my dead comrades – who do you think you are? You saw me or one of my men steal these drugs?'

Natasa shook her head.

'You really are a great help, Grundy,' she said. 'Letting him drag my family reputation through the mud. Say something, damn it.'

'Say what? If it's true then it's true. Do your work and then get back to town. We have business, Natasa.'

'This area is restricted,' Muha said. 'If you have finished your business here, leave.'

She looked at each of them in turn.

'Jesus, Grundy, don't lay that male Masonic rubbish on me. Okay, okay, push the woman out. I'm good enough for a cold screw on a winter's night and I'm good enough to put bandages on you when you're screaming for your mothers and I'm good enough to try and make sense of a mutilated body when there's nothing but blood and tangled guts on the table and I'm good enough to spill your heart out to when you're shit-scared and you're going to shit yourself; but when it gets down to it, when it gets right down to it, you're all a bunch of testosteroned queers. They say that about soldiers, real professional soldiers, men who like it, all the camaraderie, all the crap about death, that you're all just a bunch of scared queers who can't bear to come out. So you'd rather just die. Next time you make a joke about some effeminate bastard who's done that, you just consider that, just consider how much more guts he has than you. Fuck you, Grundy, you're a shit husband, you know that, a shit husband.'

Natasa spat at Grundy but her saliva went to the right of his body.

'Your wife, Grundy?' Muha said.

'Yeah,' Natasa said, 'now there's a real joke, Muha, doesn't it make you laugh?'

'I am not laughing,' Muha said. 'And you should control your wife, Grundy. Or perhaps someone will control her for you.'

'Butt out, Muha,' Grundy said.

'You get those bodies buried, Muha, they're a health hazard,' Natasa said. 'And two of them were mutilated before they were killed, I'm pretty certain. Maybe Husic'll want to have an inquiry, but I don't think so. And I want my fucking drugs, I want them. And if I don't get them there'll be hell to pay, you hear?'

'Do not threaten me, doctor,' Muha said, 'do not threaten me.'

'Get them in the ground.'

'Hey, respect them, they have done their duty,' Muha said. 'They will receive their reward. Remember that.'

He moved down the line of stretchers and said a prayer over each of the bodies.

He went down on his knees before each of his own men and put his hands palm out and prayed facing Mecca.

And he fixed things on the bodies of his own men.

He closed one man's battle vest and touched his head. The man was maybe twenty-five and his eyes were only partially closed and you could see his pupils under the eyelids. Muha tried to close the lids but the muscles were rigid and the man looked as if he was smiling.

The medics brought in five more bodies from the line while they were there. A cart came from the trees and two men in overalls and face masks pulled the bodies down by their hands and feet because they had no stretchers now, and laid them with the others.

'We will have peace among the dead,' Muha said. 'That's not from the Koran, that's from me. Okay, Grundy?'

'How many more you got comin' in?' Grundy asked Muha. 'I do not know.'

'What do you mean you don't know? They're your men.'

Muha stood up and stepped in front of Grundy.

'When they have examined all the pieces maybe I can tell you.'

Grundy lit a cigarette and started to smoke it and lit another and walked over to Muha and gave it to him. Muha smoked the cigarette with Grundy and went down the line of bodies again and talked about each of his men and what they had done before the war, what their hopes had been. He did not say anything about the other dead.

Then he swung around to Grundy suddenly.

'We will co-operate, Grundy,' he said. 'Yes? For them.'

Grundy just nodded his head and turned away.

'I still wanna see the Russian, Muha,' Grundy said.

'You are an irritating man, Grundy. I believe you to be
unbalanced, you know.'

Grundy was going to answer, but he suddenly swung his
eyes across to Luke Ryan, coming from the direction of a dirt
track leading to town.

Ryan followed Grundy's eyes and stopped at Natasa and
let his mind undress Natasa because he needed the release
it brought. His head was still throbbing and he had blacked
out once and vomited. He did not know if it was all due to
his wound.

Natasa looked at Ryan and then thought of something she
knew and he did not and dipped her eyes and watched a hole
in the ground fill with water and overflow.

The water rolled over round pebbles in the ground and
brushed away fine grains of limestone into the hard iced
mud.

'All fixed?' Grundy said to Ryan.

Ryan shook his head and then turned to smile at Natasa.

'I just knew you'd find your way here, Luke,' Natasa said.
'Where Grundy is, can Ryan be far away? Tweedle bloody
dum and tweedle bloody dee.'

Then she slapped him across the face. There was a pregnant
pause that seemed to last for ever and Luke Ryan felt that
the burning sensation on the side of his face had opened his
skin up and every nerve ending he had was exposed to the
weather.

'That's for not telling Grundy what I told you to tell him.
And other things.'

Muha frowned.

'They're lovers,' Grundy said.

Ryan came forward and kissed Natasa and held the kiss.
The taste of her lips soaked into him and she put her tongue
in his mouth.

Celo started to laugh and clap his hands and some of the
soldiers whistled. Muha glared at Celo and the big Sarajevan
went slightly pale and stopped. When he stopped, the soldiers
stopped.

'That what you wanted?' Ryan said.

'Yes. I'm sorry for hitting you, Luke,' Natasa said. 'But you must do as I say. You bloody must. Do you know where the Russian is?'

'No. I don't know where anyone is.'

She touched the place where her hand had struck his face. She let her finger run down his cheek and then turned her hand over and stroked his face with the back of her hand and her skin was cold and it cooled his face.

'Did I hurt you?'

'No. I don't feel pain any more. I feel like shit. You got anythin'?'

'Ask Muha,' Natasa said.

'It is not right for you to kiss in public like this, doctor,' Muha said. 'I would prefer if you would keep your sentiments to yourself when we are in a public place. I do not expect you to observe the laws of the Koran but I do expect you to respect my men's observance of it. Personally, I have no interest in your affairs, doctor, but Islamic women do not disgrace themselves with such public displays. You would do well to remember this, too, Ryan.'

'I don't give a fuck what you think about anything, Muha,' Ryan said. 'You wanna peddle all that *fatwah* bullshit around here, you do it, but keep it away from me, just keep it away from me.'

'Very western and very liberal,' Muha said. 'Conscience doth make cowards of us all. Am I right?'

'Ah, fuck off, Muha. Odjebi.'

'I think you should go home, Ryan, you are the wrong peg for the wrong hole here.'

'Hole's the right word,' Ryan said.

'Alas, I must depart,' Natasa said, 'to a less testosteroned environment. I'll see you, Luke. You too, Grundy.'

Muha looked towards two of his men and they came in beside Natasa. She looked at Grundy and Grundy nodded and the two Black Berets led Natasa to a white four-wheel drive with black UN markings on the doors.

'We'll get drunk tonight, Luke, good medicine, make love!' she shouted at Ryan.

She blew a kiss at him and he blew a kiss at her.

'Beautiful missus you got there, Grundy!' Ryan said. 'Beautiful.'

When Natasa had gone, Muha shoved up to Ryan.

'Ryan,' he said, 'you will stay away from my sister, please. Grundy, you keep this man away from my sister or I will take action.'

He touched his nose.

Ryan looked at Grundy, and then at Yves and Spit, looking for support. He got none.

Grundy watched Muha cross the pockmarked ground that had been the gardens of the ski hotel. He watched until Muha and his men had vanished into the hotel. Then he turned to Ryan.

'So you never found her?' Grundy said to Ryan.

'There was nothin' to find, Grundy,' Ryan said.

'Muha's sister a Chetnik whore and there's nothin' to find? I'm wonderin' what you've got for brains. I'm wonderin' where you're workin' these days.'

'I don't have to take this, you know? I came here on my own, and I make my decisions the way I see it.'

'She give you what you wanted?' Grundy said.

'More than you'll know.'

'You better have Natasa treat you for clap then. What's her pussy feel like after half the Chetnik army? A tad wet?'

'Jesus, you're a real pisshead, you know that, Grundy. You and him, Muha –' Ryan pointed at the ski hotel – 'you deserve each other. You get some kinda kick out of this, Grundy? You know you should look after your wife.'

'Or you will?'

'Bollocks. You know I used to think you were somethin', Grundy, I used to think that with you with us then we'd win. Now you're just lookin' like a run-of-the-mill asshole, Grundy. She's a victim, Grundy, Emira, she's a victim – what we're about here, or had you somethin' else in mind? What did you want me to do, break her fingers? Or did you think you'd have to do it, because I couldn't do somethin' like that? It works both ways, Grundy, you keep me blind maybe I keep you blind.'

'You wanna try somethin', Ryan?' Grundy said. 'You wanna try somethin'?'

He shoved Luke Ryan in the chest and smiled at Spit and Yves. Neither of them smiled back.

'Come on, try somethin',' Grundy said again. 'Come on!'

Ryan hit him in the face and knocked him across the row of bodies and when Grundy went to pick himself up he found he could not. He held his jaw.

'Don't mess with me, Grundy,' Ryan said. 'Don't mess with me.'

'Jesus!' Grundy said.

He rubbed his jaw again. Then he looked around him and at the dead, and he started to laugh.

Ryan began to walk off.

'Hey it's on, Luke, it's on,' Grundy shouted after Ryan. 'Husic said yes.'

15

That night tracer fire cut the sky in the darkness of the curfew and the falling snow twisted the tracer lines and pierced the darkness, and the darkness showed the barest outlines of the buildings around him. The snow fell in short lines from right above his head, in heavy drops, and the ground broke under him. The sound of his feet clashed with the sound of the tracer fire across the valley. And the whole valley was black.

Ryan stopped at a corner and pulled his identity card out before running across the street to the police post. The two policemen were sheltering from the snow, warming their hands on a brazier, AK47 rifles hanging over the backs, scarves around their heads. The brazier had only a few coals, the rest of the fuel was wood. The policemen smiled when Ryan showed them his card and one of them asked if he had cigarettes. Ryan said no. The other asked Ryan if he wanted a woman. Ryan asked about her even though he did not intend buying her. When the policeman had finished describing the girl, Ryan shook his head and said he did not have enough money. The policeman shrugged.

Ryan stayed warming his hands on the brazier flames. They were weak flames and the wood was old furniture and the snowflakes dropped into the flames and turned to steam immediately. One of the policemen pulled out a flask of *Sljivovica* and passed it round. Ryan drank and gave the policemen a square of chocolate each. Then the figure in the doorway across the street came out into the tracer light and walked across the rubbled street.

'I thought it were you, man. I wasn't sure. How's your 'ead then?'

Tahir Khan nodded at the two policemen and put his hands over the fire.

'You're alive,' Ryan said.

'Can't kill me, I'm already dead. But me bloody leg's stiff as a board. I keep feelin' it's gonna split any moment.'

'Where you been?'

Tahir nodded in the direction of Crna Gora.

'Back up there. Bloody mess, it were. And guess what?'

'Newcastle won away?'

'I dunno about that; no, I'm gettin into the Black Berets. I was talkin' with Muha. I'm gettin' in.'

'Should we celebrate that?'

'Ah come on, Luke, it's really what I wanted. Islam, like. You wouldn't understand.'

'So you're a mobster now. When do you make your bones?'

'That's just Grundy talkin', Luke, and Grundy's a fuckin' Jew. You ever see them para wings he carries in his pocket?'

Ryan hadn't.

'They're Israeli, man. Muha says he's a fuckin' Israeli spy. Fuckin' Zionist. You just don't know, do you, Luke? Them wings, they're from the Mitla drop, 1956, I know about it. I recognise 'em. A fuckin' Zionist, 'ere to do us down, maybe.'

'Yeah, Tahir, you believe that. You been workin' with us for two months.'

'I'm not sayin' he is a spy or anythin', I'm just sayin' what Muha said. Just that. We're all on the same side. I heard you hit him. Grundy.'

'Don't believe everythin' you hear.'

'You wanna have a coffee?'

'I'm goin' to meet someone.'

'Oh, right. That lass, Natasa, the one at the hospital? Grundy's missus?'

'You're very well informed these days. Must be the company you're keepin'.'

'Bonnie lookin' woman. Adultery, though, Luke.'

'You wanna stone me?' Ryan said. 'You'll have to give up women and all that now. Hope you're up to it, Tahir.'

'You've got Muha all wrong, Luke. He's a man of vision.

Things'd happen round here if Muha were in command. Husic's afraid to piss without a committee meeting first. He's tryin' to protect himself. They're all pretty pissed off with him. I am, too. It's down to him we're losin' this war.'

'You know that girl we brought in from the Chetnik lines was Muha's sister?'

'I heard that, too.'

'I'll bet. Jesus, Tahir. I hope you're happy. Look, if you wanna come along, you're welcome to have a coffee.'

'Ah, no, man, I'm no gooseberry. I was goin' somewhere else anyways. We'll have a coffee again. You hear about what's happenin'?'

'No more than you.'

'Okay ... okay ... I'll see you then.'

Ryan was standing at the counter in the *kavana*, trying to pick up too many drinks at once, when Emira Kusturica came in. He did not see her.

Behind him, Mihalj Dutina sat with Natasa at a table in the middle of the floor. One of the candles in the *kavana* went out when Emira opened the door and the owner cursed and raised his hairy arms and said something she did not hear. Emira stood and looked around before she went over to Natasa and Dutina.

There were three soldiers at one table, playing backgammon, and two men who were probably policemen because they were dressed in blue jackets, and armed with AK47s and automatic pistols and because they looked like policemen, even from behind. Then there were a man and woman who did not look up when Emira came in, and the soldier at the counter with his back to her, trying to pick something up with two fingers and hold three bottles at the same time.

'I have to talk to you, doctor,' Emira said to Natasa Ruzic. Emira nodded at Dutina but she did not address him.

Natasa put out her hand.

'Of course, and how are you?'

'I am still alive.'

Then Natasa took the chair beside her and moved it towards Emira.

'But I must speak with you. Yes?' Emira said then.

'Yes, yes. Sit down. Dutina here is another doctor.'

'I know Dutina. But I must talk with you. Please.'

'There's time, there's time. I've been working so long now I can't remember what time it is. I must have my drink. You must drink too. Luke!'

Natasa looked at Luke Ryan as he made his way around tables from the bar counter with three bottles of beer and a bottle of *Sljivovica*. The shadows from candles in the *kavana* hid most of his face and then showed his head bandage and the mud streaks under his cheeks, then his eyes, and his eyes stopped at Emira.

'Hello there – again,' he said. 'How are you? Eh, *kako ste?*' He stood looking at her for more time than he could hide.

'Oh, for Heaven's sake, so this is your mystery girl, Ryan?' Natasa said. 'What taste.'

'We met at a Chetnik party,' Emira said.

'Oh, do tell,' Natasa said. 'And close your damn mouth, Ryan, before your tongue falls out. Is the electricity back or am I imagining it? Go and get her a drink, Luke.'

The shelling had started again. Every two minutes, maybe a little more, and they were landing on the old end of Evkaf and Ryan felt he could tell which street by now, almost which building and each individual apartment. Sometimes he felt he could hear the screams. And there was another sound.

It was nine o'clock and a *muezzin* was calling people to the last prayer of the day from one of the mosques near the *carsija*. The *carsija* mosques were just heaps of rubble and pieces of old timber now and people used them as a kind of supply dump for timber and bits of furniture for firewood and books and newspapers for lighting fires. Sometimes there were fights between the people who owned the wood and the books and the other property that was taken and the people who were taking it. Once or twice people had killed one another over pieces of wood or maybe a stale loaf of bread, and often the police had to fire shots to break up crowds.

'I'm very drunk,' Natasa said to Emira in Serbo-Croat. 'Mihalj is very drunk, too, and he has to work in an hour. And there are three hundred more people with various illnesses and wounds coming in from Banja Luka at the weekend and we have two sticking plasters and a laxative. The Chetniks called the UN and just announced it. Just like that. They say they have hundreds of people who want to come here. Who wants to come here? The Chetniks say they're going to send them all. To sunny Evkaf. Bosnia's St Moritz. And they'll just bring them to the lines and make them run. Oh, shit . . . it only gets worse.'

'Where did you hear this?' Emira asked.

'Our headquarters told us. We have a radio at the hospital. Husic and Muha told the Chetniks to fuck themselves. Husic knew the Chetnik colonel, I think. He called him Lazar. Yes, he knew him. And Lazar called Husic Jusef. I asked Husic if he knew the Chetnik colonel but Husic wouldn't say. Husic's like that.'

'It's difficult,' Dutina said. 'No one wants to admit how close together we are. It's a real fool who fights his brother. And no one wants to be a fool.'

'What was all that?' Ryan asked Natasa.

He had brought a beer for Emira. She did not pick it up.

Natasa told him what had been said. Ryan nodded. Dutina downed his beer and stirred some sugar into his *turska kava* and the *kavana* owner brought Ryan a coffee and asked if any of them had cigarettes. The internal black market in Evkaf was running on cigarettes now, and even Deutschmarks weren't as prized as cigarettes unless you were buying from outside or planning on leaving. Inside Evkaf, cigarettes were the basic currency, drugs and booze came next, and then food. But people didn't trade basic foods, only things like chocolate and maybe pork if they had it and any mutton that was still around.

There were American Meals Ready To Eat in circulation after NATO had done a night drop. A lot of them had fallen into the wrong valley and the Serbs got them, and a few had actually fallen on people's heads and killed them. One family was in their living-room, ripping up a Tolstoy novel, people said it was *War and Peace*, to make a fire, when a whole load of MREs came crashing through their roof and killed the father and two of the kids. For days afterwards they said it was a Serb mortar and even when they were burying the family in a football field at the edge of town, they said it was a Serb mortar, but the whole area around the house was covered in bits and pieces of MRE.

'So here you are again,' Ryan said to Emira and felt stupid as soon as he'd said it. 'I've been tryin' to find you. I thought you were gone or somethin'.'

She threw her eyes up and took a cigarette from the packet Ryan had used to pay for the coffee.

'And I thought you would be dead,' she said to him. 'You should be dead. There are many dead.'

Ryan got embarrassed. He looked at Natasa for support.

'I want him to sleep with me,' Natasa said. 'I'm getting him drunk. You will sleep with me, Luke? He's a wonderful lover.'

Ryan knew his face was going red and he tried to laugh it off by making a joke about his masculinity, the kind of thing he used to despise.

'You're lookin' better,' he said to Emira. 'More life in your face. If I can do anythin'?'

'Hey, hey, Ryan, you're with me, okay?' Natasa said. 'Jesus, men, they're so fucking fickle. What do you think, Emira?'

'I don't very much.'

'No, of course not.'

'Have you more money?' Emira said to Ryan suddenly. 'I can use your money. How many Deutschmarks have you?'

Ryan looked at Natasa and she frowned and he looked at Dutina.

Dutina stared into his coffee. Ryan took a sip from his cup. It had a bitter taste and he squirmed at the bitterness. Three mortars impacted near the Bratstva i Jedinstva Trg. They were hollow impacts and were followed by heavy artillery which made noise when they flew and were sharper when they impacted.

'I have no more,' he said. 'I'm sorry.'

'Wow!' Natasa said. 'Mr Ryan, are you and this girl lovers?'

'You're pissed, Natasa. So shut up. Don't mind her, Emira, she's English.'

'*Hrvatica*. Croat!' Natasa said.

She slammed the table.

'English by accident of birth. Foolish by design. Romantic by grievous fault. I think Mr Ryan has a soft spot for you, love. Mr Ryan, you would be advised to go softly here.'

'Butt out, Natasa!'

'You have wonderfully desperate eyes, Ryan, know that? I just want to eat you right now. Couldn't you eat him, Emira? He is a good lover.'

'I said, shut up, Natasa.'

'Men. Fuck you and fuck you. All you ever get with them is fucked. Take it from me, love.'

'I know this.'

There was a pause. Natasa realised her mistake and put her hand to her mouth.

'Oh, there I go again with my foot in it. I'm sorry, love, I am. I'm a fucking stupid cow sometimes. Booze does that to you. I didn't—'

She shook her head.

'It's okay,' Emira said. 'I think you are right.'

'About his eyes?'

'That, too.'

Natasa touched Ryan's arms and then stroked them. He wanted to pull away but it was too nice.

'Tonight. Midnight. We'll make love,' she said.

Ryan almost spat his coffee out. Dutina laughed and Ryan turned his head and Dutina shouted over to the *kavana* owner to bring three *Karlovac* beers and more coffee.

Emira smiled.

'I embarrass you, Luke,' Natasa said. 'Good. I mean to. They're heavy now, listen, that's heavy stuff, the boys on the line will be taking a pounding. What do you think, Luke, will they be taking a pounding?'

'I suppose. Everyone is. And will you see Grundy again?'

'Sure I'll see Grundy. He's my husband, a gentleman all the way. Sure I'll see him. I'll see anyone I like. You want to see me, Mihalj?'

'I am too old now, Natasa, too old and too tired.'

'I'm a bit of a bitch, Dutina,' she said.

She picked up a glass of *rakija* and drank it in one, then

poured herself a beer and drank some of that and wiped her mouth.

'You see, Luke here –'

She pointed at Ryan and then touched his shoulder.

' – Luke here is a little bit, just a little bit, in love with me. Luke is a lover, aren't you, Luke? Luke falls in love with things. Takes one to know one. You know Grundy bet me Luke would fall in love with me. However, and this is a big however, he did not bank on Luke falling in love with someone else.'

'You're gettin' too drunk,' Ryan said.

'Pissed out of my head. I'm better in bed that way.'

She raised her glass. Emira laughed.

'You are a nice man, Luke,' Natasa said. 'Your eyes aren't dead yet. Everyone round here has dead eyes but you don't, so you must still believe in something. Please don't tell me what it is. Yeah, he's a nice young man and I'm pissed. God, my head's lifting. I'm going to feel rotten tomorrow. I hope I don't kill anyone on the table.'

'I'll take you home,' Ryan said.

'Which of us are you talking to?'

'You.'

'Jesus, no. I can't bear another night in that bloody kitchen – and all the damn people who just sit there watching the ceiling, counting the hits. Eighth floor went the day before yesterday, did I say that? I'm talking too much again. There's a hole in my wall. Something came through last night – I was at the hospital – and it's stuck in the bathroom wall. I was looking for Luke last night, that's why I want him so much now. What do you do at night, Luke?'

'Listen to Grundy's stories.'

'Oh! He's always telling stories, Grundy. We made love on the floor of one of the hospital rooms, Luke and I. Very romantic.'

'Shut up, Natasa,' Ryan said.

'Oops,' she said. 'Kiss and tell. Hell hath no fury, eh? You're very lovely, Emira. And I'm very jealous.'

There was another pause and Emira drank what was in front of her, then picked up the bottle of *rakija*, poured it into an empty glass and drank that.

'So what story did Grundy tell you last time you were with him at night, Luke?' Natasa said.

Ryan felt there was something more than the question in the words but he was too interested in Emira and too numb from his wounds to pursue it.

'Nothin' . . .' he said. 'Just Diocletian's Tears. He's always goin' on about it now.'

'Not to me,' Natasa said. 'Christ, you know something about Grundy I don't. Well, fuck you, Ryan. Do you know about this, Mihalj?'

Dutina drank the glass of *rakija* he had poured and then picked up his coffee and finished that, and Ryan could see the particles of *turska kawa* grit between his teeth.

'Yes. It is a legend. There are many legends.'

'Wait a minute, wait a minute,' Natasa said. 'What's this story? Grundy's told me all his stories. What's this Diocletian's Tears?'

'It's just another Grundy story,' Ryan said, 'like all his stories. This country's full of stories. Ask Grundy.'

'I'm asking you. I'm asking you who's going to make love with me, I'm asking you, Luke, I am drunk and I am – I want to know what you know, you see, I want to know about Diocletian's Tears, so tell me.'

'It's a kind of treasure – or it's supposed to be. A weddin' gift or a bribe, dependin' on your point of view. Silver or somethin'. It's supposed to be around here somewhere. Grundy says he knows where. But he's usually drunk when he says it.'

'He never told me,' Natasa said. 'He should have.'

'And it is silver?' Emira said.

'I don't know. Dutina'll tell it to you. He knows the story.'

'Diocletian was the Roman emperor who cut his empire between east and west,' Dutina said. 'And so it remains. Orthodox one side, Catholic the other.'

'And Muslims in the middle,' Emira said. 'Like in a sandwich.'

'Maybe the three of us should try that,' Natasa said.

'Natasa!' Ryan said.

'No, I'm sorry, I'm sorry.'

Natasa took Emira's hand.

'Please, forgive me, I'm a bitch, I know it. You should hit me or shoot me. Grundy always says he will shoot me.'

'It is okay,' Emira said. 'Look, can you go away, Ryan, I want to talk to the doctor. You and Dutina leave us. Please!'

Ryan thought about it and tried to figure out if there was a question in there somewhere. But he could not.

'Sure, okay,' he said. 'We'll go over here, Dutina. You can talk to me, Emira. Is it somethin' I can help with?'

'I think I'm going to throw up, Ryan,' Natasa said. 'Piss off like the lady asked. Mihalj?'

Dutina nodded.

'It is my business, Ryan, my business,' Emira said. 'When you are dead I will see they give you flowers and tend your grave.'

'And I'll take your organs,' Natasa said. 'How about now?'

The two women talked for ten minutes and three times during the conversation Natasa slapped the table and Emira shook her head. Once, Ryan was going to go over and find out what was happening, but he did not. Then Emira stood up and walked to the door and Natasa shook her head and downed two drinks very quickly.

Ryan pulled himself up from his table and went after Emira. He caught her at the door.

'Please, don't go,' he said. 'Look, it's curfew out there. I'll bring you home. Come and have a coffee or somethin'. You owe me a coffee. Remember? Look, I'm sorry for Natasa bein' stupid, she's a bit drunk. Please! Eh, *molim!*'

He had his hand at her waist and she looked at it and dipped her head and smiled without showing it.

'No, please, leave me alone, please. I must go. You stay. You talk. You make love. Please, Ryan, you will stay here. I thank you for the coffee, for the *rakija*. Doctor Ruzic – Natasa – is a good woman. She is a good woman. And I hope you will stay here and I hope you are okay.'

A shell landed close to the *kavana* and the impact shook the building and the candles flickered and one of them went out.

Emira went out into the street between the impact of two heavy shells. and after she had gone the door swung open and the *kavana* owner, who had a bad arm, had to run over and close it.

'What the fuck happened?' Ryan said to Natasa. 'What the fuck did you say to her?'

'We talked about – what is it? – Diocletian's Tears,' Natasa said. 'She wants to know where they are. And I don't know.'

'You hurt her, you damn bitch,' Ryan said.

'That's me all over, Luke. You're a bigger fool than I thought.'

His head was turned to the door. The sound of shells hitting buildings nearby and the dents in the steel-reinforced door and the sandbags at the window spilling their sand on to the tiled floor of the *kavana* distracted him. Mihalj Dutina came over to the table.

'I must go, too, Natasa,' he said. 'Are you all right?'

'I'm a damn bitch, Mihalj, a damn bitch.'

'Then you are all right,' he said. 'Look after her, Ryan.'

He nodded and tapped Ryan on the shoulder but Ryan was not paying attention.

When Dutina had left the *kavana*, Ryan turned back to Natasa.

'Listen, I think I'll go out and see if she's all right,' he said. 'It's comin' down heavy now. We shouldn't have let them go. Either of them.'

'Bloody hell, you do have it bad, my boy,' Natasa said. 'I should say something like open your eyes, but I can't be bothered. And don't worry about her, lover, she's a survivor, that one. God, you look nice here. You bastard.'

'You stay here,' he said. 'I'll be back.'

'Story of my life. I'll have a different lover then. I won't be here, lover, I won't be here.'

He backed towards the door.

'The judgement is in the perspective, Ryan,' she said. 'And you can have that for free. You will always be disappointed, Luke.'

Ryan fell over tins of American cooking oil and a piece of a car which had been blown apart at the top of the street. The shells were impacting further down the town towards the fortress and the *carsija* and he could see flames from the area around two of the mosques.

When he could not go any further, he sat down in a doorway, rested his head on his knees and listened to the shelling. For a while he wished a shell would land beside him and he took his automatic from its holster and flicked the safety catch on and off and put the barrel into his mouth once. And when he got back to the *kavana*, Natasa was gone and the owner was closing.

16

The snow had stopped again and the cloud was lifting. The mist rose with the cloud and the cloud broke to the north first and the mist there lifted from the top of Crna Gora. The snow was a blanket on the mountain which pushed through the rising mist, and the shapes of trees and roofs appeared like stains on the snow.

Grundy pulled the table away and powdered snow fell on to the balcony. A sharp wind touched the heat in the room and Grundy felt the cold on his chest. Three snowflakes landed on his skin and dissolved. He stood at the wall and watched the skyline. A long block of apartments curved around for about three hundred metres to his right and behind that was an Orthodox church and the remains of a tower block. His gaze drifted from the tower block across the white roof of the apartment block and down to a cluster of small houses and sheds and allotments. There was a woman out on one of the allotments, dressed in black, and Grundy could hear the sound of one of her children calling to her from the balcony of one of the apartments. Grundy went with the sound and the sound carried beyond the mother in the allotment and made it to the football field which was spread out between the blocks and sloped up towards Grundy.

Rows of headboards stuck out of the snow and a dog moved around them stopping now and then to mark its territory. A young woman in a long coat and wearing a headscarf broke off from a group of people praying at one of the graves to chase the dog. The dog barked and then disappeared over a dip towards the allotment where the woman in black was working. Grundy pulled a bottle of *Sljivovica* from the cabinet beside him and

put the neck to his mouth and drank. Then he took a cigarette
from the Marlboro packet, lit it and watched the gravediggers.
They were a tall man and a fat man and one of them had a cap
and the other a moustache and they had already dug two holes
in the football field nearer to Grundy. The tall man was in the
hole and he wore a denim jacket. His pick was clogged with
mud and there was a heap of rocky soil beside the grave where
the second man leaned on his spade and smoked a cigarette.
Then there was firing.

The firing was small-arms fire from around the valley;
Grundy could not tell exactly where it was coming from.
The gravedigger stopped his work and pulled himself out of
the hole, and his colleague crouched down and continued to
smoke. The family at the headboard kept praying with their
arms spread out at a sharp angle and their hands open in the
Muslim way. The dog reappeared and there was a long burst
of automatic fire and the dog turned and went back over the
slope. Grundy turned his head to the room and his eyes made
their way across the splintered floor to the figure in the bed
and up the wall to where the ceiling had been gouged out by
a piece of shell fragment. The fragment was in another wall
and Grundy's gaze was going over to that wall when there was
a sustained burst of automatic fire and then the dull thud of a
mortar impact.

The gravediggers were back in their hole. The fat man
lifted his head above the level of the ground and looked in a
semicircle at the football field. Grundy left them and his glance
went to the family at the graveside. They were running back
to the apartment block and one of them had tripped and fallen
but the others had not stopped for her. Then she called out and
they stopped and hesitated, then turned back and, pulling her
up, dragged her towards the apartments.

'Close the damn thing up, Grundy, will you?'

Natasa pulled her head out from under the bedclothes. She
let the bedclothes drop and her breasts hardened when the cold
touched them. Grundy watched her nipples colour and extend.

'I'm freezing,' she said. 'And put some bloody clothes on,
man. You're fat, you know. I can see goosebumps. Jesus,
Grundy, what on earth are you doing there?'

Grundy lifted up the table and wedged it back into the broken balcony door window, pushed a second table in behind it. Then he went over to the bed and took a mattress propped up against it and wedged it in behind the tables. There were three more mortar impacts nearby and the rifle fire was almost continuous.

'What time is it?' she asked.

'Eight-thirty.'

'They're early,' she said.

'Puttin' the pressure on. They think they have us.'

'And do they?' she asked.

He sat down on the bed and pulled his trousers on, then leaned over Natasa and took a t-shirt from the floor and pulled it on. Natasa threw the covers off the bed, jumped out and ran across to a chair, pulled his combat jacket off the chair and put it on.

'Christ, it's cold,' she said. 'Your leg still hurting?'

'Some.'

'You should get it seen to, you know. It won't get any better unless you get it seen to. Can you move it much, the leg?'

'Not so much.'

'Do I ask too many questions?'

'Of course.'

She sat on the bed beside him.

'I don't want you to think I'm easy or anything,' she said. 'Just because I still sleep with you. I still want your friend.'

'He's not my friend.'

'Yes. Well, I want him. You look fine, you know. You are a lousy husband, Grundy. Am I a bitch for saying that?'

'You're a lousy wife.'

'We were good lovers.'

'Were?'

'There's a legal technicality here, I think. I'll have to go to work. Will you take me?'

'Sure. You got a procedure? I mean, if things get worse?'

'Evacuation? No. We just all run down to the Red Cross. There's a man called Selby, he'll be here today if he can get through. So I hope the bloody Chetniks aren't in a bad mood.

You're not going to do anything to put them in a bad mood, are you?'

'You know me.'

'Yeah. I'm not sure I'll go even if it's necessary. Very dramatic, aren't I? But I'm not sure I'll go. I needed you, love.'

'I'm flattered.'

'I think Selby thinks he'll get me into bed if he saves me from a band of marauding Chetniks. He's a nice man but an awful seducer. Englishmen either make magnificent seducers or awful ones. There's no in-betweens. The Irish are usually awful – that's why it's so wonderful to find one with all that romance and technique. You'll have to get him to stop chasing that bloody girl around. He's mine. You can order him, Grundy, can't you?'

'I'm not sure I want to.'

'I broke ethics telling you anything about her,' Natasa said. 'I shouldn't have. But he had to go and say her bloody name when we were making love. Her bloody name and he didn't even notice it. Fuck him.'

'What's a name? You shoulda seen the look on Muha's face. Bastard. Thanks.'

'Always my pleasure, Grundy. You found your Russian?'

'No, and we won't. But it gives me leverage.'

He touched her face.

'I missed you,' he said.

'Don't go getting sentimental, Grundy. It doesn't become you. I'm frightened, you know? I used not to be frightened, but now I'm frightened all the time.'

He ran his hand down to her neck and touched the chain around her neck and fingered the opal on the end of the chain.

'I told you this'd protect you. Don't you believe me?'

'I want to. God, I hate being like this. It's all so damn complicated. I want him, Grundy, I want Ryan so much now it hurts. Did I say his name last night?'

'Maybe. I didn't notice.'

'You wouldn't.'

He leaned over and kissed her forehead.

'Do you want a divorce?' he said.

She smiled and took his hand and held it between hers and stroked it.

'God, no,' she said. 'You're my husband.'

Later, in the street, they stood beside a cargo container pocked with fragment holes with the metal rusting around the holes. Broken glass protruded from the snow and a long black cat carried something away from a rubbish heap down the street. The snow covered most of the rubbish and the cold cloaked some of the smell and there were rat-prints in the snow beside the rubbish.

'It's not *zbogom*,' Natasa said, 'it's just *dovidjenja*.'

'*Shalom*. And thanks. It was good.'

'We could be sitting at the marina in Trogir now, you know, fishing. That was a nice time, Grundy. Why do I call you Grundy? I should call you by your first name.'

'You are a bitch, Natasa. I think I married you for that. Some kinda masochism, I think. I want you to take care of yourself. You might think again about goin'. We got a paper line holdin' 'em back. If it collapses ... I don't think the Chets are gonna be very understandin' when they get here.'

'When?'

Grundy shrugged.

'Well, I'm fighting my own battles,' she said. 'And today, among other things, I have to buy back my own drugs. I want to tell you so much, Grundy, but I can't, I just can't. Maybe when we're away from here. You think you know people, then they smile at you and offer you lives at a discount and make it sound like a favour. Jesus, it's all a bloody pain in the neck. So unpredictably predictable. Sometimes I think there's a secret cabal running this war for themselves. And when I'm really depressed I imagine Milosevic and Karadzic and Tudjman and Izetbegovic, all sitting round a table, sharing out the spoils, all laughing at how clever they are. But that's just my nightmare. And the enemy changes with the wind.'

'Yeah. You know, you could be a spy,' he said. 'We're fightin' Croats in the Lasva. Maybe I should shoot you. Maybe I shoulda shot you before.'

'Don't joke about that any more, Grundy. Please. I often wonder what'd happen if we ended up against each other some time. That really scares me. So don't tell me what you're going to do or what will happen, don't tell me that, just look at me and give me a big hug and let me feel you close to me. You're the worst husband a woman could ever dream of, you know. You're a faithless bastard, Grundy, and you see right through me and I hate you for it. I hate when people know me too well. It's awful, isn't it? And I still can't figure you out. Tell Luke I want him. Tell him we were together and see if that makes him come to me. Is he going to live?'

'Jury's out.'

'Don't get him killed. You read about it, about jealous lovers having their rivals killed.'

'I'm not jealous.'

'Of course you are. I'm jealous of you. Do you have many other lovers? No, don't tell me, I couldn't stand it if you told me. I can't stand the thought of Luke with her. She is beautiful, but she's very desperate. And now I'm treading into professional ethics and confidentiality again. All very Catholic. I wish I really was a prize bitch. Oh, well . . . Don't die on me, Grundy. You're a love, you know.'

'Go on, fuck off or I'll shoot you. You're still the best medicine around.'

'Tell Ryan that.'

'Take care.'

The front of the apartment block he walked to was lined with holes running from one window to another. Further up, near the attic, three of the apartments were blown out.

Spit was lying between a girl's thighs and the girl was lying over a map. She had short hair and small breasts. The bottle beside them was almost empty and some of it had spilled on to the map and smudged the marks Grundy had made. Yves was asleep on a bed in the corner with his rifle beside him and a girl and three bottles of beer and a packet of cigarettes on the floor. A bra hung over the bedpost and the sheets were stained where a second imprint had been made in the mattress. Grundy picked up a cigarette and lit it, then walked round the room and into a small kitchen. Horst was on the floor in the kitchen, under a blanket, surrounded by bottles. Grundy kicked him and Horst opened one eye, nodded his head and put his arm up.

Grundy went back into the bedroom and when the tip of the cigarette was cherry-red he touched Yves's backside with it. Yves jumped out of the bed, hit his head off the wall, rolled back to the shelter of the bed and cocked his rifle. Grundy leaned over the girl on the floor beside Yves and put his hand to her mouth to stop her scream. He smiled.

'Rise and shine,' he said to Yves. 'It's the war game.'

The girl on the floor scrambled for her clothes and Grundy pulled a sidearm out of a holster on one of the chairs, cocked it and walked over to Spit. He watched the Englishman snore with an open mouth, shoved the pistol into it and put his own mouth to Spit's ear.

'*Zdravo, druze!*'

Spit opened his eyes and froze.

'Ah, fuck you, Grundy, man, fuck you, I thought you was a Chetnik, fuck you, fuck you.'

The girl beneath him screamed and jumped up, and Spit's head hit the floorboards and he cursed her.

'I mighta been a Chetnik,' Grundy said. 'You'd be all over the wall now, Spit. Get your pants on, Yves. Get these ladies back to their homes and sober up. Get the *rakija* off your breath. I don't want Husic thinkin' my men are a bunch of drunks. You may well be a bunch of drunks but I don't want him knowin' that. These aren't anyone's daughters, Yves?'

'*Non*, Grundy. *Pas de famille. Triste.* Jesus, my ass is fucking flambéd, man. You are an animal, Grundy. Let's kill him, Spit.'

Grundy took a pot, went over to a row of bottles on top of a wardrobe and started filling the pot with the water from the bottles.

'Come on, start drinkin',' he said. 'Then we're gonna run to the *carsija*, full kit, then we're gonna do the rest of our soberin' with snow. Naked, if you're not the way I want you.'

'You get your fuckin' nuts off last night, mate?' Spit said. 'Where'd you go, Grundy?'

Spit was pouring more water over his chest than was

going down his mouth. He wiped his lips and passed the
pot to Yves.

The two girls dressed silently, picking up their clothes
around the room, and when they had dressed they stood
together at the wall, running their hands through their hair.

'Pay them, Grundy, will you?' Yves said.

He was strapping his boots.

Grundy went over to the girls and looked at them. Their
faces were drawn and sad and their skin was grey like the
valley mist. He pulled out two Deutschmark notes and gave
one to each of them. The girls did not say anything and the
expressions on their faces did not change. They took the notes,
folded them and slipped them into their clothes and left.

'You got that terrain survey, Spit?' Grundy said.

'Yves's tart sat on it. 'E was fuckin' her on it, 'e was.'

'Where is it, Yves? Jesus, if it's all come stains, I'll make
you fuckin' lick it clean. And where the fuck's Luke?'

'Who knows?'

Horst stood at the kitchen door, drinking from a bottle
of beer.

'He did not come back, Grundy. We thought maybe he was
with you.'

He looked at Yves and Spit and they all smiled.

'Get me the fuckin' terrain survey, Yves. You worked out a
play for the Accuracy, Spit?'

''Course, mate. It's marked in over there. Somethin's brewin'
down the valley, hear that?'

They listened for a while and Grundy picked up a list of
equipment Yves had made out, detailing numbers of items
and weights per man. Then Grundy went over to a map
they had pinned to the wall and pushed his finger along
the preliminary route they wanted to follow. The route was
marked with Xs where they would hold up or change direction
if necessary.

'These photographs, Grundy?' Horst said. 'You want to
show them around?'

'Not the Sljiva ones. I don't want anyone who doesn't need
to knowin' where were goin'.'

'That include Muha's men?'

'If that fuck has told his men, I'll slit his fuckin' throat. Put the photographs in the bag.'

Yves brought the terrain survey out of the bathroom. It was stained, and Grundy looked at the stains and shook his head before unfolding the map.

'It is a problem if we lose men, either in the weather or another way,' Yves said. 'The numbers are so exact. And the size is a problem. I have been thinking about the space – fifty men.'

'Yeah,' Grundy said. 'Well, if we run into trouble, we break, to minimise casualties. Each group has one man who knows the destination. Then maybe we can still do it if we take losses.'

'What kinda losses, Grundy, man?' Spit said.

'Like Yves said, the first man we lose is too much.'

'And Luke?' Yves said.

'He'll come.'

'He is perhaps fatigued. It is dangerous to bring a fatigued man on such a job.'

'Who would we have, Yves, who would we have?'

'I think he should go and get his hole from Muha's sister and then he'd be fine. I seen this before. Lad can't get his leg over – fuckin' useless till he does. It's fuckin' nature, man.'

'You gonna hollow out some of those Lapua slugs, Spit?' Grundy asked.

'Already doin' it, Grundy, man.'

'We should have killed her,' Horst said. 'Muha's sister. I have seen them like her before. I know their eyes. They will live over all. She does not care for him. Maybe I should go fuck her and show him.'

They all stared at Horst for a few seconds and then laughed.

'You and Spit co-ordinated, Horst?' Grundy said. 'I've been lookin' at this hill you're gonna operate from, Spit. When the pontoon's blown you'll have a job reachin' home.'

'That's the challenge, innit? When have I ever let me old mate Grundy down?'

'Never, Spit. Yves?'

'If there is more than one company in Bor when we attack, then we are in trouble.'

'There won't be.'

'It's imperative we get into the mosque,' Grundy said. He pointed at a map of Vrh and touched the area around the mosque. 'The Bor mosque'll give us in position what we lack in numbers. We'll have 'em pinned down this side of the mountain between the front line and the village and we'll stop their reinforcements gettin' down there. So they're gonna be desperate to get us out.'

'It will be a tight one,' Yves said.

'Yeah,' Grundy said. 'I hope he fucks her.'

'Muha's sister?' Horst said.

Grundy nodded.

'It would not be good for us if Muha knows,' Yves said. 'All this would go in smoke.'

'A failin' of mine, Yves. Anyone want to leave anythin' with the Red Cross do it now and I'll hand it in.'

They all smiled. Then there was silence.

'You sure about Ryan?' Yves said.

'Sure I'm sure,' Grundy said.

'Maybe she's a lesbian,' Spit said.

'Who?' Grundy said.

'Luke's skirt. Muha's sister. I knew a bird was a lesbian once. Bloody shame.'

'You should have fucked her anyway,' Yves said.

'I did, mate, I did.'

17

The breadline shuffled forward two metres and then stopped. It was about fifty metres long and stretched around the corner into the Ulica Marsala Tita. Ryan stood on the corner at the other side of the street and watched. The line moved again. Five women passed around old copies of *Hello* magazine and two men played magnetic chess. There was rifle fire in the mountains. The line moved again. The rifle fire stopped. The line stopped.

A Bofors 20mm anti-aircraft cannon began firing from a Serb position in the valley. The rounds hit the top floor of a residential block beyond the Bratistva i Jedinstva Trg. The rounds tore chunks of concrete from the block and the people in the breadline threw their eyes up and watched.

Then the mortar rounds fell: three streets back from Marsala Tita, east of the breadline.

People stopped what they were doing and shoved themselves in closer to the wall. Smoke rose from the direction of one of the mortar impacts and the people in the breadline discussed where the mortars had landed and who might be dead. None of them moved.

Ryan crossed the street and nodded when he passed three women he knew. They nodded back and he walked on and three more mortar rounds landed at the other end of Marsala Tita. The impacts were close to one another and the ground shook. The line crouched against the wall and two of the men said they were not going to wait to die, the Serbs had them in their sights, they would put the next one on top of them. But no one else would move and the men stayed.

Ryan picked himself out of the doorway he was crouched

in, looked at the breadline again and crossed the street
to the shaded side where the buildings gave protection
against the Serb positions on the south side of the valley.
Another mortar round hit home. Two policemen watching
the breadline ducked into a doorway and crouched down.

The people in the breadline shouted at them.

The policemen told them to fuck off or they would arrest
them all. The people laughed. The policemen pulled out their
cigarettes and started to smoke. Four more mortar rounds
came in to the north of the breadline and three windows
were blown out of an office building down the street. They
were the last windows in the street and they shattered before
they fell out.

The breadline moved again. Ryan watched a woman
running with her bread ration. She was a tall woman and
her scarf kept coming off her head and she tried to replace
it while she ran. The mortar rounds were landing at random
now – up one end of the town, down the other, in the centre
around the square, to either side of it, every two minutes.
The breadline moved again.

The line was thirty metres long now, maybe a little longer
because some more people had joined it during the shelling.
The next mortar landed to the right and the one after that
to the left and the one after that in the street behind them.
The breadline crouched again and some people closed their
eyes and others held hands. A group of five men and women
held hands and one of the men was crying. His face was
covered in tears and a woman beside him, who was younger
and might have been his daughter, was telling him to calm
down, it would be okay, their turn was coming soon.

Another two mortar rounds fell and Ryan looked left and
right, then ran. He was still running when the burst of fire
rang out across the valley. It was heavy machine-gun fire
and the tracer rounds disappeared into a building on Marsala
Tita. Ryan looked around at it while he was running and
saw the breadline break up, but he did not see the man who had
been crying lying dead in the street.

He cut through some shattered buildings and across open
ground covered in debris to the shelter of an old school which

had been used as a feeding centre till the Serbs blew it up with long-range artillery. There was a dead woman in the street in front of the school. She was old and small and fat and her skirt was up to her underwear. There was a shallow mortar impact hole in front of her and a handcart was tipped over further down the street. The small sticks she had collected in the handcart were scattered about and two young girls were picking them up and stuffing them into their coats. The dead woman's face was white and her eyes were open and her head tilted back as if she was looking at the sky. The sky was blue except for small transparent clouds that dashed across it. Ryan smoked a cigarette.

Emira was standing at a headboard in a cemetery beside a mosque when he found her. The mosque was small and built of brown stone and its minaret was white. The top of the minaret was gone and the dome had a shell hole in it and a black streak running from the shell hole. There were cargo containers and buses, two and three high, around the mosque. Emira wore a scarf and a long coat and she had her hands out, showing the palms. An artillery shell landed down the street.

'Shit, Ryan,' Emira said when she saw him. Colour slowly drained from her face. 'Are you following me? Are you with Hasim – Muha?'

'No, no, I want to see you. I want to see you.'

'But you were with the doctor. Why did – are – you not with the doctor? Did she send you?'

'No! You. I want you, damn it. There's somethin' ... somethin' between us. You know it. You can feel it, too. I know you can.'

'You know so much.'

'Damn, my head still hurts,' he said.

He patted his head. Then she touched the bandana he was wearing over his flesh wound bandage. Some colour had returned to her face.

'How did you find me?' she said.

'Dutina. He told me he saw you last night and I just walked around. I was gonna give up. But I found you. You see! You shouldn't be outside.'

'She was killed in bed,' Emira said.

She pointed at the grave.

'I was at school with her. Her husband was killed, too. That's him. They had a baby girl. That's the baby there, with her mother. Did you make love with the doctor? Last night?'

'No. I came after you. You were gone. I came down this way but it was too dark. So I slept in a doorway. I'm very cold. Is there somewhere we can go?'

'For what?'

'To be alone.'

She looked past him to the other side of the street. Ryan followed her glance. There was a shadow in the doorway of one of the blocks – it might have been a man – wedged between the door and the wall.

'They go with me,' she said. 'Everywhere. Hasim's orders. You should remember that.'

'I don't care.'

'Hasim will be angry. I tried to get away. Do you know that? Hasim caught me. That made him more angry. I think Hasim likes being angry. Do you have any more money?'

'No. Do you have any food?'

'Only for me. There is a war.'

'You owe me.'

'And the doctor?'

'Fuck her, I wanna be with you.'

'I think you mean that.'

She looked past him, but he kept his stare and she brought her eyes back to his and they looked at each other.

'Okay, I will make you coffee,' she said. 'I have bread and cheese, too. Hasim gives me food. He does not want me to have money. I have been selling some of my food for money. I have other things, too. I will sell them. I will get the money. Hasim will not stop me.'

'Fuck him.'

'He is my brother.'

Ryan sat on her bed with his back to the wall and chewed on fresh bread and cream cheese and picked up a china cup with a flower motif and sipped the *turska kava*. Emira tried to get her pine cone fire started but the cones were new and wet from the snow and they would not catch fire.

'You are very cold?' she said.

Ryan swallowed his bread and cheese and shook his head.

'I don't feel it so much now. Come and sit with me.'

'The fire.'

'Let it be. It'll find its own way. Your bag is packed.'

'It is always ready. I am going to try and go away again soon.'

'You won't get through.'

'I will walk to the coast if I have to. I am strong, I can do that.'

'I'll bet. You're beautiful.'

'I know. I am a genius, too. Did I tell you that? My father made me take a test when I was fourteen and I am a genius. A boy who loved me killed himself when he was seventeen because I did not love him. I did not speak for six months. I am strong.'

'Come over here, please.'

She stood up, walked over to the bed and sat beside him. He gave her a piece of bread and cheese and she ate it.

'Are you rich?' she said.

'Extremely.'

'Do not lie.'

'I can't help it, I wanted to be a journalist,' he said.

'And you were in love?' she said.

'I want to kiss you.'

He leaned over and kissed her.

She did not respond. Ryan gave up.

'You have no right,' Emira said.

'I'm sorry.'

He kissed her again and she sat still and did nothing. Ryan gave up again.

'Your mouth is stale,' she said then. 'You have bad breath.'

He kissed her again. She reached into her coat pocket and pulled out her knife.

'Okay, I will kill you if you do that again,' she said.

He looked into her eyes to see if he could tell what she was thinking and then pulled back.

'I'm sorry,' he said again. 'I was wounded. I think I'm still sick.'

'You may put your arms around me,' she said. 'And hold me. I want to be held. We can hold each other, would you like that? I would like that. You have a good face, the doctor was right. She loves you. You are lovers?'

They held each other and Ryan stroked her hair and she touched his head.

'We made love once,' he said.

'Did you talk about me with her?'

'No. I don't wanna share you. I want you. I love you.'

'That's stupid.'

'Okay, I'm stupid.'

'You should wash.'

'I'm a soldier. You're beautiful. I want to touch you all over, I want to kiss you, I want to lick you with my tongue, I want to kiss your breasts and lick them with my tongue and I want to put my tongue between your legs.'

'Would you kill him if I asked you?' Emira said.

'Muha?'

She laughed and pulled her head away from him.

'You're hard. I mean the man who follows me now. He has dark skin and his eyes are bright and he has a good smile. He says good morning to me when I go out and he says good night to me when I come in. If you killed him for me I could leave now without trouble.'

'I want to sleep with you.'

He moved his hands around her body and pulled her closer to him and she moved her hands around him and they lay there, holding each other close and moving their hands around each other. Then she stopped.

'You must stop now,' she said, 'or you will not control yourself.'

'I don't want to.'

She took her arms away and sat up. Then she stood up and went over to a chair at the table.

'I have what I need,' she said. 'Will you kill him for me?'

'No.'

'It is okay, I do not really want you to. Do you get afraid?'

'All the time.'

'In the line?'

'More out than in.'

'I do not understand you.'

'Me neither. I like it that way. I'm a foreign country to myself and I don't speak the language. And I don't want to.'

'I like you, Ryan,' she said.

'I want you to love me.'

'If you get me money, I will love you. I will need money when I go away. I will go to Paris. Have you been to Paris?'

'It's full of Americans.'

'I will go to London.'

'It's full of Americans.'

'I will go to New York.'

'It's full of Irish. Go to Paris or London. Americans are better than Irish.'

There was a pause and they listened to the gunfire outside.

'I hate the war,' Emira said then.

'I like it,' Ryan said.

'But you are afraid and you may die.'

'Yes. It's a bitch, isn't it?'

'You are very stupid. I should be somewhere, with money and clothes and lovers. I would have many lovers. How many did you have when you were in – Dublin?'

'Just the one.'

'What was her name?'

'Rachel.'

'Jewish?'

'No. She played hockey.'

'Why did you leave her?'

'She had a baby.'

Emira got up and poured another cup of coffee for herself and drank it. Then she came back to Ryan.

'You did not want the baby?' she said.

'It wasn't mine.'

A flood of memories brought Ryan to a point where he wanted to cry. He leaned into Emira so that he would not cry and held her tighter and she kissed his neck and whispered a song he did not know. Then she looked at her watch.

'It is time for you to go, I think,' she said.

He looked at his watch.

'So I don't get my end away?' he said.

'I don't understand you. What does that mean?'

'It means you're the most beautiful girl I've ever met and I respect you and want to cherish you all the days of my life. Will you marry me?'

'You are a fool. You are crazy.'

'I have a passport. I can go from here.'

'But you will not.'

'You're right, I am crazy.'

'Many girls here have had babies for the Chetniks,' Emira said.

'Yeah, I know. Poor little bastards.'

'Do not say that, it is not their fault.'

'It's a figure of speech.'

She shook her head.

'I lost my virginity to an AK47 . . .' she said. 'Then there was an automatic pistol, I don't know what. And after that I cannot remember all the weapons and other things I had as lovers.'

'I understand.'

'No, I do not think you do.'

She sat down on the floor and put her hands on his legs and rubbed them. Then he leaned her head against his knee and he rubbed her head.

'That is nice,' she said. 'They asked me who was Ustasha, who was Mujahideen . . . Muslim, Croat, it did not matter to the Chetniks. Ustasha this, Mujahideen that. They took us to an old school near Prijedor. Do you know Prijedor? There is a railway line there and the trains come from Doboj and Banja Luka. It was summer and the sun was hot and the grass was burnt. The Chetnik officer was a very tall man.

He had a long face, like Hasim – like Muha. And his eyes were green, very cold bright green, and they were back in his head.

'The Chetniks took me into this school and they were questioning prisoners. There were prisoners from many places. The Chetniks did not ask them too many questions, they hit them and they drank beer and *rakija* and they hit them more and the prisoners said to them: "Why do you hit me?" and "Please do not hit me" and "I have done nothing". I remember this.

'It was a cold room. Where I was. Outside in the sun, it was hot and the men were standing and I saw their skins turning red. They did not wear anything except their pants. Some of them were naked but that was because they had – you know, ... in their pants – yes?

'So, the Chetnik officer, he says to me: "Muslim girl, you will say yes when I ask you if a man is an Ustasha or Mujahideen?"

'And I said, "But I don't know. I don't know any Ustashas. I don't know any Mujahideen". And he hit me. He hit me in the stomach and then he picked me up and put me in a chair and called two of his men in. They were small men and they wore Chetnik beards and they took me into another room where there was beer and mattresses and they raped me. Three, four, maybe five times. The last time they raped me with a bottle of *rakija*. And after I am raped, I am taken back into the Chetnik officer.

'He is sitting at a desk and there is a man tied to a chair in front of him. I know this man. I have met him and he and my father were friends. So the Chetnik officer, who is a handsome man, you know, in that kind of way, and he can smile and it is a nice smile, he smiles at me and offers me *kava* and a cigarette, he pours my *kava* and then lights me a cigarette and he touches me on the face. His hands were big and there were scars on the knuckles and one big scar on the finger here, like it had been cut off and put back.

'The man they had was Izmet, and he was a baker, and he was a Communist once. He worked for many years in Bundesrepublik Deutschland – West Germany – okay? He was an old man and his hair was grey here and his wife was dead maybe ten years. I knew his son who was also called Izmet. But he was not a baker. Izmet the baker tried to be proud and brave when they had him. The Chetniks stood away from him and he was alone where he sat in the chair. And the Chetnik officer called a man over and told him to get some water and the man came back with water and a cloth and he wiped my face and gave me the cloth and I wiped my neck and down here.

'The Chetniks looked away when I did that and the officer asked me if I was okay and if I needed something more to eat and if I wanted more *kava* and cigarettes and I said no. I said no and then I said thank you. Then one of the Chetniks hit Izmet.

'Izmet shouted when the Chetnik hit him. The Chetnik hit him here, across the face, like this, and Izmet fell over. I thought the Chetnik had used his fist but when I saw his fist it held a gun. Izmet said to me they were going to kill him, he kept saying it when they were hitting him and they broke his jaw and he was – what's that word?'

She made a spitting noise. Ryan told her what it was.

'Yeah, spitting blood,' she said, 'and he could not speak so good any more and he said to me they will kill me ... But what could I do? They broke his arms and the Chetnik officer asked me again, "Is this man Ustasha? Mujahideen?" I said, "No," I said, "no, I do not know, I know he is a baker." And the Chetnik officer stood up from his seat and he took me by the hair and made me kneel down in front of Izmet. "He is a fucking Ustasha, he is a fucking mujahideen, you are all fucking Ustasha, fucking mujahideen, you are motherfuckers. Is he?" he said.

'They shot him. Izmet. He was crying. He said to me to tell his son. He was saying prayers. Allah, the prophet, anyone. He was not a brave man, he was a baker, and he did not die well. I think I was angry with him, I think I felt that he should not betray us that way. He pissed in his pants and one of the Chetniks took out his pistol and shot him. I was glad when they shot him. He fell over to that side with his arms tied behind the chair and his body – went smaller. Then they raped me again.

'I did not feel it so much that time.

'So they took me back to the Chetnik officer and he has – had – more *kava* and cakes, yes, cakes, and more cigarettes. We were sitting, drinking *kava* and eating cakes and he is telling me about his wife and kids. He has good teeth. Many Chetniks have bad teeth, but not him. And he has aftershave, very strong. I remember the aftershave. So, we are drinking coffee and I can see men outside in the afternoon sun and they are falling down on the ground and the Chetnik *policija* are walking up and down the lines shooting the men who have fallen, in the head. Like this, like this. And each time there is a shot, there is silence and I try to swallow.

'Another man is Spahic. This man is a town official, but he is a member of Alija's party – of the SDA. Izetbegovic, you know? He is a member and he is saying he is a Muslim and he will die for Allah, saying *Allah u akbar*. So they shoot his knees. First one, then the other. He starts to cry. The Chetnik officer takes my cake and my *kava* and he asks me if this man is a mujahideen? I say I don't know. The Chetnik officer leans over his desk and touches my face. "I want you to say it," he says to me, "I want you to say he is a motherfucking mujahideen shit, I want to hear you say it, you Muslim bitch." He called me a whore and said I would be raped by every Chetnik in the camp, every one.

'There is more and then comes a woman. She is blonde, she wears a uniform, her name is Nada. The officer says Nada this, Nada that, so her name is Nada. She is beautiful, I think she is beautiful. Spahic is crying in the chair and I cannot say what he is because I do not know. I say this to the Chetnik officer, I say what I know, I say I am a student and I know nothing. Then this woman – Nada – she steps forward and she cuts Spahic with a knife and each time the Chetnik officer asks the question she cuts Spahic.

'And Spahic is crying and the Chetniks are telling him to shut up and hitting him with their pistols and rifles and he will not stop crying. "Say he is a mujahideen," the Chetnik officer says to me. "Say it. We know he is so all you must do is say it."

'"Say it, say it," Spahic says to me, "say it and let them kill me, say it, please say it, say it." But I cannot say it, I don't know it, I want to say it and I know how easy it should be to say it but I cannot say it. He had a high voice, you know, this Spahic, like a girl's, and when he was crying and screaming at me, I thought it was my sister and I kept looking around to see if it was my sister, and I remember thinking, I remember this, where is Hasim, where is Hasim?

'The woman, Nada, killed him – killed Spahic – with the knife. I did not see it but I know she did it. They were raping me again. When I came out he was in the corner and he was dead and Nada and the Chetnik officer were talking about football and tennis and drinking *rakija*. When I came out and I sat down and the Chetnik officer poured me *rakija*, I drank it and when he put his hands on my shoulders I put my head against his arms and I felt safe, I felt safe when he touched me. He whispered in my ear that I should do what he said, he whispered in my ear that I was a beautiful girl and that all Muslims were really Serbs and that I could change my religion and my name and come back to the family of the Serbs. He said that. Many of them say that. I said I was not a practising Muslim. My father was a Communist. The Chetnik officer gave me a cake.

'They did not rape me for anything this time, they just raped me because they were drunk. And when they raped me they did it without hurting me. And I was grateful. They put me in a room for the night and gave me bread and *kava* and some books. And the Chetnik officer kissed me goodnight.

'I said yes, the next morning – I think it was the next morning – I said yes, when the Chetnik officer asked me if a man I did not know was Ustasha. I was drinking *kava* and eating cake and the Chetnik officer was talking about his kids – one of them had been messing with drugs and he did not know what to do. He thought that because I was a student I would know something. He shot the man I had named as an Ustasha and he shot four more when I named them and then I was raped by three of his men and they killed eight factory workers from Banja Luka. I knew three of the factory workers a little and one of them cursed me and asked me why I was saying he was mujahideen.'

'You don't have to do this,' Ryan said.

'Please do not interrupt me. I do not interrupt you. I have not finished. When I have finished you may speak. The Chetnik officer took me to his room . . .'

'Please, Emira . . .'

'Shut up. You fucking don't know when to shut up, Ryan. He took me to his room and I slept with him. I slept with him and I enjoyed it. I even said I loved him after it. I lay with him and I said I loved him and the next day we went into the classrooms where they were holding the men and I picked men out for him. I did not know most of them, I just went around and I looked at them and if I felt like it I picked them out and I said they were Ustasha or mujahideen or whatever. Sometimes I would say they were criminals – rapists or murderers – and I would say I had seen them kill Serbs or rape Serbs or something like that. These men were led away to a pit across a football field and shot. Some of them were tortured. I saw one man tortured. He was a nice young man and he had been a student with me and once he had asked me to have dinner with him. I will not say his name but he was a good friend of mine. He had moved to the back of the crowd and I walked through the men and picked him out and said he was a rapist and a murderer of Serbs. He said my name and begged me to say I was lying and pleaded with me that they would kill him. They took him to the small white room and they castrated him. I saw that. Nada castrated him and my Chetnik officer and two of his men shot my friend's arms and legs away and I sat and drank *kava* and ate cake.'

She looked at Ryan.

'He was kind to me – my Chetnik officer,' she said.

'I'm sorry.'

'There you go again, saying you are sorry for something that has nothing to do with you. It is not your problem, it is my problem, and I will solve it. I am a genius. I must go before winter or the mountains will be too hard to cross. Do you think there is silver here – the way Grundy says?'

'Diocletian's Tears? It's a legend. He's a good story-teller, Grundy.'

'It would be good to find it. The silver. I could go to Paris or London or New York. I could be anything. Oh, that is a nice dream. I had stopped dreaming, you know, and I had forgotten what a dream was.'

'It's a story, Emira, just a story.'

'Maybe that's all mine is,' she said. 'Sometimes I think so. Then when I must go out, I think everyone I see on the street knows me. And I am afraid. One day, I will meet someone who knows what I have done. There are people coming in from Banja Luka, maybe they will know me. If Hasim finds out ... sometimes when I look at him I feel he knows already. I feel that. I have to get away, Ryan, I have to get away.'

'I'm here,' Ryan said.

He touched her hair and wrapped it round his finger. She took his hand and kissed it and he kissed her head.

'I would kiss your body, too,' she said, 'and I would put my tongue ...'

She smiled.

'I can say it, too,' she said. 'I can say anything you would like. I am tired now, so I would like you to go.'

'I don't want to go.'

'Yes, I think you do. And I want it. You must go now. You can go out the back way, so Hasim's man does not know how long you were here with me. It is better that way. And do not look at me with pity in your eyes, Ryan, I do not need your pity, I need your money. If you can give me money, I will be happy, money will get me out of here, money will give me a life, and I will get as much money as I can.'

'I'm in love with you,' he said.

She kissed his hand.

'But I am not here,' she said.

She brought him to the back of the building and kissed him before he went. The kiss was more a ritual than anything.

The snow was falling again and the shelling and firing had

stopped. Ryan had to climb two walls and get under a wire fence and cross open ground unprotected by sniper screens to get back to the Ulica Marsala Tita. When he was crossing the open ground he could feel a sniper's sights on him, but the cloud was down on the mountains and he could not see anything up there. He shivered when he walked through the snow and he wished for something, but he would not allow himself to think about it. He did not see the five masked men who came out of the bombed buildings and walked behind him.

18

The body was found in a bombed-out bakery, covered with old baking trays. The bakery had been used as a UN food depot after the baker had moved out and then the food depot ran out of food and the Serbs shelled the building into disuse.

A small boy had found the body during a lull in the shelling, while he was scavenging for old pieces of bread and any flour left behind. He found three stale cakes and a crust of mouldy bread and some beans. The beans were spread out individually on the floor and he had to pick them up singly.

He had sat down to chew on them when he saw the feet. The feet were crossed over each other as if the body was resting.

Then the boy saw the blood. The blood ran away from the body towards some old paper bags and a broken steel tray and then ran around the tray and pushed through the dust on the concrete floor. The dust held the blood back and the stream broke up into smaller streams and disappeared under the remains of old pieces of machinery, destroyed when the Serbs had shelled the bakery.

The boy told his mother and his mother told a neighbour and they went to a policeman, sitting at a guard post beside a public building. The policeman did not want to leave his post, mainly because the Serbs had started shelling again, although his excuse was that he was guarding a public building and could not leave it to the mercy of the Serbs. The women went alone and looked at the body and then came back to the policeman.

The policeman got hold of a colleague and they went with the mother and her neighbour to the old bakery. There were torn UNHCR stickers on the windows and an old UN jeep sat in the forecourt, without wheels and rusting, peppered with gunfire.

When Grundy stood over the body, he could not help reaching out to feel if there was any warmth left in it. He let his hands rest on the face. There were streaks of blood around the mouth, on the cheeks. Grundy placed his fingers on the eyelids and tried to close them but the muscles were tight, so he took a handkerchief from his pocket and unfolded it and placed it across Natasa Ruzic's face.

'There was an opal,' he said to himself.

'What was that, mate?' Spit said.

Grundy turned to Milan Husic and Yves.

'Where're the fuckin' medics?' he said.

'An apartment in the *carsija* has been hit. Sixteen are dead,' Milan Husic said.

'I should get mad and shout at you and say she was worth more than sixteen,' Grundy said. 'Where the fuck's Luke, Yves?'

Yves just shook his head and said something in French.

'Who knows, mate?' Spit said to Grundy.

'She wore a chain, with an opal on the end of it,' Grundy said. 'It's gone.'

'Her throat, Grundy,' Yves said. 'It was taken then, the opal, I think.'

Grundy let out a deep breath and looked around the old bakery.

'Come on, let's get her to the morgue, I don't want her here like this,' he said.

Grundy stood up from the body and stepped back.

'I don't feel anythin', Yves,' he said, 'I don't feel a fuckin' thing. I think I should. Jesus Christ!'

He swung round at the two policemen standing back from the body. They were smoking and talking, quietly.

'Put those fuckin' things out,' Grundy said. 'You want a Chetnik sniper across the river to get you?'

The two policemen looked at each other and then stubbed their cigarettes into the concrete floor.

They put the body in a cellar in the hospital, along with twenty-three other bodies. Selby, the United Nations representative in Evkaf, was a short, bald Englishman. When he saw Natasa's body he cried and tried to smoke and dropped his cigarette to the ground and cried again.

Grundy just sat in the corner of the cellar, legs crossed, looking at the body. Sometimes he drank from a small hip flask and occasionally he felt his body shake as if something was trying to get out. But nothing did.

'I will do everything in my power to apprehend the killer,' Jusef Husic said. 'This is a terrible crime, terrible, just terrible.'

When Muha came, he stood at the door and allowed two of his men in ahead of him before he moved towards Grundy. Celo stood back a metre.

'You have my condolences,' Muha said very slowly to Grundy. 'I am shocked. Genuinely shocked.'

Grundy did not look up at him.

'Just get out, Muha, just get out,' Grundy said. 'I don't need this. Go on, just get out.'

'I understand. But I assure you my men are investigating this with the police,' Muha said.

'Just tell 'em to look up their own asses.'

Muha nodded slowly.

'You are distressed,' he said.

Then he knelt down by the body and said a prayer.

'That's nice,' Grundy said. 'In New York they send flowers.'

'I will not be provoked on such an occasion as this, Grundy,' Muha said. 'I will restrain myself. Dignity.'

'Fuck dignity. You think lyin' with your throat cut has any dignity, Muha? Get the fuck outta here before I lose my fuckin' temper, Muha, and bite your fuckin' head off.'

Yves and Horst stood beside Muha's two guards and Spit came in behind Celo's shoulder.

'I think perhaps it would be best,' Jusef Husic said to Muha.

'I did not do this, Grundy,' Muha said. 'You have my word.'

'Don't you know you should never give your word? Someone might just come along and break it for you. Go on, get out, Muha.'

'My men did not do this.'

'There'll be a time, Muha, there'll be a time.'

'Jusef?' Muha said.

'There is work to do, Muha,' Husic said. 'Prepare your men, Muha, prepare your men. We will talk later. Please.'

Muha thought for a while and then nodded.

'She is in paradise, Grundy. She is in paradise,' he said.

'I don't give a fuck.'

Muha thought for a few seconds more and looked at each face in the room in turn.

'Well,' he said then, 'perhaps you will know now what our people suffer every day, Grundy.'

'Muha!' Husic shouted.

'Is this just, Jusef?' Muha said. 'This man may accuse me of murder. This is the second time he has made such an accusation. I do not have to tolerate this, no matter what the circumstances. You are becoming Grundy's lapdog, Jusef. I think you have stayed too long for any good you have done.'

'Get out, Muha!' Husic shouted. 'Get out!'

Grundy stood up and slowly walked over to Muha. He stood so close he could hear Muha's heart beating.

'When the time is right, when the time is right,' he said.

'Your Russian escaped, by the way, Grundy. Broke free – or was let free – from this hospital – where you insisted he should be sent, Jusef – broke free and climbed down a drainpipe with a broken leg. Tough bastard. When I find those responsible, I will punish them.'

'And I will punish you, Muha, if you carry on with this insubordination,' Husic said. 'I am your superior officer, you will obey my orders.'

'For as long as that is the case, I will, Jusef,' Muha said.

Then he smiled.

'I will not argue any more out of respect for the dead,' he said.

Grundy was going to say something else but he could not work up the energy. He turned away from Muha and sat on the floor again.

Then Selby started to cry once more. Grundy told him to shut up.

The Serb shelling intensified.

Dutina was the last to visit the body. He had been crying, but when he came into the morgue, he was almost matter-of-fact. He looked at Natasa and then at the other bodies around her, nodded at Grundy and left the cellar.

Later, Grundy sat with Dutina on the floor of one of the empty hospital wards. Occasionally a bullet came in over their heads and embedded itself in the wall. The disinfectant smell of the hospital was escaping through the holes in the walls and the empty window frames.

'Luke should be here with us,' Grundy said. 'Where the fuck is he?'

'I am just glad it is her and not me,' Dutina said. 'What do you think of that?'

'I suppose I should cry and be full of funny stories about her life. But I don't really know much about her life. I'm almost embarrassed she's my wife. I wish she was someone else's wife.'

'Who do you think did it?'

Grundy shook his head.

'It should be important,' he said. 'To get who did it. But it's not important right now, is it? Not here, in this place. There's other things. She had a good heart, you know. She wanted to do things. I don't think she knew what, but that doesn't matter, does it?'

'Give me some of that *rakija*.'

'You drink too much.'

'I'm scared.'

'I was gonna kill him,' Grundy said. 'Muha. I was gonna put my fuckin' knife into his fuckin' neck. But I didn't.'

'Why not?'

'Beats the hell outta me. I'm a Jew, you know?'

'I heard. Mauthausen.'

'I was a kid. There were guys like Muha all over the camp. There was this huge bastard from Austria, Benny, he was called, and he ruled our hut. Like you couldn't take a leak without havin' Benny's say-so. Step outta line and Benny'd kick hell outta you, cross him and he'd kill you. He killed three guys from Italy when they bought black market food from another hut without Benny's say-so. I hated the bastard. Then we were gettin' near the end, and the Germans were panickin' – the SS guards were drunk all the time – and one big fat NCO – I think maybe he was Ukrainian or Estonian, somethin' like that – he comes along one day and lines us up for *appel* and starts screamin' about murder, betrayal, Jewish conspiracies, all that kinda thing. I was keepin' my head down and his German wasn't great and mine was worse. I was only about nine or ten but I was big. I knew single words, that's all, then. Anyway, he's screamin', sayin' he's gonna kill all of us, and we're all shittin' ourselves, because we've heard the Russians or the Americans are near, and sometimes you can hear the guns in the distance. After about fifteen minutes of this NCO guy screamin' at us we finally work out what's eatin' him. He had a bar of chocolate stashed away under his pillow and someone stole it. So he says he's gonna kill all of us if the one who stole it doesn't come forward. He says it doesn't matter to him how many of us he kills – then there's more shit about Jewish conspiracies and betrayal – and he's wavin' his pistol around. It went on for an hour.

'So no one's sayin' anythin', and – Jesus, I can't remember the guard's name, can't even remember his face. But he's gettin' ready to shoot someone. Then this guy Benny steps out of the line. Just like that. "It was me," he said, "I took the chocolate," and we're all bowin' our heads so the German NCO doesn't see us, and we're all thinkin', yeah, it was him, listen to him, he's sayin' he did it, kill him, kill him . . .'

Grundy took out a cigarette and lit it and drew on it three times.

'So what happened? The German shot him?'

'No, they just took him away. I saw him in Tel Aviv about twenty years later, he was runnin' a fruit business.'

'But he saved your hut from the German NCO.'

'They hanged eight guys that mornin'. The two boys either side of me were hanged. The rest of us they took to the quarry. One hundred and eighty six steps. Fifteen more died there. The war ended then.'

'I have heard of this quarry. Bad times,' Dutina said.

'Interesting times.'

Grundy looked up to the sound of the voice.

'Pity the man ...' he said. 'Hello, Jusef, come to join the wake?'

The colonel closed the door and bowed his head below the level of the window and then sat down on the floor. Grundy slid his flask across to him.

'They are looking for you, doctor,' Husic said. 'More wounded have come in.'

Husic picked up the flask and drank from it, then he sent it back across the floor to Grundy.

'I think the colonel is tryin' to get rid of you, Mihalj.'

'If you are going to discuss killing then perhaps I should leave.'

'I want to know how this affects your disposition,' Husic said to Grundy. 'If you need to be relieved.'

'What do you think, Jusef?'

'I would not blame you.'

'Always the diplomat, Jusef. When we took Jerusalem in '67, I lost my best friend near the Rockefeller Museum. Sniper got him. He was lyin' in the street, dyin', and we couldn't get to him. So we had to leave him. I had my own battalion then, Jusef. There's a picture of me goin' through the Lion's Gate somewhere.'

Grundy shook his head.

'That was a good one, that war, Jusef. That was a hell of a time to be alive. That was a hell of a time to be a Jew. You could get drunk on that. Shit, we were good. Jesus, I'm gettin' nostalgic. That's a bad sign. Gimme a couple of hours,

Jusef. You don't look good, Jusef, I think maybe you should take a holiday.'

'Sarajevo, perhaps. Doctor, you have heard from your sons?'

'No, Colonel. I saw a boy I knew among the Chetnik dead the other day. He was at university with my sons. Perhaps my sons are out there. I dread the day their bodies will come in. I dread that.'

'It is difficult for you. For how long were you in the Israeli army, Grundy?'

'On and off, since I was able to carry a weapon. It was like a love affair, Jusef, started with stars and music and ended in acrimony.'

'Always the way, Grundy.'

'And a mercenary?' Dutina said.

'When I fell out with my first love, I always found another love. Another war.'

'Very romantic,' Dutina said. 'So how is our war going, Colonel?'

'We are having a few problems, doctor. I think perhaps we were premature in our declaration of an independent Bosna-Hercegovina. Maybe we should have asked the Chetniks what they were planning. But it wasn't our fault, really. Once Croatia went, we had to go.'

He laughed.

'I was going to say that otherwise we would have been at the mercy of Milosevic and Karadzic. I blame Germany and the Vatican. If they hadn't recognised Croatia, then maybe we could have talked this out.'

'I don't think so,' Dutina said. 'There is a madness among Serbs here, the madness of the oppressed, and the madness has been fed by the war: they have fulfilled their own prophecy. The Chetniks. I know Serbs. I don't like to say it, but there it is. So, we're not winning?'

Husic smiled and his teeth showed and he nodded at Grundy.

'I have spent two hours on the radio with the United Nations, begging them to come and help us. They have promised to fly over the valley and stop the Chetniks using aircraft. The Americans or the British or the French will drop food on us. It is a difficult position we are in. Grundy, I need you to go about our business now.'

'And Muha?' Grundy said.

'He is ready.'

'That wasn't what I was asking,' Grundy said.

'I know.'

19

When Emira Kusturica opened the door, the light from the fire touched the body of the figure sitting in a corner of her apartment and threw his shadow on to the wall. But she could not see his face. She stopped at the door.

'I've been here five hours,' he said. 'Where were you?'

'I have been out,' she said.

'I've been here five hours.'

She came in and closed the door and lit a candle on the table and another on the mantelpiece. The man's face appeared from the darkness.

'God, what happened to you?' she said.

'Where were you?'

'Why do I tell you?' she said. 'There is a lot of shelling. I had to move through the sewers. Look, I got very dirty. Do I smell? I was arranging things. I'm going to go away now. I just came back to get my things. What happened to you?'

'I was in a big fight.'

She walked over to him, touched his face and ran her hand down to his and lifted his hand and kissed it.

'I did not think I would see you again.'

'You say it like you know somethin',' Ryan said. 'I'm a stubborn bastard.'

'Hasim? Muha?'

Ryan nodded. She touched the bruising below his eyes and brushed his hair back with her fingers. He was cut above one eye and the side of his upper lip was swollen. Then she went over to a cupboard, opened it and pulled out two bottles of water and a cloth. She sat on her bed and wiped her face and hands with water from one of the bottles and took her boots off and wiped her feet. Then she drank from the bottle of water. She passed the cloth and the second bottle of water to Ryan and he wiped his swollen lip and cleaned the bullet wound at the side of his head and slowly wiped his hands until they felt clean. And Emira watched this.

'I fought for you,' Ryan said. 'Where were you?'

Emira came over to him and reached out. Ryan stood up.

He pulled her head to his and kissed her. She backed off and turned her head but he moved towards her and kissed her again. She backed off again.

'I waited for you,' he said. 'You weren't here.'

Then she turned to him and kissed him and ran her hands through his hair. And he kissed her.

'I must get away, I must,' she said. 'I did not think you would come back.'

He slammed his right fist into the palm of his left hand.

'I was fuckin' waitin' for you. I came here for you. Here! Where the fuck were you?'

She kissed him and he moved his hand around her body and Emira reached down and touched him between the legs and Ryan kissed her.

'I can't help it,' he said.

He kissed her and moved his fingers under her sweater and touched her skin and she shivered.

'You're beautiful,' he said.

He pulled her sweater up.

'I am still dirty,' she said.

'You're not.'

'Clean me.'

They held each other and then she opened his jacket and he kissed her neck and she kissed his hands and lifted her arms. He kissed her arms and pulled her sweater up and she pulled his jacket off his shoulders and kissed him.

They continued to kiss and Emira pulled Ryan's green t-shirt up and he pulled the t-shirt over his head and she saw the bruising on his body.

She kissed the bruises and ran her tongue over his body and whispered into his ear. And she undid her bra.

Ryan pulled the bra from her breasts and kissed her breasts.

He lay back on the rug beside the fire and she kissed his body and ran her hands down him and kissed his neck and his mouth and they held the kiss. They put their tongues in each other's mouths and he ran his hand down her body and she lay on him beside the fire.

The fire was soft in the darkness and the flames were small tongues, licking at the gentle darkness and Ryan watched Emira move her body over his.

She put her finger to his mouth and kissed him again and his hands touched her between her legs and she moved her head to his shoulder and held him.

He did not push his fingers into her and she moved herself very slowly when he was touching her with his fingers.

And she kissed him again.

He moved his body against hers and he kissed her and she moved faster and her breathing was quicker.

She slid down his body and licked him and slid down further and kissed him.

He held her hand and pushed up to her and said her name and kissed her hair.

And she came up and they kissed and he moved over her and kissed her breasts and she held him.

He moved down her body and she was wet and he kissed her there. And she moved her body to his lips and he put his tongue into her and that was the first time she came.

He held her hand and she put her legs around his back and closed her eyes.

And when they were coming together they kissed and when he came again she moved her mouth over his body and he kissed her breasts and she held him.

When they had come together the third time and he was lying on his back, just touching her hand, she leaned over and kissed him.

'I didn't hurt you?' he said.

She kissed him and touched his bruising.

'And I?' she said.

'No.'

'Will you come with me?' she said.

'I have already,' he said.

She did not get the joke.

'I would like you to,' she said. 'Away, now.'

'I want to. You don't know how much, but I can't get out of my contract. I've a bad agent.'

'Do not say stupid things. You say stupid things. Do you have any more money?'

'Sure. Don't you know, I'm rich? I'm a rich bastard and I do this kind of thing for fun, to relieve the boredom of havin' too much money. We rich kids do it all the time. I know this bloke and he's done two tours with the Legion and five other wars, all because he's bored with a fortune of fifty – no, a hundred and fifty million. Fights with a goldplated M16 and carries silver grenades.'

'Are you rich, Luke?'

'Moneywise?'

'Is there any other way?'

'Blessed are the poor in spirit,' he said.

'I do not understand your humour, Luke. I think you are probably the only one who laughs at it.'

'It's in that contract. Put my jacket over yourself.'

She pulled his jacket over her back and rested her head on his chest.

'Do you think I said I loved you because I want to take advantage of you? Is that right – take advantage?'

'Yeah, you've very good English.'

'I am a good student. I do not know if I am taking advantage of you.'

She kissed him and smiled.

'I would like to be rich. I would like to be able to say no more often. Do you understand?'

'You're very beautiful,' he said.

'Massage me,' she said.

He touched her arms and moved his hands down her arms and then over her shoulders and her back, and she moved her hands over his chest and around his stomach. And he rubbed deep into her skin and she kissed him and moved her hands down to his legs and touched him between his legs and he kissed her.

'You're beautiful, too,' she said. 'So we are both beautiful.

We must talk more. We have made love and we are happy. You are hard again. I can feel you are hard. Do you want me again?'

'Your nipples are hard,' he said.

He touched them.

'Kiss them,' she said.

He kissed them.

'Are you warmer?' he said. 'I'm warmer. Keep rubbing me. It's very strange.'

She moved her hands to his legs and went down his legs with her hands to his feet and she stayed a while at his feet. Then she started moving up his legs again and Ryan moved over her back to the backs of her thighs and rubbed them and asked her to part her legs so he could rub her more.

She parted her legs and moved the way he asked and she kissed him and he moved the way she asked and he kissed her and they massaged each other.

'I'll come again,' he said.

She did not understand and he made a gesture to show her what he meant.

'It is okay,' she said. 'It is good for you. I like it, too. I would not let the war destroy that. I will never let that. Keep touching me. I feel warmer – do you feel much warmer? – and the fire is good now, I can feel the fire.'

He came when they were rubbing one another's backs. Emira had her head on his shoulder and she was making circles on his back and the warmth of the fire was touching the base of his spine. He had his hands at either side of her spine and he was rubbing her back in deep movements.

It was a very gradual movement and he knew it was coming and did not try to stop it, and once or twice he thought it would come and it did not. When he did come he cried out and held on to her and she kissed him and watched him and held him while he came.

'Do you feel better now?' she said.

'I think I'm embarrassed. I wanted it to be with you.'

'It is natural. I wanted to see it happen. We are lovers, it is natural.'

She held his head in her hand and kissed him and then

pulled her head back from him. Then she touched her stomach.

'See, you are on me. You are very nice.'

He kissed her. She touched him between the legs and let her finger go down the inside of his thigh. She showed him her finger and then put her finger in her mouth.

'You are very beautiful,' she said.

He smiled and kissed her. Then he closed his eyes.

'I'm tired,' he said.

'Yes, it is always like that with men.'

'You've been with so many?'

'So many.'

He let his mouth drop.

'It means much to you, Luke? Yes, I have been with many. I have been with so many I do not remember most of them. I have been with men who hit me and used bottles on me and spat at me and called me bitch. They were my lovers. When I lost my virginity, there were four men in our kitchen and then five men in a bean store on five sacks of beans – and all the rifles and the bottle of *rakija*. Who was your first, Luke? Have you ever made love to a bottle of *rakija*? It is something to tell my grandchildren, you think? I had a lover once, he was a bottle of Chetnik *rakija*. But I do not think like that and I will not let them make me think like that. You are my lover. And I will still want men and I will still be a woman. Now be still and talk to me.'

'I'm a bit of a pain.'

'You use too much idiom. I would like to hear about your life, Luke. You have had many lovers? Tell me about your lovers.'

'I haven't had many lovers.'

'That is good. I want you again,' she said, 'but it is okay, I will wait, it is better to wait, is that not right? Just touch me. Were you rich?'

'Does it really matter?'

He moved his hands between her legs.

'It always matters. Rich people have power. I am interested in power.'

'I wasn't rich. Rachel – my girlfriend – she had more money than I did. She was an options trader.'

'Was she beautiful?'

'A little bit.'

'Did you love her?'

'I don't know. I said I did a lot, but I don't know.'

Emira's breath shortened suddenly. Ryan stopped what he was doing.

'No, please, don't, please. I want to be erotic. Am I erotic?'

'Very.'

'Talk more. You made love to her a lot – Rachel?'

'I think so. We lived together. You forget things like that when you're livin' with someone. I feel like I'm talkin' about someone else. What time is it?'

'So where is she, Rachel?'

'I'd like to think she's still at home. We had a flat – apartment – well, it was hers. Everythin' was hers. I was hers. She used to call me that, hers. I wasn't a very good lover.'

'And you left her?'

'Yes. She's probably still lookin' for me. I should feel bad about leavin' her there. I should have sent somethin'. My folks'll be crawlin' the walls. They're the kind that crawl walls over everythin'. We were supposed to get married, Rachel and I. Her mother was a beautiful woman. I think I went after Rachel just to get near her mother.'

'You made love to her mother?'

'No, she died. I think that was the beginnin' of it.'

'Why did you stay with her, Rachel, when she had another man's child?'

'I don't know. Maybe I liked the indignity. I have a low self-esteem. I'm a bit of a coward sometimes. I'm good in battle. But I'm afraid even that's passin'. I think maybe some time soon I'll do somethin' really stupid. I wish I was like Grundy. I don't know why I'm tellin' you all this. I'm not good at this kind of thing. I don't like what it turns up. It's hard to lie when you're tellin' the truth.'

'Slowly, please,' Emira said, 'go slowly ... and hold me. Oh, very slowly ... very slowly ... all men want to be asked about themselves by girls they love. I know this. I know a lot about this, you know. You would like to spend the rest of your life talking about yourself. I know this, too. I know men. I am not a very good Muslim girl, am I?'

'I think you are.'

He touched her face and she kissed the inside of his hand.

She leaned her head into his chest and began to move on his hand and her breath was faster and she kissed him and held his head and kissed it.

She came slowly first and then very quickly, as if something had been released and she reached down and held him and moved him with her hand when she was coming and leaned her head over his shoulder and held his back and cried out.

'Did Rachel love you?' she asked later.

He was lying on her and she was moving her fingers through his hair.

'All the time,' he said.

She lifted his head and looked at him.

'You are going to cry,' she said.

'No, it's the smoke. Fire's smokin'.'

'She was with many other men? Rachel?'

Ryan thought back to the other life and tried to question the other man in it but they did not understand one another.

'Just the one.'

'You wanted to stay with her?'

'Women run away from me. I mean, they like me when they see me and then they know me and then they run away. But Rachel didn't run away. There was this girl, I remember ...'

He looked around him, at the room and the smoke rising from the fire and the cold taste of the room and the smoke and he could hear the sap in the burning wood and smell the sharp acrid smell of the fire and then her body.

'I'm borin' you,' he said.

'Another joke? I want to hear about you, about that world. I have heard about it and some piece of me remembers some of it but it was so far away and so long ago I do not think I can any more. You can tell me what it is like. The small things.'

'I don't remember much about it either. There was this girl and we got off at a New Year's party and—'

He knew by the way her eyes moved she needed an explanation.

'Got off – you know – just kissin' and stuff. But it was nice. Anyway, then she just ran away and made me feel like a hole should open and swallow me, and any time I was near her she just ignored me. I remember one time she shook my hand and made like she didn't even know me. She said she was drunk when we got off and that was supposed to do somethin' but I don't know what. It made me feel this small. That's what I mean. Rachel didn't do that. Even when she went with this other guy, she didn't do that. I was tryin' to make somethin happen' with Rachel. She had sandy hair – like sand.'

'Rachel?'

'No, the girl who shook my hand. It doesn't seem like much out here but it hurt even worse than Rachel. I bet if I went home now and walked into a place where she was she'd ignore me. That's what it's like there, just a whole load of people goin' round ignorin' each other. You wouldn't believe the amount of ignorin' goes on. All the chances that get missed. That's what I like about here. Every chance is taken. I wasn't a soldier when I came here. I'm not like the rest.'

He ran his hand through her hair and leaned down and she pushed her breast up to him so he could kiss her nipple.

'Nor am I,' she said. 'I did not know if I could be with you. Say if I hurt you.'

She touched him between the legs and he started to come hard again.

'You would like to?' she said. 'Together.'

'We can hold each other for a while.'

'I would like that.'

'Are you still warm?'

She pushed herself closer to him and put her hands to his chest.

'Lie back,' she said.

She pushed him down and when he was on his back again she lay across his body and rested her head against his shoulder and kissed him. They held the kiss and then Emira kissed the swelling on his upper lips, very gently.

'We can lie here,' she said. 'Until the war is over.'

There was a pause.

'I can't stay,' Ryan said then.

'I know. I was just saying it because I wanted to believe it. Sometimes when you say something and you want to believe it enough it comes true.'

'I want to stay but ...'

'You have had me now and you are able to think.'

'No. Stay another week, please. One more week. I'll be back for you.'

'All men say that. I am hungry,' Emira said. 'Are you hungry? You are very hard now. I will touch you until you are ready.'

She rolled off him and closed her eyes and they held hands apart. Then Ryan moved over and lay between her legs and pushed himself into her. It was the slowest movement and she held him tight when he was just inside her and then let go and threw her arms back when he was inside her and moving.

'You will kiss me?' she said.

'I can feel it comin', here. It's beatin' like your heart.'

They made love very quietly and Ryan let Emira come once before he let himself go and they came together then.

'I'll have to go soon,' he said when she was pouring the coffee.

She was wearing his combat jacket and breaking pieces of a *burek* and placing them on the rug.

'Did you have many boyfriends before the war?' he said then.

'Many.'

'But you didn't sleep with any?'

'I was waiting for someone.'

'And what happened?'

'The war. He was very shy. He would have slept with me eventually except for the war. He was from here. I heard he was killed but that was someone who did not like me and I do not believe it. But I do not love him any more, that time has gone and I do not care if he does not sleep with me now. But before the war, I lay awake at night, thinking about him.'

'Will you wait for me?'

'Why?'

'Because I ask you to.'

'He did, too. My love before the war. And we made love many times when I was alone in my bed before the war. When I was waiting. He was a good lover then.'

'I'm very jealous.'

'That is good. And now I will cry when you are gone because I am in love with you. I am angry for that. But I will not let it affect me. You should go when you have eaten. Will one more soldier make a difference? You are a foreigner, you do not have to fight.'

'That's the reason.'

'Come with me, please.'

He kissed her.

'I'm tempted,' he said. 'You don't know how tempted I am.'

'But you love Grundy more. Natasa – Ruzic – she said this to me.'

'I have a purpose. I want to find out who really shot Kennedy.'

'I do not understand. What can you do? The Chetniks will be here in a week or two. I know this. What can you do?'

'We can drive 'em back.'

'Do you believe this?'

'I don't know.'

'But you have had me and now I am not a mystery any more and there is no challenge left, so you will put me aside. I have seen this, too. You are not so different, Luke Ryan.'

'That's not it. Wait for me, I'll be back. I promise, I promise.'

'And I should believe you?'

'Grundy'll make it happen. We'll knock 'em out of the valley.'

'He must have you with him? Grundy?'

'It's a hard move. And Grundy needs me. I hit him, you know. Knocked him over. But he needs me.'

'And Hasim? He will know about us,' she said. 'About this.'

'I can take care of Muha.'

'Look at you. You will die just like the rest. There is nothing to win here. Do you wish me to give you something? Sometimes girls give soldiers things, but I don't have anything to give you. I do not want to do it anyway, it is a stupid tradition.'

'I have this,' Ryan said.

He reached into the pocket of his combat jacket and pulled out a small blue book.

'It's poetry,' he said. 'Someone gave it to me. I want you to look after it. It's yours now.'

'For the fire,' she said. 'I said it was a stupid tradition, very stupid.'

She stood up and went over to a cupboard, opened it and pulled the bottom up. She took out a metal box and brought it over to Ryan. She then went over to her bed and reached under the mattress for a key. When she opened the box it was stuffed with Deutschmarks.

'I am richer now,' she said.

'Jesus, where'd you get it?' Ryan said. He did not say what was in his head.

'None of your business,' she said.

'I'm sorry. How much is there?'

'Enough for you and me. You see, I do wish for you to come with me, Luke. I know this is stupid and you will refuse but I wish you to come.'

'I will be back,' he said.

She smiled.

'But I will not be here,' she said.

'You will,' he said.

'You do not really understand anything, do you, Luke?'

He shrugged and ate his pieces of *burek* and drank his coffee.

'What was his name? This great love of yours?' he said.

'Frejzo,' she said.

'Not Frejzo Ceric?' he said.

'No,' she said.

And the room shook and the walls cracked and the mattresses and steel wedged in the window frame blew out and the ceiling came down in lumps and there was a sheet of flame dancing on the rooftops and Ryan threw himself on Emira Kusturica and said her name over and over again.

20

Ten minutes after the Turkish bridge in Evkaf blew up, the Serbs attacked the southern suburbs across the Thread. The Bosnians could not reinforce their positions on the south side of the river without the Turkish bridge and the Serbs drove a wedge into the thin Bosnian line along the south bank of the river as far as the remains of the bridge. Then they stopped. The action took eight hours and effectively cut the Bosnian positions in Evkaf in two.

And Jusef Husic ordered Grundy to move out that night.

Grundy sat on his bed cleaning a silenced MP5. He had it stripped to retractable butt stock, grip and receiver, barrel and silencer mechanism and bolt and firing mechanism. Each of the parts was laid out on the bed in order of their replacement. Beside them, Grundy had a webbing belt and a small knapsack, and on the pillow, a commando knife still in its sheath and a Hush Puppy in its shoulder holster. He had six grenades laid out in a line ahead of the MP5 parts. The grenades were still in their containers. He picked up the MP5 silencer and looked through it.

Luke Ryan stood at the door and hesitated before coming in. His face was hidden in the shadow of the hall. Grundy did not stop examining the MP5 silencer.

Ryan stepped out of the hall shadow and into the room. His skin was still purple under the right eye and his upper lip was black. There were specks of coagulated blood still on his face.

'So you decided to join us?' Grundy said. 'I was beginnin' to think you'd bugged out.'

'Who did it?' Ryan said.

'I thought you'd know,' Grundy said. 'You been fightin' across the river? I musta missed you, 'cos I could swear you weren't there, Luke.'

'I mean Natasa,' Ryan said.

'Get your kit together, we're pullin' out. You look like someone dropped you from a great height.'

'Either I had great sex or six guys jumped me. I want to believe it was the former. I'm an optimist. Now who did it? Who killed her?'

'How the fuck do I know?' Grundy shouted.

'Do you even care?'

'Don't be a joke, Luke. Where the fuck were you when she was waitin' for you?'

'So you just accept it and move on?'

'Whada you want me to do?'

Ryan didn't answer. He closed his eyes and sat down on one of the beds.

Grundy put the silencer down and picked up the Hush Puppy. The Hush Puppy is a modified version of the Smith and Wesson Model 39 Pistol. It was designed for use by US Navy Seals in Vietnam. It is equipped with special caps for the barrel and plugs for the chamber to allow it be carried under water. And it has a side lock to keep the mechanism closed and silent while firing.

The Hush Puppy shoots a special green-tipped 9mm Parabellum round with a subsonic muzzle velocity.

Subsonic ammunition is necessary because standard supersonic ammunition degrades the effectiveness of the silencer insert. With subsonic ammunition, an insert is good for about 30 rounds; with standard velocity cartridges the insert sometimes has to be replaced after six shots.

'Any beer left?' Ryan said. 'I could do with a beer.'

'I gave it away,' Grundy said.

'How bad's it?'

'About as bad as it can get,' Grundy said. 'They've done us the way I wanna do them. They got good brains over there. We're tryin' to rig up footbridges behind the fortress, but their snipers'll have a field day. They had us watchin' Donje Selo and they hit us over there. Smart move. Andre was right, they got someone in here all right. If Muha hadn't fuckin' killed the son of a bitch I could have got it all out of him. I thought you and Muha's little sister'd be in Australia by now. That's where you were – yeah?'

Ryan nodded and shoved his hands in his pockets and sniffed. A small trickle of blood dribbled down from his right nostril to his swollen lip.

'Did he do it?' Ryan said. 'Muha?'

'Are you comin' or not?' Grundy said.

Ryan nodded and then winced and held his side.

'Yeah, I'm comin',' he said. 'I was at the hospital. Dutina's in bits.'

'So who isn't? Get your kit, we're goin' tonight.'

'Jesus Christ, Grundy, you just go ahead and keep fightin' for these people when they can do somethin' like that?'

'And you couldn't?'

'I'm supposed to give a smart answer, I suppose. I don't feel like it, Grundy. We know he did it.'

'Do we?'

'You're protectin' him?'

'We need him now.'

'And that's it?'

'We don't have the time, Luke. Move.'

'Yeah, sure. It'll get me outta here, I guess. It's gettin' a bit claustrophobic. There's all sorts of things I shoulda done, shoulda said, I suppose. Jesus Christ, she was a fuckin' doctor. I mean, you just don't kill doctors. I wish I was her friend.'

'So do I.' Grundy said.

'I don't miss her, Grundy.' Ryan said. 'Oh, Jesus! Jesus Christ!'

'I hope it was worth it,' Grundy said.

He gestured to Ryan's face.

'I think maybe one of my ribs is cracked. Dutina says no, but look at the fuckin' colour. It keeps changin'.'

Grundy put the Hush Puppy down and went over to Ryan and touched his bruises. He moved his fingers over each individual rib.

'Nothin',' he said. 'You with us?'

'Yeah. I wanna fuckin' nail him, Grundy, I just wanna

fuckin' nail him. Bastard. Jesus, I can't even get angry without it hurtin'. I wanna get that bastard. If he touches her . . . if he touches Emira . . .'

'I told you, don't be such a joke, Luke. You can be a big joke, you know that? You gotta be the biggest joke in all the jokes around here sometimes. If you're comin', then get your damn kit ready. We got a briefin' in an hour. Time's runnin' out.'

'If he does anythin to her, Grundy . . . I mean it.'

'You'll what? You kill him and the Berets'll get you and we'll be down two men instead of one girl.'

'You just don't like her, do you?'

'I'm sure she's a fine young woman and if I have the time maybe I'll try and fuck her. There, that's what I'm thinkin'. Satisfied?'

'I don't want you sayin' that. You could have had Natasa back, Grundy. I was givin' her to you. You shoulda been with her, you know.'

'Jesus, Luke, you better watch your mouth or I'm gonna get mad. Jesus Christ, you almost have me on his side now. I should fuckin' shoot you right here for sayin' that. They catch you in the sack?'

'I don't want to talk about it. I shoulda been watchin' out, I shoulda been. I was careless.'

'That's right. He'll kill you next time. Or maybe he'll just kill you to get at me. But he won't get at me if he does it. So you just be thankful they roughed you up and didn't cut your fuckin' throat, and concentrate on your job.'

'It was him, Grundy, you know it was him.'

'Do I?'

'What is it, man? She was your fuckin' wife.'

'It was a bad marriage. Don't you go gettin' married.'

'I'm in love with her, Grundy. With Emira. She wants me to go with her.'

'Jesus, you sorry bastard.'

He went back to his MP5D. He cleaned each part. The room stank of gun oil and sweat and cordite residue and tasted of burning and masonry.

When it was ready he loaded his spare magazines and placed them in the pouches of his webbing belt. Then he stripped the Hush Puppy, replaced the parts and plugged and capped it and put it in its holster, then took his Luger from its shoulder holster and stripped it and loaded a new magazine.

He went along the line of the grenades on the bed and took each of them out, unscrewed the detonator and checked the grenade, replaced the detonators and placed the grenades in a bigger canvas pouch on his webbing belt.

When he had finished with his weapons he pulled on a thermal vest and took a mountain camouflage combat jacket that was hanging over a chair and put that on, then pulled his webbing on and tightened it around his shoulders. He checked the pouches were secure, pulled on his shoulder holster and adjusted it around the webbing and strapped the holstered Hush Puppy around him.

Finally he taped a spare nine-millimetre magazine to the magazine in the MP5D, cocked the weapon and placed it on safety and adjusted the fire selector to single shot.

Then Yves came into the room with a G3 rifle over his shoulder. He picked some magazines from the corner and turned to Ryan.

'How many?' he said to Ryan. 'Muha men?'

'Six, I think. Two, maybe three of 'em, held me from behind.'

'Then you were lucky. This man is lucky, Grundy.'

'One of them was Tahir, Grundy. He held me. Bastard.'

'You oughtta choose your friends better, Luke Ryan,' he said.

Yves looked closely at Ryan's bruises, made a face and left the room.

'So what about Natasa?' Ryan said to Grundy.

'She's dead. End of story. She was a good poke.'

'You're a sick shit, you know, sicker than Spit.'

Grundy slammed his fist into Ryan's stomach and Ryan buckled and Grundy brought his left heel into the back of Ryan's knee and Ryan went down.

Then Grundy put his arms around Ryan's neck and grabbed his left arm with his right hand and put his left hand behind Ryan's head.

'Now all I do is pull the neck up and back and then twist,'

he said. 'But you gotta twist hard so that it snaps, you know, necks are tough suckers – and you're an ex-joke, Luke.'

He let go and kicked Ryan forward. Ryan lay on the floor, moaning.

'Jesus, what a fuckin' army!' Grundy said.

Ryan gradually pulled himself up.

'She didn't fuckin' deserve that, Grundy, she didn't.'

'What are you, a karma expert?' Grundy said.

'I didn't kill her, Grundy, I didn't fuckin' kill her.'

'Are you comin'?'

'I said I was.'

'You talk too much. Get your kit.'

Ryan started picking up pieces of his kit lying around the room.

'You ever been in love, Grundy?' he said after a few minutes.

'Every day.'

'We should get some *rakija*.'

'We should.'

Spit, Horst and Yves sat in the back of the jeep in autumn-coloured, mountain-camouflage combat jackets and khaki combat trousers. Their MP5Ds were on the floor with three camouflaged backpacks. All of them were wearing double-strapped combat boots and Yves wore his Foreign Legion beret with the para winged hand and dagger of the 2nd REP at the back. He carried a small tin with a mixture of cooking oil, mud and soot in his right hand and placed it in one of the pouches on his webbing. Spit had his Accuracy sniper rifle stripped down in his backpack and Horst carried a fibreglass longbow in his. The jeep was an old American army vehicle and there was a mount for a light machine-gun bolted to the floor but no machine-gun on the mount. Ryan put two knapsacks in beside Yves and climbed into the passenger seat and Grundy got into the driver's seat and turned to Yves.

'Plastic?'

'*Oui.*'

'How much?'

'Enough. It's good. I have checked it. I almost blew Horst's balls off with the detonator cord. He was too close.'

He threw his hands up and blew air out between his closed lips.

'I brought some of the nice hollow stuff for the Accuracy, Grundy. And I done a bita doctorin' and I got a subsonic round, I think. We'll see. Anyways, we got somethin' of everythin' to fuckin' blow some cunt's head into little pieces.'

Three shells landed two streets back from them and two of them hit an apartment block and blew out the remains of a window that had already been blown out. They felt the vibration beneath the jeep and watched the glass fall from the building and smoke rush out of the hole and then fire. There was screaming and the siren went and people who were on the street began to run.

Grundy started the engine and a shell hit the street to their right and shrapnel broke left of the explosion and hit a wall and the burnt-out remains of a car. The car moved and there were small jets of smoke from the holes in the metal. Grundy drove down a narrow street blocked off from snipers by piles of cars, trucks, buses, juggernaut containers and shipping containers and the jeep bounced on the cobbles and they could hear the shells move up the town from their right and see the impacts.

A mortar shell landed behind the jeep and shattered a window and two rockets hit a building in a parallel street. The mercenaries tucked down in the jeep and Grundy put the pedal down and headed up the cobbled street and they passed a small park and a Christian church with the steeple sandbagged for a watchpost. The house windows and the shop fronts were boarded up and taped with masking tape and there were rubbish heaps in the side streets and burnt out cars and UNHCR stickers and now and then you could see a face or hear a voice shouting or smell something cooking over the smell of the cordite and the rubbish.

Two lines of young soldiers, maybe twenty in each, sat against two broken stone walls on opposite sides of the Turkish fortress. They were bent over and dirty and their hair was long. They wore dirty combat fatigues and some had shoes or Wellington boots or woollen pullovers and they all carried AK47s.

Rain had begun to fall and it fell cold and drove into the two lines of soldiers and melted the snow on the flagstones in the courtyard of the fortress. And when the snow was melted to slush the rain started to take the mud and rubbish from around the fortress courtyard and the rain and the mud and the rubbish ran over the boots of the soldiers and down to the street gutters.

The rain sat heavy in the long dirty hair of the soldiers and they bent against the rain and around them the Serb shells hit the *carsija* every few minutes. There was cloud descending on the town from the mountains and soon the cloud covered the town and you could not see the mountains any more.

Muha was sitting on the steps of the fortress, surrounded by ten of his Black Berets. Tahir sat against a wall. Ryan did not make eye contact with him.

Muha stood up when Grundy stepped out of the jeep. He put his hand out.

'To success,' he said. 'And no hard feelings, as they say in America.'

Grundy did not take his hand. He brushed by Muha as if he weren't there and the other mercenaries did the same. Only Ryan looked at Muha.

'Hey, Ryan,' Muha said. 'I will protect what is mine. It is normal. It is natural.'

'*Odjebi,*' Ryan said.

'I understand. You have had misfortune with your women.' Muha looked at his men and shook his head.

'Bastard!' Ryan yelled.

He threw a punch at Muha but the punch went wide. Muha stepped to the right and Ryan fell forward. Muha kicked him in the stomach. Ryan tumbled down the marble steps of the old fortress and tore his bruised face in the gravel. Muha followed him down. He pulled a small knife from the sheath at his shoulder and grabbed Ryan by the hair.

'Give me one reason why I should not cut your fucking throat,' Muha said.

He pressed the knife into Ryan's neck and drew blood.

'Because I would not approve. I need that man.'

Muha looked to his left. Jusef Husic stood flanked by his military police guard and his son. Milan had unfastened his holster and had his hand on the handle of his pistol.

'And because we have more important business, and because we are soldiers and not New York gangsters.'

'It's a thin line.'

Grundy stood at the door of the great hall, holding his hand outstretched.

'So what say we shake, Muha,' he said. 'I don't think you wanna do that. Colonel's right. There's more important things. We have to put aside personal feelings. You hear that, Luke?'

Ryan did not answer.

'I said, do you hear me?' Grundy shouted.

Ryan made an attempt at a nod.

'Please!' Husic said.

Muha looked around him. Spit and Horst had gone either side of Grundy and Yves was now right in front of him. They were all armed but their weapons were pointed to the ground.

'Of course. I'm not a murderer, despite what these mercenaries think of me.'

He dug the knife further into Ryan's skin. Then he pulled away. Ryan fell to the ground.

'To work, I think, Jusef,' Muha said. 'We have a war to win.'

When Muha and his men had followed Grundy and Husic inside, Tahir Khan came forward and helped Luke Ryan up.

'Jesus, man, you know how to make enemies,' he said.

'Fuck off, Tahir,' Ryan said.

'Ah, come on, man, we're still mates, aren't we?'

Ryan touched one of his bruises.

'This one yours?' he said. 'You think a fuckin' balaclava would hide you?'

'Ah, come on, man, come on – I didn't know it was gonna be you, man, I swear, honest, I didn't. How're you feelin'?'

'Just fuck off, Tahir.'

'The man said he was protectin' his sister. You wouldn't understand.'

'And I'm a pervert or somethin'?'

'You look at your fuckin' skin man, look at it. You ever had anyone call you Paki? You ever get yourself hammered because of your skin? I've been hammered since I were a fuckin' lad, a fuckin' bairn. Paki this and Paki that, always the fuckin' same. Well, I've had enough o' bein' Paki, I'm someone now, and no one in the Berets calls me Paki, not Muha, not anyone. You think about that.'

'No dogs, no Irish – ring a bell?'

'Years ago.'

'Still there if you look.'

'I've said I'm sorry. Shake?'

'Piss off.'

'Some of Muha's boys, they're not like me,' Tahir said, 'they hate you lot worse than the Chetniks – you're just westerners to them – it's fuckin' dangerous even to talk to you. So I suggest you keep watchin' your back, Luke, because I won't always be here tryin' to natter with you.'

Ryan shoved him away.

There were four eight-man sections of Bosnian mountain troops, sitting on a canvas tarpaulin, in the nuclear shelter beneath the Turkish fortress when Grundy came in.

The mountain troops carried canvas knapsacks and rope and their camouflage was an alpine autumnal design with pinks and reds in with the greens and browns.

Grundy watched them from behind when he came into the shelter and Husic shifted nervously at the table in front of the soldiers when he saw Grundy and his men enter. He shifted again when Muha and his men came in five minutes later. Muha made something of a theatrical entrance and the shelter went silent while he walked to the table between two bodyguards. The rest of Muha's men sat behind the mountain troops. The mountain soldiers were not too pleased.

When Grundy was walking through the shelter a mountain soldier near him turned his head, looked up and smiled. Two of his teeth were missing and he had a scar across his forehead and a chunk of skin missing at his eye. He had a netted scarf around his neck and his skin colour was brown going cream, laced with cold-water dirt. His name was Ibrahim Abdic and he was a section leader. Ibrahim was not a young man. Some of the soldiers were young men, but at least a third of them were over thirty-five. Grundy found himself having to defend them by referring to his own age.

Grundy smiled at Ibrahim. Ibrahim held his AK47 across his chest and carried his spare ammunition in pouches to the side of his webbing. And he had an automatic pistol on his right side and a long two-sided commando knife on his left.

Grundy acknowledged any of the soldiers he knew by name and stopped to shake hands with them, and behind him, Spit and Yves did the same. Ryan did not. He was shaking.

The shelter was cold and some of the water which had gathered on the walls had frozen. Some of the soldiers sitting on the canvas tarpaulin were rubbing their hands.

Grundy shook Husic's hand more out of reflex than anything. Then he looked at all the faces in front of him.

The faces were worn and the uniforms hung over the bodies as if they were sizes too big. The hands fidgeted with weapons and kit and the eyes darted around the room in a kind of anticipatory panic.

For a moment, Grundy just wanted to thank them for turning up and then say it was all futile, the plan had a negative chance and it would be better if they all took their families and made a run for it through the mountains for Travnik or Zenica that night. He was sure some of them realised that, and when he had composed himself he turned to Yves and Yves winked and Grundy winked back.

Muha stood at ease behind him.

21

The first man crossed the lines to the southeast of Evkaf, where the Bosnians still held sharp mountain peaks on the south side of the river, during a sustained Serb bombardment; the others, men, women and children, followed every five minutes and the whole group spent the next day in a pine forest a kilometre behind the Serb lines, sitting in small holes, camouflaged by branches. And the rain came.

An hour before the sun set, they moved again.

The forest broke ahead of them and then there was a meadow and the meadow fell away in a sharp drop which made a fold, then rose again and climbed at a steep gradient at first, flattened and started climbing at a shallower gradient.

The meadow grass ran into thickets of oak and the soil became rocky with flints of rock sticking up from the soil like small teeth. The wind came from the northeast along the line of the mountains and blew pieces of soil ahead of it. And there was snow on the ridges of some of the mountains.

They moved in a line through the trees, each one ten metres from the one in front with two men out a hundred metres to each side of the line and one man a hundred metres ahead of the line, for lookouts.

There were five rows of pine trees between them and the meadow and the wind moved the pine needles in the trees and whispered through the dead winter meadow grass. Red dust lay on the grass and there were small patches of ice at the edges where the sun did not fall. The sun was very low in the mountains and there was a cold sheen on the landscape as if it was being frozen for preservation. The cold on the mountains was a sharp cold and they could feel it on their faces like steel.

They stopped beside a winding mountain track.

There were tyre marks in the track and the ground was hard. The tyre marks were shallow and fading and probably came from a lumber truck or a digger.

There was a lumber mill to the west of them in a gorge. The water there was brown and red up high and then milky green and white below and the river narrowed in the gorge and cut through, white and foaming, pulling at the banks. There were tall thin oaks running down to the banks and the brown leaves rustled in the wind from the northheast and were a gentle counterpoint to the river.

The lead man raised his hand and the line picked itself up and started down towards the river along the treeline. They could hear the river below them and the sun was dipping to the sound of the river. The last colours of the early winter freeze caught the landscape and made it hard and for ever. And, one by one, the line climbed down to the river.

Fifteen minutes later, Emira Kusturica put her foot in the fast-flowing water of the river and the water whisked her foot away and Emira unbalanced and fell into the water on her back, rolled over on to her stomach and grabbed at a stone under the water.

Her companions, two men who had been cement workers before the war and were deserters now, held her fast with a hemp rope and started to pull her in to the bank. The bank was steep; it climbed fifteen metres to the river gorge which went up a hundred metres on both sides of the River and then flattened out into the small grass fields before the pine and beech forests climbed over the surrounding mountains.

The sun's still dying light licked at the mountain forests above them, and there was a phosphorescence on the swollen river water when the snow started to fall. Emira crawled on to the bank and let her head rest against an outcrop of rock.

'It's too fast,' she said.

She sat down and one of the cement workers helped her undo the rope. Emira shivered.

The cement worker had a single eyebrow and long matted hair and his cheeks were sunken. One of his hands had been mutilated and there were scars on the palm of the hand and two of the fingernails were gone. He looped the rope around his shoulder and elbow.

'Too fast for the bloody kids,' Emira said. 'We'll get across but they won't.'

'I never liked kids,' the man said.

He smiled.

'Bad joke,' he said. 'Maybe we should go back. You'll freeze.'

'I won't. I'm made of stronger stuff. We can try further up. There might be a better place to cross. More rocks. I'm not giving up. You may do what you like.'

The cement worker was about forty and his stubble was approaching beard status. Three of his teeth on the bottom row were gone and there was the beginning of a scar at his neck when he bent his head. The pupils of his eyes dilated each time the light faded a little more and the dilation took away the remaining colour in his eyes.

'What's your name?' Emira asked him.

'Kemal. And you?'

This was the first time anyone had asked a name.

'Emira, Kemal. My name is Emira.'

They did not ask surnames.

Emira looked at the group of people sitting on the river bank. There were seventeen of them, twelve adults and five children. Six of the adults were army deserters, four were men and women over sixty-five and all of the children were under seven. Emira closed her eyes.

All the faces were tired, all the bodies undernourished, all the spirits were low. All of them were afraid. It did not seem like such a difficult journey when you studied it on a map and drew a line, but the mountains were higher than they looked and the rivers were swollen from the rains and the cold was everywhere.

Kemal pulled a piece of stale cake from his pocket and gave it to Emira.

'We'll have to stay here,' he said. 'It's getting near night and we won't cross this at night – not with them.'

He pointed at the children. Two of the smaller boys huddled close to an old woman in black. The old woman's hands were white and shrivelled and she was moving slowly back and forth and muttering to herself. Three of the deserters sat on a long rock and pulled weeds from the stones around them. One of them said something to the woman and threw a stone over at her. The boy on her right swore at the deserter. The deserter asked him if he would like chocolate. He threw the boy a piece of chocolate and smiled. The boy threw a stone at him.

'Another night in this, without shelter, and then another,' Emira said. 'They won't make it.'

'We have a choice?' Kemal said.

'No. You're from Evkaf?' she said.

'No, no. I'm from Skender Vakuf. We came to Evkaf when the Chetniks took Skender Vakuf. Like this. That's my mother.'

Kemal looked over at the woman with the two boys.

'They're your sons?' Emira said.

'No. My sons are dead. My wife and my sons were killed by the Chetniks when I was fighting. They burned the house. You know the way. No, I found those boys in the street. They had no father, I had no sons, so we kind of did a deal. Their grandmother likes it. She's an old woman. I don't know if she can do this.'

'What about this fighting in the Lasva?' another deserter said.

He walked over to them, stooped and with his hands in his pockets. There was a young girl sitting with two old men, arms folded, trying to smile at him. He smiled at her and blew a kiss.

'One of these lads says the fighting in the Lasva's getting worse,' he said. 'I'm Croat, you think they'll do anything to me when we get to Zenica?'

'You want to go to Travnik?' Kemal said. 'The Seventh Brigade are all around the Lasva. I heard this from a man who heard it from a guy who came from there last month. I don't want to run into the Seventh Brigade. I don't want to have to explain myself to them.'

'The Seventh Brigade are in Zenica, too,' Emira said.

'Stjepan,' the young Croat deserter said.

He held his hand out.

'Kemal,' the cement worker said. 'Krajl Turtko Kompanie?'

'No, they're assholes,' the Croat deserter said. 'I was on Crna Gora with the second mountain company. Jesus, we took a lot of shit from the Chetniks. You?'

'Donje Selo.'

'Fuck. Bad?'

'Worse than bad.'

'You been out of it long?'

'Since those fuck-ups at the end of the summer. That was it for me.'

'We just left – that's my girlfriend over there – we just decided to go two days ago. What's the point? Those three over there have been hiding out in Evkaf since June. This is their fifth attempt to get out. Jesus, you think it'll take that long? Got any cigarettes?'

Kemal shook his head.

'That's his last one over there,' Stjepan said.

'He was at Donje Selo,' Kemal said. 'I know him. He's a tour guide from Jajce, I think. I thought he was dead. He had a brother. He's dead. We'll have to move out of here, get back up into the woods. It's better for shelter. Emira, maybe you and I could take a stroll down the river and have a look? You from Evkaf?'

'Years ago,' Emira said. 'I lived in Jajce and Banja Luka, too.'

He knew not to pursue it any more than that. He got up and went over to his mother and the two boys and talked to them. The other cement worker started climbing the bank.

'I'll go and check out a place for us to make a camp. At least we have water,' he said. 'You're a pretty girl, Emira, you think we could have a date when we get to our lines again?'

'I'll think about it,' Emira said.

He smiled a very happy smile and it made Emira smile.

'We should eat,' Emira said.

'I'll see what our people feel like,' Stjepan said. 'I feel lousy myself. So what are you running from, Emira?'

She paused before she answered, to see if he knew something more than he was saying. Then she spoke.

'My lovers,' she said.

'Yeah, sure,' he said. 'It's always the way.'

He went over to an old man, who was anything from seventy to eighty, and his wife, who was about five years younger, but looked like a piece of dehydrated fruit. The old man had a stick and the woman carried their possessions in a bedroll. She wore a gold chain and a head scarf and her facial hair was hard and sharp. Her husband's skin was soft and hung low from his eyes, making it look as if his eyes might just fall out of his head. He had a wart, too.

Two girls and a boy sat beside them, eating bread, and the old man had a small flask of *Sljivovica* which he passed around. One of the girls had had cholera and one of the boys was still swollen from mumps. Kemal had told him to keep away from the adults who had not had mumps but the little boy was afraid and had a habit of cuddling up to the first adult he found. Kemal was sure one of the deserters, who had not had mumps, would come down with it, he had carried the child so much the previous day.

'You're still feeling bad about leaving?' Emira said to Kemal.

They were sitting in the shelter of the river bank. The gorge was melting into the darkness now and the clouds were showing pinprick starlight. In the distance they could hear the sound of guns, but it was far enough away that they could pretend it was thunder. They had had a conversation the first night about the thunder, just to keep the children distracted, and one of the deserters had told a story about thunder, and then cried to himself because he remembered telling it to his own kids years earlier to help them when there was a storm.

'The soldier's ethic,' he said. 'I did not think it would be so strong. There is something very basic about it, very, very basic. I would go back except for my children. Does that sound crazy?'

'No. Sometimes, when I wake up in the morning, I look for strings. I was a prisoner of the Chetniks. They kept us in places that were cold, and I would only sleep when the sun came up. Then I would wake suddenly, very tired, and begin to check for the strings. I was convinced there were strings attached to me. But I never found any. It did not stop me checking. I still check for those strings. Some day I may find them.'

'It's not so easy, is it?' he said. 'To make a decision? I think I preferred when my decisions were made for me. I'm like that.'

She rubbed her eyes.

'I'm in love,' she said.

'Bad way to be at this time. Is he a soldier?'

'Sometimes I can feel him. I don't mean just imagining it but actually feeling it.'

'Yes, I am that way with my wife. I think I see her in the street. I do it all the time. Once I was sitting in a trench and I thought I saw her coming from the Chetnik lines.'

'You miss her so much and you know she is gone,' Emira said.

He pointed to his family.

'Without them I'd shoot myself,' he said.

Emira threw a stone at the river. Then she kicked some stones.

'Okay, let's go and look around. You ready?' Kemal said to her.

She nodded.

'Of course, I'm really interested in money,' she said. 'That's what I want. You know, like in the Beatles' song?'

'Sure.'

He put his finger to her face. She smiled.

The second cement worker came over the edge of the gorge and started making his way down the steep slope, holding on to rocks and small scrub plants and thin oaks and weeds. He slipped once and slid ten or fifteen metres, then picked himself up.

'There's a hollow up there, maybe three hundred metres to the left, well covered. The wind doesn't get in there.'

Kemal started moving up the slope towards him. Emira stood where the river bank touched the gorge and Kemal disturbed rocks while he climbed and they fell down around Emira.

Then the second cement worker fell again. He rolled ten metres and then jumped up and stood for a moment. The people on the river bank tried to figure out what the noise was and they looked at one another and at the small landslide of rocks tumbling into the river to Emira's right. Then the second cement worker fell again. He fell forward and rolled over once, and Kemal tried to catch him but he was too far away and it was too dark. A bullet ricocheted off a rock beside Emira and flew past her head.

A burst of automatic fire hit one of the little girls sitting with the old couple. Three of the rounds which hit the little girl hit the old woman, too, and she dropped the flask of *Sljivovica* she was drinking from and told her husband she was hit and tore at her clothes to see where she was wounded. Two of the bullets had entered her chest on the right side and struck bone and gone back down through her body to her hip. They did not come out. The third round came out at her shoulder joint. She fell back on to the river bank and the little girl pitched into her lap. Then there was shouting and screaming and the firing came from everywhere.

The husband of the old woman threw himself on top of his wife and put his hand into the remains of the little girl's skull and cursed and was shot by five Serbs coming along the river bank in front of him. They were strung out and shouting directions to each other, and one of them had a PK machine-gun.

He held the PK with one hand and the ammunition belt with the other and fired the machine-gun in a wide arc. Eight of his rounds hit the old man on top of the little girl and his wife. They forced him up and back and he rolled and tried to shelter behind the body of his wife and asked his wife's forgiveness for doing it, but the other men on the bank had fired, too, and their rounds went through his wife and into the old man.

They killed the boy who had had mumps. The old man had pushed the boy away but he could not run far because he was still tired from his sickness, and the AK47 and PK rounds caught him at the river and passed clean through him. He was dead when he hit the water. The river carried his body away.

More Serbs were coming along the far bank and from the other direction on that bank and there were Serbs above the bank, at the top of the gorge, shouting and screaming and firing.

Two of them shot each other from different sides of the river and their officer, who had a beard and a walkie-talkie, shouted obscenities at the acned young man who had killed his comrade. A PK machine-gun above the gorge swept the river bank below it.

Kemal pulled out a Tokarev pistol and shot one of the Serbs trying to make his way down the slope to the river.

The Serb cried out and held his back and called a friend. Then he toppled off balance and came rolling down with the rocks to the river bank.

One of the deserters went to grab his rifle but the PK machine-gun caught him in the stomach and knocked him back on to two big rocks. He cracked his spine in the fall and he could not reach the rifle any more.

Kemal yelled for everyone to scatter. He fired three rounds at the Serbs who had shot the old couple and the children, but his rounds went wide.

The Serbs shot him from three sides. One round entered his mouth and another five hit his torso and three more hit his left arm.

He spun and tried to fire again but the Tokarev had jammed and six more rounds hit him below the abdomen and in the legs. He fell back and tried to get up but another PK burst from across the river took the back of his head off and pushed him on to his face.

The two kids he had adopted were trying to run up the river bank with their new grandmother when Kemal was shot.

The grandmother was hit from three different firing positions and her body was held in the air by the rounds, until it just dropped. The kids scrambled into the river. They managed to swim out ten metres when two Serbs down the bank knelt down and killed both of them with shots to the back.

The deserter who'd managed to pick up the dead Serb's rifle fired off a burst in the direction of the men coming down the bank with the PK machine-gun. He hit one the Serbs and two others stopped firing to help their friend.

'Into the river!' the deserter yelled.

He was dead when he hit the river. His body jerked in the water and the large stain changed colour in the silver light from the trees.

Stjepan and his girlfriend made it to the the river behind the deserter but Stjepan was hit in the foot and he fell forward. His girlfriend came back to help him. He told her to go and tried to raise himself up, but she would not go and he could not get himself up.

A Serb round caught him in the back. He cried out and cursed. His girlfriend tried to lift him, screaming at the Serbs around her. She was hit eight times. She spun away from Stjepan. Stjepan crawled towards her and reached her head and four more rounds killed him.

The Serb with the beard and the walkie-talkie examined the first two bodies.

'Shit!' he whispered to himself.

From where she was, Emira Kusturica could still hear the firing, but it was far away now and she was not sure which direction it was coming from.

22

The following dawn, three kilometres to the southwest, Luke Ryan checked his compass bearing and watched the sun break through the trees. The early morning sun was a weak yellow without much heat and if you looked around, you felt that it was kept back by glass, but when you put your hand out to touch the glass it was not there.

The trees filtered the light and the cold was damp and he could see shafts of thin, weak, yellow light hanging from tree to tree and lines of raindrops on the pine needles. The raindrops touched his face one by one and the damp, cold smell of the forest stung his nose and pricked his brain.

Ryan moved towards the water.

The trees thinned out before the river and you could hear the water in the silence of the dawn before you could see it. When he broke through the trees the river was green and swollen and fast flowing, and at the edges the green turned white and the white foam ate at the stony banks of the river and pulled rocks and stones away from the bank and into the water.

He took his woollen hat off, cupped some cold river water and poured it over his head and face. Then he thought of Emira Kusturica and when the thought was getting too strong and Frejzo Ceric was pushing into it he let it go. He could do that there.

He came along the bank of the river inside the first three lines of pines, his body bent at the waist, his MP5D extended right to left, slightly dipped, safety catch off, his finger over the outside of the trigger guard. He moved left ten paces and then cut right and when he reached the point where he knew the Bosnian pickets should be dug in he stopped, crouched down and made a low whistle which did not sound as much like a bird as the wind.

All the time his eyes moved left and right of him and his lungs drew in large gulps of the frosted air. He expelled the carbon dioxide through his teeth so that it would not cloud around his face and give his position away.

He picked up two twigs and a stone and rolled them in his fingers while he waited. Then he whistled again and moved forward to a tree and some scrub and held his position.

A sharp whistle returned and Ryan saw a man in mountain camouflage appear from the trees ahead of him for a moment with an AK47 levelled at him. Then the man disappeared and Ryan moved again.

The Bosnian pickets were in concentric semicircles around their camp at the river, by sections, and in an angled formation so as to provide crossfire killing grounds.

A small dark Croat called Njofra was moving around the eight-man sections of Bosnian mountain troops and Black Berets, giving out orders. Njofra is inverted slang for Franjo.

Njofra was the commander of the mountain troops and he had a hooked nose and a hare lip which he covered with a thick moustache and his ears stuck out. He had been a hill farmer before the war and wore a camouflaged sheepskin vest under his combat jacket and a sheepskin bandana around his head. He had very thick legs and his cheekbones were depressed, giving his face the look of someone who had been punched once too often.

He looked at Ryan and that look asked a question and Ryan shook his head.

Grundy was sitting above the river bank, against a rock, examining a map. Spit sat on the roots of a tall tree. Ryan sat down beside Grundy. Grundy did not look up when Ryan sat beside him.

The river bank dropped maybe three metres to the rocks at the edge of the river. Ryan could only see the tips of the rocks sticking out of the water because the river was flowing too fast and too deep even in the shallows to see the bottom. The mud and limestone coloured the foaming water there and Ryan watched the colours change before he spoke.

'Any trouble?' Grundy said.

'Good to see you, too,' Ryan said.

'What was the firin'?'

'Good fortune, I'd say,' Ryan said. 'It was over quickly. Maybe it was rabbits. I kept back. There's a checkpoint on this road goin' to Jajce.' Ryan pointed at his map. 'I watched it a while. They didn't do much. One car came. That was it. You?'

'Nada. And those guys we saw yesterday?'

'They did the shootin', I think. I didn't get too close.'

'You reckon there was anythin' in it?'

'I swept for two clicks. What do you think?'

'Nothin' happens for nothin'.'

'Well, I'm fuckin' frozen. Jesus, I think I'm gonna collapse. What's happenin' here?'

'There's a village up there. Njofra thinks it's for lumber workers. Yves's gone on ahead with Horst to scout it out. We're layin' up here till dark. So put your head down for a coupla hours. Definitely no one behind us?'

'Definitely.'

Grundy turned from Ryan, picked himself up and went over to Njofra. Ryan went to say something but he stopped himself and could not figure out why. He saw Tahir over with three Black Berets, praying, but Ryan did no more than glance at them.

The dawn was a purple black now and the morning light crept over the shoulder of the highest mountain and across the purple black carpet of the dawn. Luke Ryan watched the light touch the leaves around him and show their shape and the dry bark of the trees on the side sheltered from the rain. He thought of Emira again, and Frejzo Ceric was holding her hand for some reason Ryan could not understand.

The trees were creaking in the wind when Ryan woke, and the light which had now crept over the shoulder of the mountain and along the purple black dawn carpet was filling the river valley and the purple black was turning deep green and brown and the shapes of the mountains and the forests were more defined.

Muha sat beside a tree, reading.

'You have made love to my sister?' he said to Ryan without looking up from his book.

Ryan stared down the river bank at the water. There was a kind of stone outline below the surface although it was only marked by the current of the river. He stretched and yawned.

'Jesus, go to hell, Muha,' he said.

'You do not have to insult the prophet, Jesus, peace be upon his name,' Muha said. 'And you will answer my question, please.'

Two Black Berets sat at trees ten metres either side of Muha. Both of them had their rifles in their laps. One fingered worry beads.

'Would it make a difference what I said?' Ryan said. 'Why don't you just go to hell!'

'Hey, she is my only sister, you know,' Muha said. 'I did not see her for many years, but we are bonded.'

'By blood.'

'That is all that counts in this life. Without blood there is nothing.'

'Maybe she doesn't think so.'

'She is young. She will learn. Young people are foolish. I was foolish when I was young. You think I am wrong?'

'As Clark Gable said, frankly, I don't give a damn, Muha.'

Muha smiled.

'I know this movie. That is good. But it is American. Everything in this world is American, yes? Coca Cola and McDonald's, that is the world now. Even our war has to have Americans if anyone is to take notice of it. And the Americans do not like Islam. I know this. They will do anything not to help us. They are Zionists.'

'Nah! They're just scared, Muha. Vietnam. They keep seein' Vietnam everywhere. But you've a better chance with the Yanks than the Europeans.'

'Yes. The French, the British, they are for the Serbs. UNPROSerb. Think about it.'

'I don't give a fuck, Muha. I don't speak for them. And they don't speak for me. Most of them don't even know who the Serbs are and they sure as hell don't give much of a shit.'

Muha put his book down and threw some stones into the river.

'That is Christian for you.'

'I'm fairly pagan myself, Muha.'

'I am trying to keep my country together,' Muha said. 'I would die for this.'

'Be my guest,' Ryan said.

'You are afraid – of death?'

He pulled an apple out of his combat jacket. Ryan had not seen anyone else with an apple in months but Muha always had them. Muha cut the apple and handed half to Ryan. Ryan's hunger overcame any sense of anger or pride. The apple was sweet.

'Of dyin', I suppose,' Ryan said. 'All people are. I'm ready, I think, but I'm afraid. There, I said it. You think I'm a coward? Well, I don't really care much what you think, Muha.'

'Good apple?' Muha said.

'Yeah, sure.'

'Good. You are still sore?'

Muha touched his ribs.

'I'm cold now,' Ryan said.

'I cannot help that. You look at my sister again and I will kill you with my bare hands. Understood?'

Ryan stared at him and then at the two Black Berets either side of him and touched the MP5D beside him.

'I think the snow's comin',' he said.

'I have killed men with my hands,' Muha said.

'I believe it.'

'But you are not a believer?'

'No.'

'So you are afraid to die. That is right. If you do not believe, there is nothing.'

'I'm afraid of dyin'. I don't know about the rest. I'll tell you, I'm a bit curious.'

'When we die, we are martyrs, we go to Allah. This is a Jihad.'

'Is that what it says in there?'

'You have read the holy Koran?'

'In the name of Allah, the compassionate, the merciful.'

'So you know it?'

'Only that.'

'You should read it. Christians never read it. They all know it but they never read it.'

'I'm an agnostic. I fought long and hard all my life for the right to care less. It's a sacred right. You ever read *The Satanic Verses?*'

'Yes.'

Ryan was caught off guard.

'Well, I haven't,' he said. 'It's blasphemous.'

'Perhaps. I read it in English, so I did not understand all of it. And I was very drunk in those days. Alcohol does not help translations. Emira, she has talked to you about what happened to her with the Chetniks?'

'Not much.'

'They made her a little crazy, I think.'

'She's your sister.'

'I think she is very confused.'

'I'm in love with her, Muha. I'm in love with your sister and she's in love with me. Do you understand that?'

'It says here: "If anyone attacks you, attack him as he has attacked you." In here. In this book. Al-Baqarah, verse one-ninety. I read this part a lot. It is about war. It is about life. Life is war.'

'And war is love.'

'This is ridiculous.'

'I'm not very clever. Emira's a genius.'

'Yes. She is beautiful, yes?'

'Gorgeous. Takes my breath away. But I love her for her mind.'

'I think you make fun of me.'

'Nah, it's too easy. I'm asleep. I'm just dreamin' out loud.'

Ryan closed his eyes. He did not sleep again.

When Yves came in from patrol, Muha stood up, put his book away, picked up his weapon and went over to Grundy and Njofra, who were sitting around a map. Grundy was chewing something.

'Nine houses,' Yves said. 'In two lines, like this.'

He drew a line with a stick in the pine needles at his feet.

'There is a – how do you say it? – a control, here, at this end, with one, maybe two guards. They just sit and listen to a radio. Sarajevo is cut off again. Chetniks shot at a French plane. Up here, there is another control, but I could not see anyone in it. Horst is still there. The road is a mountain road and it goes into the trees here and then like this –' he drew again – 'up the mountain. There are two dogs. Big bastards.'

'Can we get by?'

'Sure. Down the wind. We go wide, here, and through these trees. It is a . . . ? Like this?' He made a sign with his hand.

'Steep,' Grundy said.

'Yes. But we can do it. And Grundy – there is an antenna for a radio transmitter. On one of the houses. I think the radio is with the guards. There is a wire.'

'Then we must destroy it,' Muha said.

Yves bit his lip and moved his head from side to side.

'Not possible,' he said. 'Without they know.'

'No way, Muha. We're goin' round quietly,' Grundy said. 'We can do that.'

'It is your decision to make?' Muha said.

'Yes. Take it out and we'd be writin' a message to the Chetniks, tellin' 'em we're around. No contact, that's the way it is, no contact.'

'And leave it there and they only have to see a footprint or hear a dog bark and they can radio it in. Then we are found out maybe.'

It had begun to rain sleet and the sleet was turning to snow on the pine trees and the snow was heavy even though it melted when it hit the ground. Heavy drops of sleet settled on all of them and on the men in the forest and on the logs that were caught in the rocks at the edges of the river, and on the far bank where the mud and the limestone flint was breaking away in a tear and falling into the water.

'Njofra?' Grundy said.

'No, Muha, we must keep out of contact,' Njofra said. 'We must.'

'See, you're outvoted, Muha. You're outvoted.'

'By an Ustasha and a Zionist.'

'We go round,' Grundy said. 'Unless you wanna make an issue of it, Muha?'

Muha looked at the ground for a while.

'I am the senior officer here, I will be treated with respect, Grundy.'

Grundy snapped to attention and saluted.

'*Jawohl!*' he said and laughed.

Muha might have responded but Yves remembered something and interrupted.

'Hey, Grundy, there is a small valley over there,' he said, 'like the Evkaf, about five kilometres that way, to the south, and it is like a tear, too. You can see it from up there. High.'

Grundy grinned, shook his head and laughed again.

'Yeah, but is it the right one?' he said. 'You gotta have the right one, Yves. Anyway, we're headin' this way. Right, Muha?'

Muha turned and went over to three of his men. Grundy followed him and Ryan watched Grundy. Ryan saw Tahir out of the corner of his eye, shaking his head.

'But it is just like a tear,' Yves said to Grundy then.

'He that believes in me . . .' Grundy said.

'Fuck you, Grundy,' Spit said, 'you still goin' on about that? 'E's been goin' on about that since Croatia. 'E was sellin' shares in the tears to these two Yanks – bastards – had 'em eatin' out of his hand. Joe and – what was the other bastard's name?'

'Tom,' Yves said.

'Yeah, Jerkoff Joe and Tom Thumb. Stupid pricks. One of 'em was from this military school, wasn't 'e? Looked like a burst airbag. Joe. What was it that the school 'e went to did?'

'The entire graduatin' class of 1863 died in Pickett's Charge at Gettysburg.'

'Yeah, that was it. So old wimpy Joe wanted to do some soldierin'. Get some snaps for his mum and dad. Remember he shot off a PK without grippin' proper. Bastard nearly killed this Croatian colonel. Big fat bastard, that colonel.'

Grundy returned to examining his map and Spit went back to cleaning the Accuracy. Yves pulled some bread from his backpack, drank water from his canteen and crouched down at Grundy's map.

'So what happened to the two Americans?' Njofra said, turning away.

Spit looked up. He had the Accuracy in his lap and he was messing with the bolt. Njofra stopped.

Grundy looked at Spit. Spit saw him out of the corner of his eye. He did not look at Grundy.

'They died,' he said.

'And I inherited their share of Diocletian's Tears,' Yves said. 'I already had some so I have sold some of my share to Spit, and now Horst has bought a new issue from Grundy. There are always shares available. Is that not right, Grundy?'

'That's right, Yves.'

Njofra knew he was missing something and tried to understand what they were saying, but his English was not good enough and he was too tired and cold to try and make sense of it then.

'The men taken their salt?' Grundy asked Njofra in Serbo-Croat.

He put out his hand and showed Njofra some salt. Grundy carried it in a small plastic bag for all of them so they could maintain their salt level in the mountains. Even in the cold you need to keep up your body salt levels.

'Once upon a time soldiers fought for this, Njofra. Once upon a time,' Grundy said then.

'Maybe when we're done and you're still alive, mate,' Spit said in English, 'Grundy'll sell you some shares to Diocletian's Tears, Njofra.'

Grundy took Njofra's hand and poured salt into it. The salt stung a cut in Njofra's hand and he winced.

'It can heal you and hurt you,' Grundy said.

'Grundy is giving us some of that home-town bullshit he is famous for,' Yves said, in English too. 'In Africa, he once made a whole town surrender just by talking to them. Many of them killed themselves.'

'You are joking?' Njofra said.

They all laughed.

'You laugh too much, Grundy.'

Grundy swung his head. Muha was behind him, crouched down beside a tree, holding his rifle out.

'You should have been watching your back. You would all be dead now.'

'You first, my friend.'

Ryan had his pistol to the back of Muha's head.

'Put it away, Luke,' Grundy said.

Three Black Berets cocked their weapons. Two of the Iranians went left of them and took up position.

'Go ahead, Ryan, shoot,' Muha said.

'Jesus, do you ever stop?' Grundy said. 'Sit down, Luke. Don't you know, violence never solved anythin'. One for all and all for one, Luke. That's how it is. Right, Muha?'

Ryan sat down and put his pistol in its holster. Muha made a gesture to his men and they went back to what they were doing.

'I'd fuckin' kill you now myself if I thought there was any gain in it,' Grundy said to Muha. 'But I need you now. And you need me. There's a symbiosis there. Here, come on, have some food, set a spell. You got some of that cream cheese, Yves?'

Yves took his knife from its sheath, scooped into the cream cheese he had and handed the knife to Grundy. Grundy ate some of the cheese off the knife and passed the knife to Muha. Muha hesitated.

'Look, if I wanted to kill you I wouldn't waste my food doin' it.'

Muha touched the cheese with his tongue, then ate a piece and chewed it, ate some more and then cleaned the knife. He passed it to Ryan. Ryan dipped it in the cream cheese.

'Maybe it is all a big joke for you, Grundy, for you and your men,' Muha said. 'That is a luxury I cannot afford.'

'Didn't you know, Muha? That's what bein' Jewish is all about: humour. We just can't help it, it's in the blood. Just gotta crack a joke. I get withdrawal symptoms if I don't crack a joke once an hour.'

'You make fun of me,' he said to Grundy. 'Like him.'

He looked at Ryan.

'You don't need me for that, Muha,' Ryan said.

'If I see you are even thinking about my sister, Ryan, I will kill you,' Muha said.

'Why don't you just fuck off, Muha, just fuck off.'

'Hey, come on, boys, smile and the whole world smiles with you, cry and you cry alone,' Grundy said.

'"Make war on the unbelievers and the hypocrites and deal rigorously with them,"' Muha said to Grundy. 'That is from the Koran.'

'"We will hurl Truth at Falsehood, until Truth shall triumph and Falsehood be no more,"' Grundy said. 'Al-Anbiya, eighteen.'

Muha grinned.

'Very good,' he said. 'You have taken instruction?'

'Okay, Njofra, everyone not on watch bed down,' Grundy said.

'Diocletian's Tears,' Muha said then. 'I have heard of this before. Old men talk about it when they are drinking *rakija*, old men with old dreams and no hope. They have to get drunk to talk about it because they are so empty inside. They have nothing.'

'Then maybe it's just a story for old men.'

'So tell me a story, Grundy.'

'I don't much feel like it, Muha.'

Muha reached over with Yves' knife and dug into the Legionnaire's cream cheese.

'The old Roman road, it went through Evkaf. It was a place for soldiers – I forget the English word.'

'Barracks,' Spit said.

'Barracks, yes. And the road went from the coast to the Danube. The fortress in the *carsija*, it is built on Roman ruins. The tunnels, they are Roman. There were baths, I think. I know this story, Grundy. So what do you know about the tears?'

'They were mercenaries, the men guardin' them, emperor's guard, a select group of ex-gladiators from all over the empire. The Romans were takin' all comers into the legions at that stage, and some of the talent wasn't so good, but these guys were the best hired soldiers around. And they fought for Rome because – well, who knows why? Who knows why a man fights a war? I bet none of us does. I bet if we were to chew on it maybe we'd find that what we thought we were here for wasn't the truth. Right, Luke? But then I've always found the truth an unhelpful ally. Truth is somethin' someone else told you. You don't know the truth for yourself. Maybe that came to them, whoever they were, the men guardin' the tears.'

'You believe they took them?'

'No. They were the emperor's guard, I don't think they ran off with the tears. But then I'm a bit of an idealist somewhere and I like a romantic bent to a story. Maybe they gave them to the poor, maybe they died defendin' them, to the last man. And the tears stayed with them until they were found – and then the tears moved on.'

'And who found them?'

'The Bogomils.'

'Yes, I know this, too,' Muha said. 'And around here were many Bogomils. Their *stecci* are in these mountains. You can read the inscriptions carved on them.'

'What the hell's a Bogomil?' Ryan asked.

He was still standing behind Muha.

'They were Christian heretics in the middle ages,' Grundy said. 'Said the earth was the Devil's domain. Didn't believe in possessions or authority or anythin' like that. So they weren't liked by the Christian churches. Said they buggered people. They always said that about heretics. Bugger comes from the localese for Bulgar. The Bogomils had a connection with the Bulgars. It means God have mercy or somethin' like that, Bogomil. They kinda converted to Islam when the Turks came. Their leaders were a bunch of bastards, if I remember, Muha, that's why the peasants jumped at Islam. The Turks let 'em continue with their beliefs so long as they were nominally Muslim. Maybe that's what you guys are, Muha, a bunch of Bulgars – buggers.'

'You make fun of things very easily, Jew,' Muha said to Grundy. 'So you think the Bogomils found the tears?'

'Oh, they found 'em, all right.'

'You know this?'

'Look, I like to think the Roman guards are still out here in these mountains, still guardin' the tears for their emperor and givin' shit to anyone who wants them. And maybe they are.'

'And it is much money?' Muha said.

'It's a story, Muha.'

'So how do you know all this, Grundy?' Njofra said.

'I have the words of a man named Bar Shimon, Yitzhak Bar Shimon. He says two of the valleys round here – one's the Evkaf – look like tears when you look down on 'em from above. Then he says you gotta line 'em up and then follow his code. That's the tricky bit. He was a good codester. Bitch of a thing to decipher, the way to the tears. But I'm gettin' there.'

Grundy looked at all the faces around him and smiled. Spit shook his head and snapped the Accuracy bolt into place.

'He was a Sephardic Jew,' Grundy said. 'They came here from Spain in 1492 when good old Ferdinand and Isabella threw 'em out. Well, the way of the world for Jews, bein' thrown outta places. I think it's our table manners. Or our jokes. Anyway, this expulsion got relegated down the runnin' order of good stories in 1492 when Columbus ran into Haiti or wherever and Ferdinand and his old lady fucked the Muslims outta Spain, too. We share somethin', Muha. The Spanish Jews came to Sarajevo. There were fourteen thousand of 'em in 1941. There's about two thousand now, I think, probably less with this mess. I hear Tel Aviv's been doin' its Exodus thing again. The Germans and the Ustasha did for the rest.

'This Yitzhak Bar Shimon was livin' in Sarajevo in the sixteenth century. The Turks had taken Bosnia and they were movin' west. So Yitzhak comes on a tradin' trip to these mountains and spends the night in an old monastery and meets a bunch of these Bogomils, these guys who either denied temporal power and wealth and lived good Christian lives or buggered anythin' that moved, accordin' to which history you subscribe to.'

Grundy leaned over to Yves.

'You got any *rakija*?' he whispered. 'I talk better when I'm tight.'

Yves pulled out a small flask and passed it to Grundy who drank and rubbed his lips.

'And . . . ?' Muha said.

'Well, they're all gone now, the Bogomils. The rest . . . who knows?'

'And what about this Jew fellow?' Muha said.

'I'll get the share certificates,' Spit said.

'You want to buy some of mine, Luke?' Yves said.

They were smiling.

'Well,' Grundy said, 'the Bogomils told Bar Shimon – I don't know why – they told him how their people found the tears centuries earlier, during the Magyar crusades against them. And they showed Bar Shimon where they were.'

'And you know where they are,' Ryan said.

'Oh, I'm gettin' tired now. I can't think of any more. Go and bed down.'

'You wanna buy some shares in the tears, Muha?' Spit said.

Muha brushed Spit's hand aside.

'So you know where they are, Grundy?' Muha said.

'In your eyes, Muha,' Grundy said. 'In your eyes.'

He smiled. Muha did not smile. Ryan put his hand on his MP5D.

'Luke, get kitted up and move off about a click down river and then swing back this way,' Grundy said. 'Muha, get two of your boys out that way. I want my flanks covered if we're gonna swing round this place. And rotate it around, Njofra. All day. Yves, get back up there and send Horst down. Spit, do another sweep back.'

When Ryan was moving off Tahir signalled to him and threw him an apple. Then he looked over at Muha and put his finger to his lips. Luke nodded and winked at Tahir.

23

The lumber village was a straight line of red tiles in the snow and the new rain was melting the snow which had fallen during the day. There were dark green patches on the mountainside where the rain had melted the snow and the line of red roofs fell away at an acute angle from the mountain ridge to where a mountain track hairpinned. And the track was of hardened snow which had been compacted by an earlier fall and the rain did not melt it.

The trees beneath the village were mountain beech and oak and above the village were rows of pines going up towards the ridge until the land could not sustain trees any longer and they gave way to scrub which was light brown and even grey where the snow had melted. And then there was not even enough for scrub to cling on to and the scrub disappeared into black streaks in the snow and then the snow was a blanket.

They could see lights moving along the roads to Skender Vakuf and Jajce and Banja Luka in the dusk. The roads dipped into the mountains and wound round them in thin strips. The higher peaks and ridges were white and silver in the dusk light and the lights dipped into them and disappeared.

Grundy kept looking at his watch.

They had been climbing for an hour and the beech and oak below the village were dripping melting snow and some of their smaller branches bent with the snow which had not yet melted. Dust clouds of snow powder exploded in men's faces when they touched these branches.

Grundy swung his head, looked back to where they had bivouacked and watched the line of the river break away from them and snake through a valley and a steep gorge. There

were pines futher down towards the river and they broke at
the fields in a small saucer valley behind and then continued
up the other side of the valley to the last ridge they had crossed
before the river.

Yves came out of the trees ahead of Grundy. He was wearing
a white snow jacket and his green Foreign Legion beret was
caked with snow and ice. Grundy could see sweat lines running
down the Legionnaire's red face and scratch marks in the skin
from the trees.

'No lights,' he said. 'Two vehicles – like, eh, four-wheel drive,
yes?' He made a gesture with his hand.

'Animals?' Grundy said.

'Perhaps the animals are inside now. The cold. I could see
none. I think one, maybe two, Chetniks in the guard post.
I could not see them. There is a fire – brazier, yeah? The
Chetnik I saw, he is an old man, you know? Maybe sixty.
Just an old man.'

'Old men can rape and murder, too,' Muha said.

He had come in behind Grundy's shoulder.

'We're goin' round, Muha,' Grundy said. 'And tell your men
to keep ten metres apart, they're bunchin' up.'

He sat back against a tree and rested his head on the
rough bark. Some of the snow still clinging to the bark fell
on to his forehead and mixed with his camouflage paint. The
camouflage came off with the melting snow and mixed in with
the sweat on Grundy's face and then ran with that to his white
beard. And he had streaks of mud and oil and soot and sweat
and snow in his beard.

The map case was wet and Grundy shook it to get the
snow off it.

'We'll drop a tad here and skirt this piece of forest and go up
this line of the mountain. It's an exposed ridge, and if we get
caught on it we're sittin' ducks. But it's dark and it's cold and
if we move fast we can get over before anyone has a chance
to see us. Okay, Yves, get back to Horst and set up a coverin'
position, watchin' the village. Don't go any closer. Muha, get
Njofra to split the sections, I want us spread right out so that
no one can bring the whole group down if anythin' happens.
And put it round, no talkin' – at all.'

Muha was tempted to argue but he did not.

Njofra broke the Bosnian line into its sections and then split the sections into bricks of two-by-two cover. Then Njofra went ahead with Spit and found the line Grundy wanted to follow. Above them, to the northeast, below the village, Horst and Yves set up their cover position, down wind of the village.

They were about a hundred metres from the garden of a three-storey house. The garden had a brown wooden picket fence which had seen better days. Part of the fence had collapsed at the southwest corner, either under the weight of the snow drifts which had built up at that end of the garden or because of the high winds. There were small trees stripped bare in the garden and some metal bars strung across each other. An old Yugo car was wedged up against the back wall of the house and there were cracks in the wall on either side of it where the building seemed to be slipping.

Horst set up a PK machine-gun facing this garden and Yves dug in to his right.

Below them, the Bosnian line moved across the mountain parallel to the line of the village houses, three hundred metres away. Njofra and Spit marked the perimeters of their path of movement between two lines of trees.

There was an area of rocky open ground before the exposed ridge. Njofra slipped on one of the rocks and fell. The men in the first two-by-two cover brick picked him up. He was cut on the face and embarrassed. He took up position and signalled to Spit.

The first brick covered each other across the mountain and turned up towards the open ridge. Spit covered their southern flank and watched the vehicle lights move through the shoulders of two mountains to the west of him. The first brick moved through each other along the trail and then set up a cover position when they had cleared the line of the village.

Then the next brick followed, and when they had cleared the first brick they moved further up the mountain through thick pines towards the open slopes beyond the treeline where the wind was strong and the cold tore your flesh.

Grundy and Ryan held the back door below the village with Muha to their left and Tahir to their right.

When Ryan looked over the red roofs of the village houses he could see the next level of the mountain and he knew there would be more.

Five of the men were walking with wounds already and two had near frostbite, and he wondered if another night in the cold with the snow on those ridges would break the group up so much that they would not be able to attack Vrh.

And he thought of Emira again. And Natasa with her this time. He thought of Emira first and in a way that made his heart beat faster. He did not think of Natasa in any kind of special way, just as a diversion to his other thoughts. And he was sad about that. Sometimes he touched the Tokarev at his side.

When Muha moved off there was only the sound of the wind and his first step into a patch of hard snow, and the wind almost drowned that. He followed the path of the cover groups and then Tahir backed off from his position to move into a cover position ahead of Muha, and Grundy fell back behind them. Ryan would have moved through them when they were in position.

The explosion shattered everything.

Ryan picked himself up and ran.

Two men lay on either side of a small hole. One of them was dying. His stomach had been opened. The other man lay away from him, face down, holding his leg and trying not to scream. The trees beside them were flecked with pieces of human flesh and fragments of combat jacket material.

Four Black Berets bent over the dying man, trying to do something for his pain.

The melting snow around the hole beside him was dripping into the hole and there was blood in the melted snow. Ryan went to the second man, knelt down and rolled him over.

It was Tahir. His right eye was gone and the left one was bleeding.

'Ah, Jesus, me fuckin' leg,' he said, 'I think me fuckin' leg's gone, man. I can't get up, Luke. I can't fuckin' get up, man.'

Grundy took a look at the dying Black Beret on the other side of the hole.

'Shoot him,' he said.

Muha frowned and knelt down and whispered into his man's ear. Then he stood up, took out his Hush Puppy, unplugged and uncapped it and fired two rounds into the man's head. Grundy went over to Tahir.

'Can you walk?'

Luke shook his head.

'Help me up, Luke,' Tahir said. 'Please, man.'

'I'll help him,' Ryan said to Grundy.

Two Black Berets and the balding medic got down beside Tahir. The medic examined Tahir's wounds, wiping the falling snow from his eyes. His steelrimmed glasses fogged up and he had to take them off and wipe them.

Muha shoved in.

Ryan and the two Black Berets lifted Tahir to his feet and Tahir cried out. Ryan held him and rested Tahir on his shoulder. Tahir bit to try and hold the pain but it was too much. The medic examined Tahir's eyes and shook his head.

'I'll hold him, Grundy,' Ryan said. 'I can hold him.'

Grundy looked at Tahir's wounds.

'I can walk,' Tahir said. 'I can walk. Tell him I can walk, Luke. I just need a hand. Jesus, I can't see, man.'

'He's gone,' Grundy said.

'Stand back,' Muha said.

'What's happenin'?' Tahir said. 'Luke?'

'I can help him,' Ryan said.

'He's dead. We gotta move.'

'Oh, Jesus, man. Luke, tell him. Luke. Muha, I can walk, Muha. Jesus, I can't fuckin' see a thing, Luke.'

'You think I want this?' Muha said.

'Oh, Christ, Luke, tell him, Luke, tell him, I can walk.'

'Allah is merciful,' Muha said.

'Grundy!' Ryan said.

Tahir started to slip on Ryan's shoulder. Ryan tried to pull him up. The wind was blowing the snow directly into his eyes.

'Oh, shit, Jesus, don't let 'em kill me, Luke,' Tahir said. 'I'm cold, Luke, hold me, where are you, man? I can't fuckin' see, Luke, I can't fuckin' see . . .'

Muha shot him four times, two in the head, two in the

body, and Tahir fell back against a tree and slumped down in a heap.

Ryan watched the dead body for a few seconds. He was going to say something but he saw the rifle first.

The barrel was levelled at him. His eyes ran along the length of the barrel from the forward sight to the bolt and then the receiver and the rear sight, then the arms on the end of the hands that held it, in their camouflaged combat jacket and sleeveless overvest and scarf and up the camouflaged sleeves to the collar which was up over the neck and the scarf to the face. The face was long and angular and the colour was somewhere between grey and olive. The mouth was wide with a bigger lower lip than the top lip and above the lips the nose was long and almost hooked and slightly bent to the right. On either side of the nose the eyes were middle-aged and black and deep-set with maybe a powder burn beneath one of the eyes. The eyebrow of the other was torn away.

The Serb fired.

Nothing happened because he had forgotten to take off the safety catch.

Ryan shouted a warning, dived to one side and rolled over four times. The Serb pulled the trigger again. Grundy went flat. Muha and his men swung their weapons. Ryan aimed his submachine-gun. Muha fired a single shot with his pistol and missed. The Serb panicked and threw his weapon to the ground, then turned and ran.

'Get him!' Grundy said.

Ryan was already up. Muha barked an order at his Black Berets. The Serb disappeared into the trees.

Three dogs were barking and four lights were on in the houses and there were voices from the village.

The nightwatch was two grey-haired lumber workers at the barricade at the lower end of the village, sitting in the cargo container with the remains of a brazier beside them. They were wearing peaked caps, woollen greatcoats and Wellington boots and carrying AK47s with retractable butts and wearing automatic pistols. They had a shotgun, too, but it was propped up against the wall and not loaded.

The two nightwatchmen came out of their cargo container

and Yves and Horst had moved in closer to them in the woods below the village. The nightwatchmen shouted a name and then one told the other to radio headquarters.

'Maybe it's only Miro, hunting again,' the other said.

'Best radio it in.'

'But Miro'll get into trouble. That's company explosive he uses.'

Miro was thirty metres ahead of Ryan. Ryan had lost sight of him and then the Serb had spun round when he was running to see where Ryan was and Ryan had seen his outline again. Ryan fired a single shot which hit a tree above the Serb's head. The Serb spun to see where he was, hit a tree and glanced off the trunk and hit another tree tearing his face and hands. He stumbled and fell.

Ryan moved wide of him at full speed and the Serb desperately scrambled up towards the village, digging his hands into the snow-covered soil. Then Ryan lost sight of him.

Ryan slowed, checked his weapon and listened. Then he saw the Serb again and fired and missed again. The Serb tried to move out wide of Ryan, and Ryan cut inside him. Ryan fired but there were trees between them and he hit the trees.

The Serb disappeared again and then his silhouette reappeared further up the mountain, near the village.

Muha and his men had lost the Serb and were to the right of Ryan below a back garden with a child's rusted swing. Muha moved into the garden, covered by two of his men. He was running noiselessly when a dog attacked him.

He killed the dog with three shots from an MP5 fitted with a home-made silencer.

The first nightwatchman turned and shouted at his friend to get on to brigade. He may have already known it was too late.

Yves came up out of the trees behind him and shot him with a burst of his MP5D. The Serb's legs collapsed and he tried to spin when he was hit in the shoulder with the second silenced round. The round struck bone and tumbled across his lungs and out his side and a third round went through his neck.

His legs crossed beneath him when he collapsed and he

could not even get to his rifle. He tried to say something, but Yves's next round went into his head and he fell back.

His companion did get his rifle up but only that. Yves's next three rounds hit him across the chest and even if he had intended to fire, the message never made it from his brain to his finger.

Ryan had stopped running now. He was listening again. He could hear breathing, but the wind was too strong and the breathing was smothered by the wind. Then the body came at him.

Miro knocked Ryan back into a tree and Ryan's weapon fell out of his hand. The Serb made a grab for the MP5D and punched Ryan at the same time. Ryan kneed the Serb in the balls and rammed his fingers into the Serb's throat and the two men rolled over twice.

The Serb headbutted Ryan and Ryan fell back and the Serb went for Ryan's knife in its sheath at his shoulder. Ryan brought his knee into the man's plexus and the Serb cried out and sank, then tried to get up and made a grab for the knife again.

But Ryan pulled the knife out. He backed off and held the knife up to the Serb and made a few thrusts, and the Serb called him friend and said the words father and money. It was the first rebel Serb who had ever spoken to him and Ryan stood fascinated by the man, wanting to say something to him. But he did not.

In the village, the relief nightwatch were already up and preparing to come on duty when the explosion happened. One of them, a tall lumber worker who kept a few sheep, was at his front door when Yves killed the first two Serbs. The tall man's name was Dusan and he did not see Yves kill his father and the other Serb guard, but he saw one of their bodies lying in the street.

Muha came at him from the left of some poplars and maple trees and between two Yugo cars. One of the Yugos had bullet holes in it and the other had a sticker proclaiming: *Necemo rat, necemo kir*, which means, no war, no peace.

Dusan had his rifle by the grip and was reaching down for the fire selector when Muha fired at him. He fired a three-round burst and the third shot was not slowed down sufficiently in the home-made silencer and broke the sound barrier with a crack. Dusan fell through his half-open front door and cracked his head on the tiles. His rifle fell against an earthenware pot and smashed it. Muha shot him on the ground again.

Below him, Miro backed off from Ryan and put his hands out and said a few more things in broken German and Serbo-Croat and his mouth turned down. Then Ryan lunged at him with the knife. It was not a strong movement and Ryan did not know if he intended to kill the Serb but the knife went into the man's ribs and cracked two of them and Miro's eyes nearly came out of their sockets. And when Ryan tried to twist the knife he could not do it and the Serb continued to speak.

Ryan hit him and then stood off and watched him on the ground, blood in his mouth, trying to breathe. The knife moved with Miro's breathing and there was very little blood at the wound. Ryan watched the Serb and heard his words without understanding what all of them meant.

For a while there was silence except for the wind.

Then Grundy and more Bosnian mountain soldiers were scrambling up an embankment to the back garden of one of the lower village houses.

The garden was laid out for planting but because it was winter there was nothing in it and the snow ran along the furrows in deep drifts. The ridges of the furrows were exposed and the sticky clay had hardened in lumps and it made moving over it in the darkness difficult.

There were chickens in a coop and a pig and another dog. The dog was barking.

Two of the Bosnian mountain soldiers tried to shut it up by making a hissing noise with their lips, but the cold meant that they could not get their lips to pass the requisite air, so they shot the dog without silencers. Grundy cursed at them.

Then there was a scream. It was not a loud scream and the wind muffled it and gave it an animal sound.

Muha was standing over Dusan, touching his face with his boot when the Serb lumber worker's wife came out of a bedroom with a piece of bread and a glass of water, asking

about the noise. She was a round woman and her nightdress
was torn. One of her toes had a corn on it.

Muha shot her.

She fell back against an icon of the madonna and child and
the icon cracked and fell off the wall on top of her. There was
a cup of sweet tea, which is a Serb drink that tastes like jam,
steaming on the table behind her.

Muha switched off the light.

A boy of about thirteen came out rubbing his eyes. The
boy saw Muha and the shadows of his dead parents before
Muha saw him and made a bolt for the door. Muha fired and
hit the boy in the head, but he did not fall. He caught Muha
off balance and Muha fired again and his silenced shot went
wide of the boy and into a glass and some pottery and then
into the wall beside an oak cabinet.

The boy made it to the picket fence in front of the house and
Muha shot him when he was trying to get through the gate.
Muha fired a burst and again the final shot was not slowed
down enough and the noise shattered the silence.

But it did not matter any more.

Three Black Berets had entered a house across the street
and caught the father and mother trying to get their children
out the back door. The father made a move that looked like he
might be reaching for a gun and the Black Berets opened fire.
They killed the mother and one of her children with the father
and the other two children when they were just over the back
fence. None of the shots was silenced.

Another boy came out of a third house and made a run
for his back fence. He was shot and he fell against the fence
and rebounded, then reached out to hold himself up, then slid
slowly down the fence still holding on to it.

Grundy reached the body of the boy Muha had shot. The
boy lay with his eyes open and his hands holding his
wounds. Blood seeped through his nightclothes to the thin
snow around him.

'Aw, Jesus Christ, Muha!' Grundy said.

'Grundy!' a voice shouted.

Grundy swung round. A Serb man was running at him
with an automatic pistol. Horst shot the Serb with three

single bullets across the back. The man jumped and threw his pistol away and a round went off and the man spun and started to shout. Grundy shot him. Horst nearly fell over the body in the middle of the road.

'Cut all the fuckin' wires!' Grundy shouted. 'Cut everythin'. Jesus, Muha.'

But Muha had shoved past him.

Two men and a woman came out of a house down the street. The woman was screaming and one of the men had a hand gun. Muha and Njofra shot them. Then Muha moved off towards the guard post where the small brazier had tipped out of the cargo container on to the road and the bodies of the two guards lay where they had fallen, smouldering in the fire.

Three women came out of another house, shouting. Three Bosnian mountain soldiers coming out of a garden shot them in the middle of the street and there was another long burst of gunfire from a small house wedged between two three-storey houses.

Then two Serb men opened fire from a top-storey window.

Rounds hit the ground around Grundy and Yves and caught one of the Bosnian mountain soldiers who was emerging from the garden across the street in the head and chest. He fell back over a garden fence and the fence collapsed and he was buried in a snow drift.

Grundy opened fire with the remainder of his MP5D magazine on full automatic. The rounds hit the house from where the Serb firing had come around the window. Then Grundy dived for cover and called for support fire. Spit had entered the village with eight more Bosnian mountain soldiers and they opened up on the two Serbs.

Grundy and Yves moved round each other and flanked the house, while two Bosnian mountain soldiers opened fire on the front door and smashed it in. The first of them was killed the moment he entered the house and the second took a round to the shoulder. Grundy pulled out three grenades and threw them in over the body of the dead Bosnian mountain soldier.

When they had gone off, Grundy reloaded his MP5D and scrambled into the house, firing. Yves followed him in. They got as far as the top of the stairs when they heard a burst of gunfire from one of the rooms. Yves broke the door down.

One of the Serbs had shot three women and two children and then killed himself. The other Serb man was dead against a wall and there was a teenage girl in the middle of the floor, shot by the Bosnians.

Ryan came running up the stairs and almost fell into the room, gasping for breath, trying to take in everything around him.

He stood for a few seconds without saying anything. Then Grundy grabbed him.

'Blow it!' Grundy said. 'Torch it all. Come on.'

A Serb man ran from a house at the bottom of the village and Njofra shot him while he ran. He fell dead in the snow. Njofra then tried to calm the situation, yelling at his men to hold their fire unless fired on.

Two more Serb men tried to escape into the forest. Spit's team gunned them down.

A young girl screamed from her front door when she saw her mother and father dead in the street. Three Black Berets and two mountain soldiers shot her.

At the other end of the village, the Black Berets cleared two houses near the cargo container guard post, lined the families up against their front wall and shot them while Njofra was yelling at them to hold fire.

But when four Bosnian mountain soldiers brought out a family from their cellar in the middle of the village, Muha shouted for them to be shot. Njofra just lowered his rifle and turned his head.

Vinko Herak, a Serb section commander with the Bosnian mountain soldiers, was the last into the village. He came running along the street with his men strung out behind him, roaring at Njofra and Grundy to stop the killing. Njofra, who was shaking his head at this stage, told him to shut up and clear three houses out.

'What the fuck do you want, Vinko?' Njofra said. 'What do you want?'

'Jesus Christ, Njofra,' Herak said. 'Jesus Christ!'

The mother of the Serb family the Bosnian mountain

soldiers were holding, a good-looking woman in fur boots, begged for mercy for her children. Across the street, Ryan turned to Grundy and went to say something, but Grundy had turned his back.

'Don't say a fuckin' thing,' he said to Ryan.

'Grundy!' Vinko Herak said.

Grundy looked at Muha and walked on. Muha gave three of his men a stare.

The Black Berets shot the Serb family. Muha shot the mother on the ground.

And Vinko Herak had to be held back from attacking Muha by Njofra and two Bosnian mountain soldiers.

Muha just kept pointing at the circled M on one of the smaller houses in the village, but Herak continued to curse at him.

And Luke Ryan just watched.

It was all over in eight minutes. There were thirty-three dead in the village. Njofra shot his own wounded man. They stripped the Bosnian dead and put civilian clothes on them and put them in the burning houses. And Grundy kept looking at his watch and yelling at people to get a move on.

Ryan did not move from where he stood next to the dead Serb woman with the fur boots.

'What the fuck are you doin'?' Grundy said to Ryan. 'Do what I said and torch this fuckin' place. Take a good look at 'em, that's you if you don't move. What did you wanna do, tie 'em up? They were dead before we got here.'

Grundy stared across at Muha again and then turned away.

24

Mihalj Dutina's hand shook as he wiped the wound clean with cotton wool. The wound was a shallow gash in the flesh and there were small pieces of stone and grey clay in it and the flesh was pink and weeping. Dark blood had clotted on the skin around the wound.

'I won't stitch it,' he said, 'it doesn't need it.'

Then he moved down to the leg. The leg had a similar wound, only longer and neater, in fact so neat that Dutina thought it looked like someone had used a geometric instrument to help inflict it. There was no foreign matter in the wound and the denim around it had stuck very neatly to the edges where the blood had clotted. The blood was not as dark as that on the shoulder.

Emira Kusturica let out a small cry when he touched her leg with alcohol. She felt the alcohol burn into her wound and suddenly the stiffness in her leg was gone and the pain made her move the limb.

'Just fix her,' Celo said.

His radio crackled and a voice came over it. The transmission was coded.

'Maybe you could cut me into small pieces and feed me to the fish in the river and I can get out of here that way. Maybe that, doctor. I'll give you five thousand Deutschmarks, Celo, if you let me go.'

'Where would you get five thousand Deutschmarks?'

'I'm resourceful.'

'I'll take payment in kind. How about that?'

'Drop dead, you creepy bastard.'

'I wouldn't be so free with your mouth, Emira.'

'Touch me and Hasim – Muha – will have your balls, Celo.'

'You think? Maybe he wants a good man for his sister. Maybe you could give me what you gave the Irac.'

'Where is Hasim?'

'Who knows? Out winning the war. I'm looking after you. Muha trusts me. You can trust me.'

He touched her hair. She moved her head back.

'I can't work if you're going to make love to her,' Dutina said then. 'Look, give me some time to get this right, will you?'

'You're a cheeky bastard for a Chetnik,' Celo said.

Dutina threw down the cotton wool swab he was holding.

'I'm not a fucking Chetnik,' he said. 'I fought fucking Chetniks when you weren't even a dribble down your mother's leg. You bastard.'

Celo scratched his bald head and smiled.

'Okay, okay, like I give a shit. Just patch her up. I got some morphine, doctor, you want to trade for it?'

'With what?'

'Let's have a coffee and talk some business. You got some new stuff in, I heard.'

'That was a shipment stolen from us. The UN bought it back. Maybe you know something about that, Celo?'

'You're getting very brave all of a sudden,' Celo said.

'That's despair. You going to cut my throat, too?'

'You think I did that?'

He grabbed Dutina's collar and pulled him up.

'You better watch who you accuse, doctor. You could find yourself under arrest on spying charges. You think I'm a murderer? You think I would do that? Okay, okay, you know, I do a little survival here and there, who doesn't? But not that. I liked her, you know. She had spirit. But don't worry, we'll find the shit that did it. In time. Hey, people die here every day. One UN doctor gets it and all of a sudden CNN and the BBC are screaming about mujahideen and gangsters and all that shit. What about our people?'

'Just get out, Celo,' Emira said. 'I don't want you here when he's examining me.'

'Maybe someone's trying to tell you something, *draga*,' he

said. 'You were about as lucky as you can be this time, *draga*. Next time, well, I wouldn't think about a next time. Shit, Muha'd chew you alive if he knew. Maybe I could keep it from him. I'm always open to a good deal. You the only one who made it?'

'As if you give a shit.'

'It's good for propaganda. We can inflate the numbers. No, I don't give much of a fuck for deserters, *draga*.'

'Call me that again and I'll stick something in you,' Emira said.

'I love your spirit. I'm jealous of the Irac. Ten thousand Deutschmarks and we can talk about doing a deal.'

'Shit.'

Celo laughed.

'Almost as hot as your brother, but I wonder ...'

'You're very brave, Celo.'

'Black Berets. Bravest and best. *Allah u akbar*. Ten thousand, *draga*, think about it.'

'I'm thinking very hard.'

'Good. I bet the Chetniks taught you a few tricks, *draga*.'

'I bet they did, Celo.'

Celo made a face and then walked out of the small cubicle.

'I'll be out here if you need me,' he said. 'Treat her well, doctor, or you'll answer to me.'

He closed the door.

Dutina blew out. Then he wiped his brow.

'Oh, shit,' he said, 'what did I say all that for?'

'He scares me,' Emira said.

'He scares you!'

'I am not my brother, doctor, I am not Hasim. I am not Muha.'

'No, you're not. Forgive an old man his fears. I loved her. Natasa. Dr Ruzic.'

'I do not feel such things any more,' Emira said.

'I understand. Sometimes I try and analyse the whole situation – like a good psychiatrist should – and I am left to conclude that all that is left is paranoia. Who was it said the lunatics have taken over the asylum?'

'Ouch!'

'Sorry.'

'I think he is right – Celo – I am destined to stay here for ever,' Emira said. 'Like there is an invisible fence and I cannot go beyond it. Or no matter how far I walk I keep coming back to where I started. That is a punishment worthy of the ancient underworld.'

'I don't know much about the ancient underworld. But it cannot have been as bad as this.'

He told Emira to take off her jeans.

'Do I have to?'

'I could get a woman.'

'It's not that.'

'Sometimes with Muslim women I have to get a woman. Even with Serb and Croat women this is the way it is.'

'I will take that as a comment on our society, doctor,' Emira said.

She pulled her jeans down. Her panties were heavily stained with blood. Dutina looked at them and then at her.

'You have heavy periods?' he said.

'No, doctor, I think I've had a miscarriage. I was in cold water for a long time, very cold water, so I didn't feel much and I don't know when it happened. I cleaned as much of it as I could with beech leaves. They have healing properties. You look surprised?'

'I didn't know you were pregnant.'

'I didn't advertise it.'

'And the father?'

'Does it matter?'

'Only to your brother, I suppose.'

'And you will tell him?'

'No. God, no!'

'It was a different life – over there. Much of me had to die. What is left . . .'

She shook her head.

'I understand,' Dutina said.

'Natasa – the doctor – she said I should have an abortion,' Emira said. 'I didn't want one. I just wanted to get out. She was going to help me, you know. She made a promise. The

UN are going to evacuate people. You think I could still get out that way?'

'They've cancelled the evacuation,' Dutina said. 'And they won't send another doctor till the murderers are caught.'

'Shit. I wanted the baby – this is all confidential.'

'Of course. Like a priest or a lawyer.'

'Muha.'

'Indeed.'

'Vengence has its own mind.'

'I thought you were going with the Irac, Ryan.'

'He's in love with someone else.'

'You want me to examine you, see if you are okay?'

'Please. I think I will be sick.'

She bent over to the side and vomited.

'Excuse me,' she said when she was finished. 'I have a son, you know.'

Dutina did not make a comment.

'I have to say it sometimes, to remind myself. My life is for my child, I tell myself. He is with the Chetniks.'

'Please don't tell me any more. I don't want to know. Just do what you have to. Okay?'

'I do.'

Dutina called a nurse and Celo came to the door and smiled.

'You have pretty legs,' he said to Emira.

'Drop dead, Celo.'

'Not yet.'

When the nurse and Celo were gone, Emira was drinking water from a plastic bottle.

'I remember things,' she said to Dutina. 'Things I try to forget. It is always difficult. Most of the time I can keep it back but sometimes it creeps up on me. It is frightening.'

'I just want to see my wife again,' Dutina said. 'Just one more time.'

'Do you know where they are, Ryan and Grundy?' Emira said, as if she had not been listening to him.

'I haven't seen them in a few days and they haven't come in with the dead and wounded. There's a lot happening down at Donje Selo now, maybe they're down there. Maybe they've run away.'

'Do you have an address for Dr Ruzic's family?' Emira said. 'I would like to send a letter when I get out of here.'

'No. Ask Grundy. I think he's her family. I don't know. Look, I've got more patients and then I want to sleep. We had seventy wounded yesterday from south of the river.'

Celo stood up when Emira came out. She was limping slightly on the wounded leg. Her face was pale. He commented on her pale face.

'Maybe we can have a coffee and talk about things, doctor,' Emira said. 'I would like to talk about some things.'

Dutina was rubbing the bridge of his nose. One of his eyes was so tired that it was closing of its own accord.

'I'll think about it,' he said.

She walked in front of Celo.

'Have you considered my offer?' she said. 'Five thousand marks if you let me go.'

'Ten thousand. And show me the money and I'll think about it,' he said.

'Hey, have you ever heard of Diocletian's Tears?' Emira said.

25

Ryan woke to the sound of a bird and the chill of dawn and felt his teeth shake and then his muscles. A sharp coldness drove through his spine and then his whole body was shaking. Beneath him he could smell the sweetness of the pine resin and the mustiness of the earth and he touched his MP5D on the barrel and the cold of the barrel took away any warmth remaining in his hand.

They had marched through the night after the Serb lumber village, up the same mountain, through a high pass that was covered in deep snow and then down a sharp ravine to another river and along the north bank of that river, a bare bank with nothing but stones. The moon was low down there and there were only a few stars between the snow clouds, and the low moon sometimes disappeared behind the high mountains when they were marching, depending on what angle they were at. And the stars looked as if they were resting on the tops of the mountains.

The Serbs had patrols out on the mountains the next day, and a helicopter flying cover, and the Bosnians lost time and ground trying to avoid the searches. They did not stop to rest all the next day and night and they lost two men from exposure during the march. But new snowfalls had covered the Bosnian trail and the Serbs did not follow them.

After the river, there were two more high mountains.

The mountains rose steadily and the climbing was hard and monotonous and the snow was blinding. When they reached one level and thought they were at the top of a mountain there was always another level to climb to, and the climbing was hot in the freezing cold of the night when the snow was falling. Another man died of exposure and two of the mountain soldiers had frostbite. And at the end of that march one of the frostbite victims had to be shot.

After a day and two nights of constant marching, the Bosnians had bivouacked in a cave because they could not go on any further. The cave was colder inside than the mountains outside but Grundy would not let anyone make a fire. There was no talk in the cave except to ask for specific things and the Black Berets sat away from the others.

Grundy and Yves went out on patrol for five hours when everyone else was sleeping. There were no Serb patrols that day and the snow was so bad even the helicopter did not fly. That night the Bosnians marched through the snow again and lost a Black Beret to exposure. But they made it to Sljiva with a day to spare.

The sun had a gentle hint of warmth in it and Ryan pulled himself up from where he lay in a small hollow. He was still shaking and his head was sore from lying on his backpack and his back hurt from the magazine pouches in his webbing. He tried to straighten his uniform and his webbing, then tucked himself up warm in a kind of ball against a tree and rubbed his hands and legs.

Ryan walked through the trees to the top of the mountain. The trees were packed tight up here and some of them had been blown over and rested on the ones next to them. There were deep furrows filled with snow, and the snow and the trees made it hard to move. Small alpine flowers grew where the sun came through and they were surrounded by pieces of melting ice. Ryan picked a flower when he was tying his boot lace. He came over the top of the mountain and crawled through the trees to a line of rocks where Grundy lay, looking through binoculars. The rocks were covered in snow and moss and there were fallen trees around them and a stream came out of the rocks and went down the mountain on that side.

'Thar she blows,' Grundy said.

He pointed. Three kilometres northeast of them was the Evkaf valley; and at the west end of the valley was Vrh; and on top of Vrh was Bor and its mosque.

'Like I give a fuck,' Ryan said.

Grundy passed the binoculars to him.

Ryan could see the Evkaf valley clearly now, and the town and the river and the road running out of the valley along the line of the river and the front lines and then Vrh.

The river was a rusty colour because of the thaw and there were animal carcasses and other things in the water.

Ryan looked at Vrh. The mosque in Bor was brown stone and white behind the tall pines and it looked like a fortress. Ryan moved the glasses to the main Banja Luka road.

The Serbs had cut tracks through the trees from the main road up the south and west sides of Vrh to Bor. The nearest track ran through the cover of pine trees which stood up like crew-cut spikes on the mountainside, and there was a military police checkpoint at the junction of the track and the main road.

Three Serb military policemen with green berets and AK47 rifles stood near a pockmarked cargo container at this junction. There was a small armoured personnel carrier at the checkpoint, green against the white patches of the snow around it. And on top of the cargo container was a red, blue and white Serb flag with a symmetrical cross adorned by four mirror image Cs. A banner beside it said, '*Ovo je Srbija*': 'This is Serbia'.

There were more military police checkpoints along the main road to Banja Luka where the other mountain tracks intersected it and single APCs stood at these intersections, too.

The Evkaf river cut the Serb lines in two and there was a pontoon bridge about a hundred metres back from the last military police checkpoint before the front line. Small tracks ran up the river banks to allow vehicles to climb out of the gorge and into the mountains around. The river had lost some of its rusty colour down there and was turning green-brown and there were large pieces of flotsam clogging up the banks.

Before the pontoon bridge there was a boom stretched across the river to stop Bosnian attempts to float explosives down or launch attacks that way.

Below Ryan, the slopes of Sljiva were covered with the skeletons of beech and oak trees which had shed many of their leaves, and the melting snow left patches of parched limestone and dull grass between the trees. There were small villages in the next valley to the west of the Evkaf, Serb villages now but many had been cleansed, and there were patches of pines around the fields and meadows there. The pines rose up the mountains and fell away in lines and then met up further on into the valley to the left.

Then there was the sharp sheen of a lake, many kilometres to the west, and the sun and the clouds threw patterns on the lake and across the pine forests on the mountains. The mountains were dark and the snow patches shifted according to where you were and it all seemed to be asleep.

In a deep valley surrounded by bare pointed hills, between Sljiva and Vrh, there was a small Serb army camp with APCs and Serb soldiers in training. They did not have any buildings in this camp, which was set in farmland among a series of lacing woods, and cattle wandered around the soldiers.

The soldiers were older men and very young men, some with grey hair and some with no hair and some with very long hair, and they did not always have uniforms. Some had Chetnik beards and some had old woollen Chetnik hats with skulls and crossbones and others wore t-shirts with slogans like 'freedom or death' around the skull and crossbones. The mountains in this area were all very small.

There was still a mist in the valleys which gave them the look of an impressionist painting behind a fogged window. Some of the soldiers were starting fires and washing themselves in makeshift washhand basins, taking water from the small rivers flowing into the Evkaf and the streams flowing into the small rivers. The steam from the cooking and the smoke from the fires rose up and mixed with the disintegrating mist of the mountain valleys. The men drank *Sljivovica* from bottles and passed the bottles around.

An APC started up under a camouflaged netting hide and moved out a few yards before stopping.

Then there was a burst of gunfire to the right, where the Serb lines pushed into the south side of the Evkaf valley. Ryan could not make out where the gunfire came from. And then there was the sound of a *gusle* and a Serb singing and Ryan felt his spine twist. The *gusle* is a one-stringed instrument which looks like a violin, is played like a cello and sounds like a cat being tortured.

'Anythin' you noticed?' Grundy said to Ryan.

Ryan looked at him. Grundy had been taking pills to keep him going and his eyes were popping out of his head.

'I'm gonna go with Emira after this, Grundy,' Ryan said. 'I've made up my mind.'

Grundy just nodded.

'That wasn't what I asked,' he said.

'Wasn't it?'

'There's no fuckin' tanks,' Grundy said. 'I can't see a fuckin' tank. Andre said they were there behind Vrh.'

'What do you think?'

'I think I hope they've moved 'em round to Crna Gora maybe or into the south side of the valley to support the move into Evkaf. I don't see 'em there either, but that could be good camouflage. It's too far away to be sure.'

'I'm still goin',' Ryan said.

'I want you to watch Bor and count everyone you see,' Grundy said. 'I'll send someone to relieve you in a couple hours.'

'I might not be here in a coupla hours. I think I'm dyin' of hypothermia, Grundy,' Ryan said then. 'I can't feel much any more and I'm gettin' giddy.'

'Yeah, well don't die till you've done this. I can't afford to lose any more men.'

'I'll try. If I'm goin', I want my share of Diocletian's Tears, Grundy.'

'Don't try to be too smart, Luke,' Grundy said. 'Where'll you go?'

'That's it, isn't it? Is that sun warm or am I just too optimistic?'

'I want more snow. There's not enough snow round Vrh.'

'Reckon we'll take it?'

'I wish I knew where the tanks were. How many Chetniks you seen in Bor?'

'Thirteen so far, three mighta been the same guy. What's the time?'

Grundy told him the time and pulled a biscuit from his pocket, broke it and gave a piece to Ryan.

'How are they?' Grundy said.

'Unarmed, first thing in the morningish. How many you expect?'

'In the village? One company, I think. It's what's in the line that counts. What Jusef has to break through. I reckon they've moved most of their strength to Crna Gora and the southern suburbs. That would tie in with the tanks bein' gone. Bad move, the southern suburbs, you know. You fuck her? Muha's sister?'

'Jesus, shut up, Grundy,' Ryan said.

'I only asked you a question.'

'I don't like the way you asked it.'

'I told you not to be such a fuckin' joke, Luke. How many now?'

'Fourteen. One guy's definitely come back twice. He keeps goin' into that house near the end of the village, with the wooden shutters. You can just see it through the trees. There's a combat jacket hangin' out the window. Look, I know what you wanna talk about, Grundy, and I don't wanna talk about it. It's done, so drop it.'

'Sanctimonious little bastard,' Grundy said. 'Maybe you should just fuck off now. Go on, Luke.'

Ryan took his eyes from the glasses and turned to Grundy.

'No, you're missin' the point, Grundy. There's a legend back home about a guy who goes to an island of eternal youth, called *Tir na nOg*. Anyway, after a few hundred years he comes back and the minute he touches home soil he ages and dies. That's the way I feel.'

'Jesus, you should hear yourself. Just keep your eyes on the fuckin' village.'

Ryan put the binoculars back to his eyes.

'I think I'm gonna kill Muha, Grundy. I don't think I can stop myself. I mean I never wanted to kill someone in my life. But I wanna kill Muha. I mean, I want it because I know I'll like it. Tahir was a gobshite.'

'What's that?'

'It's someone like me.'

'Look, when I was a soldier first,' Grundy said, 'I said – you know? – I'm not gonna do this or this or this . . . but it's like tellin' a woman you'll love her for ever . . . You heard of Sabra and Chatila?'

There was a pause for a minute while Ryan watched the village.

'Sure,' Ryan said then. 'The two Palestinian refugee camps in Beirut. The Christians massacred the refugees in them. I was havin' a flirtation with an Israeli girl in Vienna when it was happenin'. Ruty. Gorgeous.'

'Yeah, one of the bonuses of bein' an Israeli – the women. Well, I was there, I was in Beirut, watchin' it, the killin', from a buildin' nearby. And I watched and I listened and I did nothin'. None of us did. And that was it.'

'Ruty walked away on me. Or I walked away on her. I never really know. I was goin to Dachau. I stayed in Dachau fifteen minutes. I shoulda stayed with Ruty. Maybe I shoulda stayed with Rachel, too. I want to stay with Emira. What was it like? Mauthausen?'

'You know you come out of somethin' like that and you swear this and you swear that and one day you wake up and you've become what you swore against,' Grundy said. 'And that's it. All for the best reasons. You can never have it all, Luke.'

'That's five more. Two of 'em takin a piss in the woods. She didn't know Frejzo – Frejzo Ceric. Emira. Jesus Christ, I thought she did. I shoulda got to him.'

'He should have had a personal weapon.'

There was another pause.

'I would have been up to interrogatin' the Russian, Grundy,' Ryan said then. 'I would have.'

'Would you?'

'I don't wanna end up like you, Grundy. This is my first and last war, my first and last.'

'You think? At least he was right about this place,' Grundy said then. 'Andre. He said they had nothin' here. On this mountain.'

'And his spy shit?'

Ryan laughed softly.

'Yeah,' Grundy said. 'He was a smart bastard, Andre.'

When Ryan came back down from his watch shift, the four-man Bosnian teams were spread out in formation down the slope, camouflaged in small hollows and slit trenches, eating, checking their weapons, bodies bent and tired, faces stiff and pale, shivering. They did not seem to Ryan to be alive any more. Grundy sat with Njofra and the section commanders. Muha stood about five metres away from Grundy. He kept turning to his Black Berets, huddled around a tree.

'Are you gonna do it?' Grundy said to Muha.

'I think you are trying to manoeuvre me, Grundy,' Muha said in Serbo-Croat.

'Yes or no?' Grundy said in English.

He had a map of Bor and was pointing at a *kavana* at the west end of the village.

'I will need more men,' Muha said. 'We will be exposed in the *kavana*.'

'You had better be there when I come in,' Horst said to Muha.

'Don't threaten me,' Muha said.

'So you'll do it?' Grundy said. 'You'll hold the *kavana*?'

Muha began nodding.

Grundy turned to Ryan.

'How many you count?'

'Fifty-six.'

'Get someone else up there, Njofra,' Grundy said. 'Muha?'

'My men will do it, Grundy,' Muha said. 'We will hold it.'

'And don't get drunk on any booze you find there,' Grundy said.

'Don't try my patience, Grundy,' Muha said. 'I will only tolerate so much. Remember that.'

'You remember it, Muha,' Grundy said. 'And you hold your ground till you're relieved. I mean that.'

'Do not lecture me on my duty.'

'I'm tellin' you, son,' Grundy said. 'I'm tellin' you. And once this is done, Muha, all bets are off. You understand?'

'When it is done, Grundy, when it is done.'

He turned and went back to his men.

Ryan went over to a small stream running in a narrow gully

to his right. The water was running fast and, further down, the stream divided into three and then five streams, then joined up again before it flowed into a tributary which ran into a bigger tributary and finally into the Vrbas.

Ryan dipped his hand into the stream and felt the cold mountain water prick his nerves. He cupped the water in both hands and threw it on his face.

The sky was clear blue and cold like the water and there was a jet trail over one of the mountains. The mountains were topped with snow and the sunlight reflected in the snow lit up the lower mountain slopes.

'The Hour of Doom is their appointed time.'

Muha crouched down, scooped water from the stream and drank it. He looked at Ryan and grinned.

'That is from the book,' he said. 'I think it refers to the Chetniks, don't you?'

Ryan looked around for the usual Black Beret bodyguard, but they were alone. He touched his pistol handle.

'Perhaps,' he said.

'You are thinking about using that on me?'

Muha nodded at Ryan's holster. Ryan took his hand away.

'I do not think you should be in this war, Ryan, you do not understand it. You do not understand what it is about. You watched too many news broadcasts. I know this. The international press, they don't know what it's all about. They think they do, but they are always one, two steps behind. It is about power, Ryan, plain and simple, power, about who has power in a place with no frontiers. You see, I can be frank. And let us be frank. That is the right word? I learned my English from tourists – a bit here, a bit there – and I sometimes forget which word goes where. You know anything about power, Ryan? I don't think you do. English is power. Okay, you learn my language a little bit, but you don't need to much because many people here has some English – have some English. That is power. Very simple, very strong. Power is that simple. It is in the language we use, it is in the skin we are born with, it is in the faith we profess. Profess?'

Ryan nodded.

'So, we are barbarians to you – no?'

'What do you want, Muha?'

'I am a reasonable man. I wish to reason. We are for now comrades. That will change some day maybe. We have time. We can talk. You do not wish to talk with me?'

'No.'

'It is always the way. Muslims are barbarians. Serbs are barbarians. Even Croats. But Croats are Christians – Catholics, so they are not so much barbarians as Serbs, who are also Christians but very different. They have priests who wear beards and they are a little crazy. But Muslims – oh, yeah, Muslims is – are – just barbarians. And you think this. I know. So who wants Muslims in Europe?'

'And the kids?' Ryan said.

'It was necessary. For what we are doing. And one day they would be men. That is how it is. It is logical. I do not think about it. I do not have that luxury. That is your problem.'

'If you're tryin' to tell the truth, Muha, forget it.'

'You are calling me a liar?'

'Not at all. What I'm sayin' is, there's a whole heap of stuff you have to leave behind when you do this. Ordinary rules don't run. It's like bein' in a black hole in space. Everythin' is warped or squashed out of existence. It's not possible to tell the normal truth. It doesn't exist. There are different truths for different occasions. Somethin' like that. See what I mean? Now I'm gettin' all existential.'

'What is that?'

'It's another word for bullshit.'

'I think you are insulting me again.'

'It's like love, Muha, it never works out the way you think it will. I love your sister.'

'I should hit you for that. You are trying to provoke me again. I will not retaliate. This mission is important. And Ryan, *recht oder unrecht – mein vaterland. Verstehen?*'

'*Ja, ich verstehe.* You're still a shit, Muha.'

'Do you still want to kill me?'

Three Black Berets had moved to either side of Muha now.

'Yeah, I do. You killed her, Muha, you killed her,' Ryan said. 'You killed Natasa.'

'And you know this? You have seen me do it?'

'I know it, I know it.'

'Well, then, kill me.'

Another Black Beret took up position. Ryan touched his Tokarev.

'I'm thinkin' about it,' he said.

'Of course you are. I think you are more afraid to die than you say. You say I killed your friend, yet you do nothing. If you are sure, kill me, that is what I would do. Kill me or shut your fucking mouth.'

'Look, some other time, Muha,' Ryan said.

He pushed past Muha. Muha watched him and then came after him very quickly and spun him round.

'Here, I am unarmed. My men will not interfere. Kill me.'

He faced Ryan off. Ryan shook his head.

'Jesus Christ, you know you're not worth pissin' on, Muha,' he said.

Muha laughed.

'Very humorous, very humorous,' he said.

Then he turned and swung his rifle butt at Ryan. The butt caught Ryan on the temple and he fell back against a tree, cracked the back of his head and rolled down the slope for about ten metres. Muha went after him. He raised his rifle again.

Grundy's kick caught Muha below the knee and Muha's leg bent. Then Grundy put both his boots into Muha's belly and he went down at right angles to his legs. Grundy came up and smashed his fist into Muha's neck and grabbed his knife from its shoulder sheath.

Muha's men were pulling their weapons into position when Spit and Horst cocked.

The Black Berets and the mercenaries stood off each other.

Grundy looked at each of the Black Berets in turn.

'I'll cut his fuckin' throat,' he said softly in Serbo-Croat. 'Now, back off.'

'Grundy, let him go,' Njofra said.

'Stay out of it, Njofra,' Grundy said.

'What are you going to do,' Njofra said, 'kill him? Here? And what will that do?'

Vinko Herak pushed through between two Black Berets.

'Njofra is right, Grundy. Do you think I would not shoot the fucker if I could? Let him go. What we are doing is more important.'

'Very noble, Chetnik,' Muha said. 'But you had better kill me, Grundy, because I will kill you now, I promise it, I will kill you and carry your fucking balls around my neck as a souvenir. Bastard. You Zionist bastard.'

Njofra ordered the Black Berets to lower their rifles. They did not do it. Njofra opened his side holster.

'You will let him go, Grundy,' he said.

'Butt out, Njofra.'

'Let him free, Grundy, or I will shoot you,' Njofra said

'You'll have a real problem then, Njofra, you can shoot me and Muha here might just live, or I might slice his fuckin' jugular, or you can let me kill the motherfucker and rid us both of a big headache. Or you could kill both of us. In that case, I would advise you to kill these guys and Yves too if you do, because old Yves and me go back to – well, we go back, and he'll kill you. And I'm sure Muha's boys aren't gonna like it if you kill their boss. But that's your choice, Njofra.'

'No, Grundy, it is your choice,' Vinko Herak said.

Ryan was picking himself up, trying hard to understand what was being said.

'Please, Grundy,' Njofra said in English. 'Let him go.'

Grundy looked around him again. Njofra's mountain soldiers had come in from their positions. He looked at all of them.

'Yeah, I suppose you're right, Njofra,' Grundy said. 'I gotta learn to control my temper, that right, Spit?'

'Difficult at times, Grundy, man,' Spit said. 'Specially with bollockses like 'im. But I'm sure you're makin' the right decision given the circumstances.'

Grundy smiled and nodded, relaxed his grip on Muha and let his head drop into the pine needles. Then he shoved his knife back into its sheath at his collarbone and pulled his MP5D into position.

'You're gonna get me into deep shit, you know,' he said to Ryan. 'Come on, let's see this thing through.'

Muha pulled himself up on his hands and took deep breaths before pushing himself on to his legs.

'You should have killed me,' he said to Grundy. 'You should have killed me.'

'Get your men ready, Muha,' Grundy said without looking behind.

He was walking back up the mountain.

26

The firing from across the river had slowed to single shots. Jusef Husic stubbed his cigarette into the steel ashtray in front of him and drank the last of his coffee. He rubbed his eyes and imagined their colour and pulled a sheet of paper from the bottom of a pile.

'Have you eaten? I can have some food brought in.'

Celo shook his head.

'I need to lose weight,' he said. 'It's good for me. Healthy.'

'Yes, of course. Sometimes I forget about things like that. Perhaps we should have a greener image. You know, plant trees every time we cut some down, only use environmentally friendly equipment, ask the Chetniks to give us a truce so we can pick up the garbage. It might attract more attention from the outside world, get intellectuals on our side. They like that kind of thing – I am being sarcastic.'

'I had noticed, Colonel. I don't know many intellectuals, sir, we didn't move in the same circles back in Sarajevo.'

'You miss it?'

'Sarajevo?'

'I don't know. I just said the words, I'm not sure why, but since we're on the subject of Sarajevo – yeah.'

'All the time. I have a wife and a kid. I don't miss my wife much, she's a fat woman, but I miss my kid. I'm uncomfortable with this, Colonel.'

'Yes, of course, I'm sorry. I don't mean to make you feel uncomfortable. If I sound too cerebral just say so. I believe in frankness.'

'What's cerebral?'

'It's people who like to consider the world in their heads and run a million kilometres when they have to face the actuality of doing anything. I am one of them, so you will appreciate the transition is somewhat painful for me. That is not an insult to yourself.'

'I know what you mean. We are not popular with the intellectuals. I think our struggle is too basic for them, it irritates their sense of superiority. Personally I understand a man who kills for his family a lot more than one who kills for an abstract idea.'

'I think you're not quite as proletarian as you would have me believe. And Allah?'

'Gives me strength, Colonel. A friend in a world of few friends. But I am not Muha.'

'No.'

Celo pulled a piece of chocolate from his pocket, broke it in two and offered one half to Husic.

'My health kick is not a doctrine,' he said.

'I'm glad to hear it.'

Husic accepted the chocolate and they both ate.

'You're a good man, Colonel,' Celo said.

'I'm glad you think so. So we're ready?'

'The pieces are in place.'

Husic nodded.

'I haven't yet learned to trust my irrational; I'm not used to it. You think they're there?'

He pushed the sheet of paper he had in front of him across the table.

'It's a village between here and Jajce. The Chetniks are claiming we massacred all of them. I don't care about it. All I care about is the bad propaganda and Grundy making it into position. Do you think they're there?'

'Muha'll crawl if he has to. He's like that.'

'Yes, certainly. But I am still uneasy. This is not my natural state. I'm a lawyer. Good argument, that kind of thing. Fine wines, Milan Kundera, classical music, Pink Floyd. All this is strange for me. I am surprised I have these instincts at all.'

'I'm where I've always been, Colonel, only now I have rank and people who used to despise me look up to me because I will kill to keep them alive. This war's been good to me. I still want to see my kid.'

'I find I admire brutality more than I did. Cunning, all that. There is a good feeling underlying all the questioning, all the doubt, a feeling of being alive. So close ...'

'It can wear off, too.'

'It's a novelty for me. I was a soft kid, always studying, always with a book or a new song. I was lousy when I was a conscript.'

'I dodged it. I was too busy making money. It interfered with business.'

'And our asset?' Husic said then.

'Our asset is out of our control now,' Celo said. 'It is all in the hands of Allah.'

'Mischief thou art afoot ...' Husic said.

Celo did not betray his ignorance. He glanced down at the piece of paper detailing the lumber village massacre.

'It is from Shakespeare – the English playwright,' Husic said then.

'I did not study much when I was a kid,' Celo said.

'I studied too much. There's so much compromise, so many things I must ignore – all the judgements I would make are nothing except for what they can do for our war effort. Life is very simple in that sense – once you accept it. Accepting it is the problem.'

'Tell me, Colonel,' Celo said, 'what are you prepared to lose in this war?'

'I don't want to lose anything.'

'When I was a gang leader – a teenager – we used to have fights with knives and things. They were not serious fights, just maybe nicking your opponent or slashing his clothes. Now and then they got a little more serious, but still they were stopped by something, and when the first blood was drawn there would be some excuse to stop and friends would intervene and honour and face would be saved with a compromise. However, once every so often, very rarely though, someone would come along who was prepared to go all the way. I don't mean go all the way and kill someone – that could always happen – no, I mean, he was prepared to be killed. I have not seen many of these people in my life – Muha is perhaps one of them – but they have a great strength because they have no fear of death, of losing everything. Do you understand me?'

'Are you sure you were never an intellectual?'

'I'm a debt collector.'

'I am prepared to die.'

'That's not enough, is it? These guys weren't just prepared to die, they didn't care if they did or not. And in a world where people prize life above all things, such people are very powerful. They conquer death.'

'I will bear it in mind.'

'They will be preparing now,' Celo said.

'I hope what we have prepared works, Celo. I feel I have thrown my dice into a dark hole.'

27

Spit turned the last Allen key in the Accuracy, picked up the rifle and snapped a magazine in. Then he fitted the telescopic sight and started to customise the weapon to his own personal feel. He had ten .338 Lapua Magnum magazines in his ammunition pouches, evenly divided between hard, hollow and mercury noses. It was still dark and the wind blowing full from the northeast sang with a low whine through the needles on the trees and threw the small snowfall around the air in spirals. And the moonlight slid over the mountain ridges and under the snow, and between the wind and the ground, the whole night had a silver sheen beneath the black.

'You ready?' Grundy asked.

There was a burst of gunfire from the hills around. Then there was the wind and more gunfire. Spit looked behind Grundy and saw the assault team lined up in arrowhead formation by twos, each man using a tree for cover. Grundy checked Spit's equipment and Spit went over his webbing one last time and adjusted his green headscarf. Then he slipped a Colt Commando over his shoulder and wrapped netting around the Accuracy.

'*Moritur* – what's that fuckin' thing the gladiators said, Grundy?'

'*Morituri te salutant*. Those who are about to die salute you.'

'Yeah, that. You better take this place, mate, I don't wanna be out there on my fuckin' own. You boys fuck up and I'll get the 'ump.'

Grundy slapped Spit's side arm.

'Havoc, Spit,' Grundy said.

'Be seein' you then, Grundy, man,' Spit said.

Spit smiled through his camouflage paint. And then he was gone.

Thirty-five minutes later, Yves moved off to centre point. He went almost in a direct line towards Vrh, and sometimes he could see the moonlight skipping on the white minaret of the Bor mosque. He took up a position on a low hill between two higher peaks where the land rose and fell in wide hollows. The hill he had taken up position on was covered in oak and beech trees and the remaining leaves were wet and even the heavy wind could not move them very much. And the snow swirled and brought visibility down to a few metres.

When Yves had moved off to his position, Horst slung his fibreglass longbow over one shoulder and a G3 rifle over the other. Then he cocked his MP5D, placed his trigger finger over the edge of the trigger guard and pointed the silenced barrel of the weapon down from the horizontal and moved off to Yves's right.

Then Njofra led the first two-by-two brick of mountain soldiers forward into the snow and the wind and the moonlight and darkness.

It took four hours to make the river. They skirted two Serb camps and three villages and Yves killed a Serb who had wandered out of his village, drunk. They dumped the body in a small ravine.

The wind died before the river and the snow came dropping slowly. The sound of the river was heavy. The snow stopped falling and the moon broke through.

The Serb pontoon bridge had four guards, two on either side.

The Bosnians moved into position above the south bank of the river, east of the pontoon bridge, between it and the mined boom, where the river bent northwest around Vrh and headed towards the Vrbas. They were on a wooded slope, stretched out in arrowhead cover in two-by-two bricks.

Ryan came up the slope and tapped Grundy on the shoulder. Grundy looked at his watch. The moonlight passed over the face of his watch and Grundy nodded to Muha. Muha stood up and checked his Hush Puppy and started walking down the slope. Ryan followed, and Grundy followed Ryan and Yves followed Grundy.

The night was starting to die now and the dawn was a deep blue to the east and there was sleet. The sleet came irregularly on the wind and the moon was a fat crescent below the shoulder of one of the bigger mountains. The mountains were rough outlines in the deep blue to the east, threatening something more than was there.

Grundy slipped into the water and it made him shut his eyes and hold his muscles. The current was strong and it caught him and pulled him down towards the pontoon bridge. Yellow from the weeping eye at the shoulder of the mountain spread out like milk on the river and where the clouds broke, the stars crossed the sky in lines. The others followed Grundy into the river.

They moved down in a line, riding the current, and Luke Ryan could hear voices on the bank. He looked up and there were two Serbs at the top of the river bank, pissing into the water. In the moonlight their faces were tight and dark and sharp and their mouths were worn. They carried bottles and spoke in whispers as if they were afraid someone would hear them.

The river slowed before the pontoon bridge and Luke Ryan could see Grundy's head ahead of him in the water against the pontoon. He could see a checkpoint on the dirt track which led up the river bank to the main Banja Luka road and a Serb soldier at the checkpoint, and then there was water in Ryan's mouth and his head was under the water.

For a moment Ryan thought he was drowning. He felt he should struggle and tried to, but the weight of the water was too much and his combats and his equipment helped take him under and he fell deeper into the cold water and felt the cold invade all of him so that it wasn't cold any more, just peaceful, and he was giving up.

Then he was up again, water rushing around him, a strong burning in his throat and lungs. He took a deep breath and dipped his head under water again.

When he came up, Ryan had overcome his desire to cough. He floated on. He could see the main road and the lower slopes of Vrh. The woods on those slopes stood tall in the moonlight and the early morning blue.

Then Grundy was at the bank below the pontoon on the northern side. Grundy lay flat for a while and Muha came into the shallows behind him. They could feel the rolling stones of the shallows under their feet and on their hands when they were pulling themselves in against the current of the river. And the river went off ahead of them into the silver of the moonlight and between the bridge pontoons.

Ryan watched Grundy move up the bank and then fall flat. Yves had passed Ryan and was moving up the south bank. Away in the distance the crescent moonlight had caught the snowcapped peaks of far-away mountains and they seemed to glow in the darkness. Grundy edged along the river bank and pulled himself up on his feet again. Then Muha followed him.

There were trees to the left of the pontoon bridge climbing the bank towards the road in a heavy group. Right of the trees was a line of white limestone boulders and then smaller brown stones and the trees and other vegetation moved in and around these stones.

Grundy looked across the river and made a signal to Yves and then pulled out his Hush Puppy. He unplugged and uncapped the Hush Puppy, checked the weapon and removed the safety. Then he started to move up the bank towards the guard post. There were loose stones and pieces of root and branch sticking out that did not hold when you pulled on them and when Grundy pulled on a piece of stick coming from the soil he fell back and almost trumbled down the slope. But he got his hands and elbows into the bank and dragged himself up. When he was at the top he lay flat and then brought his head up.

The guard post at the bridge was less than twenty metres away and Grundy could hear them talking. There were three he could see. They were standing at a brazier made out of three biscuit tins soldered together. There was a caravan across the dirt road and maybe a man in it. An aerial stuck out of the top of the caravan and ran into the trees and up the rest of the river bank to one of the houses further along the main road.

There were two steel anti-tank barriers beside the caravan and behind it, almost hidden, was a BTR-40 armoured personnel carrier. The BTR-40 carries a crew of ten but its weapon is only a 7.62mm machine-gun. Grundy waited, and below him Muha took up a covering position on the bank.

Across the river Yves had pulled his own Hush Puppy out and was moving up the bank to the cargo container on the dirt road into the mountains on that side. He stood with his back to the container and listened. Luke Ryan covered him from the river below. Ryan could feel nothing and his mouth was dry.

They waited. The moon disappeared behind cloud and there was a gust of wind down the line of the river and a series of low-calibre mortar impacts from the Evkaf valley area.

Grundy watched the three Serbs at the brazier and listened to their conversation. They were all in their thirties and were talking about a woman and blowing into their hands. Two of them had their AK47 rifles over their backs and the other had his lying against a box beside the brazier. He was drinking coffee.

Ryan looked at his watch and held his breath.

Then Grundy stood up, levelled his Hush Puppy and shot the Serb drinking the coffee. The silenced bullet entered the back of the man's skull from a distance of three metres and blew out the left side of his head. The next bullet went into his neck. He fell forward, his coffee cup tipped into the brazier and a column of steam rose out of the embers. The man to his left was trying to get to his rifle when he died. Two bullets hit him in the head and sent him back on the dirt road. The third Serb soldier tried to catch the man who had been drinking coffee and reached for his AK47, slung over his back, at the same time. He dropped his friend and tried to get the rifle to bear on Grundy's figure, but it was too late and Grundy's fifth bullet hit him in the chest. The next bullet hit him through the right eye and he saw Grundy's foot come up and kick him in the stomach but he did not feel the kick and was already dead when his body hit the broken road. Muha moved into cover for Grundy.

Across the river, Yves walked around to the front of the

cargo container and Ryan moved up the bank after him. There were three Serbs in the container, playing cards and drinking. One was seventy-five. Yves shot the two nearest men with a single bullet each to the head. Both fell forward on to the makeshift card table and their blood ran across the breadboard they had been using, over a heap of cards and matchsticks and over the rim of the board and on to the floor.

The third man was about to scream but Yves had shot him before he could get the sound out. Yves shot him in the throat and the head and the man reached for his throat when the second bullet was entering his head. His head kicked back and he let go his throat. Blood spurted from his throat and he fell back on to the cold metal floor of the container and twitched for a while until Yves put another bullet into his head.

Another Serb soldier had been sitting in the BTR-40, drinking a coffee when Grundy killed his friends. They all came from the same village around Banja Luka and none of them had seen any real fighting because they were guarding the pontoon bridge. The fourth Serb heard the bodies of his friends hit the ground and heard a small muted shout from the second man and the sound of his AK scraping the stony road when he fell back. The fourth Serb put his head out and called one of their names.

Muha's pistol was pointed directly behind Grundy.

The Serb jumped out and levelled his rifle.

Grundy froze.

Muha fired.

The bullets hit the Serb's head and took the top off his skull. He jerked violently, as if someone had punched him, and fell into a thorn bush and wet, icy grass.

Muha shot him one more time in the back of the head and gave a single whistle.

Grundy blew air out between his teeth and looked at Muha. Then he pointed to the caravan.

Muha crouched down, picked up a pebble and threw it at the caravan window. Then he moved across the dirt road and stood against the caravan. There was a movement inside. Muha made a fist and knocked on the door.

'Zdravo, druze,' he said.

There was more noise inside. Someone pulling on a pair of boots. The latch on the door moved and the door opened and the man inside muttered. He was wearing combat trousers with bulging side pockets and a vest with braces over it. One of the braces was loose. He rubbed his eyes and opened them and asked what was going on. Muha shot him three times in the chest and twice in the head and the man jumped back into the caravan and cracked his head on a table and a chair and broke the chair. He was not dead when Muha climbed into the caravan and Muha shot him again through the mouth while he was on the ground.

At the other end of the bridge, Yves was coming out of the cargo container, reloading his Hush Puppy. He saw the man across the road who had been in the bushes taking a piss and he saw the man's rifle aimed at him. He was an old man, with white hair, and his girth made him look a bit like Grundy and for a moment Yves thought it was Grundy. Then the rounds struck.

The Serb was lifted off his feet and his body spread while it was in mid-air and Ryan's Hush Puppy rounds continued to pump into his body with the sound of a boxer hitting a punch bag. The Serb fell back into the bushes where he had relieved himself and there was a long release of air from his lungs that sounded like a car tyre deflating.

Ryan walked over to the dead Serb and emptied the remainder of his magazine into the body. Then he changed magazines and walked back towards Yves. Yves clicked out a morse signal on his walkie-talkie.

On the north bank, Grundy grabbed the first dead Serb at the brazier, pulled him into the trees at the side of the road and took his AK47 and stood in his place. Then Muha stripped the second man and threw the body down the bank into the river.

On his side, Ryan took a Serb AK and moved out on to the pontoon bridge and took up a covering position.

Then Njofra and two bricks of men came out of the treeline above him, moved over the bridge and took up positions either side of the northern guard post. Njofra signalled from the far side of the bridge.

Another four bricks of Bosnian mountain troops and Black
Berets came out of the trees, ran across the bridge to the APC
and took up position.

Ryan was breathing so heavily he thought the whole world
would hear him. He swung his head round until his neck felt
as if it would snap.

A third line of Bosnian bricks came out of the trees and
began advancing across the bridge. One of them stopped and
took Ryan's position over and gave Ryan his MP5D and G3.
Ryan started moving across the pontoon bridge.

The sound of the boots on the sand and metal over the
sound of wind and the river was a hard scraping and
each time Ryan heard that he felt someone would yell
and the firing would start and they would be caught in
the open crossing a river, with Serbs on both side and
nowhere to run.

Yves and three of the Bosnian mountain soldiers got down
in the pontoons and set plastic explosive charges and three
booby traps.

The light was cooling the deep blue of the dawn and the
sun was throwing its scouting rays out of the ridges of the
mountain folds. Ryan looked at his watch, then at Muha. Muha
did not respond. Ryan felt like shooting him again but the
thought passed. The Bosnian mountain soldiers were crawling
up the river gorge to the main road. Ryan went over to Grundy
in the Serb APC.

The APC was almost bare inside except for an AK47
and a small football holdall. The football bag was an AC
Milan bag and there were girlie magazines and condoms
and hand-grenades inside it. Ryan picked up one of the
magazines and looked at it for a few seconds but he could
not work up any interest in it now.

'Save it for me,' Grundy said.

'You gotta buy it,' Ryan said.

'Give the grenades to Yves,' Grundy said. 'Use 'em here.
See what else you can pick up, Luke. Strip everythin'. Give
it to whoever needs it.'

Ryan nodded. He picked up the holdall and climbed out of
the APC.

'Half an hour,' Grundy whispered after him. 'We got half an hour.'

Ryan did not stop.

'Njofra,' Grundy said, 'get the RPGs set up along the road. I don't wanna get my tail shot off by a column of tanks we don't know about.'

'The APC?'

'Set it to blow. It's no good to us,' Grundy said.

He pulled himself up and checked his weapons.

'Now all we need is Jusef to keep his nerve,' he said.

Then he moved off up the bank towards the Banja Luka road.

Up on the main road at the cargo container checkpoint before the dirt track to Bor, two of the Serb military police had come out of their positions around the crash barrier and anti-tank obstacles and run across the road to see what the shout was. One of them had his pistol drawn and his AK47 rifle by the grip and pointed towards the ground. Grundy stepped out from behind a small tree.

Both men turned to him. He shot off six nine-millimetre rounds, three into each man and they fell back side by side in the middle of the road. A third military policeman came out of the cargo container still doing his uniform up. He was pulling his white webbing straps over his shoulder when he realised he had forgotten his weapon.

Yves cut him from the neck to the stomach with his Siberian Kandra and the MP slumped to his knees and spilled the contents of his body on to the broken tarmac road. Yves pulled the Kandra out of the Serb's body and cut his head off with a second swipe. The torso remained where it was, propped up on the legs, and the head rolled across the road and into the small oaks there and then down to the river. Two Bosnian mountain soldiers came out of the trees, grabbed the bloodied torso and pulled it into cover and four more covered each other across the road to the guard post. They held themselves at the cargo container and watched the Serb flag billowing. Grundy and Yves went on either side of the container entrance.

Grundy nodded at Yves and Yves moved into the container. There were two Serbs and a woman lying on a camp bed. One of the Serbs made a grab for a gun and the other dropped a bottle of *Sljivovica* he had been holding over the woman. Grundy fired.

The bullets hit all three at the same time and Grundy did not take his finger off the trigger until his magazine was empty. The three bodies danced around each other on the camp bed and Yves fired single shots at them while they writhed together on the bed.

Grundy looked at his watch.

28

The blue came slowly, like a gentle fade-in on a movie screen, and the sounds of early morning announced the day before it arrived. The pre-day darkness was a snow-streaked blue-green and brown and the blue-green was giving way to deeper green and the brown was slowly turning red at the edges of the snow streaks. The whole scene was frozen in an icy haze.

In the Bosnian lines, the first wave of Jusef Husic's assault infantry huddled close to the walls of their forward trenches, overweight with ammunition and equipment. Their faces were white and tired and unshaven and the men shivered in the cold. Some of them talked to themselves in silent mouth movements, others stared at the ice on the trench walls and the long buttresses. They all breathed through their teeth to avoid any chance of frozen breath giving their numbers away. They had been moving into position since midnight two days before, in small groups, and some of them had been there since then. Behind them were more soldiers, waiting to go in as the second and third waves.

Husic smoked a cigarette, picked up a cup of cold *turska kava*, sipped the liquid and looked at his watch. Two of his officers sat round a map of the Serb positions stretched out on the floor. Husic took out another cigarette but did not light it. Then he picked up a rifle in the corner of the room, nodded at one of his officers and winked at the other.

The first officer, a small man with a limp, who had been wounded in the leg early on in the war, took his own rifle, tightened his webbing belt and made it comfortable on his back. Then the second officer gave the order to the mortars behind Donje Selo to fire on the Serb line below Vrh.

Husic looked at his watch when he heard the first 120mm mortar cough – that dry morning cough he had grown so used to hearing.

The shell impact was long and the shell hit the remains of a wall and sent pieces of stone in three hundred and sixty degrees around the shallow impact crater. A Serb out taking an early-morning piss on the lower slopes of Vrh was caught in the back of the head by a piece of stone and fell forward into the spot where he had relieved himself. Someone yelled *Pazi . . .* !

At the sound of the first mortar impact, Grundy pulled himself up from where he lay below the village of Bor, one hundred metres to the right of the dirt track leading from the main Banja Luka road to the crest of Vrh on that side.

On the other side of the dirt track, Muha and his Black Berets picked themselves up and moved into position to cover the left flank of Grundy's attack.

Then Yves and a section of Bosnian mountain soldiers led by a fat shopkeeper called Emir, moved out of their cover on the north side of Bor, directly opposite Grundy, and ran for the last house at the west end of the village on the north side.

And Luke Ryan moved uphill at full pace behind Grundy, panting, over broken branches and rocks and across frozen packed snow, focusing his eyes on the minaret at the Bor mosque.

To his right, he heard more Bosnian mortar shells hit the Serb line in the valley at the base of Vrh.

Then there was a shout ahead of him, and then a shot, then more shouting and more shooting.

Two Serbs appeared in the trees in front of Ryan, half dressed and holding rifles. He shot them.

Muha and his team, moving in line abreast formation at the south western edge of Bor, caught five Serbs rushing out of a house at that end of the village. The Serbs had been sleeping in the cellar. All the houses in the village were destroyed above ground level and the Serbs had been using the cellars as billets for men not on trench duty.

The five Serbs fell dead in a single line across the broken street in Bor.

Muha's team then threw grenades into the *kavana* at the southwest edge of the village and smashed their way into the building, firing.

Two more Serbs came out of a house across the street. They got ten metres and never fired a shot. Yves and Emir shot them dead.

Then Yves threw six grenades in a bag into the stone house across from the kavana and the rest of Emir's section kicked their way in and cleared the house of Serbs.

On the south side of the village, Grundy led Vinko Herak's section into a small hollow between two houses. The mosque was about fifty metres away, to the right, and there was a dead Serb lying in front of it beside an armoured personnel carrier. Grundy signalled with his hand.

One man carrying an RPG7 moved to Grundy's left, supported by two covers. The centre man pulled the RPG7 off his back and took out a rocket, placed it in the launcher and took aim and fired at a Serb APC.

The RPG is a High Explosive Anti-Tank weapon and relies on a shaped charge to achieve penetration. The shaped charge is high explosive formed around a thin-walled metal cone, usually copper. The open end of the cone faces the target and is covered by a hollow ballistic cap. The fuse and detonator are at the rear of the charge. When the projectle impacts, the cone collapses and a jet forms on a central axis at a very high velocity. This high-velocity jet is what achieves the penetration.

The Serb BTR-40 opened like a tin can and the front end of its roof came back as if someone had peeled it.

Two more RPG men from Vinko Herak's section took up positions to the right of the first man. They fired their projectiles at white sandbagged houses left and right of the mosque.

The RPG is vulnerable to crosswind and needs to be operated by a skilled user but at that time of the morning there was very little wind and all the RPG projectiles found their targets.

Njofra, Ryan and Vinko Herak supported the RPG fire with rifle grenades which fell in a diagonal line towards the mosque.

And then the RPG men systematically fired rockets into every house in the village.

Then Ekrem Delic, a thin bony one-eyed man, who had been a retired professional soldier before the war, led his section through Vinko Herak's and kicked in the side door of the large white sandbagged house on the south side of the mosque.

Five Serbs were already dead from two RPGs and Ekrem's men caught three Serbs at the door, two more inside and eight in the cellar when they burst in.

And when Ekrem's section were in the house to the south of the mosque, they covered Grundy, Ryan and Ibrahim's section while they ran for the mosque.

And to their right, they could still hear the Bosnian mortars around Donje Selo continuing to pound the Serb forward line at the base of Vrh.

And Ryan was high.

He was firing three-round bursts with a G3 and shouting things he did not know the meaning of. And he did not care about anything any more, just being and firing and shouting. He shot a Serb with no boots and another man in a broken window and a third Serb coming from the front line trenches below Vrh.

He could hear the blanket sound of heavy machine gun fire from the valley floor below and he imagined the Bosnian assault soldiers there out of their trenches, running for the Serb line.

Serb soldiers in Bor were now coming out of their billets in a kind of staggered disorder. Some just ran away. Others made a fight.

Muha's men caught them from their positions in the *kavana* and the remains of the house beside it.

'*Allah u akbar!*'

Some of the younger Serbs panicked when they heard this and threw away their weapons and were shot in the back by Muha's men.

By then, Grundy's men had made it to the mosque.

Grundy threw four grenades into the mosque and one of the mountain soldiers behind him kicked what passed for a door in and a comrade threw another grenade in. Ibrahim stuck the barrel of a PK machine gun in and sprayed the inside of the mosque.

They found ten dead Serbs on the sodden carpets inside. Six of them were half dressed.

The mosque was a plain structure of old stone and whitewash, peppered with shell impact and shrapnel holes and full of brandy bottles and pieces of food and the smell of human defecation. There was old arabic script on the walls and a rack with shoes still on it from where they had been left on the first day of the war. Snow had fallen through a huge hole in the dome and gathered in the centre of the carpets. The carpets were in shreds.

When Grundy's men were in the mosque, Njofra and Vinko Herak's section picked themselves up and moved across the village street, firing as they ran.

They cleared out the house on the north side of the mosque and set up a crossfire with Muha's men at the other end of the village. And any Serbs still in the village street were cut to pieces.

Ryan and Ibrahim Abdic's men began hacking out holes in the east wall of the mosque.

Around them, in the trees to the north of the village and from the back slopes of Vrh and the valleys behind, Serb mortars and artillery had begun to respond. But it was wild undirected firing, and most of it landed away from its targets.

Two of Ibrahim Abdic's mountain soldiers knocked a small hole at a wooden balcony in the mosque wall into a bigger hole. Grundy and another of Ibrahim's men took positions on either side of the new hole ready to fire.

Instead, Grundy cursed out loud.

A thin veil of mist still shrouded the Evkaf valley floor and much of the mountainside below them, and all they could see from the mosque were the shattered roofs of scattered houses and the tops of trees and the remains of the roofs of the taller buildings in Donje Selo and the tips of the smoke columns from the impacts of the Bosnian mortars at the Serb front line.

The rising sun burned hard into the mist from behind Evkaf town and the mist was clearing from the east in streaks, but it was a slow fight. Grundy cursed again.

Then a Serb appeared from the mist, along the main track running down to the forward trenches at the base of Vrh. Grundy shot him. A volley of Serb rifle fire came back at him out of the mist and the trees.

Grundy swung back against the mosque wall for cover and cursed some more.

The mountain soldier stood on the other side of the hole, took an RPG and on Grundy's signal he went down on one knee and fired a rocket at a house directly below the mosque. The rocket hit the house and Grundy then swung from cover and opened fire with a PK machine gun, holding it at his waist in a standing position.

And, on Grundy's order, Ryan and the rest of Ibrahim's men opened fire down the mountain into the mist, supported by men from Vinko Herak's and Ekrem's sections in the houses on either side of the mosque.

Grundy looked at his watch and listened to the position reports on his walkie-talkie and called through a code word to Jusef Husic. The single reply came back.

Grundy thought and looked at the mist for a few more seconds and wondered ...

Then a group of Serbs in the trees below the mosque tried to assault the mosque position in a frontal attack. But the mosque was too difficult to take from that side because it was on a limestone outcrop that went straight up about fifteen metres and the Serbs were beaten back.

But the Serbs in and around Bor were starting to organise.

The surviving Serbs in the village were jammed into three houses in the centre of the village, caught in triangular fire between Yves's men working their way west to east along the north side, Muha's men around the *kavana* and the Bosnian positions around the mosque.

But the Serbs were fighting.

And Yves's men were held up.

Yves called through for support from Grundy.

Grundy gave a general order to secure the village.

In the mosque, Ibrahim's men dug in and covered the mountainside with PK machine guns and Grundy took Ryan and Njofra and joined Vinko Herak's section in the house on the north side of the mosque.

Herak left three of his men to guard his position and Grundy led the rest towards Yves's men, coming from the other end of the village on that side, supported by Muha's men at the *kavana*.

And on the south side of the village, Ekrem started moving along the line of houses towards Muha, using Yves to support his flank.

The Serb anchor in Bor was a house on the north side of the village between Yves and Grundy. It was a grey house with baroque decoration in the stonework, and the walls were sandbagged. The cellar had been a billet for thirty Serb soldiers. Serb stragglers from the frontal assault and the billets around the mosque had all gathered in there, too. They were not well armed, but because of Muha's men, they were motivated by sheer terror.

Yves made two efforts to take the house but his force was too small and did not have enough surprise when they attacked. He lost two men dead and Emir wounded.

Grundy's team cleared two houses and Ekrem and Muha's men broke a small group of Serbs firing from the ruins of a house on the south side of the village.

The Serbs in this house tried to get out into the woods behind the village, firing from the hip and shouting for cover. But the concentration and ferocity of Ekrem's attack, and the mess caused by grenades in a confined space, caused most of the Serbs to run out into the village street.

The Bosnians caught nine Serbs out in the open this way and killed them all with a single volley of automatic fire. Then Ekrem's men, supported by Muha, cleared the house of those left inside.

Grundy's men cleared another house on his side of the village. They based themselves around a PK machine gun and each man threw two grenades into the Serb house and fired off a full magazine and Ryan and another man swung round the back door and caught the Serbs inside in retreat.

Ryan was on his stomach, firing.

He hit a Serb in the arm and then took a barrage of fire from a new Serb position he had not seen before, in the beech trees at the edge of the forest to his right.

There were two small Serb positions in those trees now and they were firing on the two Bosnian teams advancing along the north side of the village.

Around him, Luke Ryan could see the smoke of the battle and taste the battle on his tongue and smell the cordite and the gun oil and the other smells of battle, and he could not tell what was happening more than a few metres from himself.

It was a confusion of sight and sound, an overload of emotion, and Ryan watched it and saw soldiers running left and right of him and fired at a couple of them and heard incoming rounds near his head and the sounds of bullets and shell fragments tearing pieces of masonry and rock and bits of tree. And he could smell the resin from the pine trees and the sickly smell of blood and charred flesh from the dead bodies and the smells blended and became one.

And he wondered how far up Vrh Jusef Husic's men were and what the Serbs were doing around the mountain.

On the main road to Banja Luka, fifty Serb soldiers and five T34 tanks were preparing to counterattack up Vrh.

The tanks had been in camouflaged positions to the west of Vrh, in a ravine the Bosnians could never have seen from Sljiva.

The Serb tank commander had originally been told to counterattack immediately, without infantry support, but he refused to advance up Vrh without support.

Tanks and mountains do not go well together at the best of times; tanks are too vulnerable to infantry with anti-tank equipment, and tank commanders will not readily go charging into mountainous terrain without the support of sweeping infantry on their flanks.

A unit of Serb infantry and five APCs were coming across the pontoon bridge towards the Banja Luka road at the same time as the T34s were organising with supporting infantry to advance up the dirt track to Bor. The men on the bridge were shouting at each other and at men across the river. One of the T34s stalled.

Then the bridge blew up.

The lead APC had passed the centre point and the last APC was just out enough to topple into the water. The soldiers walking across the bridge were all blown into the water and it swallowed them as if they had never been there at all. One of the APCs was blown to pieces but the others just tipped into the river and held there until, one by one, the water from the mountains brought them rolling over and over down the river bed. Now and then you could see a body emerge from beneath the flowing river water.

That was when Horst started firing.

He hit the first Serb through the head with a tungsten-tipped arrow and the second through the heart. A medieval longbow arrow could go through chain mail and still pin a man to his horse. Horst pinned a Serb to the tree he was standing beside and another to the man beside him.

When he had fired off ten arrows and killed six men, he began to fire his grenades. They landed line abreast and caught the Serb military police running along the Banja Luka road, trying to direct the armour to its counterattack position.

The Serbs scattered all over the road and down the river embankment and began firing in the direction they thought Horst was firing from.

But Horst had moved.

He had moved up Vrh towards Muha's position in the *kavana* on the southwest side of Bor. He threw his bow over his back and took out a noise suppressor and screwed it on to his G3 barrel. A noise suppressor will keep the noise of a round leaving a rifle barrel down to levels where it is difficult to pinpoint the direction of the shot and the position of the sniper. It is not a silencer, it just diffuses the gases, muffles the noise at the muzzle and eliminates muzzle flash.

Horst had killed his first Serb officer while the Serbs were still firing into the position where they thought the arrows had come from.

He shot an officer and three NCOs in quick succession and kept moving in a wide arc zigzagging up the mountain towards Muha's position.

The Serbs on the Banja Luka road were in the ditches and among the trees, taking cover, and their tanks were moving into cover positions along the side of the road, trying to avoid being caught out in the open by any Bosnian anti-tank rockets.

The Serbs on the road were calling through to their pockets in the trees around Bor, a Serb colonel trying to get an account of what was going on there, when Spit came into play.

He was directly opposite Horst, but much further away. He caught the growing Serb command post, centred on the colonel, out in the open from that side. They were sheltering from Horst behind a treeline and an APC when Spit's first round struck home. It was a mercury tip and it took part of the head off a Serb NCO who had begun to smile at the corner of the APC. The second round hit a captain in the back and the Lapua Magnum round took most of his right lung out through his chest.

A single Serb tank had begun to climb the dirt track up Vrh to Bor, surrounded by infantry, and Horst and Spit caught them in a sniper crossfire.

The Serbs dived both ways and were caught by the sniper fire. Spit's rounds were designed to cause more immediate terror and the sight of a comrade being hit by doctored Lapua Magnum rounds made some of the Serbs, already in a state of confused terror, start falling back on the road behind them. Advancing men ran into Horst's shots and then turned and ran back into Spit's rounds. They called for support from their pockets around Bor, but those men just screamed for support from the Serbs on the road.

The Serb tank stalled. It fired off three shells in the direction of Bor and the commander threw his hatch open and screamed back at the infantry around him to stop running away.

It was the last thing he ever did. Horst and Spit caught him at the same time and he slid back into the tank.

Another tank began to come forward in support. It fired half a dozen shells at Bor and one where it thought Horst's rounds were coming from. But Horst had moved again and the tank round killed five Serbs below Muha's position.

Small units of Serbs in the trees southwest of the village were attempting to force Muha's men out. Some of them had run away and come back and others had come up from billets behind Vrh. Ten of them were military police from three checkpoints along the Banja Luka road.

And in his position at the end of the village, with some of his men still trying to link up with Ekrem, Muha was vulnerable.

The Serb teams in the trees around Muha made two assaults on his position. Two of Yves's men in the house across the street, armed with a grenade launcher and a PK machine-gun, were able to help Muha beat back the Serb assaults on the *kavana*, but Serb mortar fire from around the mountain was beginning to co-ordinate with the infantry.

Fifteen mortar rounds landed in and around the *kavana* in one barrage. Then two teams of Serbs launched a frontal attack from the forest there. Muha's men beat it back. He shouted into his walkie-talkie for support.

Then the Serbs tried to force the house across the street, but Grundy and Ekrem were able to give cover and Muha's position caught the Serbs in a crossfire and they fell back again. But Muha lost another Black Beret.

He radioed through to Grundy for support again.

Grundy told him there was no one to spare. To hold his position.

Muha cursed Grundy.

The Bosnians were now in command of every house in the village except the grey house with the baroque architecture. And Grundy knew his time allowance was close to running out.

He called to Ryan to organise cover fire and told Yves and Njofra to lead flanking moves left and right of the house. Ryan and three mountain soldiers emptied their magazines and Grundy and Njofra moved forward left and right of him.

Serb rocket-propelled grenades landed behind them.

Ryan thought they would die then. It was as if the earth was in a rage and the anger was the battle.

But Grundy inched forward.

He made his way along a broken wall and down into a ditch that had been part of a garden. Yves moved towards Grundy with three Bosnian mountain soldiers behind him. And Njofra tried to use rubble and a drainage ditch to move to their left.

But the Serbs saw them and caught Njofra and his men out in the open. Vinko Herak was killed by a single round, a small hole in the side of his head, blood trickling from this on to a piece of broken limestone. Another man lost a leg and was screaming for the medic.

Grundy radioed Muha and told him to put everything he had into the Serb-held house.

Muha said he was trying to hold off the Serbs in the forest around him. He screamed at Ekrem to get a move on. Ekrem roared back that he was supporting Grundy against the grey house across the street, Muha would have to hold on longer.

That was when Muha said he was launching a frontal attack on the grey house himself.

Grundy shouted abuse at him.

Muha told Grundy he was his superior and if someone did not force the Serbs out they would lose the village.

The Black Berets ran at the grey house in a line, firing from the hip.

They got as far as the street. Two Black Berets were killed and one had to be dragged into cover by the legs. Muha covered the retreat lying on his back, but his men did not make it back to the *kavana*, instead they fell into the next house down. And the Serbs in the trees made a dash for the *kavana*.

Five of them made it to the *kavana* but they were caught from three different Bosnian firing positions and ended up down on their bellies firing in all directions.

They managed to kill four of their own men running up to help them from the pine woods to the northwest of the village. Yves's men in the house across the street fired into this group of Serbs, too.

Luke Ryan saw one Serb hit by fifteen different rounds. The man almost disintegrated under the assault. His shoulder came loose, his knee was blown out, his spine smashed and his pelvis cleaved off. His neck exploded, his right eye came out, his chin shattered and his chest spat blood. But he was still standing and his square Chetnik hat was falling from his head, very slowly. His blue, red and white Serb ribbons had come free with his severed shoulder and he spun as if he was looking to see who had shot him. Several more rounds hit him and he just stood as if he was being supported by the rounds alone.

Muha and Grundy were still in the middle of an argument when Ibrahim came in on the walkie-talkie from his position at the mosque.

'Something's not right, Grundy,' he said.

'Say again,' Grundy said.

There was a pause and crackle and Muha asked Ibrahim to repeat himself.

'There's no movement between the lines, Grundy, I'm looking at it now. The mist is clearing at Donje Selo, I can see nothing. No fighting on the mountain. Our mortars are firing but there is nothing happening. Nothing has moved from our lines.'

'Aw, shit,' Grundy said.

'What should I do?' Ibrahim said.

'Stay put,' Grundy said. 'You hear that, Muha? Our song's off air.'

Muha did not answer.

Then, suddenly, Celo's voice came in on the walkie-talkies. His tone was subdued, almost as if he was reading a prepared statement.

'You will please hold your ground until relieved,' he said. 'Hold your positions, please.'

Muha shouted at him to clarify the situation but Celo did not come back. Grundy called for Husic. Again, there was no reply. Njofra tumbled in beside Grundy.

'Something's not right,' he said.

He said it very quietly as if he did not want to hear it himself in case it was true.

Grundy called Husic again. Then he looked across at Ryan and Ryan's face was whiter than the houses.

Ibrahim came in on the walkie-talkie and said what everyone wanted to say. In a kind of strained panic.

'Where the fuck are they?'

Grundy started to laugh. He shook his head and laughed hard. Ryan kept looking over from where he was lying and asking what was happening on his walkie-talkie. Then he started to smile, because it was a choice between smiling and screaming, and his smile gathered momentum and then he laughed, too. And then Njofra laughed and shook his head and slid down the wall.

Serb rounds hit the walls and stones all round them but Ryan could not hear the firing, only the laughing.

'What's happening?' Muha yelled. 'Celo!'

Serb mortar rounds hit the area around the *kavana* and killed two of the remaining Serbs there as they tried to get inside the building. The other two made it.

At the same time, Horst was moving to link up with Muha in the *kavana*.

He lay flat in some scrub beside the ruins of a small workshop, which had made religious artefacts, just south of the village. There were some crucifixes and statues of saints and the Virgin still lying in the ruins of the workshop.

Horst reloaded his G3 and removed the noise suppressor. There were Serbs around him but he could see the *kavana* thirty metres ahead of him. He took three deep breaths, picked himself up and ran, yelling for cover fire from the *kavana*.

The first round from the *kavana* caught him between the neck and shoulder and he dropped his walkie-talkie and reached for the entrance wound.

The round had clipped his collarbone and tumbled back across the centre of one lung and out below the level of his nipple.

Horst shouted at the *kavana* to stop firing, but his shouts were drowned out by the noise of the battle.

The second round, from the trees behind him, was from an AK74 and it came from behind, hit him to the right of the spine and came out his pelvis.

He swung his weapon and got off ten shots at the Serbs in the trees behind him, and one of the Serbs, a town official from Evkaf before the war, who had held on until a visit from Muha's Black Berets made him and his family leave, was hit.

The Serb was hit in the shoulder and the bullet spun him and he took another round through the back and fell to the ground. He saw his blood leak into the snow and said something about not being able to feel his legs and how cold it was. He was a

bald man with glasses and one of his legs was shorter than the
other; he had been called up late into the Serb army because of
this. He lay on the ground watching the sky cloud over from
the northeast and feeling the cold of the wind on his face and
the cold of the bleeding in his body and reaching down for
his legs.

Horst was still running when four more rounds hit him from
the *kavana* and the trees behind at the same time. He cursed
at Muha but Muha wasn't there.

Horst tried to get his longbow off his shoulders and fire his
G3 with one hand.

A bullet hit his cheek and came out beneath his skull. Horst
went down on one knee and staggered and pulled himself back
up on his feet.

A young student who didn't know much about weapons
fired a whole AK74 magazine at Horst and most of it missed.
But the last five rounds hit him across the abdomen. None of
the rounds came out.

Horst killed the student, crashed against the *kavana* wall,
spun and fired back at three Serbs behind him and staggered
around the *kavana* and fell to his knees.

He was hit three more times from the forest.

He crawled out to the edge of the village street and loosed off
the rest of his G3 rounds. One of his bullets killed a Serb trying
to drag a wounded friend out of the village. But Horst was hit
again in the neck and in the head and the G3 slipped from his
hand and he put his hand down for his side arm but another
round caught his hand and took two of his fingers off.

And all the time he thought.

Of a small village in Bohemia where he had been a secret
police informant, of the blossoms on the trees where he met
his contact, of the athletes he had spied on when he was one
of them and the girl who killed herself because of it and the
shame he felt. And he was still shouting for Grundy.

And the Bosnian situation in the village was getting
desperate.

Muha was down to four men and five magazines each.
Ekrem had linked up with him but the Serb defenders in the
grey baroque house and the two Serbs in the *kavana* had the

Bosnians pinned down. And the Serbs in the trees south and west of the village were on the verge of moving in to reinforce their position in the *kavana*.

And added to all this, it was all around the Bosnian soldiers that something was very wrong.

The Serbs who were dug in on either side of the *kavana* on the south and west sides of the village, preparing to reinforce the *kavana*, lost their advantage when their own mortars refused to fire in support.

The NCO commanding this Serb infantry shouted into his walkie-talkie for mortar support. He had already sent two men back down the mountain for RPGs. But the mortar teams behind him insisted they could not fire any more without hitting their own men. And they would not risk it.

Muha took advantage of this and led his and Ekrem's men in an attack to retake the *kavana*.

When he was back in the *kavana* he screamed into his walkie-talkie for Husic or Celo and threatened to kill both of them if they did not answer. Then the Serbs around him launched a front assault and he stopped transmitting.

The sight of Muha retaking the *kavana* together with Yves's attack broke the Serb resistance in the grey house.

Grundy covered Yves with two grenades and two magazines of automatic fire and Yves rolled out into the open and put an RPG rocket into the house.

Ryan thought at first that Yves was hit but the Legionnaire just rolled over and moved around to another angle and put another rocket into the house. This one caught some of the Serbs trying to get out after the first explosion.

The survivors of the rockets tried to run and were cut down by crossfire from Grundy's team, Yves's men.

Muha's men ran out of ammunition at that time.

Luke Ryan slid in behind the remains of a stone shed, rested his head on a sandbag and closed his eyes.

He could hear Muha screaming for Husic on his walkie-talkie.

At that moment, two kilometres away on Crna Gora, Jusef Husic ordered the rest of his mortars to open fire.

The barrage was short and furious and concentrated on a one-hundred-metre section of the Serb line on Crna Gora.

It was followed so closely by the first wave of Bosnian assault infantry that some of the Bosnians were killed by their own fire.

But they caught the Serb front line troops on Crna Gora completely by surprise.

Husic's first wave came out of the trees and the smoke on Crna Gora and poured into the hundred-metre stretch of Serb trenches they had picked for bombardment. Men threw themselves on wire and others ran across the men lying on the wire. And the Serbs on Crna Gora broke and ran.

Below Vrh, the mist had completely lifted.

29

The flames touched the evening skyline at the level of the pine trees which stood in rows along the folds of Vrh and then down to the sides of the mountain to the west and south. The flames spread out along the lines of trees and burned into the snow and the snow caught the hard midday light and held it for the flames.

The paint on the Serb armoured personnel carrier blistered and burst in the heat of the flames and then the fuel went and the heart of the carrier shot up to the height of the highest pines and held itself there in a rage of fire. Luke Ryan sat down against the wall of the *kavana* in Bor and felt the heat of the burning APC and a burning three-storey house in front of him.

'Who won?' he said.

Grundy scooped a handful of snow and touched his beard with it, then reached into his pocket and pulled out a hunk of stale bread, broke the bread and handed it to Yves and Ryan.

'You'd think they'd have some damn chow around here,' Grundy said. 'Gimme some of that wine, Yves.'

Yves pulled the bottle of wine he had looted out of his knapsack and gave it to Grundy. Grundy said something in Hebrew.

'Pick his personal stuff up, will you, Luke?' he said then. He nodded towards Horst.

Ryan pulled himself up from the wall on his rifle, went over to Horst and crouched down at the body. He picked up Horst's longbow and the two halves of the bow fell apart in his hands and one toppled on to Horst's corpse.

Grundy opened the wine bottle, sniffed inside and took a mouthful to taste. He moved the wine around in his mouth and spat it out into a patch of snow. A snowflake landed on his hand and Grundy watched it dissolve under the heat of the fires around him. Then he looked around at the other bodies.

There were bodies lying all over the street at different angles to each other and the thin snowfalls earlier in the day had coated them in very delicate white shrouds.

Njofra came out of the *kavana*, carrying a stick of bread and some bottles of clear liquid.

'They're coming again,' he said. 'I don't think we'll hold them this time. More tanks.'

'I come as a fuckin' saviour and end up a fuckin' vulture,' Ryan said.

'That's always the way of it, Luke. Check everythin'. If he's got any cash, share it out, anythin' personal, give it to me.'

'He give it to you in his will, Grundy?' Yves said.

'Well, he didn't fuckin' give it to you, Legionnaire. Jesus Christ! Take his boots, Luke, he has good boots, and mine are fucked, and see if he still has that Swiss army knife. Come on, before the Chetniks get here. They'll take everythin' we don't.'

A mortar shell impacted on the other side of the *kavana*. 'Incoming!'

Grundy fell forward on his belly and Yves fell back. Ryan and Njofra took cover behind Horst's body. Five more shells came in and impacted in a line towards the mosque. Then there was silence and then firing. The firing stopped after a minute.

'How much ammunition you have left, Luke?' Grundy asked.

'Nothin' much. I picked up a Chetnik AK and a couple of spare mags. My G3 ran out, nine mil, too. The AK's a 74.'

'Yves?'

'Three magazines.'

'Njofra?'

'*Neman*. I was coming back to see if the Chetniks left any more. I was using this up there.'

He touched the Russian Stetchkin automatic pistol in his side holster.

'Two of my men ran out of ammunition over there – they were killed.'

The gable wall of the stone house they were looking at began to crack lower down on one side where a rocket had entered and killed three Serbs.

They could still smell the charred remains of the three men inside the house but because winter was approaching, the snow was falling and the roof was off the house and spread along the road with everything else, the men did not smell as they might have in summer.

The APC fire was starting to weaken and the snow wasn't melting around the APC as much as it had been and they could feel the wind again on their faces.

Ryan swigged a large amount of plum brandy and felt it burn into his throat and sink slowly to his belly. He felt the warm feeling it left and watched through a hole in the front wall while the gable wall started to come apart like wet paper. One piece fell out and the cracks spread out from the orignal crack. A sheet of whitewash fell off and crumbled and then a triangular section of the wall further up collapsed and some of the remaining timbers in the roof fell into the house.

None of the men sitting against the front of the *kavana* moved while this was happening. Ryan switched to the wine bottle and felt he needed to be drunk. He did not know how drunk he wanted to be and he was shaking while he drank the wine. The bottle was dark and covered in other people's fingerprints and the wine was cold from having been kept in a place which had been covered with snow. There were small beads of water on the bottle below where he was holding it and ice at the base.

The snow had hardened and it had a sound to it when you walked in it that made you aware of everything.

A few birds came from wherever they had been and dipped their small beaks into the hard snow but they could find nothing there and Yves shot one of them.

Muha came out of the mosque at the other end of the village and began walking towards them.

'You have tried Jusef again?' he said when he reached Grundy.

'Nothin',' Grundy said. 'They're still fightin' over Crna Gora way?'

'Sure,' Muha said. 'I knew I should have killed Jusef. I let my heart rule my head. Bad move.'

'That's you all over, Muha. All heart,' Grundy said. 'You have to give it to him, Jusef, it was a smart move. I didn't think Jusef had it in him. I didn't think he had it in him. A move like that.'

'So what's our move now?' Yves said.

Grundy looked at Muha.

'What do you say, Muha? You're the boss.'

Muha smiled.

'I think I see the joke here,' he said. 'You know, I thought Jusef would open the valley up to the Chetniks. That was when I was going to shoot him. If he did that. Now, I am open to suggestions, Grundy.'

Grundy pressed the transmit button on his walkie-talkie and asked each of his section commanders for a report.

As well as Vinko Herak, three of his men were dead, one was wounded and three were alive. Ibrahim Abdic was down to four men, two seriously wounded. Ekrem's section was split even, four dead, four walking wounded, and Emir's section and Muha's Black Berets were down to four men between them, including Muha. Emir lay dead in a house across the street.

'Next rush and they have us,' Grundy said to Muha. 'It's that way to our lines.'

'With what guarantees?' Yves said.

'More than we have here,' Grundy said. 'Stay here and we're dead.'

'Great options,' Ryan said.

'One more thing, Grundy,' Muha said. 'I think I have been shot.'

He opened his combat jacket and looked at his woollen undervest. There was a hole in his right side, below the ribs, and a small seepage of blood was moving over the green fibres of the undervest. And when he breathed, more blood came out.

There was more shooting from around the mosque. Ekrem came in over the walkie-talkie, saying there was a fresh assault coming up the mountain from the Banja Luka road. His man in the minaret could see it.

'So who's gonna do it for you?' Grundy said to Muha.

He pointed at Muha's waist holster.

'You think I'm going to let you?' Muha said. 'You would like that. I can still fight, Grundy.'

He pulled out his Beretta and cocked it.

'Want to come and see paradise, Grundy?'

'Not if you're there, Muha,' Grundy said.

'Hey, Grundy, maybe you will find Diocletian's Tears for me. Maybe we will share them. Get rich, live well. Paradise awaits. Shit, it fucking hurts. Go on, humour me, tell me where the tears are, tell me.'

'I told you, Muha, the tears are in your eyes, they're in your eyes.'

'Fucking Jew shit. You wanna kill me now? Go ahead, kill me. You think it is a big joke now. The joke is on you, yeah? We have a strange sense of humour in Bosna. True?'

'Jesus, you just don't get it, do you, Muha? You just don't get it.'

Grundy started to laugh and when he had been laughing at Muha for a minute Muha started to laugh, just because he could not stop himself any more.

'I'm Bosnian, Muha,' Grundy said, 'I was born in Sarajevo.'

Muha's laughter continued but his jaw lengthened. Then his laughter stopped and his eyes retreated into his head. He coughed.

'Yeah,' Grundy said. 'I'm a Sephardic Jew. My family came here in 1492. How long your people been here, Muha? Maybe you're just Serbs who changed religion to have it good under the Turks. There's a thought: Muha, a Chetnik.'

'Fuck you,' Muha said. 'Celo ...!' he shouted into his walkie-talkie.

'I think Celo's been promoted, Muha.'

'I'll kill the bastard with my bare hands. So what the fuck are we going to do?'

'We could do a Masada.'

'What's that?'

'Bunch of Jews surrounded by Romans. Killed themselves rather than surrender.'

'Any other options?' Muha said.

'You could bombard Allah or the prophet.'

'Not for you, Grundy. For me, for believers. You want to convert? Give me another option.'

'Like I said, it's straight down the mountain to our lines. One hour to dark, maybe. We can just make a run. Hey, Luke, you wanna run?'

'Sure, Grundy, I'll run. I have a girl waitin'.'

'You touch my fucking sister, Ryan, and I will ...' Muha said.

'I was a good athlete at school,' Yves said.

'Where's the fucking medic?' Muha said.

He looked around him.

'He's over there,' Ryan said.

The medic's body lay face down in some short grass. The combat jacket was smouldering and a pool of blood had run through the grass into a small ditch at the side of the street.

'Bastard owed me money,' Muha said.

'What chances we get through?' Ryan said.

'Not terrific. You probably blame me.'

'Nah, Grundy, nah ...'

The ground began to shake beneath them. It was a trembling, as if someone was rocking the mountain, and Ryan could hear the sound of metal on stones and an engine.

Grundy's radio crackled.

'Tank ... It's stopped ... It's just sitting there in a hole.'

'There is one good thing for me,' Muha said to Grundy, 'you'll be dead. I would have killed you sooner or later. This saves me the bother. You're a good soldier, Grundy, but you're a shit. So you know Sarajevo well? I worked for many years in Sarajevo. They have good food in Sarajevo. Good nightlife. Not like this place.'

'I didn't remember it when I saw it again – Sarajevo,' Grundy said. 'We used to live near the Jewish cemetery. You know it? The Chetniks have it now. There was a woman who made the best *bureks* in the whole world next to us. She was a Muslim.

When the Nazis came for us, she hid us. They shot her. They shot her whole family. You were with Juka?'

'Sure. He was a crazy shit, Juka. Didn't like Muslims much. I think that was why I became a Muslim again. Anything Juka didn't like had to be good. It's not easy.'

The radio crackled again.

'Hey, Grundy, there's a Chetnik with a white flag out there, sitting on the back of a tank. He's coming through on the radios. You hear him?'

The radio crackled again and then there was another voice.

'Grundy, is that you, Grundy? Hey, Grundy, it's Andre, Andre Koniev, remember me? I'm under a flag of truce. I want to talk.'

Grundy looked at the faces around him before answering. His mouth opened very slowly.

'It's the Russian,' he said to Ryan, 'it's the fuckin' Spetznatz sniper.'

Muha whispered something to himself.

'Sure, Andre, sure . . .' Grundy said.

'We need to talk, Grundy.'

'Not on the radio,' Grundy said. 'Face to face . . . I wanna see your fuckin' face.'

'You don't believe me, you bastard?'

'No face, no deal.'

Muha turned to Grundy.

'I'm not particular about when you apologise,' he said. 'Take your time.'

Grundy wasn't listening.

'Whada you say?' Grundy said into his walkie-talkie.

'Your word isn't exactly hard currency for me, Grundy,' Koniev said.

'That wasn't me. Anyway, you're still here.'

There was a pause of three or four minutes. Then the voice came back.

'Okay, okay, but I so much as get a sneeze from you and you're dead.'

'Deal. I keep my word. I won't kill you.'

Grundy pulled himself up, took his rifle and went into the *kavana*.

Two Black Berets and a mountain soldier covered the west and southwest sides of the village through loopholes in the walls of the *kavana*. There were bottles of *Sljivovica* and other spirits spread on the floor and crockery and bits of food and old furniture and pieces from a CD player. And there were old photographs of the mosque and the ski resort on Crna Gora and Gola Planina, on the south side of the valley – and a faded photograph of Evkaf with Archduke Franz Ferdinand sitting on a horse in the forecourt of the Turkish fortress.

Grundy leaned close to the window. He could see a burnt-out T34 tank and the pieces of another tank which had turned over into a shell hole. And between then, the turret of another Serb T34 tank. The body of the tank was hidden by a depression.

Grundy pressed the transmit button on his walkie-talkie.

'That tank comes one more metre and we'll blow it to hell like the rest, Andre,' Grundy said.

A white flag came up above the level of the T34 turret and then Andre Koniev showed his face.

'I am under a flag of truce ...' he said through the walkie-talkie.

'Shoot the fucking bastard,' Muha shouted.

Grundy laughed to himself.

'Okay, okay, you come on in, Andre,' Grundy said then. 'On your own.'

He gave a hold fire order.

'You listenin' to this, Jusef?' he said into his walkie-talkie then.

There was no answer.

Koniev came forward on crutches from behind the tank. It was a slow progress and the tank's turret followed him as he moved uphill towards the *kavana*.

Grundy came to a large hole in the west wall of the *kavana*. Koniev stood on his crutches and placed his flag in his belt. There was an automatic pistol in the belt, too.

'*Zdravo*, Grundy,' Koniev said.

Grundy nodded and gestured to the Russian to come in. Koniev hesitated.

'You wanna talk, then get in,' Grundy said.

Koniev looked back at the tank.

'You have my word, I won't do anythin'.'

Koniev thought for a moment and then moved forward. Grundy helped him through the hole in the wall.

'Nice surprise, yeah? But the leg's still a fucking mess, Grundy,' Koniev said. 'I probably won't ever be able to use it properly again. How are things, you bastard?'

'Say what you have to say,' Grundy said.

'Hey don't give me fucking orders, you bastard,' Koniev said. 'Anyway, I'm here to help, as they say. You know I was convinced you were going to break out towards Zenica or Travnik. But I think I was meant to believe that. Stupid of me. Then there was that lumber village – you had us all over the place!'

He smiled.

'We moved men, you know. Very good. Then a whisper there's going to be an attack here – but I never guessed all this – brilliant! Round and round in circles. Your colonel is a smart man. I am glad to see we were both fooled by him.'

Grundy looked around him.

Yves was standing at the back door of the *kavana*, holding his rifle and checking the magazine on an AK74 he had found among the Serb dead. Ryan sat on an old chair and held his Tokarev with two hands.

The Black Berets watched the woods ahead of them for movement.

'So what's the deal?' Grundy said.

'Surrender, of course,' Koniev said.

'You're kiddin'?'

'You will be wiped out,' Koniev said. 'What I am offering you is a chance.'

'Of what?'

'Unlike you, Grundy, and these mujahideen shit, we are not barbarians. We do not wish unnecessary death. You are completely surrounded. Your own troops cannot help you – will not help you. There is nowhere to go. You will be killed.'

'So kill us.'

Koniev smiled.

'Still the brave man, Grundy.'

'I know what'll happen.'

Koniev smiled.

'Okay, okay,' he said. 'We want Hasim Kusturica – Muha – alive!'

'And we walk free?'

'Of course – much to my own sadness. I want to have you for a week, you bastards. But orders are orders. There are more tanks waiting to attack you. They will just blow you to hell, Grundy, and I offer you a way out.'

'Generous, Andre, considering . . .'

'Too generous. But you're a mercenary, a realist, and I figure we can do a deal. What is he to you? What is this Muha to you? We know what you think of him, we know this, we know a lot about you. So give him to us. Headache solved. No more Muha.'

'And what will you do with him?'

'He is a war criminal. You are aware of this. And there was a massacre of civilians in a small lumber village south of here. I think I mentioned it. Everyone killed. Men, women, kids. We found a Black Beret dead in the woods – well, the animals found him. One of his men. We did not find anyone else. And we are not looking. We have a deal?'

'We must be a big thorn,' Grundy said.

'Small splinter.'

Grundy thought about it and looked around and scratched his white beard. He smiled at Koniev.

'You've gotta be the toughest sucker I ever met, Andre. How'd you do it? How'd you get out?'

'Aah, I like to think it was charm, but now I am not so sure. I think my escape had more help than I knew. Where is he? Where's Muha?'

'He's dead. I thought he'd killed you.'

'No. I was saved by an angel. A beautiful woman with a confused sense of duty. Spetznatz trains you for that. A real angel, she was. Fixed my leg so I wouldn't lose it, then made arrangements for me. Good woman. Then I just got into the river and floated here. Smart thinking, no?'

'And the woman?' Grundy said.

Koniev smiled again. He shrugged.

'Details. The deal, Grundy?' he said.

'Nah!' Grundy said.

'You will die. I promise you, Grundy. And I will – how did you say it? – I will make the last hours of your life more hellish than you can imagine. Is that what you said? You don't have too many friends, Grundy, so you better start making some.'

'So how bad's your situation on Crna Gora?' Grundy said to Koniev.

'I'm not at liberty to discuss that. I'm a sniper, Grundy, what would I know about situations?'

He grinned. Then he talked into his walkie-talkie.

'Please,' he said to Grundy, 'do not fire.'

The T34 moved slowly out of the hollow where it had stopped. When the tank had flattened out they could see the body stretched out across its front. It was stripped and bloody.

'Your man, I think,' Koniev said. 'I could not prevent it. Honest Serbs found him. And he was a sniper. You know what happens to snipers.'

Grundy looked at Spit's body for about thirty seconds. He did not say anything.

'I saw my death again last night, in darkened mud and fading light,' Ryan said, 'while tallest trees stood guard around and howling wind blew trumpets sound . . .'

'What the fuck's that?' Grundy said to Ryan.

'It's from a poem I wrote years ago when I was in my tragic phase. It's not a very good poem.'

'You have no more options, Grundy,' Koniev said.

'The woman's dead, Andre,' Grundy said.

'Too bad,' Koniev said. 'I suppose that's war. Nice woman. Too bad.'

'Yeah, too bad,' Grundy said.

He looked at Yves and Yves shook his head.

'It seems I do owe you an apology, Muha!' Grundy shouted then.

Muha pulled himself into the *kavana* and leaned against the doorpost.

'To my face,' he said, 'everything to my face.'

He closed his eyes and began to slide down the doorpost. Grundy lifted him up.

Koniev grinned as if he had found Grundy out.

Grundy turned to Ryan and then gestured to Koniev. 'You understand what he's been sayin'?' he said to Ryan.

'Enough,' Ryan said. 'You want me to shoot him?'

'How does it end?' Grundy said. 'The poem.'

'With a prayer, I think,' Ryan said.

'Yeah, shoot him,' Grundy said in Serbo-Croat.

Koniev's grin shrank and the colour vanished from his face.

'You gave your word!'

'I'm not killin' you,' Grundy said.

Ryan shot Koniev twice in the head. The Russian fell back against the wall and slumped to his knees. Ryan fired twice more into his head and the Russian fell over on the floor.

'Dumb fuck,' Grundy said. 'Sound battle stations, Yves.'

30

The first Serb tank appeared on the left, from the dirt track leading to the Banja Luka road, a box-like, sharp-angled T34 with a Serb flag fluttering from its turret and five Serb infantry on the back. It fired five shells at the *kavana* and blew one wall to pieces. Then the commander realised he had outrun his flanking support infantry and the tank stopped.

Two men from Ekrem's section came out of the house across the street with a PK machine-gun, fired a burst and hit one of the Serbs. The Serb cursed and fell off the tank, then stood up, said something and fell down dead.

The two Bosnians dived back into the house. The tank moved forward and stalled. Two Serb infantry teams went either side of it. The tank fired at the house from where the Bosnian pair had attacked. The first round was armour-piercing and went through the house. The second round – high explosive – took a whole corner off the house.

Then two Black Berets came out of the house beside the *kavana* and fired two long bursts at the Serb infantry advancing on either side of the T34.

The Black Berets were gone and three more Serbs were dead before the tank could line up on the house. The tank fired three rounds at the house and the flanking Serb infantry pulled back behind the tank.

Grundy came up from a ditch to the left of the tank and fired an RPG-7. It struck the tank at the engine and the tank moved forward a few metres, then the back exploded.

A second Bosnian PK team caught the Serb infantry in the open from two sides. The Bosnians fell back into the village houses.

The Serb attack halted.

Then the barrage began.

Tank and mortar shells from the slopes around Vrh hit the village.

Ryan clutched his rifle close to him and squashed his face into the wall of the house he was in. Yves was at the far window, watching the Serb silhouettes moving against the background of flames and starlight.

Two more Serb tanks came up left and right of the first and fired three rounds each through the *kavana*, then turned their guns on other houses.

The tank shells destroyed a Bosnian position in the grey house in the centre of the village. One Bosnian mountain soldier tried to get out and run across the street but the tank machine-guns caught him in the open and he was dead before he made it to the middle of the street.

Then two more tanks, T54s, bigger, more rounded and streamlined than the T34s, came up the forest track from the Banja Luka road and broke well right of the other tanks.

Yves gave the order to move.

Yves took the RPG rockets beside Ryan and Ryan took the launcher and the two of them moved out through a hole in the wall of the house, then slid out of the trench and down a low gully to work their way round the back of the Serb tanks.

Ibrahim Abdic and two of his men fired supporting bursts from the house.

One T54 flanking to the right swung left again and got caught on some logs long enough for two more Bosnian positions to get machine-gun and rifle fire into the infantry around it.

The second T54 closed up and fired off three rounds into the house behind Ryan and then stopped. The shells demolished one side of the house and then the first T54 rolled back off the logs and broke right of the second to support it.

The T34s to the left moved back into the cover of undulating ground and continued to fire at positions in the village.

Ryan cursed and heard Ibrahim scream and shout at his men.

The T34s began picking off pieces of the houses on the south side of the village. And the lines of stars in the night sky overhead looked like the eyes of spectators. Yves pulled Ryan into another hole.

Ryan watched the T54 on the left manoeuvre itself over the broken trees the first T54 tank had stalled on.

The tank stopped at an artillery crater and fired off a round at the nearest house. It missed. Supporting Serb infantry went on either side of the tank.

The Bosnians in the house fired an RPG7 rocket but it went high. Then they loosed off a PK machine-gun. Both T54s hit the house with high explosive rounds from two sides and half the house collapsed.

Serb infantry moved towards the western edge of the village.

Yves tapped Ryan on the shoulder. Ryan rolled out of the hole and Yves followed with his AK74 extended.

They moved between the fallen trees and the mounds of exploded earth and slid rolling from hole to hole around the curtain of fire which was all over the top of Vrh now and got in behind the tanks.

The T54 tank at the artillery crater swung its turret too far to the left and caught a tree. Then it swung it to the right and caught another tree. The tank commander ordered a reverse. But the driver panicked and stalled the tank. Yves moved.

He fired a full magazine in three-round bursts at a Serb infantry team working towards the south side of the village from broken ground and thin trees. Two of the Serbs were hit and their bodies collapsed, and a third was caught in the head. He was a short man and he fell into a mortar crater. The Serb infantry were shouting for support from their tanks.

Ryan loaded the RPG7, went down behind a broken tree, took aim and tried to gauge the distance in the darkness and make allowances for the wind from the northeast.

He fired. The rocket went left, hit a tree and exploded.

The stalled Serb T54 tank started again and began to reverse. Serb infantry fired at where they thought the rocket had come from. But Yves had moved left of them.

Yves reloaded and fired at four Serb soldiers who had

dived for cover to the right of the T54. They rolled into a hole. Yves threw two grenades at them.

The grenade blasts caught two of the Serbs before they could get out of the hole and Yves killed the other two. Five more Serbs came to help their comrades and Yves shot two of them.

Then the T54 reversed over one of its own wounded.

Ryan watched the man's silhouette try to get out of the way but the tracks caught him and sucked him in slowly under their muddied steel. Ryan had reloaded the RPG7.

A Serb soldier made a dash to the right.

'Fire the fucking thing,' Yves said.

He shot the Serb trying to outflank him. The man was hit twice in the upper body and the AK74 rounds tumbled in his body and came out his groin.

Another Serb came out of the trees on Ryan's left and Yves swung round at him and fired three times. The bullets hit a tree, then went wide of the man. The Serb fired back. His rounds hit the ground near Ryan.

The T54 was reversing very fast now, directly at Ryan, trying desperately to get its turret round and hitting trees on either side of it.

Ryan was aiming.

More rounds came at him from a position to his left. Yves swung there and fired and swung right and fired again.

'Fire it!' he screamed at Ryan.

A round hit him in the upper shoulder from behind and Yves swung and shot the old Serb running at him, screaming. Another round hit Yves lower down from the front and Yves roared and fell back, pulled himself up and loosed off three rounds where he thought the incoming shots had originated.

'Fire, Luke, fire,' he screamed.

The tank was coming at Ryan now and the second T54 was swinging its gun, looking for him, too. It started to turn.

Ryan waited.

Rounds came at him from three different sides and Yves fired at all of them.

Ryan fired.

The rocket struck the back of the tank reversing at him. The tank stopped suddenly, there was a moment of nothingness and then a column of flame shot up from the engine and the turret. It rose to tree height, stayed there and then fell away. Then the commander's hatch opened. Ryan watched, fascinated. The young commander climbing out of the hatch was on fire.

The man collapsed on his tank and moved, then collapsed for good over the side.

Then a round struck the log behind Ryan and he swung and picked up his rifle and fired. Five more Serb infantry were trying to manoeuvre their way round him.

Ryan fired three rounds from his rifle, then three more, and then rolled from his position and fired three further rounds and rolled again.

He could see Yves in a hole to his left, holding his chest with one hand and firing his rifle with the other. Yves's rounds were going left and right of their targets, and high.

Ryan grabbed Yves from behind and pulled him round. His combat jacket was drenched in blood and he was dripping blood from his nose and his mouth.

'I can't fucking move,' he said, 'my fucking legs are gone, man, my fucking legs are gone.'

Ryan shouted for Grundy.

A Serb moved right of them.

Ryan shot him with a single round in the chest and the Serb dropped to his knees. One of his comrades crawled out and pulled him into a hole and another two Serbs came out to cover. Ryan fired again, reloaded and fired single shots at the Serbs.

Ryan shouted for Grundy again.

Further up, to the left, two new T54s were smashing through two of the broken houses in the village, supported by the T34s, which had moved forward now.

Ryan fired in an arc, still shouting for Grundy.

Then one of the T54s at the edge of the village exploded. It bounced and then kicked forward, then smoke came from the turret and there were shouts and screams from all around it and a sheet of flame came out of the turret and two Serb infantrymen next to it were caught by the flame and were running around on fire.

The other T54 at the village reversed and the battle stopped while the Serb tank burned.

Then Ryan felt the vibration of another tank moving towards him. It came out of the smoke to his right and the starlight and the fire from the burning T54s gave it a ghostly colour. Ryan was not sure it was real until it fired its gun.

It was the first T54, which had reached the south side of the village and then turned to support the tank Ryan had destroyed.

It had fired and hit the mosque and taken part of the dome away and then smashed the top off the minaret. A third shell had impacted against the corner of the mosque and taken it away and some of the mosque had collapsed on that side. Now it was coming at Ryan.

Ryan loaded an RPG and fired. The rocket hit the T54 on a supplementary armour plate around the turret, bounced off the tank and went off into the forest behind.

Ryan cursed and fell back into the hole beside Yves and reloaded. But his fire had drawn the tank's attention to him and he could see Serb soldiers pointing out his position.

He fired another rocket. This time it went high and over the tank. The tank fired.

The tank round landed behind Ryan and Yves and showered them in dirt.

Ryan went to pull Yves but could not get him to move. Yves loosed off a magazine wildly in the direction of the Serbs, and a volley of shots came back at him.

The tank moved and pulled into a grass patch and lined its gun up again.

Ryan picked up his equipment, grabbed Yves by the webbing and dragged him out of the hole and across the downed trees and the mud to the fresh hole the tank had made with its first shell. The second shell impacted in front of them in the hole they had left.

'Cover!' Ryan shouted at the houses in the village, but there was no Bosnian firing coming from there any more.

He couldn't see anything or anyone from his own side near him. He could feel rounds going over his head at the Serbs and he could hear voices to left and right.

'Ah, fuck it, man, fuck it,' Yves said.

He was trying to open his jacket and examine his wounds. But his fingers were not working properly any more and he was coughing blood now in spasms.

The Serb tank opened up with a machine-gun and the rounds sprayed the ground around them. Ryan fired back. Then the tank fired another round high over Ryan's head. The round landed down the mountain in a group of Serbs.

The tank moved forward and three Serbs climbed on the back of it and it lumbered slowly towards Ryan and Yves.

Ryan looked at Yves and looked at the tank and wanted to run.

The tank machine-gun was firing in bursts now, but always high, and the tank kept moving and the Serb infantry behind it made their way from cover to cover, guided by one of the men on the tank who were shouting directions.

Ryan got out another RPG rocket, loaded it and watched the T54 move slowly towards him and wondered what it was like to be crushed by a tank. He watched the tank slip on broken logs and crush limestone and a dead body and he watched the tank machine-gun fire and the rounds pass over his head and he watched the tank's main gun level itself and he knew there was nothing he could do now but wait.

He aimed the RPG at the right track, only because it would stop the tank dead. The track movement was so slow that there was a flat enough space on the front of the track for a possible hit, and he heard himself praying.

'Get out, get out,' Yves shouted at him.

Ryan did not move. He brushed off Yves's hand and told him to fuck off. The tank came on. It was an old tank and the paintwork was rusting and there were graffiti on the front and a small Serb crest on the right side.

One of the men on the back had a beard and a PK machine-gun.

Ryan fired.

The rocket glanced off the rim of the track and hit the ground a few yards away.

'*Merde*,' Yves shouted.

He pulled Ryan back into the hole and took the RPG from him. His arms were shaking and his face was white and the blood was running down both sides of his mouth.

'Load me,' he said.

Ryan did what he said.

'Now, get out.'

Ryan hesitated. Yves pulled his Browning automatic and cocked it.

'You want I have to use it on you, too?' Yves said.

Ryan was about to say something but did not. He picked up his rifle and rolled out of the hole and Yves fired the RPG.

The rocket hit the tank right between the turret and the body and the tank jumped and there was a sheet of flame and then a second explosion, and the tank came on and then stalled.

Two Serbs from the back of the tank were out on the ground. They were caught by machine-gun fire from the mosque area of the village. Serb infantry backing them came running forward and dragged their men to cover. Then they opened up with a sustained volley of small arms fire.

Ryan kept moving back from hole to hole towards the village and he thought he heard a single pistol shot when he made the village again, but he could not be sure. He kept moving through the line of wrecked houses on the south side of the village, shouting for cover, firing two-shot bursts.

The remaining Bosnians were pulling back to the mosque, moving from house to house in twos, covering each other.

Ryan watched a cover pair being killed by a burst of Serb machine-gun fire. He called for support from Ekrem who was across the street. Ekrem came out and fired a burst at three

Serbs moving into the village. He killed one and wounded another and the Serbs pulled back. Ryan moved through a broken wall and over another and fired to support Ekrem and another Bosnian he could only hear. But neither Ekrem nor the other man made it to the mosque. There were four dead Bosnian mountain soldiers and a Black Beret in the mosque and Grundy was sitting at the front door, firing down the street.

A T54 came into the village through the remains of the *kavana*. The tank stopped at the end of the village and swung its turret round and fired into a house to its left. Half a wall collapsed. The tank fired again and the rest of the wall and a second wall collapsed. Then Serb infantry moved left of the tank and into the remains of the house. They used a flame-thrower in the cellar and the tank swung its gun to the next house on the right.

Ryan sank down the wall beside Grundy. Around him, the interior of the mosque was dark and the men in it were almost shadows.

Njofra sat in the corner beside the old shoe stand, drinking from a broken bottle of wine, humming to himself, holding his pistol to his head.

'If I pass out, kill me,' he said to Ryan.

'I think it's time to go,' Ryan said.

'Which direction you have in mind?' Grundy said.

Ryan wiped the sweat and snowflakes from his face.

Ibrahim fired a burst of PK machine-gun fire at the mountain slope beneath them. Then he yelled to Grundy that he was out of ammunition.

The Serb tank in the village destroyed another house and another T54 came into the village from the south, smashing through the walls of a house.

'Well, I'm not gonna sit here and wait for them,' Ryan said.

He grabbed Grundy by the webbing and shook him.

'Come on, Grundy, come on.'

'I think it's Masada time, Luke,' Grundy said. 'Where's Yves?'

A tank shell hit the mosque dome and brought down pieces of metal and masonry on the sodden carpet. Ryan crawled out into the middle of the carpet, picked up an AK74 and rolled back to Grundy.

'That was a fine move Jusef did,' Grundy said. 'Bastard. I wish he'd told me. That was a fine move though.'

Ryan checked the AK74 and snapped the magazine into the rifle.

'Come on, let's go,' he said to Grundy.

Another tank round came in. There were three tanks in the village now. A third tank round hit the mosque.

'They're coming again,' Ibrahim said.

He pulled out his pistol and fired into the darkness of the tree-lined slopes around him. The clip ran out and he pulled another from his pocket and fired again. The Serbs fell back into the trees below him and fired at the mosque from cover. A tank shell went wide and hit the house to the right of the mosque.

Ryan fired his rifle out the front door at shadows running between the tanks.

'I wonder did Jusef take Crna Gora back?' Grundy said.

He smiled at Ryan.

'You wanna go first?' he said.

'Next house. They haven't made the next house,' Ryan said. 'We can get out through there.'

He looked over to where tank fire had torn a small hole in the brickwork of the north wall of the mosque. Some of the broken bricks were lying beside Njofra. Njofra's eyes were beginning to close.

'I can't hold them any more, Grundy,' Ibrahim said.

'Grundy!' Ryan shouted.

He handed Grundy the AK74 he had picked up from the middle of the floor.

'Yeah, sure, why not?' Grundy said. 'You move, Njofra?'

'No way, Grundy.'

'How about you give us some cover fire?'

'How much will you pay me?'

'I'll give you an extra share in Diocletian's Tears. Free.'

'That's a good deal? Okay, get me to the door.'

They dragged Njofra over to the door and propped him up against one of the doorposts. Another tank shell hit the dome and passed right through the metal. Part of the supporting stone structure began to collapse into the mosque and some of the wooden beams higher up were on fire. Ibrahim started to knock a hole in the north wall.

'You would go without giving me mine, Grundy?'

When Ryan looked around for the source of the voice, Muha was standing under the wooden balcony at the south wall of the mosque, holding his stomach. He had his Beretta pistol in his right hand.

'I think I should fucking kill you now, Grundy, while there's time,' Muha said. 'You should have handed me over. Not a smart move.'

He coughed and blood came from his mouth.

'Hey, we didn't do so bad,' he said. 'My lung is bleeding now. I feel very sick, I think I'm going to die.'

'Come on, Grundy,' Ryan said.

'Well, here I am, Muha,' Grundy said.

'Indeed,' Muha said.

'Grundy!' Ryan yelled.

'Shut up, Ryan,' Muha said. 'Tell him to shut up, Grundy.'

'Shut up, Luke.'

Muha looked at his pistol and smiled.

'I know where they are,' he said, 'the tears.'

Grundy laughed.

'They're all yours, Muha,' he said.

'*Allah u akbar*,' Muha said. 'The Hour of Doom is their appointed time. And stay away from my fucking sister, Ryan.'

He almost laughed. But he coughed blood again.

'Go . . .'

The first Serb came through the low window to his right and Muha swung around and shot him. A second Serb came through the window to the left and shot Muha in the side. Grundy shot the Serb through the head.

Ryan grabbed Grundy and pulled him towards the hole in the wall.

Njofra fired three rounds from his pistol and yelled a

warning. Twelve Serb rounds hit him at once and he collapsed against the wall of the mosque.

Muha shot the first Serb in through the front door. Two more Serbs came in the side window and Muha was hit in the leg and through the hip.

Grundy and Ryan shot one of the Serbs at the front door and Ibrahim hit the man at the window. Ibrahim dived through the hole in the wall.

Two more Serbs came in the front door and shot Muha again. He made an attempt to stand after his legs had given way and three more bullets hit him from behind. He swung and shot one of the Serbs at the front door and Grundy shot the other. But two more were in the side windows and Muha was shot again.

Muha said something Ryan did not understand.

Grundy made a move towards Muha and Ryan grabbed hold of him and Grundy shoved Ryan at the hole in the wall.

'Out!' he yelled.

Ryan scrambled through, firing to his left when he was going through. Ibrahim was at the next house knocking a small shell hole into something big enough to crawl through with an empty rifle.

Ryan called out to Grundy again and Ibrahim grabbed Ryan and pulled him towards the house. Ryan struggled with Ibrahim and went to go back into the mosque. He broke free of Ibrahim's grip when Grundy was coming through the hole in the mosque wall.

A shot ricocheted to Ryan's left and another to his right. Ibrahim turned and pulled the trigger on his empty rifle. The third Serb shot caught him in the head. He made a small noise and then fell back into the mud beside an old gravestone which had not been broken by the war.

Grundy knocked Ryan over, went down on one knee and fired three single shots to his left and one to his right. One hit a Serb running at them. Ryan scrambled to his knees and swung to cover Grundy and hit a Serb at a tall tree. Then five tank rounds hit the mosque and the Serbs fell flat. Grundy and Ryan threw themselves into the next house and crawled across the floor, out through a hole in the far wall and down a slope to a garden.

Ryan looked back at the mosque and it was burning and the flames touched the yellow clouds in the sky and the snow was falling again.

They crawled across the garden and under the remains of a picket fence and through dense undergrowth to the trees to the north of the village. The firing had stopped and there was shouting and then firing began at the front line below them in the valley.

When they were in the pine trees they crawled into a ditch filled with mountain water and snow and moved through it down the north side of Vrh towards Crna Gora. There was firing on Crna Gora now, single shots and mortar impacts, and when they were crawling, small Serb units passed close to the ditch.

Vrh went down steeply on that side and there was a dip between it and Crna Gora and the ditch they were in ran down to the dip, then turned into the valley and connected up with a spread of ditches that bordered the fields there. Grundy wanted to use the ditch to get into the dip and then head northwest deep into Serb-held territory to stand a chance of getting away.

When they had crawled for maybe a kilometre and were down into the dip, Ryan stopped and fell on his face into the cold water. His hands were bleeding and he was shaking with the cold.

'I'm goin' back to Evkaf,' Ryan said when he had recovered his breath.

He pulled himself up over the edge of the ditch and looked around at the forest. There was only the firing now and the firing was everywhere else.

'Jesus, for what?' Grundy said.

'For her. I said I'd be back for her. I said it.'

Grundy wanted to laugh, but he held his laughter and shook his head.

'Jesus Christ, you are a joke, Luke. And how do you think Jusef'll greet you? Or Celo?'

'I'm in love with her, Grundy. And I said I'd be back.'

Grundy shook his head. Then he punched Ryan. Ryan's head went back and rebounded off the soft clay and Grundy hit him again.

'You stupid fuck,' he whispered.

'I have to live with it,' Ryan said.

'What'd I say about makin' a break, what'd I say?'

'You said break away from our lines, swing round, take the long way. I know, Grundy, I know. But if I do that, I won't go back, I just won't.'

'So be it.'

'But I gave my word.'

'I told you never to give your word.'

'Natasa said that, too.'

Grundy pulled out his sidearm.

'Okay, okay,' he said, 'but if you get me killed . . .'

'You can kill me, Grundy. That's a promise.'

'Smart bastard.'

'I practise in my sleep.'

Grundy looked at the forest around him.

'Okay, you ready?' he said.

Ryan pulled his Tokarev. He checked the magazine.

'How far you reckon?'

'Just move like hell and shoot anythin' you see. I reckon he's still alive, you reckon that?'

'Who?'

'Muha. I don't reckon they killed him.'

'They couldn't kill Muha. No one could.'

'He's a bastard.'

'He is for sure.'

They crawled further along the ditch and when they broke out of the pines and into thinner trees they came out of it, on different sides, rolling over. Then they fell in beside two trees on either side of the ditch.

'On the count of five.' Grundy said.

'Hey, Grundy,' Ryan said, 'I think I know who really shot Kennedy.'

Grundy nodded as if he was going to say something.

'We'll shoot that old bastard, Husic,' Ryan said then.

Grundy smiled and nodded his head again. Some of the

light from the stars caught the white of his beard. He reached into his top pocket and pulled out a packet of cigarettes.

'One for the road,' he said.

He pulled out a plastic lighter and lit the cigarette before Ryan could speak.

United Nations troops found the bodies in the spring.

Ryan had been shot through the head and Grundy was too badly decomposed and eaten by animals to determine how he had died. No autopsy was done and they were buried in a mass grave in Evkaf.

Two weeks later the Bosnians attempted to retake Vrh again and failed, and the week after that the Serbs attacked Crna Gora and were pushed back.

On the same morning in Sarajevo, Emira Kusturica came down from the seventh floor of the Holiday Inn and checked out. She picked up a Mercedes taxi behind the hotel and the taxi drove her along Vojvode Putnika, which is known as sniper's alley, to the UN compound at the old PTT building in the west of the city. The taxi stopped at the Bosnian checkpoint before the PTT building and Emira got out and paid the driver fifty Deutschmarks for the trip.

The rain was heavy and there were thick clouds down over all the hills around the city and even the tower blocks in the new town were shrouded in cloud. Emira approached the Bosnian guard at the checkpoint and pulled out a United Nations pass she had bought on the black market. The guard nodded her on. Only people with passes could go any further.

In the PTT compound Emira waited with about a dozen others for an Egyptian armoured personnel carrier to come and take them to the airport. The people stood in an orderly line and did not look at each other. An Egyptian captain cracked jokes with a magazine correspondent. Emira looked at her passport and thought. Her passport was Croatian. The Egyptian taxi was late.

When the APC came, the people waiting crammed themselves and their wet luggage into the muddy interior and sat facing the steel walls. The Egyptian captain reassured the magazine journalist about the resistance of the armour on his vehicles. The magazine correspondent had to be helped up on to the footplate. Emira sat in the last seat on the right and the luggage was stacked up under her feet.

The Egyptian captain smiled at her and then noticed something. He bowed his head and picked up a thin chain lying in a corner of the footplate. He held it up. There was a small stone on the end of it.

'Does this belong to anyone?' he said.

Emira Kusturica put her hand out.

'It's mine,' she said.

She smiled.

'I must have dropped it.'

'It's very nice,' the captain said. 'Opal?'

'A friend gave it to me.'

And he dropped it into her hand.

CONOR CREGAN

WITH EXTREME PREJUDICE

Tim McLennan. Unionist. Canny and determined. SAS.

John Cusack. Republican. Singleminded and tenacious. IRA.

This startlingly original thriller chronicles their relentless cat-and-rat battle of wills.

But behind the ambushes, skirmishes and killings, Conor Cregan fascinatingly exposes the complicated motives and human concerns of those involved in the Ulster struggle. Where there is little room for lasting relationships. And where, because of an unswerving commitment to an inherited cause, men and women spend their lives waiting to pick off a careless, nameless member of the opposing side.

As Cusack and his Active Service Unit meticulously plan an attack on a British Army checkpoint in south Armagh, the tension never falters. Right up until the final shot is fired.

HODDER AND STOUGHTON PAPERBACKS